ADVANCE PRAISE

Deeply thought-provoking. The author follows the lives of two very different mothers who live in the Netherlands during WWII. As the war presses in around them, their relationship with each other evolves from distrust to a true sisterhood that will enable them to survive and even help others during a truly horrifying time in history.
— Caroline Crocker, PhD, co-author of *Overcoming the Jackboot*, the true story of an indomitable half-German child who survived the Nazi occupation—and learned to be truly brave.

Our Daughters' Last Hope focuses on the experiences of two women, Herta and Julia, following the Nazi occupation of Amsterdam in 1940. A visceral, terrifying blend of fear and hope, violence and solidarity swirls as the two face disappearances—and sometimes unwelcome reappearances—of loved ones, growing repression, increasingly grim living conditions and the constant threat of denunciation or death. Stock raises fundamental questions: how far can you trust your friends, or family? What should you do if duty conflicts with what seems right? What if survival means breaking taboos? And what would you do if Nazis took over your country?

Like her earlier work in the "Resilient Women of WWII" series, the story draws on solid chunks of research as well as a rich vein of imagination to examine the fate of ordinary women driven to extraordinary feats by awful circumstances. Worth a look if you like historical fiction.

— Leigh Turner, author of *Palladium* and *Blood Summit*

Elaine Stock's "old world" voice immerses us in the poignant stories of two women who plumb depths of amazing resiliency and revise the concept of family to survive and protect their children during the unspeakable ravages of the Holocaust. Such deeply personal novels connect and remind us we must never forget these horrors.

— Sandra L. Young, author of *Divine Vintage*

Beautifully written. Touching. Poignant.

Elaine Stock's second instalment in her trilogy Resilient Women of WWII, *Our Daughters' Last Hope* shines with real emotion.

Grounded in the relationships between friends and the love and determination of a mother to protect her child, Stock leads us through her tale at pace, never losing the meaning behind her story. Her characters are depicted with raw honesty, drawing us in; we become truly invested in their journeys from the first page.

It is historical fiction that honours the strength of people of the past as they faced unimaginable horror, seeking to continue the memories so we never forget.

A story that will stay with you long after you finish the last page.

— Lelita Baldock. Author of *Widow's Lace*, *The Unsound Sister* and *Where the Gulls Fall Silent*.

Praise for *We Shall Not Shatter*, Book 1 of the Resilient Women of WWII Trilogy
A story which will touch your heart, and perhaps bring a few tears to wipe away, showing how love does indeed break barriers and sees beyond human labels and disabilities. You will absolutely fall in love with Zofia and Aanya, and how strong friendships were forged in the heat of oppression from Hitler's Germany despite their different faiths.
— We Shall Not Shatter earns five stars from The Historical Fiction Company and the "Highly Recommended" Award

Elaine Stock's novel, *We Shall Not Shatter,* the first of a promised trilogy, Resilient Women of WWII, is a poignant and heartfelt tale of perseverance, of friendship across boundaries, of making families in different ways, of horror and of healing. In the characters of Zofia and Aanya, and the families they make and lose in their native Poland, the barbarities of war, the added peril of Aanya's deafness, and their harrowing escape, the story is offset by the plot strands of Christians helping Jews, Germans helping Poles, hearing people cherishing the strength of the deaf, and the deaf healing others. This is a story not only of resilience, but of the victory of love and friendship over pain and suffering.
— Barbara Stark-Nemon, author of the award-winning novels, *Even in Darkness* and *Hard Cider,* Speech-language therapist and Teacher Consultant for the Deaf and Hard of Hearing

We Shall Not Shatter follows the lives and friendship of two women, Zofia and Aanya, during the frightening years of Nazi Germany and World War II. Their story highlights how two people from very different backgrounds—one Jew, one Christian—remain faithful friends through unimaginable hardships and separation. I loved how all of the characters developed along with all the twists and turns of the story. The author thoroughly researched Poland, deaf education, the Holocaust and the politics of that era. She told a beautiful story of these friends and their families, and how their friendship survives. This is a great book with a positive message about how people can see each other for what they are, as people.

— Dolores Tomarelli MS, Speech Language Pathologist

An unforgettable story of bravery, friendship, and love set against the harrowing backdrop of WWII in Poland, *We Shall Not Shatter* is a compelling novel penned with heartfelt sincerity by master storyteller Elaine Stock. This gem is beautifully layered with complex emotions and engaging characters struggling against impossible circumstances. Even so, they are buoyed by the ferocious loyalty of their friendship.

We Shall Not Shatter takes readers on a rare journey of life-tested relationships and uncompromising courage. Stock brilliantly creates a time and place that is terrible and heartbreaking only to reveal the beauty that awaits on the other side of devastation. This story will stay with you long after the last page is turned.

— London Clarke, #1 Amazon bestselling author of *Wildfell* and *The Meadows*

OUR DAUGHTERS' LAST HOPE

A WWII STORY OF UNEXPECTED FRIENDSHIP
ACROSS ENEMY LINES, WHEN TWO MOTHERS
SEEK TO SAVE THEIR CHILDREN'S LIVES

ELAINE STOCK

ISBN 9789493276444 (ebook)

ISBN 9789493276420 (paperback)

ISBN 9789493276437 (hardcover)

Publisher: Amsterdam Publishers, The Netherlands

info@amsterdampublishers.com

Author Website: https://elainestock.com

Our Daughters' Last Hope is Book 2 of the Trilogy **Resilient Women of WWII**

Copyright © Elaine Stock, 2022

All Rights Reserved. No part of this publication may be reproduced or transmitted in any form or by any means, electronic or mechanical, including photocopy, recording or any other information storage and retrieval system, without prior permission in writing from the publisher.

CONTENTS

Author's Note	ix
Prologue	1
Chapter 1	5
Chapter 2	11
Chapter 3	17
Chapter 4	22
Chapter 5	30
Chapter 6	35
Chapter 7	46
Chapter 8	55
Chapter 9	67
Chapter 10	71
Chapter 11	79
Chapter 12	87
Chapter 13	94
Chapter 14	103
Chapter 15	113
Chapter 16	120
Chapter 17	128
Chapter 18	137
Chapter 19	146
Chapter 20	151
Chapter 21	161
Chapter 22	170
Chapter 23	181
Chapter 24	187
Chapter 25	197
Chapter 26	205
Chapter 27	217
Chapter 28	227
Chapter 29	234
Chapter 30	245
Chapter 31	254
Chapter 32	261

Chapter 33	269
Chapter 34	276
Chapter 35	282
Chapter 36	286
Chapter 37	290
About the Author	295
Readers Groups Discussion Guide	299
Acknowledgments	303
Amsterdam Publishers Holocaust Library	305

AUTHOR'S NOTE

Anonymous. Southside of Damsquare, showing the entrances of Beurssteeg (left) and Kalverstraat (right). c 1860. Photo. Amsterdam, Stadsarchief Amsterdam (inv.nr. 010003004044).

While this is a work of fiction, there came a time early in writing the novel when, influenced by my research, I had to make a decision whether or not to create all fictional characters, use real names, or utilize a combination. I decided to use both: there were distinct names of true people that I wouldn't dare fictionalize because to do so would to change history. Yet, all of my main characters are fictionalized. I also wanted to honor several people who my research showed me were vital in helping to save many Jewish and other persecuted people as possible, such as Walter and Johanna Süskind, Alice Cohn, Henriëtte Henriquez Pimentel, and Fritz de Zwerver. However, I did take the liberty to create in the Süskinds what I hope I portrayed as good, caring people. Any inaccuracies are fully my own and are unintentional.

Dedicated in the Memory of my childhood friend, Diane Kamm Friedman, whose playing of the cello still plays in my mind and keeps me company while writing.

How I wish you were still with me, my friend.

PROLOGUE

Het leven moet verder gaan.
Life must go on.

2 June 1939 As the night lights of Miami twinkled farewell to the passengers yet again traveling on the M.S. St. Louis, a mixed wail spread from one passenger to another. Women sobbed, men swore and shook fists. Children gawked in wide-eyed terror, not with concern over their future, but for the unaccustomed display of tears and anger from their parents.

Herta's attention leaped from the spreading hysteria of her fellow shipmates to Edith's sniffling. She pulled her oldest daughter into an embrace, unable to recall when she'd last seen her stoic soon-to-be 13-year-old weep. "Hush now. We must remain strong. We'll be fine. You will see."

"But how can you say that, Mutter?" Edith glanced at the more than 900 passengers—the majority Jewish refugees who had counted on a new home in Cuba or America. "See the women crying. Don't you hear the men shouting? They won't hush like you want me to. It's not fair."

Her daughter was correct. The demands she placed on Edith—to be brave during this time of the unknown future—wasn't fair. Then again, life never favored everyone and certainly wasn't fair, but this wasn't the time for that horrid lesson. Especially since Herta didn't understand this tragedy, not one part of this sad reality. Her gaze swept over the troubled women and men her daughter had singled out, sparking memories to swirl before her. She remembered the three instances of fairness she'd experienced through the years. Marrying Kurt. Giving birth to first Edith, then Krista three years later—both healthy. As for the other less fortunate times, those memories needed to remain in the past, unvisited. Herta bent and gave Edith a peck on the head.

Krista inched closer to Herta and wrapped her arms around her waist. "Mama, is it true? Are we going back to Germany where the Nazis will kill us?"

"We will make sure that we stay away from Germany. That country is no longer our home." Herta dropped to her knees and pulled both her daughters into a fierce hug. With the terrors they were experiencing, nightmares would certainly follow. She leaned back to look each daughter in the eye. "My loves, right now this is what I know." She paused as Kurt stepped to her side and placed his firm, supportive hands onto her shoulders. "Yes, we've sailed away from Cuba and are now passing by America. But what counts is this—we have each other and we must cling to hope. One way or the other, we'll have ourselves a new home and a life we can enjoy."

Her lips twitching, Edith peered at her father. "Is this true, Vater?"

Kurt feathered his fingers against Edith's cheek. "Never doubt your mother." He offered a hand to both girls. "Come with me to the railing. Let's wave goodbye to America with fearless faces and hearts."

As Herta watched her husband lead their daughters away, someone tapped her on her shoulder. She turned to see Anika, a friendly woman she'd had the pleasure to meet while the ship was stalled in the Havana harbor for five days.

"I've considered what you've shared about having no family or friends to turn to." Like most of the other passengers, Anika and her sister, who was also her traveling partner, had barely escaped harm's way in their native Germany. They too, were uncertain of their fate. "If we can make it to Amsterdam, I'll connect you with my cousins to help settle you and your dear family. The Netherlands is a lovely country. I would have been living there with my relatives if my work hadn't kept me in Germany." The corners of her lips lifted in confidence. "The Dutch government managed to keep the country neutral throughout the Great War, and for that reason, it expects Germany to leave it alone and unscathed. Would you like for me to arrange this introduction?"

Herta's eyes brimmed with tears. "Yes, that would be an answer to my prayers. Thank you."

"Then why the sad face?"

"Honestly, I'm unaccustomed to genuine concern and generosity."

"We're friends. And friends watch out for each other, right?"

"Yes. I'm glad we've met." Herta hugged Anika. For the first time since parting with her Polish friend Zofia when she and her son debarked the ship in Cuba as two of the 28 passengers permitted to leave, Herta breathed light-heartedly. A new hope coursed through her veins; renewed energy quickened her pulse. "I'm not sure if I can ever thank you enough."

1

Herta Weber was thankful for many things that just a short time ago she couldn't have imagined possible, but above all she was thankful for living in the Netherlands. Her family flourished in the cozy third-floor apartment on Amsterdam's Nieuwe Kerkstraat where they'd lived for nearly a year now, within a few steps from the Amstel River. She didn't dare imagine what they might have endured if they lived elsewhere.

On this fine May day in 1940, she prepared pancakes with a topping of smoked salmon for dinner—a favorite of the girls though both Kurt and she preferred cod. She peered out of the single kitchen window at the leafy sycamore tree, lined up among other trees on the bank along the Nieuwe Prinsengracht. With her thoughts drifting over the contrasts between their new home and their roots in Germany, she jumped when the door slammed, nearly knocking over the frying pan from the stovetop.

"Mama? Where are you?"

"In the kitchen. What is it, Krista?" When her youngest daughter entered the room alone, alarm flooded Herta. "Where's your sister?"

Krista sighed dramatically. "Why do you ask about Edith? She's old. She can take care of herself."

"While you appear fine, I'm concerned about Edith since you and your sister walk home from school together and she's not with you."

"She's outside, talking with two friends. That's all she does. Talking."

Herta cupped her daughter's cheek. "Tell me what's upsetting you then, other than your jealousy over your sister."

"But I'm not—"

"Krista." Herta narrowed her eyes, aware that her 11-year-old knew better than to fuss with a challenge.

"It's Papa."

"What about him?"

"Papa works at Waterlooplein and something strange happened there today." Krista pulled away and twirled her long plait of thick auburn hair. "Ferdi said that since Papa sells his jewelry in the market, that he's a *Jood* and must be watched. I think that word means Jew in Dutch, but the way Ferdi said it, it didn't sound nice."

"You're right, love. It does mean Jew, which we are, and remember, there is no shame in believing in our faith."

"Why did Ferdi say that word in a mean way? He doesn't know a thing about Papa or our family." The corners of her eyes turned down. "I don't say bad things about Ferdi's family's religion."

One of the toxic traits of prejudice was that people welded it as a sword to attack others without fully taking the time to get to know the accused. More aggravating was that the attackers didn't want to know the target of their hatred in the first place. But how does one explain this to a child? "Take my hand, sweetheart. Let's sit at the table and talk." She led Krista to the oak table and its four chairs tucked in a corner of the compact but comfortable kitchen with its one hutch where dishes were kept, a stand with a radio on top, and two cookbooks on the single shelf. Relieved that Krista sat with her back to the window, so the outside busyness of life didn't distract her, Herta smiled at her youngest, who always reminded her of

Kurt. "Tell me what you remember of the time we lived in Germany."

"Lots." Krista lifted a questioning brow. "I had all my toys and books there. More clothes too. We were happy until..."

"Yes, my love?"

Krista reached for the cream cloth napkin before her and began to roll it. "Until the mean people ruined everything. People cried a lot one cold night. I remember we ran from home because you and Papa wanted to keep us safe. I think we went to Tante Franny's house. She hid us in the cellar. Behind boxes in a closet, right?"

Lost in the memory of her daughter, Herta nodded. Tonight, she'd say an extra prayer for her former neighbor Franny—a kind friend and not a blood relation, though the girls thought of her as an aunt—whose grace likely saved the four of them the black evenings during *Kristallnacht* and the subsequent gray days. Herta streaked a fingertip down her daughter's cheek. "What a fine memory you have."

Krista's eyes watered. "But they're not happy memories. Not like the ones you and Papa used to tell me about when you were growing up in Berlin." She blinked back tears. "How is this like what Ferdi said about Papa being a *Jood*? Will he stay safe? Will we all stay safe?"

Herta grasped Krista's hands. "I want to be honest with you, little dove." She paused to see if the pet name brought a smile to her daughter's face; it did not. "I don't understand why Jews have been picked on like bullies pick on other children. For that matter, many from other faiths and races have also experienced troubles caused by mean-spirited people."

"If Papa makes them believe he's not Jewish, would that help?"

Herta fought not to wince; not to shout *of course not* or *never!* She wanted to tell her daughter that securing their identity—their faith—would never come down to denying their heritage. Nor should it be for anyone. But with her family's narrow escape from Nazi Germany, and knowing full well she'd do whatever was necessary to keep her daughters from harm's way, Herta knew those words would be a lie. "What we do, Krista, is our very best to keep moving forward and enjoy our lives. We love each other. We look after each other. We live each day as it comes and we do not fear our tomorrows." She reached over and kissed Krista's forehead. "Your father and I will always look after you. And that's a promise."

With her fingers, Krista traced the perimeter of the butterfly pin that Kurt had given Herta. He'd crafted it only days before they'd committed to leaving Germany and fleeing for their lives to a land of freedom where they didn't have to fear condemnation. The fact that they never completed their journey to a new land of supposed acceptance was a topic she wanted to keep distant from her youngest child. She wanted to keep her daughters safe, like butterflies that are temporarily protected in their cocoon. She knew Edith had already become more jaded toward the workings of the real world, but as a mother, Herta had vowed to paint rainbows across the sky, like a kaleidoscope of colorful tulips. She'd fill the air with the cheer of Händel's music that would drown out talk of yesterday's fears. Like her own mother, may she rest in peace, Herta was one for never prematurely crossing a bridge into troubling thoughts. "Love, our own government is protecting us," she told Krista.

"The Germans?"

"Oh, no." Herta weaved her fingers through the child's hair. "The Dutch government. Remember how last month the military began to guard us? That is a way of keeping us safe." She needed to get the focus off combat. "Now, the government wants us to stay calm and go about our daily activities, like you and your sister attending school and Papa selling his jewelry."

"And you, Mama? What will you do?"

Finally, an easy question with a ready reply. One that always brought a smile to her face and heart. Eventually, when the girls would be older and more settled in Amsterdam, she would consider taking a job. And there was the possibility of joining Kurt in his jewelry business. He'd wanted her as a business partner, praising her 'eye for beauty' and for her 'smarts' in bookkeeping, which he'd always confessed was not his specialty. "I take care of you, your sister, and your father and make sure our home is nice and clean and happy."

Her daughter's eyes sparkled "A happy house? Oh, I like that."

"How about Edith? Do you think your sister would like that as well?"

"Probably." Krista sat straighter. "Edith likes what I like."

Herta knew this sibling rivalry went both ways, that Krista admired Edith and wanted to be just like her. Good thing Big Sister adored Baby Sis. When Herta was about to respond, relieved to hear Krista's lighter and chirpier tone, the door to their apartment smacked open again. As if she'd received a physical blow, Herta rocked back as the smile on her lips flew away.

"Mama!" Edith shouted, abandoning the more formal Mutter she'd been keen on using ever since turning the 13 last November.

Propelled onto sturdier feet, Herta darted from the kitchen. "What's wrong, sweetheart? Krista said you were outside talking with friends. Did they trouble you?"

"No. It's Papa. He's gone missing."

This wasn't Germany—or Poland for that sad matter. Nor was it 1939. One did not simply disappear from the streets of Amsterdam, especially in their lovely Plantage neighborhood. Herta planted her hands gently on Edith's shoulders. "Be specific, please."

"A boy from school just came by. He said Papa and a man were in a fight." Edith's words had puffed out like a staccato beat in a discordant symphony. "And Papa—he chased this man who snatched a necklace from him."

Her husband had zero tolerance for thieves that invented their own set of laws out of convenience. Another excellent reason for leaving Germany: Kurt, if he'd remained there, likely wouldn't be alive since he would have come close to throwing a punch or two at the Nazis. And she? Herta had no tolerance for a broken family, including harm to her husband. She flung off her apron, tossed it onto the sofa and ordered Edith to watch her sister.

Edith's eyes widened. "Where are you going? Will you be back?"

"To find your father. Of course, I'll be back. We will both come home."

It wasn't until she'd vaulted down the three flights of stairs and left the building that Edith's terror of losing her parents registered in Herta's mind. And to think that just the night before she and Kurt had expressed to each other how fortunate it was that their daughters had adjusted smoothly since the beginning of their travels. When she considered all that had happened—uprooting the children from their native country to escape an uncertain horror, only to be turned away from the one country they all banked upon for a new beginning. Then, they'd been forced to travel to yet another new country, the Netherlands, and to call it home. And now, Edith—the one who usually managed to keep her chin up despite fears—had asked if she and Kurt would come back? Fighting a headache jabbing between her eyes and a knotted stomach, Herta pushed on to find her husband. She had no other choice.

2

With the girls playing nicely together in their shared bedroom, Julia Arzt kicked off her shoes after a day's work at the bakery and sat at the table in the dining area next to the small kitchen. Starting with the left foot, she massaged her aches. The shoes were the no-nonsense kind, but after standing on them for nearly eight hours, her feet made her feel more like her mother's age rather than 30. The rest of her body was smarting as well, but what good was complaining? She was relieved to have work. Besides, she certainly couldn't complain to Luuk about her discomfort. He'd only tell her to quit bellyaching, and she was in no mood for one of his outbursts. Besides, she was being selfish. Luuk would barge through the door at any given second and want her full attention.

On her feet, she entered the kitchen and reached into the breadbox. Fortunately, her daughters—and Luuk—knew not to upset her by raiding for a snack. Good. A few pieces of *pepernoten* remained. She baked the cinnamon biscuit-cookie year-round, rather than only on Saint Nicholas Day when the treats were customarily tossed about a room for children to find. Thinking about how much both Annelise and Marianne loved them, she decided to let them enjoy the biscuits more often.

"Mama... Mama." Marianne ran to Julia and wrapped her arms around her waist, but not before Julia saw her youngest's eyes moisten with tears. To think that only minutes ago when she'd gathered Annelise and Marianne from her sister-in-law next door, they were both smiling. The girls adored their auntie Mila, which worked out well considering that Luuk's parents had passed away. Her own parents, as well as Luuk's other brothers' wives, had not offered to help out with the girls. Mila, who did not have children herself, was the sole person Julia could count on for babysitting while she was at work or running errands. Since Mila often remained home to look after her maimed husband and had no objections to watching Ani and Marianne when needed, Julia didn't feel like she was taking advantage of Mila.

Julia wove her fingers through Marianne's golden Shirley Temple ringlets. "Why the sad face, my little princess?"

"It's Ani. She won't let me play with her best doll."

"Let's sit for a moment." Julia grasped the four-year-old's hand and led her to the table. She hoisted her onto her lap. "Your big sister knows that she should share her toys with you. Do I truly need to remind her again?"

"No, Mama. Ani was good."

Julia thought so. Annelise might be the eldest by only a year, but she was a kind-hearted child who usually didn't lord over her sister and easily shared her toys. Marianne, on the other hand, tended to be a handful, often on the dramatic side. "By chance, were you the one who didn't let your sister play with the doll?" Marianne hesitated, then nodded. "I thought so. Tell me what's wrong."

"It's Papa. He scared us again. Last night—when he read us stories."

Luuk loved his daughters, but he was definitely the disciplinarian of the two of them. Thus far, more with his cutting words than by his hand. Neither was good, but her parents raised her on the 'sticks and stones will break my bones but words will never hurt me' adage and she'd survived her childhood. Yet, she needed to use caution. "Your father wants you and Ani to be good girls. He might raise his voice or threaten to use his belt, but that's out of love. He says scary things but doesn't hurt you." She hoped to God that Luuk hadn't changed, hadn't slipped into a more menacing role. She needed to ask the question, but feared the answer. "Did Papa hit you or touch you in a strange way last night, or your sister?"

"No." Marianne wrinkled her nose. "Papa said scary things about other people. Told us not to trust our Jewish friends. He said they're not people. What does he mean?"

This was not what she expected to hear from her daughter's mouth. When she thought about it though, she shouldn't be shocked. Luuk despised anyone who wasn't purely Aryan. He also saw the mixed marriages of Jews and Aryans as worthless, meaningless. Often, he griped that fake people had no rights, and certainly shouldn't bring children into the world. And that was why she kept mum about a few things that wouldn't please him. Yet, he didn't need to mentally program these ideas into their daughters' innocent minds.

"I'll tell you what—I'll talk with your father when he gets home from work." She hated lying to her daughters. Luuk wouldn't listen to anyone but himself, especially on the subject of his children. She helped Marianne off her lap. "In the meantime, go say you're sorry to your sister for fussing, then bring her to the kitchen for a snack."

Marianne departed in a hurry, evidently pushing aside the major upset for the late afternoon, hopefully the last one of the day. Julia would offer her daughters a nibble and then start cooking a supper of chicken and potatoes. She dreaded Luuk complaining about having no red meat again, despite the fact that the food staple had become scarce the past few years. Although the food scarcity was not his fault, Luuk liked to think that he provided well for his family, always striving to do better than other Dutch families who had suffered ever since the Great Depression ransacked the world. His pride, a strength, was also his Achilles' heel. Then again, she couldn't blame him. Throughout the past two decades, his family's once-thriving—though now defunct—industrial machine shop steadily nosedived in profits. During Luuk's teen years, no one spoke of poverty in front of neighbors and strangers. Both of his parents held high expectations of all five of their sons to not only do well financially, but also achieve high social status. They made no attempt to hide their displeasure upon seeing their sons and their spouses. Julia sniffled. Her poor husband. In their seven years of marriage, he hadn't accomplished either objective.

"Mama, why are you crying?"

Julia wiped her eyes and peered up at Annelise as she entered the room, holding Marianne's hand. "Don't mind me. Dust must have gotten in my eye and caused tears." She smiled at the girls. "I see you two have made up. Good. That pleases me, and your father will be happy to see his smiling girls greet him."

Marianne lifted a knee onto a chair and climbed up. "How about Papa? Will he smile?"

"He hasn't for a while," Ani added.

Julia set a dish with two *pepernoten* before each girl and watched as they each stuffed a large bite into their mouths. "He has a lot on his mind. It would be best if you both do not upset him, understand?"

They nodded simultaneously.

A rattling sound came from the door.

Marianne smiled. "Papa's home." Leaving the second *pepernoot* behind, she scurried from the room. Ani took one bite of her last biscuit and then also took off to greet her father.

Julia inhaled deeply and let out a slow breath. Yet, it wasn't calming enough. *Steady now*. As she walked toward the front door, she called her husband's name in the softest tone she could muster. The two-story house—with its two bedrooms upstairs and one small room downstairs that could be converted into a bedroom if there should be a new arrival—suited their needs well, but at times was confining if Luuk was in a foul mood or if the girls were nursing their own sour dispositions. Julia hadn't expected to encounter Luuk with a pleased look on his face—stretching his thin lips wide in a tender smile. She was surprised to find the girls bouncing around him like puppies and Luuk not reprimanding them or pushing them off.

"Papa has a surprise," Ani chirped in singsong.

"For you, Mama," Marianne said, her grin almost larger than her pixie-like build.

"Girls, girls," Luuk said. "Can't I surprise your mother all by myself?"

Julia had no doubt about three things: her husband was indeed in a good mood; he didn't mind the girls clinging to his trousers, and he held something—maybe a gift—in his arms which were secured behind his back. "Oh, my." She gently separated Annelise and Marianne from their father. She peered into Luuk's eyes for telltale hints of anger or disgust but didn't find any. "I can't imagine what the surprise is. I can only hope it's for all of us."

"No, Mama," the girls said, their voices in a synchronized squeal —a specialty of theirs.

Julia glanced at Luuk's face. She expected to see a frown. A charming smile greeted her instead. He swung his left arm around her, brushed his lips against hers, and kissed her with a passion that had been lost these past months.

Luuk stepped back and looked at the girls. "Go to your room. I want to talk with Mama." He waited until they skipped down the hallway before presenting her with the cloth pouch that he'd hidden behind his back. "This is for you, Julia. Long overdue."

"But—"

"No lectures," he said softly. He planted the gift into her hands. His eyes twinkled. "Go ahead. Open it. But face me. I want to see if you like it."

"I'm sure I'll love it."

"Julia…" A playful nudging, but nevertheless, a prompt.

Julia untied the satin ribbon, the red reminding her of Christmas, summer sunsets, sweet autumn apples—of all that was good and special. Like Luuk, when they'd first met. Her breath hitched as she withdrew a gold chain necklace with a jeweled butterfly pendant.

"Do you like it?"

"It's beautiful, stunning, and sparkly, like a stained-glass window in a cathedral." She noted that with each of her words, his smile grew. She handed him the necklace and held up her hair. "Please fasten it so I can look in the mirror to see what it looks like on me."

"You make the necklace lovely, not the other way around."

She blinked. Had she heard that correctly? Not only had her husband, who had grown sullen these past few months, given her a gift she knew he couldn't afford, but he was flirtatious and sprinkling sweet admiration upon her. She lifted onto her toes to give him a quick kiss and took a couple of strides toward the mirror. "Luuk, it's simply divine. Thank you for this precious gift. Thank you for thinking of me."

"Well, I know it hasn't been easy lately. I wanted to make it up to you. When I saw this little gem, I knew I had to bring it home to you."

"Where did you find it?"

He winked. "My little secret."

Impish glee overtook her. Goodness, she couldn't remember the last time her spirits were lifted this high. "Come on, Luuk, tell me."

He pulled her into his side, his bearish arm pinning her tightly. His usual scent of machine oil and damp sea air were absent. Instead, there was the clean, crisp smell of confidence and assurance—the best aroma that had wafted toward her nostrils in the longest of times.

"Where I found this necklace is only for me to know." His tone was pleasant, not biting. She wanted to believe him. "But, let's sit for a few minutes and I'll share my exciting news."

3

Herta expected to search the cobbled streets, alleyways, and hidden alcoves of Plantage before finding her husband. Instead, within seconds after crossing the Prinsengracht canal to head toward Waterlooplein, she spotted a man of a towering height with unruly wavy black-as-the-night hair moving through the thick crowd in her direction. *Kurt!*

From head to toe, Herta's knotted muscles uncoiled. She wrapped an arm around him as if he'd been limping, yet he stood on two sturdy feet. "I've heard you've been in a fight. With whom? What did you—"

"Simmer down." He sidestepped her hold and pivoted in a complete circle. "I'm fine. See, no wounds. So please, none of your fussing and worrying. I can take care of myself." He started to stride toward home. Abruptly, he stopped and glanced over his shoulder. "Well, aren't you coming? I've had enough with sour faces for a day."

With arms crossed, she stared. "Before we step foot indoors, with the girls clamoring for your attention, let alone mine, tell me what happened." Upon seeing that cocky lift of his brow that always irritated her, she rushed out an explanation while aiming for a calm tone. "I'm not questioning how you can defend yourself or why you had to. But you know having a decent conversation—one that actually gets finished—around Edith and Krista is just about hopeless." She held her breath. Part of her feared Kurt would ignore her and continue walking home; the rest of her expected her loving, good husband to approach her, grasp her hand, and lead her to a private place to talk. Thankfully, he chose the latter.

"Let's go to Wertheimpark, Herta."

"You don't mind walking past your workplace—where I suspect this trouble began?"

He shrugged. "I've always found the park calming, no?"

The suggestion suited her needs as well and she nodded. "I'm sure Edith is watching out for Krista."

"Good. Then let's go. No talking until then, if you don't mind. I need to clear my head."

Without another word, they sped along. Soon enough, they entered through the park's gate, with its two stone sphinxes. Wertheimpark, the oldest public park in Amsterdam, opened in 1812. Herta and her family visited with delighted frequency. Whenever Kurt and she went without their daughters, they always made their way to the fountain built in 1898. This late afternoon was no exception. Herta sat to Kurt's right and waited in silence. At times, it took a while for her husband to open up, but he was a man of deep, careful thought and one glance at his face, chiseled with furrows across his brows and narrow-slitted eyes, indicated that this moment was no exception. Her patience may suffer, but he'd speak when he'd be ready.

Three young girls, perhaps sisters—they shared similar high cheekbones and thin-lipped smiles—sat on a flowered blanket upon the spring grass, dolls propped up and facing each other as if engaged in conversation. Two teen boys tossed a ball to each other. Mothers sat on benches, gently pushing *kinderwagens* back and forth. A few men also sat on benches, either ruffling through newspapers or engaged in lively conversations. If Herta had no pressing concerns, she would have basked in these sights. Instead, she swallowed dryly and slipped a hand over Kurt's fisted right hand balancing on the knee closest to her.

"How much do you like your butterfly pin?" Kurt faced her and jutted his chin toward the pin. "Be honest."

"I've told you, love," she began softly, her words weighed by the surprise of this unexpected question. She swept her hand away from Kurt's and fingered the piece of jewelry she wore daily. Might he be thinking about selling it? She understood that the tiny pearls and the scattering of rubies would fetch a decent price and they could use the extra money, but she adored the pin he'd given her before they boarded the St. Louis to travel to a hopeful new home in America. She hadn't admitted it then, but she was terrified. Afraid of what was happening to innocent people in their native Germany and nervous about whether a new country would embrace them. When Kurt had given her the pin, she saw in his eyes that he readily understood the turmoil within her and tried to soothe her worries with the butterfly that represented freedom and new beginnings. She hadn't admitted it then to either her husband or herself, but to calm her jitters she wore the pin like a talisman. She slowly let out a breath from her tight lungs. "I adore this butterfly. I truly do. More specifically, I adore you. It's not only beautiful, but it's a gift you've given me. One I'll always cherish and admire."

"I'd made you a matching necklace."

The one snatched. Without a doubt. No wonder he was upset.

He nodded. Evidently, he'd read her thoughts.

"I finished it earlier this afternoon and was planning on hiding it until our anniversary to surprise you with it." He placed a hand on each of her arms. "Herta, I was looking forward to seeing your reaction, but that worthless thief has ruined my surprise."

"And you're furious." Not a question, but a statement, one without judgment. Before he could reply, she leaned over and kissed his sweet lips. "Make me another one, if you want," she breathed into his mouth, then pulled away. "Or not. You're the best present I have, and as long as we have each other, and the girls—that's all I need to be happy."

"I almost caught the no-good thief, but then he ducked around a corner, out of sight."

"Did anyone else notice him?"

"After chasing the piece of scum, I asked the others working their booths at the market if they saw him. But after a whole day of seeing and talking with countless folks, they only offered shrugs or a quick head shake."

"And you? Did you catch any details of how he looked?"

Kurt withdrew a folded paper from his vest pocket. "When I got back, I sketched him before the image of him blended with other memories." He handed her the slip of paper.

"Clever thinking." She unfolded the sketch and studied it. A nondescript man peered from the paper into her eyes and made her shudder.

"What? Do you recognize him?"

"I'm afraid not. It's just that he looks so ordinary, plain. He can be any of the countless Dutch men roaming the city."

"Yes, you're right. What my pencil drawing doesn't show is the color of his eyes." He pointed to the illustrated man's right eye. "This one is brown. The other, green."

"Oh, my. That unique feature is bound to help with tracking him down."

"Believe it or not, it's subtle. The only reason I noticed the difference was because at one point, I'd grabbed him by the collar and stared at his lousy face, telling him exactly what I thought about him."

"How did he get away?"

Kurt averted his eyes. "Kicked me in a place I'd rather not think about and ran off."

She pulled him into a hug. "I'm sorry for your troubles," she murmured. "Let's go home to Edith and Krista. We'll have a nice family dinner, tell the girls bedtime stories, and once their eyes close, we'll slip into our own bed and I'll take your mind off of our misfortunes until the pain goes away. How does that sound, sweetheart?"

He kissed her. "Like my wonderful wife handed me a piece of heaven. And that's why I took the time to craft this butterfly necklace for you." His smile faded; his hands clenched again into fists. "I've never come as close to wanting to kill—"

"Shush." She leaned closer and pressed a finger to his lips. "It will be fine. We're on the eve of a new day, one that is more spectacular than today and filled with promises. You'll see."

He tilted his head. "And if not?"

She glanced right, then left, as if looking for a stranger to walk up to them. "Oh, dear. Where is my optimistic husband? He's gone missing. Whoever you are, Mr. Stranger, have you seen him?"

A hot breath steamed the side of her neck, followed by a tender kiss. "I'm right, here, Herta. I'll always be beside you."

"Good. I thought I lost you." She stood and offered her hand. "Let's go home, shall we?"

4

Herta woke instantly when Kurt whipped off the blanket and sat up in bed. Not ready to face the day, she kept her eyes closed and fanned her fingers over his pillow. Seconds ago, he'd been lying there and had kept her warm and secure since the moment they'd turned off the light hours ago. "What's wrong?" Herta believed she was dreaming and turned onto her right side, away from Kurt.

"Did you hear that?"

Life pulled at her. Again. All Herta heard was the tension clogging Kurt's tone. "I must have slept through it. What did it sound like?"

"Pop-pop rattling, like artillery. But at a distance."

She shot her eyes open and sprang upright, clutching his arm. "Are you certain?"

He remained silent. Considering the subject, the quiet was more razor-sharp than if he'd replied with sarcasm. He lay back, rested his head on his pillow, and squeezed her hand. "Let's sleep."

"But—"

A siren blared. They both kicked off the blanket and scrambled from the bed. A cry of *Mama* burst through their closed bedroom door. Edith and Krista pushed open the door and ran into the room.

"What's wrong?" Edith asked as she flung her arms around Kurt's waist, an act she hadn't displayed in more than a year. "Is it war?"

Krista cupped her ears. "Make the scary noise stop."

Kurt backed away from Edith and then pulled Krista's hands from her ears. Over the youngest's shoulders he peered at Herta. "Deal with the girls. I'll fire up the radio and see what I can learn." He jutted his chin toward their daughters. "All of you, stay here until I say otherwise." Before Herta could reply, he slipped into the trousers he'd abandoned on the floor and stuffed his nightshirt into his pants. With the bedroom door left ajar, she watched him as he headed into the kitchen where the radio was kept.

Once Herta heard the radio chatter, she turned to comfort her girls. "Hop into bed with me and then we'll talk." She took the lead and dove under the covers, patting the empty places to her side.

To Herta's surprise, Edith crawled beside her first. "Is this the start of war with the Germans?"

"Mama," Krista whimpered, still standing. She wrapped her arms around her middle. "I'm scared."

Like her girls, Herta was also frightened. As if the warm bed, with its lumpy mattress and second-hand sheets and blankets, were a fortress and not just a place to sleep, she didn't want to leave its protective grip. Yet, for her precious daughters, she would, a hundred times over. She stood; her nightgown clung to her sweaty body. She gathered Krista into her arms, settled her in the bed, and wiggled between her daughters. "It will be fine, sweethearts. Your father and I will keep all of us safe."

Edith groaned. "The boys and girls at school say we might have to go into hiding. I don't want to go away from you or Papa or Krista."

"Hiding?" Krista said, stiffening once again in Herta's arms. "What's that, Mama? Is it like playing *verstoppertje*?"

If only they faced the children's game of hide-and-seek and not the possibility of war. Herta placed an arm around both girls. "Do not mind what other children say. Your father is listening to the news and—"

The wail of a siren blasted like a mother keening over the death of her child. Herta shook. Krista started to cry.

"What's happening?" Edith asked. "What should we do?"

So many questions that she didn't have an answer to, nor, she suspected, did any civilian. She wondered exactly what pat response Queen Wilhelmina, in keeping with the country's policy of neutrality, would offer at the ready. Edith scooched closer and pulled the blanket to their chins. Herta smiled appreciatively. She held back a flinch when her youngest poked her thumb into her mouth—a comforting act she hadn't resorted to since the age of three. "Papa will learn what the sirens are about and he'll tell us. In the meantime, we need to be brave."

Kurt, staggering into the bedroom, stopped either girl from responding. He leaned against the wall, a handful of meters away, yet so distant. "Dutch watchers saw German bombers cross over the Netherlands on their apparent way to England." He stared at his bare feet while another siren blasted. This time, both girls covered their ears with their hands. He took advantage and approached the bed, rushing the words Herta knew he'd utter. "Once over the North Sea, the damn Luftwaffe circled back to attack the military airfields around The Hague. Paratroopers dropped from planes like rain from clouds. We're at war."

Herta pulled both daughters tighter to her sides. "What do they advise? Is there a shelter available to stay safe?"

"Get dressed. Put shoes on, right away. Grab jackets… it's best to be ready."

Ready for what? On her feet, Herta extended a hand to the girls. She eyed her husband. "Where are we going?" she asked, hoping this simpler question would get a more telling response.

"As instructed in the broadcast, we're to sit in the building's stairwell—with the other people living here—and wait for further instruction."

Again, she nodded. She understood the reasoning behind waiting in the building's center, away from windows and the potential of shattering glass, but if a bomb were to hit them, then what? Kurt's pale face and set jaw spoke volumes. This wasn't a time to seek meaning and understanding, but rather to grasp onto the barest chance of safety.

Sitting on the stairs, situated between clumps of the first-floor and the second-floor families, proved more challenging than expected. Each family had young children who peppered the adults with questions and demanded an explanation of the horror unfolding around them. Extended family, such as the grandparents of the first-floor flat or the older aunt and uncle of the other family, whose quivering lips and teary eyes spoke the unarticulated memories of previous wars and lost loved ones, also couldn't be avoided. The younger adults closer to Kurt and Herta's age consisted of men jabbing their thumb between their eyes at likely knotted muscles or rubbing their mustache, and women who twisted wisps of hair or rocked in their seats as they hugged their knees. It was as if they were chained to a wall, restricted from taking charge of the situation. The constant hushing to quiet the children sent a viperous buzz through the stale air as the adults—keen on learning the latest news—kept an ear to the radio placed outside the doorway of the second-floor apartment.

German paratroopers are dropping from the sky, surrounding The Hague. Stay indoors. Do not leave your homes.

Dutch defenders are on hand to prevent German aircraft from landing planes full of troops.

We've raced to our borders to secure our bridges from the German advance—we will not be taken over. The Netherlands will not fall into German control.

Kurt, quick to get to his feet, began to navigate around the others seated on the steps as he descended the stairs.

Herta called after him. "Where are you going? We've been instructed to stay put."

He glanced at two men, daring them, Herta believed, to accompany him outdoors. Only Peter stood up. Kurt patted his shoulder. "Good. We'll have each other's back."

Words Herta wished she hadn't heard. "Kurt!" Her tone had never been as loud as then, not even during the darkness of *Kristallnacht*.

Kurt stopped and faced her. "I'm going to see what I can do to protect my family." He and Peter—a man they barely knew—stepped outside. The briefly opened door allowed the sound of whistling artillery to sail indoors and further assault their nerves. Whether the barrage was far away or close, it was one of the scariest incidents Herta had ever experienced.

As if frozen, both Kurt and Peter remained by the building's entrance. Peter's wife raced toward the door, which she pulled open far enough for an odd bronze light to streak in. "What is it? What do you see?" Peter started to speak—his voice barely audible through the chatter of the others on the stairs. Then, as if they collectively realized they too could learn of what was happening, a wave of silence spread.

Kurt spoke up. He pointed toward the southwest. "That orange-blackish plume—where the Schiphol Airport is—must be the smoke from bombs." He glanced at the ashen faces of his neighbors, and of Herta, perched on the stairs. "You're to stay here. We'll be back." He scurried down the outside steps, and like his fleeting words, vanished.

As soon as Peter left the building with Kurt, Peter's wife, Rita, encouraged her two boys to visit with Herta's girls. As Herta had hoped, Rita moved up a couple of steps to sit beside her.

"You are Jewish, yes?" Rita said.

Why did the woman speak so softly, as if keeping their conversation intentionally from the other neighbors' listening ears? It wasn't as if they were criminals. Herta leaned toward Rita, who, with her husband and young boys, moved in with her in-laws into the first-floor apartment two weeks after Kurt and she had settled in their own flat. The two had exchanged smiles and casual hellos, but not one conversation. Is that what war accomplished, making enemies from many and friends from a few?

"Yes, we are." Herta glanced at her girls, who, along with Rita's sons, played a shell game using a walnut and three cups. She turned her attention back to the woman. "My daughters appear a bit calmer now. Thanks for suggesting to your sons to keep them company. This is all quite stressful—the children need each other."

"To keep themselves away from grownup concerns."

"Exactly, to say the very least." Herta smoothed her skirt, realizing that in her haste, she'd put it on backward. Her cheeks burned with embarrassment.

"No worries. It was the middle of the night when we were awoken, and not by the best news." Rita pointed to her own blouse. "See—my blouse is all mis-buttoned. Ask me if I care."

Herta gave a little nod. "You're right." She fidgeted with her skirt. Should they talk about their religious beliefs here, in front of the children and the other neighbors who—Herta knew without a doubt—were not Jewish?

Rita leaned closer. "Have you and your husband talked about *onderduiken*? You know... going into hiding."

"Oh, I'm familiar with the word." Herta searched Rita's eyes. "I'm confused as to why you mention it, though."

"The Dutch government has told us for months not to worry. They say that since we've managed to keep out of the Great War and now wish to remain free of Hitler's battles, the German army will leave us alone. Nonsense. To believe that we're safe is like believing in the silly notion of men walking on the moon one day." She leaned closer to Herta. "The talk of the town is not if we Jews go into hiding when the Nazis invade, but when and where."

Herta stared at her neighbor, hoping she didn't appear to be rudely gawking. So Rita and her family were Jewish after all. Apparently, they'd chosen to keep that truth to themselves. Until now.

Rita touched Herta's arm. "They will occupy all of the Netherlands."

Good God. This was Berlin all over again. Having lived—barely—through the Night of Broken Glass, she knew well that Jews and Nazis didn't live together companionably. Herta and her family fled Germany for a reason. Now, the Germans had not only dropped from the air into the Netherlands but, undoubtedly, would march across the border, if they hadn't already done so. "In all honesty, Kurt and I have had too much on our plate to plan for a hiding."

"Peter says life here will be changing awfully fast. You and your husband may want to start looking into a few possibilities."

"And you? Do you have a secure place to keep away from trouble?"

"We've talked." Rita left it at that, spiking Herta's curiosity of why the woman was so secretive and guarded. She called her boys, and the three slipped downward toward the front door as if in anticipation of Peter walking through the entrance any second.

"Mutter," Edith said in a full-on whine. "I'm thirsty. Can I get a drink?"

"No!" The adults stared at Herta; the children grimaced. Judging from the way her daughter recoiled, she'd not only frightened her bravest child but the others as well. "What is wrong with me?" Herta shook her head when she realized she'd spoken those words she'd originally intended to think silently. They had to hide in Berlin... she had to bring water and food... had to pack clothing and other necessities for basic living. When they'd boarded the St. Louis, the personal belongings they'd packed in addition to two outfits for each of them were only a smidgeon bump up on the improvement ladder of luxuries. A marriage certificate. One photograph of her parents. A handful of hygiene items. The butterfly pin that Kurt had made for her. And Kurt's tools to continue crafting jewelry.

Krista placed a hand on her shoulder. "Mama, there's nothing wrong with you."

Herta smiled at the enormous statement from her little girl. "Thank you, my precious." She lowered her head and massaged her throbbing temples. This would be a fine time for her husband to make an appearance. As if on cue, the door creaked open. But the person standing before them was neither Kurt nor Peter.

5

If it weren't for what Julia's husband had told her a few hours ago, before the midnight hour slipped into the 10th of May, the whistles and pops of distant gunfire and the frenzy and commotion outside of their door would have sent her into a state of panic instead of hope. Instead, she clung to Luuk's assurances that they were aligned on the right side of what he described as the appropriate German takeover, making them protected and having nothing to fear. Good. She'd center her concentration on Luuk's steadfast confidence, not on the hidden particulars that might change their fate. As her grandmother was fond of advising: tell only what is necessary to know, not a word more.

"Are you scared?" Annelise asked. "Papa said we don't have to be scared."

Julia reached for her daughter's cloth napkin and blotted a dribble of milk on the girl's chin. "Your father is right, Ani. That's why we're having breakfast at our own dining room table, in our own house, just like always. Papa was told by important people not to worry, and I believe him. We must all believe him." Both girls nodded.

"I want to look out the window." Marianne scooted off of her chair and ran around the corner into the parlor. "I don't see any children." Her voice had trilled, which Julia knew signaled alarm for her youngest, despite the comfort she'd just attempted to offer. "They must be afraid."

Beside her at the table, Annelise slipped her hand into Julia's grip. "If other boys and girls are scared, maybe Papa is wrong."

Marianne ran into the dining area, straight onto Julia's lap. "Mama, can we go outside and play?"

"No, darling. It's best if we stay indoors today." When both girls frowned, likely in objection, Julia continued. "Your father will soon be home. We will talk and tell you what the day will be like for you both." She hesitated, searching for the gentlest of words. With the takeover going on, there was no such thing as gentle. "You two might have to change your routines a bit for the next few days."

"What do you mean?" Marianne asked. "What are routines?"

Julia glanced at Ani. Like her younger sister, her eyes glazed over in confusion. "For instance, Papa rides his bicycle to and from work at the radio repair shop. He might have to stop using his bike and walk instead."

"Why?" the girls chorused.

Oh, dear. How could she begin to explain hardship, especially when she and Luuk had agreed to let Annelise and Marianne enjoy the simplicity and innocence of childhood? Luuk had put his foot down the day after Marianne was born. *We're the adults, our daughters the children. We'll do the worrying for them.* But now, on the edge of inevitable war, life—without a doubt—would change for every man, woman, and child. Yet, with Luuk's news of him becoming an NSB collaborator, their future held brighter promises than that of others. As Luuk had emphasized to her last evening when he'd first told her about his involvement with their country's national socialist movement, the one good thing was that neither of them was Jewish, nor did they have relatives married into the Jewish faith. Julia, thinking it best not to prolong the conversation, had left that subject alone. Besides, there was no changing her husband's mind.

She clutched the girls' hands. "Although your father and I will make sure you are well and happy, others might have a more difficult time. Your friends may not be permitted outdoors to play. If Papa and I tell you to play quietly in your bedroom, you must obey and not be angry with us. Understand?"

"Even if we don't want to?" Annelise asked.

Julia nodded. "Yes, my dearest."

A metallic rumble came from the narrow alleyway between their house and next door where Luuk's brother and his wife lived. Thank goodness they didn't have Jewish neighbors to worry about—one less invitation for German soldiers to conduct searches.

"Papa's home," Marianne announced as Luuk walked indoors and hurried toward them. Joy and excitement sparkled in his eyes.

Luuk hoisted one daughter under each arm and twirled them around—a father fueled by the wings of his children. Julia couldn't recall the last time she'd seen her husband so exuberant. Sure, he was unusually excited when he gave her the butterfly necklace, but not to the extreme like now. He flashed a charming, flirtatious smile at her. *Oh my*. Were other NSB wives also humming in elation?

"Papa's happy… Papa's happy," Marianne chanted, with Annelise joining in. Marianne then quieted. "Did you bring home presents?"

Out of the mouths of little ones. Julia palmed the sides of her face and broke out in a laugh. Her family hushed and stared. This made her laugh harder; tears ran down her cheeks.

Ani pointed. "Oh no, Mama's crying."

Julia waved her off. "No… no. I'm fine. Just happy that we're all happy."

"Enough," Luuk said as he set the girls down. "Off to your room. Mama and I need to talk. Afterward, we'll come in together and tell you what's happening." He didn't face Julia until their daughters grasped hands and skipped off to their bedroom. He then sat opposite of her at the table.

"News to share?" Julia asked.

He rested his chin on fisted hands, appearing more amazed

than distressed. "We Germans have a fight on our hands, but we're winning."

German? They were not German. Julia knew better than to correct the obvious, that both her family and Luuk's were native Amsterdammers, with traceable family trees dating back a couple of centuries. In fact, they'd often shared with friends and acquaintances how fortunate they were to know their lineage. The few times she'd mentioned a peep about Germans to either of Luuk's parents before their accidental deaths a year after she married Luuk, they'd erupted in rage. She could only imagine how they'd lambaste their son for helping the Nazis, but fortunately, she didn't have to deal with Luuk's outrageous parents now. If Luuk wanted to think of himself as German during this time of strife, she was more than happy to let him. After all, wasn't it normal—only natural—to desire her husband to succeed, and therefore ensuring that their daughters would thrive rather than simply survive?

"In The Hague, it didn't go as anticipated," Luuk continued, "but Rotterdam was a different story, much more encouraging." His eyes widened in excitement. "We landed seaplanes and are capturing river crossings. I've also had word that armored vehicles and the infantry have begun crossing the borders. It's a matter of time, no longer if, but when. Good news for us, *ja*?" He folded his hands like a schoolboy anticipating a fun lesson. "It's expected Amsterdam will be spared."

And the other cities and towns? Would they face destruction? Her unarticulated question burned sour in her mouth. "Good," she managed to reply.

"Things will change, though. Likely, on a slow basis. Nothing too drastic for us. Exactly what, I cannot pin down, not until things settle."

"Settle? How can things settle during a war?" As soon as the second question flew from her lips, she gasped. "Sorry. I didn't mean to question you. It's just that… that…"

He surprised her again by grasping her hands and bringing them to his lips for a kiss. Gently. Sweetly. Luuk was not a tender man. She stared into his eyes. This man of hers was full of surprises on a day of dread and trepidation for millions.

"I understand your concerns. You're probably wondering whether they'll send me away." He shrugged. "For now, I'm to act as an informant."

"And later?"

"I'm not concerned. Don't you see, Julia? We're on the side of the Netherlands' enemy—the right side for us. We won't suffer. We'll have food. Protection. Income. What more can we ask for? If I have to eventually join the German forces, so be it. It will be my honor." He moved his chair closer and surprised her again with another kiss, but this one on her lips. As he pulled away, he murmured, "You, my dear, will be able to stay in our home, and guide our daughters to become good citizens of the Greater Germanic Reich sweeping through Europe, and hopefully, one day soon, the whole of the world. It's time to embrace our true destiny."

She stood up so fast that the chair legs scraped the floor. "Pardon me."

"Are you ill?"

She gave a quick shake of her head. A moment of dizziness made her think otherwise. "I'm fine. Just need to look after the girls." In actuality, what she needed to do was to search desperately for normality while the world around them turned upside down.

He reached for her hand and gave a squeeze. "Say when, and we'll tell our sweeties that it's in their best interest to stay indoors for a few days."

Normally, she'd retort that having Annelise and Marianne inside 24 hours a day for an unknown quantity of days would drive her batty. For that matter, she'd fret that she needed fresh air to walk or bike. Now, the only one thing she was certain of was that war had crossed the border and would visit each home, making normality obsolete.

6

Seconds ticked by until Herta realized Bram, the university student who lived next door, stood in the apartment building's entrance. Dirt had showered over his thick blond hair, spilling onto his once-white shirt. A splatter of red streaked across his upper right trouser leg. Blood, Herta assumed. Based upon his composure, she doubted it was from a personal injury. While her mind recognized Bram, it fought to comprehend what he was saying. It wasn't a language barrier causing the problem. Although German was Herta's native tongue, speaking and understanding Dutch had come to her naturally. But his words? A jumble.

"I was asked by our own soldiers to go door to door, to share the good news that here, in Amsterdam, we do not expect the trouble that the other provinces have endured." He smiled a tired, wary, and most certainly, forced expression to convey a sense of calmness. "However, you are ordered to remain indoors until further notice. You can return to your living quarters but should stay away from all windows." He turned to leave.

"Bram?" Herta called out.

The young man placed one hand on the banister as if bracing

himself against having to explain what he didn't understand. "Yes, Mevrouw Weber?"

"My husband." She jutted her chin at Rita, who had moved beside her again. "And Rita's husband, Peter, took off into the streets to see what is happening. We haven't seen…" She couldn't finish her sentence, not with her daughters beside her.

"They haven't come back," Rita added. "We're concerned."

"I understand." Bram withdrew a paper from his shirt pocket. "The mayor's office issued a casualty list. I'm happy to say this neighborhood has only one wounded—an elderly man who fell down the stairs upon hearing the sirens. He is fine, though. A sprained ankle, that is all."

"Can we venture outdoors to search for our husbands?" Herta asked, prepared to volunteer.

Bram folded the scrap of paper at a slow pace, as if it had multiplied into several pieces. "It is best for all to remain indoors, specifically in this building, where it's safer than the streets." He informed them his duties required him to move onto the next building and wished them well.

But buildings could crumble from fire, from destruction by malevolent hands, and most definitely by a bomb. If harm were intended, they were neither safe indoors nor outdoors. The ugly truth nearly choked Herta. For the sake of her daughters, she tamped down panic.

The woman who lived with her husband and children in the second-floor flat, approached Herta and Rita. Beatrix was in her mid-thirties with graying brunette hair and a few extra kilos around her middle. Herta couldn't help to think how it took an enemy invasion to unite her with a neighbor who usually appeared too busy to chat, let alone say hello. Beatrix gave a nervous nod. "I heard you two earlier speaking." She glanced away then back again. "Sorry. I didn't mean to eavesdrop—"

"No apology necessary," Herta said softly. "This stairwell is certainly close quarters."

"Thank you for understanding. You two are Jewish?"

Both Herta and Rita gave a hesitant nod.

"Are you and your husband?" Rita asked.

No." Beatrix twisted her wedding band but didn't go into further detail. "I wouldn't worry. Jews from Portugal have come to Amsterdam since the end of the 1500s, followed by Eastern European Jews a hundred years later. So, for a long time, those of us who aren't Jewish, do not think of the Jews living in this fine city as distinctly different. We are all good neighbors."

Herta remembered her school history lessons. Although Jews had lived in Germany since the fourth century, the years had not been kind to them, and they were often persecuted, fleeing and coming back into the country in waves, like a turbulent sea. After what she and her family experienced, she couldn't help but be on guard against future atrocities. Yet, at the same time, she believed what Beatrix implied as the truth. She sought words that would coverup her lack of complete trust. "Kurt and I have received acceptance, as Jews, since coming to Amsterdam. You're right, Beatrix." She smiled at her neighbor. "Here, we haven't experienced prejudice like we did in Berlin."

Rita leaned closer, away from the ears of the children, who were eager to listen. "Both Peter's family and mine have lived here in Amsterdam and the surrounding areas for many decades." She swallowed visibly hard. "I can't deny that several of us have spoken about when and how to go into hiding from the Nazis, not whether or not we should. Peter and I will have a few more discussions on this matter, likely beginning when he comes back... if he comes back."

As if a howling wind pushed inward, the front door crashed open with a bang. Kurt and Peter stepped indoors. Herta and Rita's children sang out as one. "Papa!"

Herta leaned against the doorjamb of the girls' bedroom and listened to Kurt tell them the story of *Hansel and Gretel*. They were at the age now when fairytales were a bit too childish for them, but during this radical change of being attacked by a different country, Herta believed it was fine for a little comfort. While it was their favorite fairytale, Herta wished they'd requested a different one. On this precarious evening, the last thing she wanted her daughters to hear was a tale of two siblings abandoned in a forest who fall prey to an evil, cannibalistic witch.

Kurt stopped his rendition of the story as a snore sailed from Krista's mouth. He kissed Edith and whispered goodnight. "Will you sleep well tonight, Edith?"

"Of course, Papa. You've come back to us. You and Mama told us not to worry, and I won't."

"That's my big girl." Though the night was warm, he tucked the blanket up to her chin, the way she preferred. "I want you to set an example of bravery for your little sister. She needs your support more than ever."

"Why is that, Papa? Will the Nazis come to Plantage? Will we leave the Netherlands like we left Germany? Will we—"

"Hush." Kurt glanced over his shoulder at Herta. "Mama and I will always watch out for you and your sister. I'm concerned that over the next few days—once you and Krista are permitted outdoors and to return to school again—that you may hear rumors and stories scarier than *Hansel and Gretel*. If you're courageous, Krista will follow your good example and not imagine the worst. Can you do that for us?"

"Of course, Papa."

He waited until Edith snuggled with her sister, then walked toward Herta with open arms. "Did I handle that well, or do you think I frightened them for life?"

With her own emotions swirling, she hesitated, unsure of how to express herself.

"Herta, sweetheart, I suspect there's a lot on your mind. Let's sit on the sofa and you can tell me."

"Yes, there's plenty." Without a word more, she took his hand and led the way to the parlor. She sat to his right on the sofa and he enveloped her hands. She failed to feel reassured by his touch. "This invasion… this turning our lives upside down again is beyond unsettling. I admit I'm already beginning to lose my patience, my rationale, my—"

"Confidence of a better tomorrow?" He wrapped an arm around her and pulled her tighter to his side. "Remember when we first heard those verminous followers of Hitler scream out the worst imaginable names and threats at Jews who never lifted a finger of harm toward them?"

What Herta heard were not the words from the past that Kurt referred to but rather the words he kept back, the words that he regularly called the Nazis. Though she appreciated his attempt not to further overwhelm her with worries, there was a part of her that wanted to shout expletives to exorcize them from deep within herself. The only trouble was she knew it wouldn't help. She would never manage to ignore the ugliness of people hating people. "I will never forget. But this time, Kurt? I'm not sure if I can hold up like I did back in Berlin." She bent over and started to rock.

He gently helped her to sit upright. "Not with me by your side."

"And if, God forbid, something happens to you? Then what? How could I take care of our daughters?"

"Right now, my love, you and I and the girls aren't victims. Don't live that way—fear will uproot us faster than an enemy's threat."

"Tell me, then, how should I live? I want to be strong for Edith and Krista, but how do we live in the face of doom?"

"We must make it through today. Tomorrow, we must make it through that day. And the next, and the next. We have no other choice, do we?"

She blinked twice, not to correct her vision but her way of thinking. "You're right. Absolutely right."

In the first few days of the German occupation, as shock and amazement traveled the streets throughout the Netherlands when

Queen Wilhelmina and the royal family fled the country to England from the IJmuiden port, Herta grew nervous but hid her emotions from Kurt and her daughters. She was her husband's wife, her daughters' mother. She had to remain strong. Besides, why shouldn't the queen leave? No doubt, there would be a forced transfer of power if Nazi rule were to become the norm. This way the queen might manage to reach out to her citizens from a distant shore. Besides, she and Kurt had yet to become Dutch nationals. The Netherlands had welcomed them warmly and provided a safe haven, but she and her husband, sensing a looming war, wanted to consider all possibilities of their circumstances before making an ultimate decision. Would they ever enjoy living life rather than surviving life?

Despite exhaustion, Herta and sleep were becoming strangers. Fighting this, she willed herself to remain seemingly collected when she learned about the disappearances throughout the neighborhood of people who appeared to be present one minute and gone the next. First, the butcher. Then Edith's teacher and her husband, their five children and her father-in-law. The old bachelor who lived across the street. And those who openly fled to the quays of IJmuiden to await their turn to hop onto the boats and sail away from the Netherlands to faraway lands of promising peace.

"Mama, should we also wait for a boat to take us away?"

Herta put down her knitting needles and peered up at Edith stretched on the braided rug beside her sister. They'd been taking turns reading a storybook aloud. "No, dearest," she said without hesitation. They had already tried escaping on one ship and that proved disastrous. The memory of bright hope blighted by ghoulish despair still haunted her as well as Kurt. Although Edith and Krista never talked about their trip on the St. Louis, she imagined they failed to look back at their overall experiences aboard the ship as a fond time, except, of course, meeting and spending time with Zofia and her son Eban. "Your father and I have decided that we'll stay here. All is fine and we are safe."

Edith scrunched her face; fine lines appeared as if she were an old woman, both wise and worn. "You know how dangerous things can become all of a sudden."

Herta glanced at both daughters. "Who wants to help make lunch?"

Barely a month after the Germans had occupied the Netherlands, Herta understood there was no more escaping reality. Krista, who was playing outdoors with her friends, ran inside as if a monster had chased her. Tears were streaming down her usually smiling little face. Herta untied her apron and lifted Krista into her arms.

"What's troubling you?" When Krista burrowed her chin lower against Herta's chest, she carried her to the sofa, relieved that with Kurt working and Edith at a friend's house, they had this time to themselves without interruption. Herta tousled the child's curls. "Tell me why you're upset."

"It's my friends. Erika and Wilma told me they're Jewish, like me."

"Yes," Herta said, without an inkling of which direction this conversation was heading toward.

"They go to synagogue and eat foods that we don't eat. Does that make them more Jewish than us?"

Herta's own mother's explanation rang strongly in her mind. "There are numerous ways of believing in God. None of them is wrong as long as you love God, and each other, as God commanded us to do."

"What about the Nazis, Mama?"

Nazism wasn't a religious belief but an authoritative justification and administration of hatred. Not that she was prepared to have this discussion with a nine-year-old. "If your friends said you're Jewish like they are, it doesn't sound like they said troubling things about you. Tell me why you're upset."

"Oh, Erika and Wilma are nice girls. I like them. They like me."

Krista's eyes brimmed again with tears. "You won't stop me from playing with them, will you?"

"Of course not. Please, sweetheart, tell me what's wrong."

As if seeing the villainous creatures of her storybooks come to life and step from the page, Krista closed her eyes. "They've both heard their mothers and fathers speaking. They said times will become hard because they're Jewish and the Nazis hate them. They worried about having enough food for their bellies." She opened her eyes and stared into Herta's. "Will that happen to us, Mama? Will we grow hungry? Thirsty?"

No one Krista's age should ever be in a situation where they had to inquire about dying from starvation. Herta reached for Krista, but she pulled away. "Wilma told me about a dog that used to live by her house. The dog had no home. No one fed the poor animal. It grew thinner and thinner. One day, the neighborhood children found the dog dead." Krista wiped her eyes with the back of her hand. "Wilma heard what her parents said, that the same thing will happen to us Jews. That the Germans will take away our food. That we will starve to death like the dog."

Herta pulled Krista into a hug. "Your father and I will always protect you, darling. You're not to worry." It was best to stick to normal, everyday routines. At least as long as possible. She stood and offered a hand to Krista. "It's time to gather your sister and bring her home. Want to come with me?" Without resistance, Krista stepped beside Herta and they hurried off.

When Kurt walked through the apartment door two hours later, Herta greeted him before the girls ran to him for their hugs. "We need to talk."

Kurt set down his tool case and leaned against the door. "No man will admit this, but we all tremble when our wives say those words."

She pursed her lips in wonder whether to meet his levity with her own. Her heart couldn't muster such an attempt.

"Are the girls well? You?" he asked.

"Yes... well, actually..." She crossed her arms, then remembering how Kurt always thought she appeared bossy in that position, undid them and rested them by her sides. She couldn't hold herself together a second longer. She was about to run her fingers through her hair and lifted her hand, but Kurt caught it en route.

"I can tell this isn't good news."

"Shh." She glanced over her shoulder, relieved the girls kept busy in the kitchen and that apparently, they hadn't heard their father's voice. The moment to themselves wouldn't last long, and she struggled to find a quick, pat reply. "Krista's on edge about Nazis robbing us of food."

"I see." A misplaced broad smile appeared on his face as he peered over her shoulder. Ah, their daughters were heading toward them. "We'll talk later," he whispered.

Kurt kissed both his daughters and was about to slide out of his jacket when someone pounded on the door. He looked at Herta, but she shook her head. She hadn't a clue as to who stood on the other side, knocking commandingly. Kurt took charge and ordered the girls to sit on the sofa. He gave Herta's hand a quick squeeze. "Do not worry."

She narrowed her eyes, but he'd already turned to open the door. A woman and a boy, about Edith's age, stood side by side, not a smile between them.

"Yes," Kurt said. "May I help you?"

The woman faced the boy. "Do you see her?"

The child stood on his toes, looked over Kurt's shoulder, and pointed at Edith. "That's her, Ma."

Both Kurt and Herta followed the trail of the boy's accusing finger. Edith?

"Are you positive?" the woman asked her son. After he gave a nod, she stared hard at Kurt, ignoring Herta. "My son tells me that girl there, the one with the straight, long hair—"

"Our daughter, Edith," Kurt said. "Yes, I'm aware of what she looks like."

Herta flinched. How she wished Kurt hadn't revealed their daughter's name.

The woman braced her son with a hand to each shoulder. "Her name doesn't matter to me. Just that she's a thief."

"A thief?" Herta said, unable to keep quiet. No one had ever accused her daughter of wrongdoing. "You must be mistaken."

Kurt called Edith to join them. "What's this about?" he asked once she stood between him and Herta.

"I do not know, Papa."

"Look at her," the woman said. "Of course, she won't dare look at us, not in the eye, the worthless Jewish thief."

Kurt stood tall. "Pardon me, uh…"

"No need for me to give you our name, not when it's more important for me to remember who you are and where you live, in case the authorities ask for anyone suspicious."

"Edith, do you know who these people are?" Kurt asked.

"No, Papa. I've never seen them before."

The woman's jaw went slack. The boy bit down on his bottom lip.

Kurt eyed the woman. "What item of yours has gone missing, and what proof do you have that my daughter is responsible?" Kurt inched closer to the two strangers. "I must tell you, it's the end of my workday. I'm tired, short of patience, and am in no mood to hear false accusations about my daughter."

The woman's brow wrinkled. "It's no wonder you'd take the little crook's side."

Kurt huffed. Physical harm would not be in anyone's best interest, especially in this situation, and before he could act, Herta hooked arms with her husband, but he pulled away. "She's my daughter." His voice was low, deep, and growly. He faced the boy. "I'll believe my daughter before I believe you. You haven't answered my question regarding your fictional tale."

"She snatched a coin that had fallen from my pocket," the boy said and held up his hands. "Now I have nothing."

The woman smirked. "We aren't rich like you Jews are. We need our money."

Kurt dug into his pocket, withdrew two guilders. He pushed the money into the boy's beefy palms, hard enough that his hands lowered before he raised them again and clamped his fingers around the coins. "This will compensate for the misplaced money."

"But it's not misplaced—" the boy snapped before his mother stopped him with a quick spin and push toward the hallway leading to the stairs. Without a word more, she began to follow her son.

"Wait. One more word," Kurt added. The woman and boy stopped but did not turn to face Kurt. He took a single step forward. "If we ever encounter each other again, it will be in both our best interests that you not accuse us of being Jewish as if our faith is a crime."

The woman then turned to look directly at Kurt. "It isn't?"

Herta yanked Kurt inside and slammed the door. It was either that or allow her husband to do or say worse, since she knew he wouldn't have easily held back politely for another second. Even more unnerving was her awareness that she would likely assist him in putting the woman in her place, far away from her family.

7

Before Julia thought about opening her eyes from a late May afternoon nap, she sensed Luuk stood before her. Desiring to slip back into her fantasy dreamworld and unwilling to confront reality, she shielded her face with her palms and moaned.

"Do you have a headache?" Luuk asked. "Would you like a glass of water? A cold compress?"

Water could never chase away the type of pain she had. And she certainly didn't have the patience to hold still for a cool cloth. Instead, she lowered her hands to her lap, blinked her husband into focus, and fished for a blanket statement that wouldn't provoke suspicion. Although he'd surprised her with his concern, she needed to be guarded. The last thing she wanted to deal with was his temper. "Thanks, no. I was resting for a moment. The girls are playing next door under Mila's watch. It's not often a mother gets to rest." She sat up and patted the violet sofa cushion beside her. "Come sit. I'm glad you're home early—a nice surprise."

Luuk sat and set his hands on the cushion as if prepared to spring back onto his feet. These days, he was more often ready to leave than to remain home with his family.

"I took advantage of an unexpected and quicker connection to get me home from Utrecht." He pulled at his chin, but it didn't distract her from seeing his satisfied, smug grin, a new look as of late. Confidence became him. "The meeting went well. As I'd hoped, I spoke directly with Anton."

"Anton?"

"Anton Mussert, the leader of the NSB. He's quite impressed with me."

"Is that good news?"

Luuk lifted a brow. "Yes, that is good news. Why are you questioning me as if it isn't positive? Don't you want the best for me? For us?"

"Of course," she said fast before he continued. "Tell me about Mussert and his plans for you. Has he offered you a high-ranking position?"

"With the German invasion, the party has changed." He slumped back into the sofa; the color draining from his cheeks. "More changes are expected."

"What kind of changes? Will it be like when the invasion occurred and there were hundreds of NSB members and sympathizers arrested?" She tensed, afraid he'd sense her irritation and berate her for it. Yet, she couldn't shake off a growing fear in the pit of her belly. "Please tell me, Luuk, that there isn't a chance you'll be detained. Or worse."

"Those NSB members? They were all released as soon as the Dutch were defeated by the Germans and the royal monarchy fled to London like scared mice." He chuckled. "The queen will supposedly try to rule in exile. The Germans have other plans, though. But getting back to your concern, sweetheart, I'm unable to predict whether I too will be detained. This is war. It impacts all of us." He smiled softly, but enough for Julia to breathe easier. "Like I've said several times, we're on the right side—the German side. Let's just say that though there will be more restrictions for the Jews, there will be a few more benefits for the rest of us. It's about time, don't you think? Time for us Aryans to enjoy the liberties and opulence that these creatures don't deserve."

To the relief of her reeling head, Luuk paused his rant. She was so tired of hearing about Jews. The few she knew personally made no gestures of harm to her or her family. Jews had lived peacefully in the Netherlands for centuries. To think the NSB purported that an international Jewry had accomplished control over this country and moved to take over all of Europe troubled her. No wonder her head ached. When she thought about her own past, her head would pound more, and she often broke out in a cold sweat. It was best to live in the present. At times, the way to not fear the future was to bury the past.

"But, here's a nice chunk of excellent news." Luuk clapped his hands together and then rubbed them with a frantic zealousness. "Anton is once again speaking in Lunteren at the annual *Hagespraken* to renounce the worthless royal family. We all believe Hitler will appoint Anton to be in charge of the Netherlands. There's concern that Arthur Seyss-Inquart may get the position rather than Anton, but the NSB is counting on Anton to make the Netherlands an independent state allied to Germany."

Julia tried to return Luuk's radiant smile, but her worries washed through her again. In an attempt to cover up her anxiety, she turned away. "That sounds like good news."

"Of course, it's excellent news. Why aren't you more pleased?"

In no mood to play his favorite game of trial and judge, she needed to keep the focus off of herself and put it back onto him. "With you on a first-name basis with the leader of the NSB, that's a wonderful indication that he must think highly of you and that yes, you will go far."

"I'm not doing it for myself, but for our country."

"I understand. And I applaud you."

He stood up and began to pace. Not a good sign. Why did his moods have to change as fast as a snap of the fingers?

"No, Julia. I don't think you do understand. Despite only a few words exchanged between Anton and me, in all confidence I can easily say that he has major plans for me. I want nothing more than to serve the Third Reich."

What about us, Luuk? she wanted to ask but didn't dare. *What about our daughters?*

"Can you imagine?" Luuk continued. "There's talk that Anton will be appointed prime minister of what remains of this shameful country and restore it to German glory. Do you know what that might mean for us—for you and I and our family—if I continue to demonstrate exactly what Hitler and Anton and the NSB want?" He stood straight, reaching a full *voet* above her height. Distinguished. Matchless. Leading. That was how she'd once thought of her handsome Luuk back in the days when they'd first courted. Lately, the words *overpowering* and *imposing* flashed through her mind. Next to him, she felt like a shrunken shell of a person, someone to forget about, someone to sweep aside, like dust.

With a funnel of heated anxiety swelling within her, she couldn't sit a second longer. In desperate need to see life outside of the four walls of her house, to see other people, to catch sight of either her own children or other young ones enjoying the fresh air, she crossed the small parlor to one of the two windows, slid the plain white curtain open, and leaned her forehead against the cool glass.

His hand pressed firmly on her shoulder. "I want the best for us." He fell silent, then. If he was waiting for her to comment, he was out of luck, since she knew to keep her fingertips out of the hot flame. "Thankfully, the Nazis have full control of what's left of this country. You must see that I'm right and trust my decisions. Don't you?"

Her throat knotted up. Any semblance of thought and its subsequent transition into words dissolved. She hated when she got like this but lost all traces of inner strength when Luuk was having one of his moments. She wished she could slip into a place of escape, her own personal, emotional inner sanctuary. A safe, quiet, and gentle place. But she couldn't go there now, not with two daughters to take care of. "You must know what you're doing," she said in a flat tone.

"Why won't you look at me?"

For the life of her, she didn't have an answer. The dry wooden floor jostled and groaned like an old lady. She sensed he'd spun around and headed away from her. The door—creaking open and then slamming shut—confirmed this.

Nee... nee... He was furious and it was her fault. He'd arrived home happy, full of good news and anticipation—the complete opposite of how he'd acted in the months before the invasion. Without Annelise and Marianne home to think about, she rushed after him. Once outdoors, she saw him duck around the corner. Luuk despised when people made public scenes, saying that airing personal matters is a horrendous humiliation. He especially hated it when she shouted out his name in public. He'd often scolded her. *I'm no little boy for you to embarrass. Always treat me like the husband you admire and respect.* In what way should he treat her? Obviously, it didn't matter to him. He'd treat her in any way that suited his current needs.

As Julia's strides became a full-out jog to catch up with him, she approached a canal bridge. Two white-haired men were huddled together at the beginning of the bridge's deck They were belly-aching—their tones pitched high and their hands gesturing wildly. As she stepped closer, the men suddenly ceased their ranting, stood tall as if in a salute, and smiled broadly at her. They greeted her by her married name as if they'd known her for years, though she had no clue who they were. Unsure of what to make of this, Julia continued crossing the bridge. At the far end stood a young woman about the age of a university student. Her arms were wrapped tightly around her middle; sadness streaked her pale face. When her gaze connected with Julia's, the woman's lips rounded in a tiny *oh*, and her face turned even whiter, as if she might pass out.

"Are you ill?" Julia reached for her. "May I offer my assistance?"

The woman shrieked and ran off without volunteering an explanation. A memory of this stranger flooded Julia's mind. Two weeks ago, with Annelise and Marianne teeming with excess energy as their bedtime approached, Julia, in the hope of tiring them, took her daughters on a rather long stroll. It was a Friday evening, and they were passing the historic Portuguese Synagogue when its congregation began to dribble out its doors. Families smiled. Couples held hands. Young men chatted in groups of three and four while individual women darted off into the night. This same woman that Julia had just encountered on the bridge was one of those women. She was sure of it. One who didn't belong in a family group or a cluster of friends, one who wore the look of utter loneliness. One who reminded Julia of herself before she met Luuk and fell hard for him, knowing she'd never be lonely again. Not as long as she had her handsome, caring man beside her to go through all the ups and downs that lay in store for them.

But this stranger also wore the look of alarm. Luuk had proceeded Julia over the bridge. Had the woman known about Luuk and his activities? Julia couldn't imagine how, but if she was familiar with him, would she know that Luuk was Julia's husband? Seconds ago, the animated old men seemingly expressed pride in her relationship with Luuk, yet this fearful woman reacted as if Julia was a monster chasing after her. Later, she'd have to ponder over this more. For now, as if acting on their own volition, her feet continued to run. She had to find her husband.

Luuk was at the one place she'd never expected to find him: sitting on a bench in Wertheimpark. Alone. Not that he didn't appreciate the park, or serene nature for that matter, her husband simply wasn't one to spend his spare time in solitude, let alone sitting idle. His parents had seen to it that their sons understood that it was sinful to not be productive, whether in business or in contributing to society. This man before her now, her husband of seven years, looked different from the one who ran away from her a few minutes ago. Oh, he was definitely Luuk, no mistaking that. But this? Accustomed to the extremes of anger and doubt, or the opposite—playfulness when it came to the girls, and confidence when it came to making love in their cramped bedroom—she didn't know this look of his cocked head, turned-down lips, and a furrowed brow.

"Luuk?" After a few seconds ticked by and he hadn't replied, she again called his name, gently and warmly. When no response came, she tried a different tactic. "I'm concerned about you. But, if you don't want my company, or to at least tell me what's upsetting you, I'll respect your privacy and go home." She allowed a few seconds to slip by, then turned around.

"Wait." This one word stopped her cold. Yet, she couldn't face him. "Will you sit beside me?"

A gentle tone. All right then. She could chance this unusual meeting. She sat to Luuk's right. Not hip to hip like lovers sat, but with a gap between them, more like two cautious, platonic associates. Luuk bent over his knees and scrubbed his face with the palms of his hands. He kept at it longer than she expected. Part of her wanted to reach out to him, touch him, and offer comfort. She wanted to reassure him that if he wanted to, he could speak what was on his mind, and she would listen without judgment or interruption. But with Luuk, things never were simple.

He sat up and leaned against the back of the bench. "I took off on you because you'd angered me."

"But I—"

He held up a hand to stop her. Just as well. Why should she explain or apologize? "Doesn't matter. I needed air. Needed to cool off. I kept walking and walking until I saw Julian. Remember him?"

She blinked at the abrupt mention of the man's name. "I believe so. He's a fellow NSB member—you introduced me to him and his wife a few months ago when we passed them on the street."

"Correct."

She waited for him to continue, but an awful silence once again slithered its way between them. Wanting to understand what troubled him about Julian, she rushed to prompt him. "Have you received bad news?"

Luuk faced her, his brows lifted in amazement. "Of course, bad news. Julian isn't the type to track me down from the other side of the city to talk about the weather or other nonsense."

Resisting the urge to cower in a corner and curl into a ball, she sat up straight and peered into his mixed-colored eyes, which were as confusing as he himself could be at times. "Would you like to tell me?"

"Arthur Seyss-Inquart is in. Anton Mussert is out."

"In... out? I don't understand."

"None of us do. We all expected Anton to become the new leader of the Netherlands under the Nazi flag, not this other—"

"Oh, now I recognize the name. Seyss-Inquart. He's the one who was overseeing changes in Austria and Poland on behalf of Hitler, no?"

"*Ja*, but it was more than overseeing those countries. Seyss-Inquart became the *Reichsstatthalter* when Germany annexed Austria, then the Deputy Governor General of Poland. He's to become Reich Commissioner of the Netherlands."

"It all sounds like a game of titles."

"Julia, this is no game. You don't understand what consequences this will have. With Anton out of power, all this work—building up faith in me and what I can do for the Nazi party—was a waste of time. I'm going to become a nobody. Again."

"Won't Anton put in a good word on your behalf? Why not ask him directly to speak with Seyss-Inquart... You're not about to leave the NSB, are you?"

"Me?" Luuk spat on the pavement before them. "I'm Hitler's dream come true as far as dedication to the Nazi Party goes. This new person hasn't changed my mind."

"Then why the long face, dear?"

He again drooped over his knees. When Luuk had fled the house, and she followed right behind, she didn't question herself on why it was her responsibility to cheer up her husband, who had previously accused her of failing to understand the difference between serving a righteous invading country versus honoring and caring for his family. It was her duty. She was his wife; she needed to take care of her husband and see to his needs and comforts. His reprimand of seconds ago jabbed her insides with the contrasting bolts of mortification and the need for self-assertion that he should stand by her and respect her needs. But she couldn't do it. She couldn't speak up for herself. Instead, she brushed her hand lightly over his back; his coiled muscles eased under her fingertips.

"Luuk, you're a good man. Devoted to the right cause and willing to work harder than anyone I know. Seyss-Inquart will recognize all your fine traits and desires to serve the Third Reich and he'll promote you to an officer."

Luuk kissed her on the cheek and then swung an arm around her. "No matter what happens, I will do what is necessary for you and our daughters to not only keep you from harm's way, but to make you proud of me."

She shook her head and smiled. "No dear, that's not necessary. I'm already proud of you and will forever remain that way." She stood and offered him a hand. "Let's go home and gather up Annelise and Marianne and enjoy a celebratory dinner."

"What's to celebrate?"

She didn't care if they were out in public; she'd show her man exactly what she thought of him. She covered his lips with a kiss she never wanted to end. When they pulled apart, she murmured, "We're celebrating you—the most marvelous man I know."

8

With Edith next door playing with a classmate and Krista skipping rope with a friend in front of their apartment building, Herta leaned back in the kitchen chair, lifted the second-hand pink candytuft Royal Albert teacup, and inhaled the fragrant mint tea before taking a dainty sip. What a luxury to enjoy a few minutes to herself. She shouldn't think like that, but considering the hectic days of the past few months, she couldn't help but view the tranquil moment otherwise. School, starting next month, was fast approaching for the girls. Worry over the German invasion had shifted to whether or not they'd be permitted to attend classes and see all of their friends again—both equally important. Children needed a sense of normalcy and routine. That was why Herta wished Daan—a fellow student in Edith's class—had kept his mouth shut regarding his supposed insight about Jewish children not being permitted to return to school. Children, being at times ratty boys and girls, could be cruel. She'd tried to explain this to Edith, as well as Krista, who caught her older sister's wave of anxiety like a cold. Herta stressed to them that with the German takeover of the Netherlands, rumors abounded, and now, more than ever, it was better to be cautious than to worry. So far, their school was slated to re-open its doors for both the non-Jews and the Jews. Fortunately, thus far, her daughters were excited and happy, but there was no mistaking that they kept these emotions guarded, ready for abandonment and to jump into a defensive state if necessary. This complicated state of mind clarified one of the many tragedies of war: the vulnerability of children, and how they couldn't be fooled into believing that everyday life was fine.

It wasn't just that the girls were struggling to remain in a positive spirit—not that Herta found fault with their wobbly moods. Of course, she couldn't blame them. They'd fled Nazi Germany for that very reason: they were Jewish, a faith and way of life that Hitler saw as toxic and evil. But she and Kurt also had their own concerns. Not until after they'd tuck the girls into bed could they safely talk about events and concerns, if they kept their voices low enough not to awaken their darlings. Kurt had wanted to flee Amsterdam, often demanding they take a chance and run before it was too late. When he couldn't answer Herta's questions about where to go and by what means, he'd switched the conversation from escaping to hiding—*onderduiken*, Dutch for diving under, reminiscent of the time she and Rita talked while hiding on that fateful day of the German attack. She couldn't imagine hiding. In a stranger's attic or cellar? Buried under hay in a pigpen? Would—and could—they send Edith in one direction and Krista in another, separating them for an unknown time, if not forever? And what about the two of them—would she ever see Kurt again? Would their last rendezvous take place in a Nazi work camp? They had fled Germany together, vowing to each other that they'd remain inseparable. The definition of family, at least in her mind, was people joined by love—whether by blood or adoption—able to and wanting to remain united in a vast world.

A hand came upon her shoulder and she breathed in the sweet earthy smell of her husband. Her jumbled nerves relaxed as he swept an arm around her and nibbled on her right earlobe.

"Expecting someone else?"

She brushed his lips with a kiss. "Good thing you're teasing."

"Or what?" He pulled her to her feet and kissed her deeply, answering his own question, as silly as it was. He pulled away. "Saw Krista," he huffed. "Evidently, we grownups are alone."

"Yes," she replied, examining his expression. He looked concentrated, with a thumb and index finger framing his chin. Despite his passionate kiss, he wasn't making a romantic move on her. "Why are you home so early from work?"

"A few of us men were talking at the market—things are changing. Right before us."

"Has Zes-en-een-kwart proclaimed a new edict that we need to obey?"

If this were a different situation, Kurt might have smirked at the nickname she'd used for Seyss-Inquart that many Dutch were commonly wielding in mockery of the new leader of the Netherlands, calling him Six-and-a-quarter. Instead, her husband's facial features contracted in solemnity. "*Obey* has been the word circulating, all right. He's been kind of mild in his control, but we're all wary about what's ahead."

"We're not living in the future, but right now."

"Herta?" Both Kurt's brows lifted like two question marks. "You are the same woman who escaped with me from Nazi Germany?"

She leaned away. "Kurt?" she replied, matching his skeptical tone.

"I'll get right to the point."

"Please."

"Truthfully, I didn't operate my booth at the market today." Her mouth fell open and he lifted a hand to pause her. "Let me explain. None of us did. We couldn't, not after the demonstration we saw."

"Where was this?"

"In Dam Square. Yes, it's a distance from Waterlooplein, but a few of us got word early enough and went to see for ourselves. We got there in time to hear most of the anti-German speech given by a college professor."

"Most? What happened?"

"Nothing good. This courageous man kept talking about the

evils of Nazism and the obscenities of Hitler—his words, mind you—despite the police showing up and aiming their guns at him. And when they dragged him away, he continued shouting out his message to the disbanding crowd. He kept on talking—well, at least moving his mouth, because who knew what he was saying by then. He broke away and ran off. The police captured him."

Herta gasped; she knew what was coming.

"The police clubbed him over the head, kicked him, and hauled him away, leaving a trail of blood." Kurt stared into her eyes so hard she flinched. "Herta, the horror of what happened to this man who dared to speak out was that the harm done to him wasn't by the hand of Nazis, but by the hands of the Dutch police. Hands. Collective. See what I mean by things changing?"

"I think I'm seeing too much, Kurt." When he shot to his feet and headed straight to the corner cabinet—locked securely from the girls' exploring hands—she grew more nervous. "You're already going for the *jenever*?"

"Yes. Would you like me to pour you one?"

She couldn't deny a sudden thirst for a strong drink to either her husband or herself. "After hearing your news, thank you, I'd love a drink."

He brought the full glasses over to the sofa. After handing her the piney-scented drink, he mumbled a few words. She asked him to clarify. Without delay, he lifted his glass. "We can use this."

She clinked glasses with him and swallowed a tiny sip, wanting more but holding back. "Tell me your thoughts on this things-are-changing matter we're facing."

He swallowed his drink in three gulps and reclined back. "I know you have your guard up, especially after leaving Germany and our abysmal trip on the St. Louis and denial into America, but Herta, it's again time for us to leave." He shushed her, though she hadn't uttered a peep. Could he sense her blood approaching the boiling point? "We've lived here a little over a year, just long enough for me to start thinking of Amsterdam—or to be more exact, this Plantage neighborhood—as a fine place for my family."

"Yes," she said, nodding, "I feel the same way. But—"

"Sadly, there is a but, one we can't help." He thumped his chest with his middle fingers. "A man must protect his family. Hitler won't be satisfied with simple ownership of the Netherlands—for lack of a better word. Life—for me, a poor alien who happens to be Jewish by Nazi standards only—is about to come crashing down on us. Maybe not tomorrow or next week or month, but this German madman, and his overseer Seyss-Inquart, will indeed ratchet up misery." He grasped her hand and gave it a gentle squeeze. "And you, my darling, you practice Judaism more than I do and see to it that our daughters follow the faith—"

"Not as much as I should."

"The degree doesn't matter to Hitler. It's one thing if my own life is in jeopardy, but I will not sit on my hands and deny that seeing you, Edith, and Krista have a future is the number one most important thing in my life. You three are the only ones I love, the only ones that matter."

With Kurt's grandparents and parents long gone, and no uncles, aunts or cousins, Herta and the girls were the sole family he had. As for her, other than two maiden aunts living in Germany, she only had her husband and daughters. It was the four of them against the two billion others in this upside-down world. About to wipe her teary eyes, Kurt feathered his fingertips over her cheeks as the tears trickled down her face. She pulled back. "I refuse to separate, Kurt. Please, we must stay together. Don't make me choose between breaking us apart or not."

He swallowed hard several times. Was he too struggling with tears? "Will you at least agree to a little preparation, then?" He leaned closer. A good thing, since his murmured words were barely audible. "Since we'll need cash, I will take a look around for things we can do without and sell them. I'll also see who we can turn to regarding going into hiding."

Hiding. That one word had stalked her mind since the German invasion occurred in May, three months ago. While she didn't want to flee, the idea of hiding was just as awful. Animals sought hiding places. Criminals dodged persecution. But her family? Going into hiding, intact as a family and remaining that way through an unknown time period, was an overwhelming situation that would inevitably fail. If they had to run from one hiding place to another in the Netherlands—surrounded by the North Sea to the north and west, Germany to the east, and German-controlled countries elsewhere—they would easily be seen and captured. Despite the chance of making it to the coast and obtaining passage on a boat, they'd have to then navigate through Nazi-patrolled waters, and their journey would be dangerous as well. They'd be risking their lives. She wasn't willing to put her daughters through that, let alone her husband.

She was about to offer another argument against hiding by reminding Kurt that the non-Jewish Dutch—the Gentiles—had ramped up anti-Semitism and wouldn't take in Dutch Jews, especially non-Dutch aliens like them. But Kurt stopped her short by ticking off on his fingers various scenarios and reactions. Her mind failed to register his points and observations, until he came to the end of his list and took both of her hands. "There are two more arrangements that I want you to look into immediately. And no challenges, understand?" She listened, trying not to second-guess her husband, who she'd always counted on making sound decisions. Although lately, Kurt was putting her to the test. "I want you to pack escape bags for us—assemble individual bags of one change of clothing, toiletries, and food that won't spoil. Store them in a secure place, so that if an unexpected raid happens in our apartment, these bundles won't be discovered easily."

She swallowed hard, her throat raw from the little *jenever* she'd drunk. She reached for her glass, still two-thirds full, but he motioned for her to put the glass back down on the table. What was he about to say that he didn't want her to nurse her drink? "And?"

"I've thought hard about this for several days. I want you to look into obtaining work, whether on a full weekly basis or a few hours each day."

"But, why would that make a difference?" She shook her head. "I don't understand. What kind of job?"

"Seek out a social-civil position, one that will be beneficial to the Nazis."

"Beneficial? To the Nazis?" She stared at him in disbelief. "I don't want to help them."

"Of course you don't, but you must. It's a diversion. Whether it's providing aid to children like you did before we married or a file clerk in a government office, become invaluable to them."

This time, she picked up the *jenever* and finished it in two gulps. "Kurt, I am a Jew and a non-native Netherlander. And a woman. I will never be of value to a Nazi."

"Try. You must."

Kurt had stressed that he didn't want an argument from her, but she needed to make him understand that his request was preposterous, nearly impossible to carry out. She needed to stand up for herself and defend her values and beliefs. She knew her husband, though. He wasn't concerned about morals. More accurately put, when push came to shove, regarding all things under the label of war, he'd deny their personal history before he risked his family's welfare, losing them, or ruining their future. As his wife and mother of his children, she could understand this—it was the very reason she didn't want to separate her family. She loved Kurt for this. Yet, unlike him, she couldn't deny her heritage, couldn't shake her fist at her past.

She inhaled deeply, aiming for a softer tone to not stir Kurt's ire. "Let me try another way to express—" He shook his head and opened his mouth. She needed to continue before he voiced objections. "Kurt, please. Listen to me. Tell me how, under the Nazi eye, am I supposed to obtain work. I'm asking because look at what happened in Germany two years ago, and why we chose to leave. Who will hire me?"

"I've taken care of that."

His words cut her like a frosted knife. "You've already changed our identities?"

Still seated on the sofa beside her, Kurt leaned closer. She did not back away. "We have no choice. I met this Jewish woman, Alice Cohn, a week ago. She was originally studying cabinet-making in Germany until she was forced to flee to the Netherlands. She's taken up forging documents, trying her hand recently at identity cards. Her admirable handiwork will help when it comes to obtaining jobs."

The thought of already hiding under a new name set her fingers streaking through her hair, tangling her locks to match her knotted insides. "When did you do this?" she murmured.

"Yesterday." He paused, the silence maddening.

"Did what happened today in Dam Square to that poor person who spoke up against the Nazis prompt you to finally tell me your old news from yesterday?"

"Yes." He pointed to the closet where he kept important papers hidden in one of Krista's storybooks. He'd made slits in the inside covers to conceal their documentation. "Our updated papers are in place. As far as the authorities go, our new names are Helmut and Charlotte Beck. To make things easier for the girls, Krista and Edith will keep their first names. We'll tell them about our new surname this evening. Fortunately for all of us, they're fluent in both German and Dutch." A grin twisted his lips. "Their old German accents will come in handy."

"And why did the Becks come to Amsterdam?"

A frown inverted Kurt's—Helmut's—lips. "Charlotte, have you forgotten that we both have a long lineage in Amsterdam? And that we've lived here since we were born?"

"This won't be looked into?"

"Why would the Nazis look into the past of a non-Jew?"

A groan escaped her lips. Denial of their given names. Denial of their faith and heritage. Denial of their birth country. She sprang from the sofa and began to pace around. "This is too simplistic. It won't work. And what about Edith and Krista's schooling? All the faculty and students, the girls' friends, they know their last name, which they're registered under. No one will accept a name change without immediate suspicion. This is too risky. Too absurd. Too—"

He held up a hand to stop her. "Tomorrow, we move to another apartment that I've secured in a different neighborhood. It's smaller, not as nice, but it will do. Best of all, it's in a new school district."

More uprooting—she didn't know whether she wanted to scream about this or the situation that was causing them to relocate, or both. "So, I'll have to register the girls under their new names? They'll have to make new friends and meet new classmates and teachers?"

Her husband stood tall, pinned his shoulders back, and tucked his arms in a defiant cross against his chest. He no longer was Kurt but Helmut Beck. A new man. And, without a doubt, he would stay that way. "We've all survived our days in Berlin. All I can do now is make sure we survive our days in Amsterdam. Do not worry about Edith and Krista Beck. Children have a way of persevering."

"But not necessarily thriving," she murmured. Heat rose to her cheeks and she bowed her head. This was wartime. She couldn't worry about thriving, not when they faced fighting for their lives. "And you, Helmut?" She noticed his lips crawled upward at the use of his new name. "Where will you work? Continuing alongside the other Jews pedaling their goods at Waterlooplein? And that wouldn't cause others to look at you suspiciously?"

"You've trusted me in the past. You must trust me again."

"Answer me." She expected him to stare at a corner of the ceiling or to peer at his shoes. Instead, he walked toward her and seized her hand.

"I'm to continue as a dairy farmer's helper in Amstelveen." Helmut looked hard into her eyes. "Charlotte, my dear, have you forgotten this too? It's where I've worked since we got married."

Lightheaded, she tottered toward the sofa. Thoughts of how, when, and with whom he'd made all these detailed arrangements poked her mind with more questions. Her knees grew wobbly and she collapsed onto the sofa. She didn't want to ask him this last question, but knew she must. "Amstelveen is about 10 kilometers southwest of Amsterdam. Do you plan on walking or biking that distance daily?"

He sat beside her and tucked her hand within his. "My friend, the farmer, has put me up in a spare room that once belonged to a son he lost in an accident."

"Accident..." she repeated, any approximation of comprehension fading fast.

"A farming accident, but don't worry. I'll return home on Sundays."

"Don't worry?" He'd just told her about a horrific farming accident. And that he'd be home only once a week. She wrapped her arms around her waist, trying to resist the sarcasm streaming to her lips, but unable to hold back. "Call it what you want, Helmut, but this pretense is a form of hiding."

"In a sense. Yes, I admit that. We'll be hiding in plain sight. But you get your way, Charlotte." The biting way he pronounced her new name seized her breath. "We won't go into hiding in a stranger's attic or cellar. And we stay together, as a family. At least for now."

For now. Painful words.

"Mutter... Mutter," Edith called.

"We're in here," Herta and Kurt replied in unison. They stared at each other, the unspoken words—this is between us until later—hanging between them.

Edith darted into the parlor.

"Where's your sister?" Herta asked.

Edith's cheeks tinged pink. "She's coming. I... uh... closed the door on her."

"You're upset," Kurt said. "Why is that?"

"I was at my friend's house when Maud's father came home. He made a sour face at me."

"And?" Kurt crossed the room and pulled Edith into his side, lifting her chin up that their gazes could meet. "Did he insult you or hit you?"

Edith shook her head. A curious look crossed her face. "No, he wouldn't do that. He's a nice man. But he said strange things that he'd heard at work."

"Which is where?" Herta asked, already fearing her daughter's reply.

"Mama! Papa!" Krista marched into the room, her cheeks slashed red. "Edith shut the door in my face. That was nasty."

Kurt told her to shush. "Continue," he prompted Edith.

"Maud's father works for the police. He heard that beginning tomorrow, all Jews in Amsterdam must no longer practice rituals, especially for the holy holidays next month." After a pause, Edith added, "Rituals, Mutter? What are they?"

Herta bowed her head. Apparently, as she'd just intimated to Kurt, she hadn't done a good job at teaching her children Jewish customs after all. Was she a failed mother plus a failed Jew? She ordered herself to speak calmly and softly. She didn't want, or need, her daughters to become more fearful than they already were. More specifically, she didn't want either child picking up on her anxiety. "Lighting candles. Eating certain foods and preparing meals in a special way. Saying prayers."

"Mama?" Krista plopped onto the sofa beside her. "We live on the third floor. How would the police know what we do here, in our apartment?"

An excellent question. One that carried an awful response that a young child need not know. The answer also came tagged with the paranoia of perpetually looking over one's shoulder to see who observed whom. This they knew from first-hand experience back in their Berlin days. Sadly, during those horrid days, suspicion often was warranted. And now, it wasn't any different. In need of conveying the unfiltered truth to her daughters, Herta summoned the barest courage she could at this given time. "You're correct, my dear." She looked both girls in the eyes. "The police cannot see what we do inside our home, but they will assume based solely on the fact that we are of the Jewish faith."

"Mutter," Edith said, lifting her fingers to her mouth. "That's awful. It's like me saying that all Germans are bad. When I think about my friends back in Berlin, there's no way I can say they're terrible people."

Herta couldn't reply, couldn't think of words to explain a situation that failed to stay within the perimeters of sense and logic. Instead, she did the one thing she knew how, and desired, to do. She opened her arms and pulled her daughters into a tight hold. "Your father and I will talk to you both after dinner. There will be changes to make for all of us. Do not worry. They are for the best. Go wash up, and then you can help me prepare the meal."

As she chased from her mind the image of Edith and Krista running from future horror, she watched her daughters trot off to the bathroom. She summoned the last of her courage and fortitude. This given second, this precious day, as a family, they were together and well. For her daughters' sake, she'd manage to live one day as it came. Hope. She vowed she'd never surrender this necessity from her clutch.

9

Other than a name change, a husband who worked and lived elsewhere six days a week, a new residence in the Jordaan neighborhood of Amsterdam, and a new part-time job, Charlotte didn't notice changes in their daily lives. A good thing. The girls surprised her with their ease with which they moved and adopted a new family name. They were already getting along nicely with the other boys and girls who lived in the same apartment building. Best of all, they liked their new school and teachers. However, it was quite disconcerting how easily Edith and Krista had accepted their new identities as Dutch citizens and non-Jews. They dealt too well with this deception. The question of whether they had done so out of a sense of survival—especially after experiencing *Kristallnacht*, first hand—or wanting to comply with their parents to protect their family, made Charlotte quite wary. She supposed it was like having to perpetually smother a small fire that defied the odds and kept igniting, threatening to become too large to one day contain. She prayed daily that the girls wouldn't make a slip of the tongue when speaking with an acquaintance. Lies had a way of catching up with the teller, and damning them to a worse fate.

Charlotte was grateful for her new job as an assistant at a crèche, a nursery, in their old Plantage neighborhood. Her last work assignment was to deliver the crèche's youngest child—a seven-month-old girl—to her parents' house each day. Unlike yesterday when it poured, today she was able to enjoy the crisp autumn air and warm sunlight. The baby's father held a position in the Dutch government, though the exact title was kept from her. She knew better than to pry. The mother, weak from birthing little Emma, spent her days at home, often in bed once the governess dropped off Emma at the crèche for the day. Charlotte suspected the mother's troubles were more mental than physical, but who was she to say? Like not knowing what position the child's father held, Charlotte also knew not to inquire into the murky nature of the mother's true ailments.

Charlotte turned left to cross the canal bridge that led directly to the street of Emma's home. The late afternoon September sunshine tickled the baby's face and she gurgled. "Hello, sleepyhead," Charlotte said in German, the native language of Emma's parents, and the language she'd been strictly instructed to speak to Emma. It was also the language often spoken between staff members at the crèche. "We'll be home with Mutter within minutes. She'll be so happy to see you. I'll tell the staff how marvelous and well-behaved you've been today and they will be sure to relay the message to your mother and she'll be pleased." Emma beamed at Charlotte, making her smile. "Oh, little one. I like you too."

"Have an orange carnation, Mevrouw?"

Startled by the teen boy, Charlotte stared at the flower he offered. Hitler's belief was that the Dutch were superbly Aryan, and for that reason, he wanted to annex the Netherlands to Germany rather than destroy it. Nevertheless, Netherlanders became more resistant to assimilate to German ways, at least in private businesses. While the Dutch, by and large, were accustomed to following orders and being obedient to laws, in June, many had taken to wearing orange carnations on Prince Bernard's birthday, a symbol of the Dutch ruling family in exile. Why this teenager had offered Charlotte an orange carnation on a September day, was beyond her. She certainly was not going to go out of her way to bring attention to herself. "No, thank you." She hurried away, pushing the carriage as fast as she dared.

In front of the family's house, Charlotte leaned over the carriage and stroked the girl's cheek. Emma cooed and giggled. "Stay innocent, little one." Charlotte rang the bell.

The governess appeared at the door promptly. She was young and had dark wavy hair. Charlotte couldn't help but wonder if she too was Jewish and if her position in this household would soon be terminated. The uniformed woman smiled at the baby, but not at Charlotte. "Has Emma been good today?"

Charlotte replied with the only acceptable answer, which was the truth. "Yes, indeed." She scooped Emma up, handed the child to the governess, and then waited for the butler to retrieve the carriage.

Her workday was complete. Finally, she could go home to her own darling, precious girls. Free from the cumbersome carriage that slowed her pace, she took large strides toward the bridge to return to her apartment situated on the other side of the city. Two-thirds of the way across the bridge, she gasped aloud as a woman and two girls approached her. The necklace the woman wore caught Charlotte's attention so keenly that she failed to note the woman's age, hair color or style, or how she was dressed. The butterfly pendant hanging from a gold chain matched the pin that Kurt had made for her a few years ago, the pin she now kept protected in her bedroom closet, away from strangers' notice. The craftwork of the necklace was so distinct and singular that no one but Kurt could have created this treasure. It had to be the necklace swiped from Kurt—the one that he was going to give her as an anniversary gift—that day back in May when he chased after the thief to no avail. Although Charlotte stopped and stared at the woman and girls, they continued walking without turning around as if she didn't exist. Evidently, her utterance of surprise hadn't reached the strangers' ears. Just as well. Relieved that she escaped confrontation, Charlotte moved on.

Once home, she'd enlist her daughters with their help in dinner preparation. After small-talk around the table—asking about the girls' school day and listening to Kurt talk about pending jewelry sales—she and Kurt would whisk Edith and Krista to their bedroom and then sit in the parlor where she'd tell him about seeing this woman with the butterfly necklace. Could she be the wife or girlfriend of the thief who had stolen the necklace from Kurt? Should they notify the police? Track them down themselves and speak adult-to-adult in a civilized exchange?

What was she thinking? She was Charlotte; Kurt was Helmut. And these days, Helmut wouldn't be home for dinner, let alone share a bed with her and chase away the monsters of the dark evening. Having surrendered his business, he was away from Amsterdam, living on a farm that was not his own, tending to cows and chores. If they were both fortunate, the grueling hard labor of farm life would be absent of problems, and this coming Sunday she could talk to her husband. Until that day, she couldn't entertain the thought of having a discussion with this stranger who wore a necklace likely crafted by her husband. People were going out of their way to remain in the shadows. This meant avoiding situations that would turn the slightest suspicious eye to them and to think twice about asking the police to intervene, especially without a trace of proof. That would be like inviting the Nazi Party to dinner.

What could she do? As Herta she'd promised her husband not to make a peep or partake in an action that would bring attention to herself or her family. As Charlotte? She'd have to hold her breath and tongue, and continue loving her daughters and watching out for them, and go to work four days a week. And hope to the heavens she'd never again see this stranger with the most remarkable butterfly necklace that had ever been skillfully and lovingly designed.

10

As the champagne deliciously tickled Julia's spirit, the notes of Beethoven's Pathétique Sonata, played on the Steinway grand piano, gave her shivers. When the black-suited and white-gloved servant offered another drink, she readily accepted her third flute. By her lonesome—at least at that moment—she looked about the ornate room. It was the grandest parlor she'd ever set eyes on. If this room were stripped of its pale damask wallpaper printed with Grecian potted ferns; rich mahogany appointments; an exotic floor—teak, she guessed—and floor-length velvet curtains, burgundy, no less, she'd consider it a palace ballroom and not a parlor in a private home. To think her husband and she were invited guests. She'd squeal if she wasn't concerned about drawing negative attention. Even though she was born and raised in Amsterdam, she'd never known about this house. Oh, she'd passed it often but never would have imagined such a marvelous interior, or that one day she'd be lucky enough to enjoy its splendor. For that matter, if she'd learned months ago that the Third Reich was considering her husband for promotion to a ranking officer, her mouth would have fallen open—first in surprise, then laughter.

Where was Luuk? Or another of the servers, this time bearing a silver tray of delicacies? She could visit the banquet table laden with German treats, but didn't want to venture there alone. Earlier, she'd overheard two women—dressed in formal gowns compared to her borrowed evening dress—exclaim that the German cheese assortment outdid the Dutch cheeses. The variety of salamis, chorizo, caviar, and roe, called her virtually by name. The chocolate-dipped macaroons, apricot panettone, and the five-tier gold trays of cakes tempted her to stuff samples into her mouth like a child her daughters' age rather than a proper soon-to-be officer's wife. She couldn't care less if she gained five kilos overnight.

Ah, there was Luuk. He was making his way toward her through the dense crowd gathered around the pianist. She greeted him with the largest smile she gave him in a long time.

Her attractive husband, dressed in a black tux he'd borrowed from one of his brothers, winked. "My dear, you look positively radiant. Is it the drinks and food, the stirring sound of the music, or my devilish company setting you on fire?"

"None of those." She offered a wink of her own. "It's the good-looking guest of honor."

Luuk glanced to his right, where Maxwell Friedrich and his wife stood chatting with Arthur Seyss-Inquart. He leaned closer to her ear. "Be careful, Julia. Friedrich is both mentally and verbally quick in the courtroom as a feared judge, a fierce and loyal Nazi, and…" He trailed off with a teasing grin.

"What? Don't leave me guessing. Tell me."

"His reputation, loyalty, and aggression are overshadowed by only one person."

"Hitler?"

"Maxwell's wife."

Julia observed how the blonde woman, likely in her early forties, flipped her shoulder-length satiny hair over her shoulders as a devoted audience of men gathered around her. In the hope of exuding as much, if not more, confidence than the woman or her powerful spouse and draw Luuk's attention, she too straightened her posture, lifted her chin, and fixed a pleasing smile in place. "No worries, darling. You're all the man I want." She straightened Luuk's bow tie. "So, when will it happen?"

He lifted a brow. "Pardon?"

She tried to speak past the champagne-enriched giggles flowing from her mouth. "When will Seyss-Inquart or Friedrich introduce you?"

"Introduce me to whom?"

"Come on, Luuk. I might have had a drink or two, but I recall that in order for you to move up in the Party, you must meet Göring..." She winked. "Or the big H-man himself. On that note, when will you introduce me to your new friend, the guest of honor?"

Luuk paled. "Friedrich?"

"Yes, of course, Maxwell and his beautiful wife—the one all the uniformed men flock around."

He hooked her elbow and pulled her closer. "I think you've imbibed a bit too liberally. Let's get you home."

She wiggled free of his hold. "Not before we say nighty-night to Maxxie and his wifey." She snorted and caught those nearby watching her. She laughed. "I just made a rhyme."

"Before you make a scene, let's leave. Now."

"But Luuk, I want to meet your new friends."

With one firm hand on her back and the other holding up her hand, he guided her to the cloakroom for her autumn jacket and his hat. Once outdoors, he began to tug her toward the bridge. She grounded her heels. "No, darling. Don't turn my magical coach into a pumpkin quite yet. Can we treat ourselves to a taxi?"

"You're no Cinderella. Besides, the fresh air will do you good—make you more clearheaded before we see the girls." Luuk yanked her a few steps, but she managed to stop them both. He let out an exasperated sigh twisted with a groan. "What is it, now?"

"Don't talk that way to me. You may be good-looking, but you're no prince." She rubbed her upper arm. "Besides, you're hurting me. Where you gripped me smarts like an insect sting."

He mumbled, and it sounded as if he'd threatened that he could hurt her far worse. And, since she knew he could, she tried to sober her state of mind and think a bit faster. "It's just that I can't remember the last time we've left the girls under another's watch for an evening of fun. Oh, what a fine night this was… and you were so gallant with your good manners to the women and noble to the gentlemen."

The full moon illuminated his face enough that Julia saw his lips lift in a charming grin. Good. If she continued to place attention on him, she might succeed in ending his ridicule of her behavior.

He shot her a sideways glance. "You think so?"

"Oh, Luuk, yes. I wouldn't say it just to pacify you."

"But I was off talking to quite a few acquaintances." He stared at the brick road ahead of them. "I might have been nice to others, but I probably shouldn't have ignored you for so long."

"Don't think twice about it. Please. It's enough already. Put a kibosh on your attitude and my supposed drunkenness." She gasped. She'd never questioned his attitude before and feared his reaction. "I was simply enjoying this fairytale occasion, champagne and all. What a grand occasion this was. You've made me so proud."

He again took her by surprise, this time grasping her hand, pleasantly, as if they were new lovers. They continued toward the canal bridge. "Darling?" She glanced at him. "Is there news that you're not telling me about? Was the promotion given to one of your NSB friends instead of you?" His silence as they crossed the bridge set her on edge. She tried again as they turned right toward their neighborhood. "The hard work you devoted to this organization, coupled with your determination to make things right with the Netherlands…" She swore silently at her alcohol-laden tongue, not that she'd admit that to Luuk. "Incorporate. Yes, that's the word. You spent countless hours getting the Netherlands to become incorporated with Germany. You deserve to become Seyss-Inquart's or that other man—Maxwell's—right-hand man."

He tugged her toward a windowless section of a closed shop, and they leaned against the old wooden structure. By the bright street light she could see his facial features well enough to gauge his sincerity and mood. She wanted a kiss or a gentle squeeze of her hand or a simple nod of agreement. What she saw instead was him withdrawing a cigarette and lighter from his inner suit pocket. When all she could do was stare at his first exhale of smoke, he fetched another smoke from his pocket and offered one to her. She gently reminded him she never smoked and didn't want to start.

"You should take up this filthy habit."

His sarcasm came as a surprise. "Why is that?"

"It will help calm your nerves while I'm gone."

Ah, so he had received a promotion after all. He was about to go off to Germany and rise to power, and their lives would become perfect. Maybe this was his way of tricking her into thinking there was bad news instead of the fabulous news that she was certain he was about to spring on her. Luuk played the part of the forlorn and rejected helper rather than a military hero in the making a bit too perfectly. She didn't know whether to childishly shriek in excitement like she'd wanted to earlier at the party or slump her shoulders and acquiesce to his gloomy mood. If she had to say goodnight to the evening's storybook magic of goodness, smiling faces, and hope that there would be endless tomorrows of better fortune instead of this pitiful existence of struggle that had plagued them since they married, she'd never get out of bed every morning. The thought alone of encountering yet another rough day standing at work on her achy feet, wondering how they'd provide enough for Annelise and Marianne to wear clean clothes, eat good food, and have a chance of growing into fine adults, threatened to send her fears spiraling out of control.

Like Luuk had done to her minutes ago when they left the party, she reached out to him and hooked her arm around his elbow, and pulled him to her side. She kissed his cheek. "Share your news with me. We'll get through this together."

He averted his gaze. "I never talked with Arthur Seyss-Inquart or, for that matter, Maxwell Friedrich."

"But you were an invited guest—I saw the invitation on your

desk. Weren't you asked to be there specifically to be presented to these two men of importance to Hitler?"

Luuk took another long drag of his cigarette, then tossed it to the ground and smothered it with the toe of his shiny black dress shoe. "I might have been invited, but I—along with several of my fellow NSB men—was window dressing. That's all."

"I'm afraid I don't understand."

"Of course not. And I'll tell you why you don't." He leaned closer; the stench of his tobacco breath made her queasy. Or was it the smell of deceit that was doing her in? "You're not following me because I've set you up to think that your husband was becoming a brilliant agent on behalf of the Nazis. Seyss-Inquart is no fool. He wanted to make an impression on Friedrich, that he—Seyss-Inquart—has the power, the wherewithal of the Dutch to obey his command."

"How long did you know that this was a setup, that you were being used to make Seyss-Inquart look good?" Luuk withdrew another cigarette. Julia pulled it from his fingers and tossed it into the canal. "Answer me."

"Not until the end of this night. I kept expecting introductions, a hearty handshake. An assignment."

"Nothing?"

"There was one piece of news I did receive." This time when he paused, she kept purposely quiet. She'd give him all the time he needed, whether seconds, minutes, or hours, to cough up the pride she feared he'd lose for good. "For a short while longer," he continued, "Seyss-Inquart will continue to play it low and quiet in the Netherlands. Though I haven't heard about his exact plans on behalf of Germany, this takeover—occupation—well, let's just say that the pinch will be received a bit more aggressively and I will have to do my part."

"Which is what? Where?" She gulped. "When?"

He dodged her scrutiny by casting his attention toward the water. She lifted her fingers to his chin, already stubbly after his last shave hours earlier, and rotated his face to meet hers once again.

"Wherever I might be sent. Germany or Africa. Maybe the Soviet Front."

"The Russian icebox?"

"Or, locally. Doesn't matter. I will become a foot soldier, not an officer." He stared into her eyes; his beautiful multi-colored irises widened in excitement. "Believing that the German government will become the ruling power of the world, I will serve Hitler however he sees fit."

She pressed her fingertips against her lips to block foolish words from escaping. Like questioning of whether he could say no to an assignment that would take him far away from his family, from her. Like whether he could choose a location to guard. Or the position, like a cook or office worker that wouldn't see combat. But she didn't dare. Instead, she asked the one question already clouding her mind. "And what about me? Our daughters? How will we survive?"

"I'll see to it that you'll be watched and cared for." He smirked, startling her. "There's no worries, sweetheart. You aren't Jewish or from the other social groups of louses."

Her stomach buckled when he turned away from her. To cover up her reaction, she focused on him and reached for his arm. "What is it, honey?"

"If you're disappointed in me, I can understand."

She gently guided him in a turn so they faced each other again. She slipped her arms around his waist, one that was becoming slimmer but firmer with all the hours of work he'd put into the NSP. She lowered her hands, spreading her fingers, just a bit. "How and why would I be disappointed in you?"

"Because of what I just said." When she remained silent, trying to make sense of this guessing game, he beat her to it. "Your husband's becoming an ordinary soldier—not an officer."

"Darling, that doesn't matter to me. You'll always make me proud."

"No officers' parties for us," he muttered. "No mingling with the upper crowd nor an officer's income for us nor—"

"Luuk. Stop this." Her firm tone cut him short from continuing his list of negatives. "I love you. And your love for me and our daughters is the only thing that matters to me. I will never be disappointed in you. Understand?"

His nod was tiny, so faint that if she hadn't been watching him carefully for his reply, she would have missed his affirmation. He grasped her hand. "If I have you always by my side, Julia, that's the single thing that matters to me."

With both hands, she cupped his face. "Have no worries, Luuk. I'm always here for you, whether it's wartime or peace. You're the only husband I want, forever."

11

They had become strangers. Before the German invasion of the Netherlands, Charlotte couldn't have imagined those four words ever being so complex, let alone apply to her family. She, her husband, and two daughters, united both physically and emotionally, had remained a strong, cohesive family unit despite the troubles they experienced in Berlin two years ago. Now, February 1941, her once-happy family had grown fragmented by the danger that surrounded them. She despised their usage of new identities, though she understood the necessity. She worried constantly that by her own slip of the tongue, she could be the one who invited grave trouble to those she loved the most. She feared that if this hostile takeover of the country didn't end soon, at best, she'd lose her true identity, and at worse, she and her family might lose their lives if the Nazis discovered their faith and heritage.

Most Sundays, Helmut traveled back to their flat in the Jordaan neighborhood tucked within the innermost borough of Amsterdam. There had been a few Sundays when he hadn't been able to make the trip back to her and the girls. Today, the 23rd, he'd also failed to show at his usual time in the late morning. No matter what, she'd make a pleasant day for Edith and Krista. She could pick them up from the park where they were enjoying some fresh air, which might not be an unreasonable idea considering the trouble lately. After fueled antisemitic attacks on Amsterdam Jews, who in return fought back and led to the killing of a Dutch National Socialist, and the mistaken spraying of German police officers with ammonia in an ice cream parlor resulting in the business owner being tortured and executed by a firing squad, Charlotte had ordered her daughters to remain indoors when not in school. This morning, when their friend's mother knocked on the apartment door to personally say she'd escort Edith and Krista to the park so they could visit with her daughter and benefit from seeing more than the inside of a house, Charlotte couldn't object. Sad, pouty faces always got the best of her.

She startled when the door rattled. "Who's there?" she called.

Instead of hearing a reply, the door creaked open. Not expecting a visitor, Charlotte grabbed a light from a table by the sofa, yanked the electric cord free from its socket, and lifted it like a weapon poised to strike. These days, one couldn't fall into the category of the ill-prepared.

"Charlotte?" Kurt's gorgeous smile greeted her.

She dropped the light. The yellow glass shade and central chimney shattered on the bare oak floor. "No Charlotte. I'm your Herta, always." She flew into her husband's open arms without any clue who kissed who first. He grabbed her shoulders and pressed her tightly against his chest. She cupped the sides of his face with her palms, then inched her fingers upward to trail through his hair, down his neck, to the base of his spine, to his rear, prepared to push him tighter against her, except he acted faster and pinned her against the wall. They couldn't stop touching each other, as if each needed the maximum sensory input of unequivocal proof that they were in each other's embrace and not living in the fantasyland of imagination.

"Edith? Krista?" he murmured into her ear.

"In the park... with a friend," she huffed. "Don't worry. The friend's mother is with them."

"And that's why I came home today—because I am concerned."

The moments of passion vanished so quickly it was as if they hadn't shared a scrap of affection. They sat on the sofa, the space between them filling with unintended yet inevitable angst, its cold crawling up her arms. When they became parents for the first time upon Edith's birth, their love for each other grew rather than diminished, as they had feared. When Krista came along three years later, their love expanded again, as well as their prime concern to always, always look after their children. On the fringe of war and persecution, the thought alone of their daughters' well-being would alter any course of action quicker than it would take to say yes or no.

"Concerned? Tell me the details." She patted his hand. "No need to paint a rosy picture."

"Hugo, the farmer I work for, well, I've learned that he's a member of the CPN, the Communist Party of the Netherlands."

"That sounds awful... radical."

"Not in these current situations. The German authorities have banned the CPN, but that's not stopping them from keeping their ears tuned to what's happening, which Hugo freely shares with me. Seyss-Inquart is rounding up hundreds of random Jews off the streets of this city as if they are discarded trash in need of a cleanup. They say these poor souls will soon be deported to Buchenwald—"

"Buchenwald? A camp?"

"A supposed work camp in Germany." He fisted his hands. "We're quite positive it's a death camp." Tears welled in her eyes as she visualized the loss of the innocent, but wanting to hear more, she willed herself to remain silent as he continued. "One good thing about the CPN is they're calling for strikes. That will interrupt the Germans for a while. I wanted to get home before the trams shut down, and I couldn't travel back to you." On his feet, he reached for her hand. "Let's get the girls. No delays. I want them home, safe, with us."

She gripped his hand, and they hurried to the park where, under ordinary circumstances, children would, and should, be playing in the fresh air without any concern other than what was for lunch.

Later that night, after they'd kissed Edith and Krista goodnight and tucked them in tight, Charlotte and Helmut tiptoed to their own bed. Exhausted, they settled under the covers as an elderly person might sag into a beloved chair. Their bones may not have creaked, and a groan may not have flown from their lips, but neither made a move to cuddle with each other. When she'd first set her eyes upon her husband as he'd walked into their apartment, she couldn't get enough physical reassurance that he stood before her. Mind, body, and soul yearned to devour him. Now, love-making seemed distant, like an absurd philosophical concept. With the way Helmut kept his hands folded on top of his thinning stomach, not moving toward her to close the gap between them, she believed her usually virile lover's senses were battered and fatigued, like her own perception of life.

"Helmut?" she murmured. She detested saying this false name of his, especially in the intimacy of their own bedroom, but she also had no desire to prompt his disapproval. It was bad enough that he'd reminded her several times that afternoon that she must always use his new name. All it took was one unintentional mistake, one misspoken word, and the little protection that they'd built around them could crumble faster than it would take to gasp audibly in regret.

Without looking at her, he grunted. "It's not you."

She didn't need to ask him to explain himself. That was the oddity of living under threat: communication became tangible without the aid of the spoken word. "Nor you, my love."

He surprised her then by grasping her hand. "I'd spoken to Hugo before I left. I won't be returning to the farm. Well, at least not this week. We'll see how it goes."

And he hadn't mentioned this until now? "What does your boss think of this decision?"

"It was his idea."

A practical-minded person, Charlotte fought furiously to push away thoughts of dwindling income, of what their new neighbors may think or do upon seeing Helmut suddenly living with them day after day. She also tried her best to quash her wonder over what would happen to her own fragile work security if the crèches were ordered closed.

"We'll be fine." He lifted onto his elbow and kissed her on the cheek, then rolled onto his side, his back toward her. Within seconds, one lone snore puttered through the room.

The next day brought relative quiet, both on the streets and within their apartment. Neither Charlotte nor Helmut ventured outdoors, nor did they permit Edith or Krista to step out for fresh air. That they didn't complain or whine came as no surprise. They were good, smart children, capable of picking up on their parents' cues on how to behave. Truth be told, they likely felt relieved tucked indoors under the protective wing of their father and mother. On the second morning, Charlotte awoke entangled in Helmut's arms when Krista bounced on their bed with a cry sailing from her mouth.

"Wake up. Come quickly."

Sitting up, Charlotte attempted to hush Krista before she awoke her father.

"I'm awake." Helmut sprang upright. "What's wrong, sweetheart? Where's your sister?"

"Edith sent me to get you. She's looking out the window at the crowds."

"Crowds," Charlotte and Helmut echoed simultaneously as they both slipped out from the covers. Charlotte donned a bathrobe; Helmut stabbed his legs into the trousers he'd tossed on the chair. They raced behind Krista into the parlor, the room that faced the narrow street in front of their building. There was no trace of Edith.

Helmut strode across the carpet to the window. Charlotte pulled her youngest daughter to her side, patting her head. A bang from the building's heavy front door slamming shut funneled up the one flight of stairs and through the apartment door they hadn't noticed was left ajar.

"Vater? Mama?" Edith called as she barged into the room. She shook her hand, a piece of paper waved in the air like a flag. "The man gave this to me. Read this."

"What man?" Helmut narrowed the distance between himself and Edith and yanked the paper from her hand. "Who gave this to you? Why did you open the door to our building?"

Edith took a step backward. Charlotte silently pleaded with her husband to go easy on their daughter.

"I didn't open the door. A stranger—who rode here on his bicycle—was already inside the building talking to the first-floor lady and her husband. When he saw me, he gave me the paper and told me to give it to you. He then left, and I shut the door and locked it." She glanced over her shoulder. "I guess I shut the door a little loudly. Don't blame me, Papa."

Helmut unfolded the two-page leaflet and studied the printed words, then scanned the faces of his daughters and Charlotte. "Let's stay in here, together." He motioned for Edith and Krista to sit on the sofa. He and Charlotte sat on the chairs across from the wide-eyed girls. He glanced again at the leaflet. "This notice urges all in Amsterdam to go on strike beginning today."

Edith nodded. "Yes, that's what I've heard—dockworkers and the city cleaners are already on strike." She stared hard at her father. "Vater, he said that the tram workers are expected to join the strike. How will you go back to work at the farm?"

"No need to worry about that." Helmut had spoken in a calm tone, but the beads of perspiration on his forehead indicated that he was struggling. "I've arranged that I will stay with you to look after your safety. So, no fears. Understand?"

"Will you stay forever and ever, Papa?" Krista asked as she scrunched closer to her bigger sister. Edith grasped Krista's hand.

"As long as it takes for things to calm down a bit. Let's not pin down a fixed time."

"Do you mean the strike?" Edith asked. "How long will this strike go on?"

For however long it will take to launch the Germans into action, Charlotte thought but dared not say out loud.

Helmut stood. "I'm going to step outdoors and see what I can learn. I want all of you to stay put."

"Why can't we come with you?" Krista asked. "If you're afraid that we won't be safe, then how will you be safe?"

"Let your father do the investigating. No arguments." Charlotte cast her husband a look over her shoulder and then signaled for Edith and Krista to follow her into the kitchen. "It's breakfast time. There are leftover biscuits from yesterday."

"I'll return," Helmut mouthed.

"Please," she said softly, instead of the words she wanted to say —*you better*.

―――

Thousands of people had taken to the streets in protests. Shops, offices, and restaurants closed in one of the most defiant shows of solidarity that was bound to send a distinct message to Seyss-Inquart, or to Hitler himself—that Amsterdam was not a city to mess with. Helmut practically floated indoors to share the news.

Charlotte recognized a look of eagerness in his widened eyes. He was ready for action.

She set the newspaper down on the kitchen table. "It's quite late. A whole day's gone by. Edith and Krista are sound asleep. Do you want your dinner?"

He pulled a chair closer to her side, its wooden legs scratching the bare floor. "I can tell you're upset with me."

"Of course, I'm a bit agitated with concern for you—for us—but after reading how this fervor is expected to spread beyond

Amsterdam and into the other cities, I'm more thankful you are home and uninjured."

"It's a planned strike against what has been happening under Nazi control, not a crazy display of passionate protest. It isn't one and the same."

She narrowed her eyes. "This isn't the time to quibble over semantics."

He leaned so close that their noses nearly touched. "Nor is it the time to question your husband." He pulled back and crossed his arms. "I want you to promise me one thing."

"What could go wrong if you stay safe and sound with your family like you promised me?"

He picked up the folded newspaper from the table, glanced at the first page, and chucked it back down. "There are developments that call for my help." He struck the table with his fist, cringed, then looked about as if he expected the girls to come running from their rooms, sobbing in fear, pleading with him to remain by their sides.

She covered his fisted hand with hers. "What do you want me to promise? Kurt, tell me."

"If I were to become compromised or detained—whether tonight, tomorrow, or months later—for our daughters' sake and for yours, you must deny knowing me."

12

Typical for February, the second Julia stepped outdoors, the cold dampness blowing in from the North Sea slipped under her coat sleeves and crawled up her arms and down her spine with a fierce tingle. She had no other choice but to chance the streets in anticipation of finding a market or shop with eager owners waiting for customers. And with Mila, her sister-in-law, ill and unable to watch Annelise and Marianne, she also had no other choice but to leave them behind at the house, alone. They promised to play nicely in their bedroom, not to step outdoors, nor to permit anyone inside. Although she believed they would remain safe, she quickened her steps. A strike broke out three days ago, to the shock of both the German and local officials, as well as residents. Nearly half of the city's population took part in the protest against hundreds of young Jewish men being rounded up off of Amsterdam's streets, beaten, and sent off to Buchenwald. But what did it matter? She couldn't involve herself in the foolishness of all this retaliation, not when her daughters needed food.

As she headed toward the corner to cross a bridge, a muscle spasmed and twisted the back of her neck. When she realized she'd walked in a hunched-over position, she straightened her posture.

She paused midway across the bridge, gripped in amazement that she'd returned to walking stooped forward like an old lady—not to protect herself from the cold or because she was in pain—but rather to avoid the stares of others. During the strike, Luuk had certainly garnered attention. Both the right and the wrong kind. Those participating in the event—both Jews and non-Jews, as well as native and non-native Amsterdammers—saw her husband as a traitor at best and a hand of evil at worst. The NSP and the Nazis, one and the same these days, saw him as a soldier doing what was expected: to find and gather these rioters, by force. By no fault of his own, Luuk had failed to gain exemplary status by the very group of people he was prepared to die for if need be.

Frost filled her insides. Was she ashamed of her country or of her husband's eagerness to quash those who disobeyed civil order, as seen through the Nazi view? She'd vowed her enduring love to Luuk, no matter what; told him she'd always stand by him, would never feel shame or embarrassment of his dedication to the Nazi Party. In fact, it was this praise that she'd murmured into his ear two nights ago after they'd made love and he was finally able to fall asleep. That was the last time she'd seen him.

"*Goedemorgen*, Mevrouw Arzt."

Julia peered into the eyes of her neighbor who lived two houses down on the left, a grandmotherly woman who had enjoyed baking for the neighborhood children before the invasion. Julia greeted the woman who, judging from her sacks, evidently was returning home from errands.

"No smile today on your pretty lips? Are your daughters well?"

"Oh, yes, they're fine," Julia replied without hesitation. The last thing she needed was for the well-meaning but nosy neighbor to surprise her with a visit later that afternoon. "Forgive me. I haven't stepped outdoors since the strike, and I'm a bit nervous."

The white-haired woman smiled widely. "With loyal men like your husband and mine, we're in good hands. Do not worry. And have you heard the latest about the mayor?"

"No, I haven't heard a peep."

"He's concerned with German punishment—well, that is, more discipline, I should say. The mayor is trying to calm things down. He's ordered city officials back to work. Hopefully, others will follow this example. Life must go on, must return to normal."

A new normal. Although, one could debate these days how to define the ever-changing meaning of normal.

"My husband Herman is willing to help as well of course, but he's not as young and fit as your Luuk." The woman's eyes twinkled. "I'm happy I can count on your soldier husband."

"Reassuring words," Julia said, simply because she wanted to sound pleasant while unable to think of other polite expressions. "Well, I must be off to, hopefully, purchase a little meat for tonight's supper and a loaf of bread."

"Try the butcher's two streets over. If you can't find bread, stop over when you return home. I have plenty of flour."

They exchanged farewells, and Julia continued across the bridge, her thoughts alternating between wondering how long one's personal stash of food might last before the city's occupants became competitors over milk and eggs, and contemplating how she'd dodge this nice but intrusive neighbor. Once on the other side of the canal, she turned left and headed in the direction of the butcher's shop that her neighbor suggested. She once again stopped short when she saw Luuk trotting toward her, as if a ghost gave chase. The closer he came, he slowed his pace, and looked about as if anxious that others would take notice of his activities.

"Where are the girls?"

"Mila couldn't watch them so they're home. They're fine, though."

He grabbed her upper right arm and spun her around. With fingers digging into her arms, pinching, he started to shake her. "Are you mad? What kind of worthless mother are you to leave young children at home when the country has turned upside down?"

Fear and anger ripped across her chest, where she'd pulled Annelise and Marianne into a hug before leaving the house, promising she'd bring home tasty foods for their lunch and supper. Luuk's beady-eyed stare warned her not to antagonize him further. His fury didn't need her help to detonate more of his ugly side, and she ditched her arguments. "Can you tell me what's happening, Luuk?"

"Let's hurry home," he said through gritted teeth. "We'll talk under our own roof. Let's move it before we no longer can."

They continued the short trip home in a cutting silence between them. Once home, Luuk slammed the door and locked both locks, a new practice he'd begun about a month ago when their once safe, peaceful neighborhood had become stripped of chatty neighbors and playful children. It now resembled a geographic location on a useless old map rather than a once-lively community.

"Papa! Papa!" Marianne squealed as she ran from the bedroom. Annelise followed. The girls hopped around him like bunnies.

"Do you have surprises for us?" Ani asked boldly but not unexpectedly since Luuk usually brought home surprises when he had been absent for a few days. "We behaved. Just like Mama told us too."

"Your mother had no business leaving you here alone."

"But we were good," Marianne added to her sister's plea.

Before Luuk could reply, Julia shooed the girls off into their bedroom. She faced her husband. "Tell me fast what is happening. Why are you home when this city is on the explosive side?"

With a hand on her shoulder, he led her into the kitchen, pulled out a chair, and ordered her to sit. He then sat down close to her and leaned toward her. "Where were you going?"

"To the butcher shop. We need food."

"After we talk, I want you to stay put. If the shop isn't closed down, I'll get the meat and bring it home before I must leave again."

"Why do you have to leave?"

His glare cut off the other questions storming through her mind.

"This strike and the counter-demonstration that I've been ordered to—"

"You personally?"

"My fellow soldiers and I." He pulled away. "Listen, we've talked enough about this—I don't need your doubts and questions breathing down my neck when I have plenty of orders from those who matter."

Like the two warring colors of his eyes, there was no mistaking that she was dealing with Luuk's uglier side of his personality. She needed to shut up and listen, or she'd end up with regrets to last her a week or more—time, she assumed, she'd have to face without him. She waited in silence for him to speak.

"You and the girls will be safe for the next few days. If you remain home. No exceptions. We have orders to seize civilians—man, woman, or child, Jew or non-Jew—whoever disobeys the command to stop protesting. No harm will come your way, so there are no worries, since you will remain home. And you will obey me, correct?"

Never before did her hand itch with the desire to slap the arrogance off his face. Had he changed, or had she? Yet, Julia nodded.

"Good. Then you won't have the misfortune to get hauled away like the miserable vermin that I had to deal with earlier this morning."

It was then that she noticed he rubbed gingerly at his arm. "Are you hurt?" She reached for him. "Let me see."

He waved her off. "I'll live."

Wanting to encourage him to continue, she leaned back. "Want to tell me about this poor person you had to deal with? When you say 'hauled away,' is he now imprisoned?"

"Poor? Don't pity the worthless bastard. Yes, he's imprisoned." Luuk pulled at this stubbly chin. "Perhaps worse."

"What was this man doing?"

"Standing on the street. He was talking to the wrong person, at the wrong time."

"I see," she said, but failed to understand. "You appear shaken. Do you know this man?"

"Not by name. But I recognized him, and I can tell he recognized me." He stared at her bare neckline. "Where's your butterfly necklace?"

Her breath pinched. She stared beyond him, toward the stairs that led to their upstairs bedroom. "Where I always keep the pretty piece—in my jewelry box on my dressing table. With all this commotion lately, I've stopped wearing necklaces."

"Well, I hope you won't stop appreciating it after what I have to say. Do you recall the jewelry maker I told you about, the one where I found the necklace?"

Actually, at the time he'd given her the necklace he'd teased her that it was his little secret where he'd gotten the piece of jewelry. She'd assumed he'd purchased the necklace from an artisan, perhaps in a specialty boutique. No way would she correct him now. "Yes. Was this the same person you arrested this morning?" She grasped his hands. "Luuk, you can tell me."

"Yes, this was the same person. We believe his wife and daughters—unless she was a mistress with their two brats—were watching."

Although Annelise and Marianne weren't in the kitchen, Julia could mentally visualize them before her. See their smiles. Their hopeful eyes. The shape of a tiny "oh" in expectation. They'd burst into tears if they ever watched their Papa get hauled away. She looked into her husband's eyes. "How did this wife and his children handle the way you... treated him?"

"Not well. The woman yelled and begged for his release, yet oddly, she never claimed they were married. Probably a whore. The two girls cried." He stood, scraping the chair legs against the floor. "Let me see about food for supper, and get what I can, what's available." He pecked her forehead with a wet kiss. "Stay here, indoors. I want you and the girls safe." He proceeded toward the front door.

"Of course." After hearing that awful story, she wasn't going to step foot out of the house or permit her daughters outside until Luuk said otherwise. "Luuk," she called.

He stopped and faced her.

"I want you to know that I truly treasure the butterfly necklace and promise to wear it. Please, try not to associate it with today's incident."

He didn't reply. A minute ambled by, a painfully long time to worry if he'd cut her with words he knew how and when to hurl at her, or slice her with worse things. Instead, he opened the door, walked out of the house, and shut the door behind him. She'd likely have only seconds before Ani and Marianne bounded into the room, but Julia shut her eyes. She wondered what the arrested man's wife and daughters were experiencing this very second, whether they were his true family rather than terrified observers, and whether the woman was, like Luuk thought, just a lover. But one needed love and needed to return love. What difference did a marriage make? And what about true love in her own marriage? Could she continue to love the man she feared?

13

When the police officer rapped loudly at Charlotte's apartment door, she had no other choice but to open it. He peered over her shoulder at Edith and Krista sitting behind her on the sofa, who remained quiet, just like she'd instructed them to. She debated whether to throw herself at his feet and beg him for information about her husband. Then, she remembered what Helmut had demanded. She hoped her daughters would keep mum.

"Frau Beck?"

Alarm flooded her insides at his easy usage of German. She remained silent.

He frowned. "*Sprichst du Deutsch?*"

Deny. Deny. Deny. She willed herself to look confused, easy enough to do. Having dyed her hair blonde just that morning only added to her new self-image in light of her changing circumstances.

The officer stabbed her with a sigh of disgust and exasperation. He mumbled more German under his breath.

Easily understanding her native language, she held back a flinch at his slur of "stupid bitch." She'd been called worse over the past few years, especially for being Jewish. She proffered him a smile, determined not to help this smug idiot score back-rubbing points with the police commissioner. Not on her watch.

"Only Dutch?" he asked in thickly German-accented Dutch.

"*Ja*."

"Very well," he replied, continuing in Dutch. "Identity papers."

She retrieved them from a once-lovely burled walnut stand beside the door. Like the old piece of furniture, she too, was distressed. Would she ever see better days?

The officer examined her papers, then extracted a sheet of paper he'd pulled from his shirt pocket. "How long has your family been living in Amsterdam?"

She plunged her hands into her apron pockets to hide their sudden shakiness. "Both my family and my husband's have lived in Amsterdam for hundreds of years." She chuckled. "Why live elsewhere when the best of life is right here?"

"Do you know a Kurt Weber? Where is your husband?"

She shrugged. Her husband had used his true name? She glanced at Edith and Krista then back at the officer. In a lowered tone, she added, "The louse took off on me. Again. Right in the middle of the strike, he disappeared. A neighbor saw him with a red-haired, tall woman. Have you seen my Helmut?"

"I asked you about Kurt Weber, a Jew we picked up yesterday morning. Do you know him? Have you seen him?"

"No, officer. My husband is Helmut Beck."

"It's been reported that you yelled hysterically when we arrested Weber."

Deny. She shook her head. "I was annoyed at all the protestors marching by. They acted like they own the city—that's who I yelled at. It was at the poorest of times when this Burt—"

"Kurt." The officer was practically growling. "Kurt Weber."

"Did this dreadful man ask for me? Why, I can't imagine." She leaned closer and purposely lowered her voice to a whisper, as if she was ashamed and wanted to keep it from her daughters. "Helmut may fool around, but I don't mess with another man."

"He did not ask for you." The officer handed her back the identity papers that regulated whether or not she could be validated by the authorities, or for that matter, if she should be permitted to be treated like a human being. "Your documentation is good." A foul grin spread his lips thin. "I'm personally glad to see that you didn't have to register with the other Jews back in January. I advise you and your daughters to stay put in case we have more questions." Without a word more, the officer turned and left.

Charlotte shut and locked the door, crumpled to the floor, and then welcomed Edith and Krista into her arms, unsure who needed the hug the most.

The dark of the February night struck fast. *All fine*, Charlotte thought. If she couldn't perpetuate certain customs and traditions, she took pleasure in the fact that the control of the seasons and the sun, moon, and stars were free from dominating human hands.

From across the table, the rattle of Krista's glass as she set down her drink caught Charlotte's attention. She eyed both girls' untouched supper plates. "Are you well, my loves?"

As if one, they both nodded. "And the food's good too," Edith said, always the reassuring one.

"Then why aren't you eating the *stamppot*? Are you two tired of Wurst, kale, and potatoes?" She hoped not, especially since her choice of meats, or food in general, narrowed by the day.

Krista lifted her fork and swooshed the mashed blend of potatoes and kale away from the sausage then back again. "It's tasty."

"So tasty that you play with your supper instead of eating it?" Without waiting for a response, she stood. "If you like, you can eat later. Let's tell each other stories."

Edith and Krista exchanged looks as if questioning each other's hearing ability. Charlotte smiled, though she didn't want to. "Yes, you've heard right." She jutted her chin toward the sofa. "Let's cuddle over there."

Though her girls didn't return the smile, they both opened their eyes wide with obvious excitement and curiosity. At the sofa, Krista toed off her shoes, sat on Charlotte's left, and drew her knees into a hug. Edith sat a bit more daintily to her right, but the way she twirled a strand of hair signaled that though she was a teen, she was a child and rightly nervous about the happenings in her upside-down family, let alone the world. Charlotte remembered her husband's telling of the fairytale the night of the bombing, and how it had surprised her that the girls took to it, and with no protests that they were too mature for a child's story. Perhaps she'd try again.

She draped an arm around her daughters. "Shall I tell a story about a handsome prince who once visited my childhood town ages ago? Or an evil fairy who snatched a bicycle from a little boy?" She hoped the girls would opt for the first suggestion. Relief flooded her heart when they chose to hear about the prince. There was certainly enough evil in their lives to warrant an escape. "Once upon a time, a prince was born to the king and queen of Noble Island. A good-natured baby, he never fretted, enjoyed many foods, slept well, and giggled lots and lots for his mother, father, and all those who loved him. He adored the family home of a big white-brick castle and played many games in the large rooms and hallways. Although he was never a difficult child, there was one particularity that made him quite different from his other brothers, sisters and cousins." Charlotte paused and glanced at each girl. "Can either of you guess what that was?"

Krista shot up straight. "He had a hidden talent."

"Why, yes. He did."

Krista pressed tighter into Charlotte's side. "What's this prince's name?"

Edith perked up. "Can we call him Vater's real name, not his pretend name?"

"Yes, of course. Prince Kurt." With her husband's name flowing from her lips, she settled back against the sofa as if she was leaning into Kurt's embrace. She prayed he'd walk through their door any second. If not, how could she continue taking care of their daughters, alone, in a neighborhood of strangers, in a city of people turning against each other, in a country occupied by Jew-hating Nazis. It was too large of a mystery for her to handle right then. Actually, it wasn't a mystery. The Nazi invasion was a crisis that should have never occurred.

"Prince Kurt, indeed, had a special talent. Unlike the rest of his family, his talent was singing. As he grew into a teenager and then a young man, his voice became better and better and charmed each fair maiden he came across, making them sigh dreamingly. His singing was so good that all the men who courted these fair maidens couldn't be jealous. Instead, they patted the prince's back in admiration and praised him for entertaining them with his songs."

"Did Prince Kurt make up his own songs or did he sing other people's songs?" Krista asked.

"He composed his own songs, and that's what made them so special."

"Did the songs cast a spell on people?"

"Not fair," Edith said. "It's Mama's story. Let her tell it."

"It wasn't quite a spell," Charlotte said. "What he did was create a different and special song for each person he met. Not once did the prince ever duplicate his words. For older folks, he composed melancholic pieces that made the listeners think of their childhood days and would bring smiles to their faces. For serious thinkers, he'd compose funny songs that would make them burst out laughing so hard they'd cry happy tears. For those lonely people who had no one special in their lives to love, the prince sang songs about a surprise romance that would come their way if they stopped looking."

"Like how you and Vater met?"

Charlotte averted her gaze for a moment then looked into Edith's eyes. "Yes, sweetie. I thought I'd never meet a man who would accept me for who I was and who would fall in love with me. But happily, I was wrong. As soon as I convinced myself that a good, kind man wasn't in my future, your father came along."

"And you fell in love instantly?" Krista asked.

Charlotte kissed both girls' cheeks. "Yes."

"Mama?" Edith asked. "Did Prince Kurt fall in love with a woman he wrote a song for?"

Charlotte glanced at the mantle clock that, without a fireplace, let alone a mantel, was propped on the corner of her husband's writing desk. She'd hoped a story would soothe her daughters and not excite them, so they could drift off into a good night's sleep, but now she wasn't sure if it was a good idea. "Yes and no. He tried to create a special song for the woman he wished to marry, but she refused to listen to it."

"Why?" both Edith and Krista cried out.

"Because she wanted to love the prince for the special man that he was. Not for the lovely songs he wrote. Her heart told her that if the prince didn't realize this, all he would do in their lifetime together was to spend bunches of hours making songs to please her. Instead, all she wanted was for him to shower her with his love, and she wanted to return this love to him. The fair maiden wanted him to understand that although she admired his talent and appreciated his songs, she loved him because he was who he was—a special man."

"Is Prince Kurt Papa Kurt?" Krista pulled at her bottom lip. "Did Papa make a special bracelet or necklace for you, but you didn't want it, so he got arrested?"

Wanting to dodge the topic of Kurt's arrest, Charlotte sat up straight. With a hand on each of Krista's shoulders, she peered into her daughter's eyes. "I love your father, whether he gives me presents or not, just like he loves me whether I cook him a delicious meal or one that he never wants to eat again."

"Does this story have a happy ending?" Edith murmured. "There has to be a happy ending."

Yes, each story deserved a happy ending. She leaned back again. "Well, the fair maiden opened a gift-wrapped package from Prince Kurt. It held a piece of music with lyrics written across the parchment. He sang the song about a prince and a fair maiden who didn't fall in love over a song, but rather over each other's hearts that ached when they were away from each other and—"

"Mama?" Edith broke in. "Are you achy without Vater here with us?"

Charlotte's eyes stung with tears. She batted her lashes in hope they wouldn't streak down her cheeks. "After the song ended, the prince surprised the fair maiden once more when he gave her a small silver box with a silk white ribbon bow. She opened it and there, before her eyes, was the largest diamond engagement ring she'd ever seen. The fair maiden accepted the prince's declaration of his love for her, and he accepted that her love wasn't based upon what he sang about or did or didn't do for her. And they lived happily ever after."

"I like that story," Krista said. A yawn eclipsed her face. "But you did not answer Edith's question about if you're achy without Papa being home with us."

"Let's get the two of you tucked into bed." Charlotte reached for their hands, relieved her daughters didn't resist.

In the depths of early morning, Charlotte's mattress dipped, followed by warmth enveloping her in a distinct sheath of protection. Or, was that someone clinging to her in need of her care? She cracked open one eye to see the moonlight shining upon Edith.

"Can I stay with you, Mama?"

"Of course, love." She couldn't remember the last time Edith had crawled into her bed. "Are you and your sister all right?"

"Krista is asleep. She's snoring. I can never sleep when she snores."

Charlotte reached over Edith and turned on the light. A little brightness often worked wonders. She propped herself onto her elbow, facing Edith. "I suspect it wasn't your sister's snoring this time that had you jumping into bed with me. You can tell me. Maybe I can make it better for you."

"You can only make it better if you tell me that Papa is coming home soon."

Papa. Not Vater. Charlotte feathered her fingers across her daughter's cheek. The softness of the child's face was a balm for her soul. "Your father will come home to us."

"No, he won't. He can't."

She averted her gaze from Edith. "Why do you say this?"

"Because of what the officer who visited said—that the man they arrested used his real name, Kurt Weber. So, they must be watching for him. Besides, you said that you're Mevrouw Beck and that Helmut Beck, your husband, left you. Maybe that means they're also watching us. What does it matter? You're denying that Papa is Papa. Papa denies he's Papa and that he doesn't live here." She groaned. "And you won't look me in the eye as I speak to you, like right now. You've always said that liars look away, not people who tell the truth."

She looked into Edith's eyes. "Yes, you're right. And I'm sorry. I am lying. Your Papa is lying. It is not the right thing to do, but in time of war—and make no mistake about this German occupation of the Netherlands, it is war—people must do what they can to survive." Confusion, not understanding, scrawled lines across her daughter's face. Would the right words ever surface to offer a measly bit of comfort to her young one? "And this is what your father and I have decided to do to protect you and Krista because we love you so, so very much."

"In the story you told us, was Prince Kurt actually Papa? Were his beautiful songs like the jewelry he makes? Like the butterfly necklace he said he made for you before a thief took it?"

Her daughter always managed to hear the sad reality from which she and Kurt had tried to shelter her. Charlotte's eyes welled with tears.

"Don't cry, Mama," Edith murmured.

Charlotte wiped her wet cheeks. "When did you become so sharp that I can no longer keep things from reaching your ears, when all I want to do is to swaddle you in a protective blanket like a baby, and keep you safe and content?"

Edith grasped Charlotte's hand. Who was comforting whom? "Do you think Papa will come back to us?"

Charlotte looked about the bedroom. Kurt's nightstand stood on the other side of the bed where his wristwatch was still set on a red velvet cushion. His clothes were tucked in his half of the wardrobe. Each time she opened its door, a fresh outdoor scent reminded her of his lingering presence despite his current absence. In the corner of the room were his extra pair of shoes she'd placed safely so no one would trip over them. "Your Papa will make sure we're reunited. It might be tomorrow or in a few months. And I, too, will do what I can to protect you and your sister. Meanwhile, you two must be courageous." She wrapped an arm around Edith. "Will you do that for me?" Edith nodded. "Would you like to stay with me the rest of the night?"

"I think it's best if I go back to my own bed. That way, when Krista wakes up and sees me, she'll know there's at least one thing about our family that is the same."

Her daughter's last words snatched Charlotte's breath. She couldn't verbally reply. Instead, she embraced her child and rocked her, wishing and praying that one day, when she would be 75 and Edith 54, she would still have the joy and privilege of hugging her child.

14

On an early August morning, six months after Charlotte had last seen her husband, she began to cross the bridge over the Singelgracht. Blaming the rationing of coffee for her weariness, she stopped, leaned against a light post, and rubbed her eyes, then gasped. There he was. Kurt... Helmut. Her husband. He stood on the other side of the bridge, his clothing ragged, his face gaunt, not a smile adorning his thin, sweet lips. He stared at her; she at him, afraid to move, to blink, terrified that she'd once again see him vanish. Or worse, that this was not a man, not her husband, but an apparition of her imagination and desire. A sneeze overcame her and she shook so hard that she pivoted half around.

A hand landed on her shoulder. Had Kurt approached her when she'd sneezed seconds ago and regrettably removed her gaze? With a smile in place, she turned around. No Kurt, but a fellow worker from the crèche. The woman greeted her and asked her if she was all right. Charlotte nodded and the colleague hurried past as if she too were chased by ghosts of either the deceased or the missing. Lately, there had been sightings throughout Amsterdam of the lost.

Charlotte craned her neck to look over the handful of people crossing the bridge—women wearing light summer dresses and men in white shirts and dark pants, but without ties or jackets. None of them remotely resembled her husband. Just like the other times she'd seen him dodging into an ally, blending into a crowd watching a protest, or pedaling away on a bicycle from Edith and Krista's school. If this phantom, this hallucination, was indeed a real person—her husband—then he'd make his presence known to her when the time was right. But, if not? Then, like other women who had lost their husbands by either death or wrongful imprisonment, she'd have to renew her determination to remain strong and move on, or she'd fall apart into pieces once and for all. She needed to find out, or she'd perpetually live in the void between yesterday, with its memories, or tomorrow, with its hopes. Even so, tomorrow would still have its demands, like caring for her daughters, protecting them from harm, and reporting to her job—a job that she was lucky to have, unlike her fellow Jews. This wasn't the time to capitulate to the madness and come apart. Instead, she rushed on and plowed into a trio of NSB men approaching from the opposite direction. Their distinctive uniforms included black shirts—like Mussolini's fascists.

Nervous, she flexed her fingers and her purse fell to the ground. The tallest of the men dropped a satchel and papers flew out. She squatted to scoop up the papers. He bent to retrieve her purse. Their heads collided. With raised brows and open mouths, they stood and rubbed at their smarting heads. The other two men broke out in raucous laughter. She glanced at the man—the tallest of the three—she'd bumped into. In an unsettling way, he looked quite familiar.

"Pardon me," the stranger said. He raked his hand through his short brown hair, chuckling. "This isn't my usual way of meeting people."

"Especially women," said the older-looking man of the trio. He'd slurred his words as if he was drunk. He smacked his lips with a finger and made a shushing sound. "But I won't tell his wife."

"Give us a *hou zee!*" commanded the other man beside his

drunkard comrade. "All good soldiers should be saluted and—" He spat off the bridge and swore. "Protected from worthless idiots and people who have no right to live."

The man she'd collided with shook his head. "Don't listen to my associates."

"Associates, are we?" the drunk one barked.

"Ignore him," the tall man said, again apologizing for bumping into her. He took off his sunglasses and smiled at Charlotte. "My name is Luuk. You look familiar. Do I know you?"

His two pals howled in laughter and snorted, finally stepping away when Luuk shot them a warning glare. When he faced Charlotte again, she swallowed back a gasp. *His eyes!* One was brown, the other green. Hadn't Helmut said—once upon a time when he was Kurt—that he'd had trouble with a man that fitted this description? She blinked and brushed her bare neckline where a butterfly necklace should have been—one that matched the butterfly pin Kurt had designed exclusively for her; one that had been snatched by a man with different-colored eyes. This couldn't be the same person. Certainly, there must be several people in Amsterdam with mismatched eyes. She caught him staring hard at her. She stepped back.

"You needn't be afraid of me." He reached out and touched her arm. "Please, I hope I haven't hurt you." He grinned a boyish and horribly charming smile. "As my wife is fond of saying—I have a hard head."

"I'm fine." She willed her nervousness away. "Thank you for your concern."

"Good, then." He released her arm and rubbed his clean-shaven chin. "I'm sure I've seen you before, but I can't quite place you or the situation of our meeting."

She perused his clipped, military-short hair. His crisp black uniform with red, gold, and black patches on the collar was as haunting as the brown shirts she'd begun seeing more and more of as the number of Dutch men swelled the ranks of the Waffen-SS. Luuk, with his slim but muscular build and those startling eyes, might have made a perfect foot soldier for Hitler. Still, as far as her concerns went, she wanted to never see him again. Then it all came back to her. She tried all she could to not gape, or worse, shout the ugliest words she could summon at this man. She prayed her dyed blonde shoulder-length hair would continue to cloud this soldier's memory and he wouldn't realize she was the dark-haired woman who had screamed when he pulled Kurt away from his family back in February. With a tightened grip on her purse, she forced herself to smile at Luuk. "I don't believe we've met, but please pardon me or I'll be late for work."

He gave a little nod and let her pass. As if she'd walked through a blackberry shrub, a distinct sensation pricked the base of her neck. She immediately knew that Luuk was staring at her. She refused to turn around and check. Well, she finally had a first name to relay to her husband about the possible necklace thief, if she ever saw him again—a name and a face she'd never forget, but wished she could.

Edith stormed indoors with Krista at her heels. Shaken from her encounter yesterday with Luuk and his two laughing friends on the bridge, Charlotte jumped. Beside the oven, her hand flew out and she smacked her knuckles hard on the door handle. A rare expletive flew from her mouth. Both girls stopped short of entering the kitchen. Their mouths dropped open, eyes widened.

"No worries," Charlotte said. She wiggled her fingers, ignoring the burning pain. "See, I'm fine. I'm more curious about the two of you. By the way you barged indoors I'm wondering if you're all right." Krista started to nod, but Edith shook her head. "Sit at the table. Tell me what's upsetting you." With the girls hesitating, Charlotte crossed the small room to the table, pulled out two chairs, and sat on a third.

"It's what Greetje told me," Edith said, sitting down first, though Krista was fast to follow.

Charlotte summoned her patience, a difficult task as of late. She remained quiet, allowing Edith to speak when she was ready. Instead, Krista spoke up.

"Mama, Edith's friend said that she can't go to school in September like us. Why is that? Why are we different?"

"Silly you," Edith murmured and rolled her eyes. "How can you not know?"

Charlotte folded her hands on the bare table. "Enough. No bickering. What did Greetje say, Edith?"

Usually the stoic one, Edith surprised her with a sniffle and eyes brimming with tears. "She said that she and her brothers aren't allowed back in school next—"

"Tell Mama why," Krista said, then blushed. "Sorry for interrupting."

Charlotte gave a curt nod and eyed Edith again. "Did she say why?"

"Because they're Jewish. Like we used to be."

Used to be. Charlotte sighed; her belly bunched in a knot. Should she again try to explain the necessity for the ruse that had her family denying their faith? "Is your friend certain? How did she learn of this news?"

"Greetje said that all Jewish parents received a notice from the Dutch government." Edith wiped the tears trickling down her cheeks. "She wants to go but can't, because Jews aren't allowed to step foot into public schools. Now she has to attend a Jewish school in a different neighborhood, but her parents doubt it will be long until that too is prohibited. Mama?"

Quite certain of what her daughter was about to ask, Charlotte swallowed hard. Despite her reluctance, she nodded in encouragement for Edith to continue.

"I didn't tell her," Edith resumed. Her tone was so soft that Charlotte had to lean forward, and strained to listen. "Didn't tell her we were Jewish. Should I? Is it wrong that Krista and I pretend that we're Christian?"

An uncomfortable silence slipped between them. For seconds?

Minutes? As if unable to support one more emotion, good or bad, Charlotte's mind emptied of all thoughts. She so badly wanted to escape the reality of what life had become. The screech of a chair leg dragging over the bare floor from Krista standing up hooked her attention and pulled her back to the present. "Where are you going?"

"I'm going into the bedroom to read a book."

A frown dragged Edith's lips downward. "How can you have fun when my friend, her brothers, and other children can't attend school and we also shouldn't be going to school?"

Krista shrugged. "I'm doing what Papa told us to do. I don't understand. Anything. But I'm just a little girl and don't understand many things." She left the kitchen.

"Are you going to punish her?" Edith asked.

"Punish? Your sister did no wrong."

"But the Jewish children didn't do wrong either. Nor their parents." Edith stood. "When we were Jewish, we also didn't do wrong. Why are the Nazis taking over countries that don't belong to them and ruining life for people who don't believe in their ways?"

Charlotte might have been a grown woman, but she'd never understand why one group of people had successfully seized power to rule over others, dictating who qualified as belonging to the human race. "Edith, I'm going to catch a breath of fresh air. Will you be a darling and watch your sister?"

Edith sighed, whether it was over her unanswered question or having to watch over Krista or both. Charlotte hated to admit it, but against the backdrop of the shocking and daily changing landscape around them, it sadly didn't matter why her oldest was pouting. They'd lost the ability to control their lives, to shape their future—circumstances she couldn't explain to a child. She reached over and kissed the top of Edith's head. "I'll only be a few—"

"Yes, Mutter. You'll be only a few minutes, and meanwhile, Krista and I will stay indoors and no matter what happens we are not to open the door to anyone but you."

Before sobs escaped her burning lungs, Charlotte strode to the door and hurried down the flight of stairs. The second she set her feet on the cobblestone street that ran alongside the canal, the early afternoon sun struck her eyes and she squinted. Wishing she'd worn a hat, she shielded her eyes with a hand, turned, and gasped. Her husband stepped beside her, hooked his arm around hers as if they were enjoying a leisurely stroll, and started to lead her down the street. She wanted to plant her feet firmly and root herself until he explained why he was suddenly here and where he was taking her. She wanted to jump into his arms, wrap her legs around his waist and kiss him until they both couldn't breathe. And she also wanted to press her finger against his delicious lips to prevent an explanation from escaping and instead tug him upstairs to their daughters for shouts of glee and dances of joy. Instead, as his grip on her tightened, she allowed herself to be whisked around the corner, guided across a street, pulled into an alleyway, only to exit and end up behind the post office. He seized her hand and they crouched between two garbage cans. With a little maneuvering, she managed to tug him toward her and they kissed hard with the passion of the enduring love of a long-time married couple—comfortable yet excited over each other's bodies and souls. No one understood them as fully as they did each other.

"Let me explain," he puffed into her face when they pulled apart. "Before I can't."

"Tell me you've come home," she said, though she knew he was about to tell her the opposite.

He fingered her hair. "You're lovely as a blonde, but you're beautiful no matter what."

"Kurt... please. Explain away."

His hands slipped into his lap and he leaned against the wooden structure. "The Dutch... German police—whoever they are these days—imprisoned me. Two weeks ago, they were transporting me to another location. A place I'm uncertain of—perhaps out of the country to a work camp. Herta..."

Could he not continue? The sound of her real name, spoken

lovingly as only Kurt could, also rang with anguish. She grasped both his hands and pressed them against her heart.

"I escaped, barely. I'm a fugitive. If they capture me, I'm certain the consequences will be far worse than living off the streets and perpetually being on the run."

"We'll hide you... in our apartment." With each word she said, he shook his head. It didn't matter, though. "The girls need you. I need you."

"No. I can't put you in that kind of danger."

"But you didn't commit a crime."

"Back then, during the strike—that's correct. I did not commit a crime. But now they know I'm Jewish and that is a crime. Plus, I've escaped on their watch—another crime and strike against me."

She understood he wasn't exaggerating or being dramatic. Seyss-Inquart and his Nazi pals might have worn smiles and whisper mere warnings at first, but since 1941 rolled around, day-by-day life was changing for the Jewish population in the Netherlands. It was no wonder her wise husband had insisted upon identity changes and a relocation to a different neighborhood. More changes—like stopping Jewish children from attending public schools, as she just learned mere minutes ago—were bound to happen. Would it be only a matter of hours or days until they were ratted on, and their true names and faith would be discovered? And what would happen after there were no more Jews upon whom to cast blame at for ruining the Aryan's nice lifestyle? Would the Nazis then go after another faith or race, if they hadn't started already? She squeezed his hands. "What will you do?"

"I have two options. Three, if I want to consider surrendering myself."

"Don't you dare."

"Okay, then. My first option is to try to escape to another country, but I don't want to because that means leaving you and the girls. For how long, I can't guess at this point. And of course, there's the likely chance I might be captured."

She couldn't think about an arrest or imprisonment or worse. "And the second choice?"

"Like I've been doing since my escape from the transport, to keep moving and living on the streets here in Amsterdam, where I can remain close to you."

So, she hadn't imagined the sightings of Kurt, after all. "But you can't be with us," she said, using the words she believed he held back. The prospects of him remaining free of recapture by the police—or the Nazis—grew slimmer each minute that ticked by. That was the last thing she wanted for him. She rested her head on his shoulder, aware that this long-treasured sensation was a fleeting moment. "You must leave. I can finally see the necessity." She blinked back tears. "Right away, without one word or glance at the girls. You must promise me to run and run and run... Go to Switzerland. That might mean entering other German-controlled countries, but you must. Palestine is a possibility, if you can make it that far." He surprised her, not with another kiss but by pursing his lips. "What is it, Kurt? You won't go? Won't try saving yourself so that one day we can be reunited and make all these horrible wrongs right for our children and grandchildren?"

"I'll go. I'll leave this minute, but first, you must also promise me one thing." She sucked in her breath and waited. "Herta, I want you to put the girls and yourself into hiding. No delays. Agreed?"

She nodded. About to stand, he placed his hands firmly on the front of her shoulders. She couldn't move. Didn't want to.

"Close your eyes, my pretty blonde sweetheart."

She knew what he was about to say, to do, and shook her head in defiance. Her eyes welled with tears she couldn't wipe away because of the way he held her, but that wouldn't have mattered. She wanted him to see her cry. "No," she murmured. She peered into his brown eyes, the shade that always reminded her of honey, of autumn leaves, of the sand on the beach on which they used to walk together, hand in hand, when they first came to the Netherlands. Shades of splendor. Shades of tranquility. He was asking her to close her eyes as if he was about to shoot her and didn't want her to see him holding the weapon. Although it felt as if she was about to receive a blow of death, this was no gun he was firing. Yet, it might as well have been, since it essentially had the same result—his absence from her life. "Please... no..."

He leaned closer. "Do it for me."

"Or what?"

"Or..." His voice choked, squeezed around the words that she feared he also didn't want to say. "I won't be able to continue if you don't. And I have no other choice but this one. Do it for me, Herta. Because I love you. Always will."

"I love—"

"Shut those gorgeous eyes of yours. Now." She closed her eyes. He released his grip. "Keep them shut and count to 20."

Aware that he'd be gone away from her within a handful of seconds, she opened her eyes at the count of 15. As if he'd never appeared, she only had her own company, which she didn't enjoy. Taking a deep breath, she willed herself to be calm and returned to the street. A glance to her right and left failed to show Kurt, or any other person. Her husband, the apparition, had disappeared once again, but this time, permanently. She placed one foot in front of the other; she too would continue. She was a wife, but foremost, a mother. She had two daughters to hurry home to and to care for.

15

Where was 1941 stampeding toward? Julia found it not only difficult to believe it was the first of September, but also that she had the house to herself. Home from work early, and with her daughters under the watchful eye of her sister-in-law, Julia didn't waste one second. She slipped out her work shoes and flung them against the hall closet door with a grunt. All she could think about was the day-long aggravation she suffered from putting up with her supervisor's cutting remarks. Good thing she was alone.

"Julia? What's wrong?"

She snapped her head up so fast that her neck smarted and she winced. "Oh, Luuk. I wasn't expecting to see you home. Sorry to upset you. Nothing other than a miserable workday is wrong—what else is new? But why are you home from your job?" Is the war advancing? Are we in danger?"

He pushed off against the wall he'd leaned upon and narrowed the distance between them. "Come." He grasped her hand—his own hands sweaty to her suddenly cool ones. He started to tug her toward their bedroom.

"What do you have in mind?" She giggled. "Two little ones, darling, are plenty enough for me to handle."

He stopped short of opening the bedroom door, his face too solemn for her comfort. "Julia, although I'd love to pull that dreadful work uniform off of your sexy body and hop into bed with you, you need to see something."

Wary of his surprise that she sensed wasn't going to be good news, for a scatter of seconds, she wished she was back at work and not home with her husband. When he pushed the door open and gestured for her to enter first, the first oddity Julia saw was the sight of Luuk's rucksack open on the bed. Pairs of black socks and white boxers, a few shabby shirts and a pair of plain trousers were piled beside the unbuckled bag. She turned to face him and that was when she saw the uniform hanging from the closet door, its gray-green color resembling a cloud-heavy sky about to burst and release a downpour. "That's not your NSB uniform. What's going on?"

"You're right. It's a Dutch Waffen-SS uniform," he said unnecessarily.

She'd seen plenty of men wearing them lately, especially as they said farewell to their families and marched off into the vanishing day, prepared to give their lives on behalf of Hitler. "I won't be returning to work at the radio shop."

"Have you been conscripted, or did you volunteer?"

"I volunteered, of course." Luuk crossed his arms and his eyes darkened. "It's been almost a year since the invasion—too much time if you ask me. I want to help the Germans complete their plans. Aren't you proud of me for wanting to make this world a better place for you and our daughters to live in?"

"This has nothing to do with me or my taking pride in you as my husband." He'd never see it that way. She had to act fast to smooth out the tangled knot she was making. "I'm concerned for you. What wife wouldn't be? You have to admit, this is a surprise, yes?"

"I've talked with you about moving beyond the NSB and entering the SS. I see joining the Waffen-SS as a natural progression to the full-out SS, where I'll be able to then enforce the racial policies of the Nazi party rather than remain in combat. That's what I want for Germany and our control of the world." His last few words left no doubt in her mind that he saw no distinction between himself as a Dutch national and a German-born citizen. If she had to be honest with herself, her husband's need to be recognized by others as an achiever would lead him to claim any status that would ultimately elevate himself over others, making him the ideal Nazi.

With two large steps he reached her, clasped his fingers around her wrist, and steered her onto the bed. "If you truly trust me, you'd put aside your concerns and start cheering for me." He sat beside her, pressing tightly against her, not out of passion, but control. That was his way. Looking back, she could admit to herself that in the past—and not that long ago—she'd received a certain sensual thrill from his force. These days, his force—whether physical or emotional—had become a turn-off. Even worse, she knew bold, ugly words would follow, implying things that were not so. "Just for once, Julia, especially before I go off and face the unknown with all its dangers, I'd like to count on your trust and admiration."

It was indeed the horrors and the unknowns he faced that troubled her, and it had nothing to do with trust or admiration, but she couldn't talk sense to him when he was in one of his moods. She glanced at the scar on her inner wrist, the one she acquired just a few months ago. Maybe it wasn't so much how he acted and what he implied, but how she caved to his pressure. "You most definitely have my trust. And yes, I also admire you for being brave and becoming a soldier."

"It's not the rank of officer that I'd wanted and hoped for."

They'd talked about this subject the night they attended the party for Seyss-Inquart. She thought he'd be over it. Aware of how she might be able to ease his discomfort, she seized his hands and pulled him toward her to kiss him. His mouth welcomed hers, and he pulled her back onto the bed and rolled on top of her, his desire for her obvious.

"Julia," he breathed into her face. "I want to make love with you one last time before I have to leave. Tell me you want the same." While staring at her, waiting for a reply, he began to unbutton her blouse, his fingers trailing to the hem of her skirt.

"Make love with me, Luuk." She silently cursed herself for wanting him.

"Where are the girls?"

"At your brother's. No worries... we have time."

"Good." He kicked off his pants, unzipped her skirt, and pulled it down. The blue scratchy uniform dropped to the floor, along with the last of her dignity. "Right now, it's you and me, Julia, and that's all that matters. The Nazis can wait."

Certain she'd never hear those words flow from his mouth again, she longed to keep him tangled in the hot and sweaty sheets of their lovemaking until Hitler got what he wanted and the war ended.

Julia could say with ironic certainty about her husband that he was a man of surprises and mystery. After they simmered down, she expected him to light up a cigarette and start chatting about the merits of killing in the name of bettering mankind to soften the blow of being sent to the harsh Soviet cold or the African heat, or at the very least, to reassure her that she and the children would manage to stay safe. Instead, he hurried out of bed, tossed her bathrobe at her, and dressed only in his boxers, urged her to follow him into the parlor. For what, she couldn't imagine.

She didn't want to disturb the lighthearted mood he was in and stepped gingerly behind him. By the time she entered the room he was loading a record onto the Philco radio-phonograph. He'd brought it home from his job at the radio repair shop when a customer said he couldn't afford to have it fixed, and it was Luuk's if he wanted it. And oh boy, Luuk had wanted this top seller of the year. Badly. He loved music. They couldn't afford this deluxe model on their own, let alone a halfway decent phonograph. She'd offered an approving smile when he'd first presented it to her, despite his confession that the player's broken piece could have easily—and inexpensively—been repaired, but Luuk had hoped to discourage the owner by quoting an outrageously high price. They enjoyed their little record collection nearly on a nightly basis ever since. On occasion, though they seldom wanted to hear the news, they'd tune into the radio.

"I love this piece!" she said when a sultry mix of saxophone, clarinet, and piano fluttered through the air from one of their old records. He mumbled something about the record being a warm-up then knelt before the sofa and slid his hand underneath. A little squeal slipped from her mouth. "Ooh! Did you bring home a surprise for me?"

With a grin on his face, he stood and waved a record peeking out of its brown-paper sleeve. "Now I know where Ani and Marianne get their screech—uh, their charm—from."

Ignoring his attempt at humor, and already forgetting about the record presently playing, she eyed the surprise of the new one. "Aren't you going to tell me who's on the record?"

Luuk returned to the console, removed the previous record that had just ended, and then put on the new one. He flashed a playful scolding look as if to say: now, now, no cheating by looking at the cover. He set the player in motion and stared at her, waiting for a positive reaction. When the first words of a crooning Frank Sinatra vibrated across the room, she let out a hearty sigh.

"That's *Blue Eyes*! I don't recognize the song, though."

"'This Love of Mine.' Will you dance with me, my beautiful Julia?" He offered a hand and whirled her around their improvised dance floor, reminding her of the times they danced under the moonlight to songs on the radio. Having a sharp ear for music and a rich baritone voice, Luuk sang along with Sinatra but altered the words and sang about his own forever love for her and that she would always be on his mind. When the song ended and the record player automatically switched off, they continued to dance.

"And it's true, Julia. You will always be on my mind, no matter where they send me, no matter what I do. I will always love you and our daughters."

"I will always love you as well."

Their dancing slowed to a shuffle and then ceased. They held each other—captives in still life—clinging to each other for, possibly, one last time.

"This is silly." Luuk pushed away, the moment spoiled. "Get dressed and fetch the girls."

She couldn't speak or move. Not with the spell of Swoonatra replaying itself over and over in her mind, chasing away the reality of life.

He batted the air. "Don't stand around like a fool."

"Can't you bring Annelise and Marianne home. They'd love it if you surprised them."

His left eye twitched, a sign of stress for him. "They will not like the news I'm going to tell them at dinnertime." He started toward the bedroom.

"Luuk?"

He stopped. "Tomorrow morning. Normandy, France."

"Pardon?"

"Weren't you about to ask when I'm leaving or where I'm assigned?"

She cinched the belt of her robe tighter. "Actually, I was going to ask how the girls and I will get along without you."

He leaned against the doorframe to their room. "Let's not go through this again. You work and have income. And I'll be sending a hefty percentage of mine home to you. You will manage quite well."

What was that supposed to mean? There was much more to be concerned about than finances. What would happen if... when... the war worsened? They were Dutch and Aryan, and thankfully not Jewish, but a bomb dropped by a plane wouldn't distinguish them from others. War was called hell for a reason.

"And you have my brother and Mila next door," Luuk added. "Liam's useless hands make him unsuitable for military service, but at least he'll be around to keep an eye on you." He squared his shoulders, towering over her. "Bring our daughters home, Julia. Is having one last family meal before I leave for a great cause too much to ask for?" He stepped into their bedroom, where they'd just made love. Likely, he'd finish packing the few personal items he was allowed to take with him to the front.

16

"Mama, Ani's not being nice."

They were at it again. Just when Julia was musing how lucky she was to have this late September day off from work, a day that felt more like summer than autumn, she had to put up with her bickering daughters. Although increasingly edgy as of late, like a lit firecracker about to blast off, for her daughters' sakes, she tamped back her snappy mood and glanced up from the red and white-checkered picnic blanket she was spreading on the grassy park surface next to the children's play area. Annelise, Julia's budding artist, sat on the opposite end of the park bench from Marianne, and busied herself coloring with a red crayon on her tablet of paper. Then again, if her squabbling daughters were Julia's only complaint, she could easily say life was grand. She smiled gently at her youngest. "Your sister is keeping herself busy with her drawing. She isn't bothering you."

"But she said nasty things to me."

Having not heard a peep from either child until Marianne started to grouse, Julia sat cross-legged on the blanket and patted the spot beside her in invitation. "Come join me and we'll watch the ducks in the pond."

"Can we feed them our lunch?" Marianne asked as she plopped next to Julia.

"Let's first see if there are any scraps leftover from our meal." While her daughter grew silent while observing the ducks, Julia took in the houses and apartment buildings that surrounded the park. If these residences could speak, she imagined she'd hear them groan and shriek, parroting their occupants. *We're not leaving. They can't make us. This is our home, not theirs.* Such words were uttered from passersby on the streets ever since the roundups of Jews had started. Each time she grew nervous by these haunting pleas, Luuk's attempted reassurances—as recited by her brother-in-law—toyed with her: "Don't be fooled, Julia. The new accommodations at the Westerbork camp are quite nice with schools for the children, plentiful food for all, and include the entertainment of an orchestra—far better than what those Jews were enjoying lately in Holland. As for rumors about the camp at Amersfoort being a work camp, don't be fooled, dear. It's a transit camp, nothing more." Julia wished folks could keep back their unpleasant opinions. Her own husband was serving the Dutch government on behalf of the Nazi Party and he wouldn't do anything illegal or inhumane.

The lunch hour passed fast enough. Fortunately, the girls behaved well. Even Marianne didn't voice one more complaint about her older sister. Despite their predictable objection that they were too old for a nap that only babies took, Julia announced it was time to go home and settle down. She needed peace and quiet and this was the one way she could guarantee it. Along with her irritable mood, exhaustion was a constant visitor lately. She looked forward to lounging on the sofa while the girls remained in their bedroom. Whether they'd actually sleep was beyond her, but she could use the rest.

With the picnic hamper empty after lunch, the poor ducks would have to seek scraps from elsewhere. With Annelise's crayons and pad and Marianne's doll tucked in a tote bag and slung over Ani's shoulder, they lumbered homeward and arrived at their doorstep 20 minutes later. Thankful to have a little privacy, Julia was quite relieved that Liam and Mila were visiting Mila's parents across town. She unlocked the front door for the girls, telling them she wanted to check on the dahlias and see if the blossoms had opened up yet—they were a couple weeks late this year. She loved the pretty colorful flowers more than tulips, though reluctant to admit this preference in a country that had enshrined the tulip as its national flower. As she turned right to head to the side garden, a blow came to her head, knocking her backward and onto the ground. Her world turned black.

Julia blinked her way to consciousness seconds—or minutes—later. She was stretched out on the parlor's rug. Annelise and Marianne were seated next to each other on the sofa. Pale, round-eyed, with mouths gaping open, they appeared gripped with fear. Neither of them uttered a word—an oddity in itself. Annelise pointed to behind Julia. Julia propped herself onto an elbow, a curse flying from her lips when the room spun.

"Mama!" Marianne called.

"*Hou je mond!*" a voice shouted.

Julia stood. Her hands splayed to her sides as if clinging to the air would steady her wobbly feet in the rotating room. A man stood beside her, towering over her, just like her husband. Unlike Luuk, this man's scraggly beard, stringy, coal-dark unwashed hair, and lanky build, repulsed her. He couldn't have been more than her age, 31, maybe 35 at the most. "Who are you? Don't you tell my girls to shut up! Leave immediately!"

He snickered. Then he held up a knife and gestured with it like a schoolteacher using a pointer before a map of the world. "I'd tell you to shut up as well, but I doubt you'd listen." His Dutch was perfect without a trace of an accent. Her inkling, though, said he wasn't from around here. Actually, she doubted he was from any town or city in the Netherlands.

"Listen to him, Mama," Annelise said, though Julia wouldn't

take her eyes off the man. Ready to report him to the first authorities that came along, she memorized every one of his miserable features. "He said he'll hurt us. We don't want to get hurt."

This beast had threatened her daughters? Taking two strides forward, she shoved the man onto a nearby chair. The knife fell from his hand and clanked to the floor. Perfect. She swooped to pick it up, but he seized her hand and forced it open. As pain shot up her arm, he yanked her against his chest and pressed the cold knife blade against her throat.

Annelise screamed. He ordered her to keep quiet or he'd hurt her mother. Marianne broke out in hysterical sobs. Annelise wrapped an arm around her sister and they both rocked as silent tears flowed.

"If you do what I say," the beast hissed into Julia's ear, "you and your girls will live. If not, best you say your goodbyes right now."

She nodded. He removed the knife and ordered her to sit. The thought of sitting where his dirty trousers had touched the chair's fabric made her stomach lurch. She gagged and pressed the back of her hand against her mouth, pleading silently for him to leave them alone.

The stranger continued to stand between her seat and the girls on the sofa. "I have no other choice but to stay here."

"Why here?" If she could keep him talking, there was a chance he'd calm down, see his foolishness for what it was, and scamper off like the mongrel that he was. "My husband will be home soon."

"That's what the last lady said." He tossed her a sour grin. "I might have entered your lovely home without an invitation, but I'm not stupid." He glanced toward the sofa and then back at her. "Annelise and Marianne—my new friends—told me their father went away to fight for the Nazis. More reason for me to take advantage of that."

He knew her daughters' names? Knew about Luuk? "Are you Jewish?" she asked.

He laughed. "No, pretty Julia."

She swallowed dryly. So, he also knew her name.

"I'm Dutch by birth, born to a church-attending family," he continued. "But those Nazis aren't going to cram me onto a train and ship me to a German factory where I become a sitting duck for a British bomber ready to wipe me off this lousy planet. That's what happened to my brother in June when Dutch labor conscripts were sent to Germany, but there's no way they're taking me."

"What's your name?"

"Getting friendly, are you? Name's Henk. No last name necessary."

"Tell me, Henk. How long will you be staying here?"

"As long as I need to."

"Can I sit with my girls? They need comforting."

"Let's get this straight, Julia." Although Henk had stopped brandishing his knife, he kept the weapon in a tight grip. "I'm no criminal. Just want to live like you. So, of course, go to your daughters and take care of them. Besides, I could use a hefty dose of quiet." A knock came at the door. "Guess fate thinks otherwise." He ordered Annelise and Marianne to remain quiet. They nodded. "Are you expecting guests, Julia?"

"No one."

"Go to the door and tell the person that you're ill and want to be left alone. I'll be right behind you, with my trusty knife."

He wasn't mistaken about her physical condition. Her head throbbed and her belly churned. Feeling the tip of the louse's knife on the base of her spine, she cracked the door open to find Mila holding a small basket.

"Julia? Let me in. You don't look well."

"I have an awful headache. In fact, I'd like to rest. How may I help you?"

"Liam and I just returned from my parents, and they had extra cheese and bread. Where they got the food during this time of rationing is a mystery. You know Mama, though. She needs to feed as many people as she can." Mila narrowed her eyes when Julia frowned. "Oh, I'm sorry. You're not well and I'm not allowing you to rest. I'll come in to help you with this basket so you don't need to fuss." Mila touched the door, but Julia placed a hand over hers to prevent her from pushing the door open. "You don't want me to at least look in on Annelise and Marianne? Would you like me to bring them next door to supper with us? I can have Liam bring you a plate."

"No, thanks." She took a step back to shut the door.

"Wait." Mila thrust the basket toward her. "Take the cheese and bread. There are two chocolates on the bottom as treats for the girls."

Julia clamped her hands around the basket wishing it was freedom she'd seized instead. She murmured her appreciation and an apology for her unintentional rudeness, then she closed the door and shoved the basket in Henk's hands. "Enjoy your cheese." She gagged, alarm poking her backside where the tip of Henk's knife had pressed firmly against her. "Pardon me." she said and ran toward the bathroom, not caring if he followed her. If he wanted to watch her vomit, he was more than welcome to.

Upon awakening at three in the morning, Julia couldn't remember what happened in the hours before she'd drifted off to sleep. Had she fed Annelise or Marianne dinner? Had she eaten a bite of food? Had she tucked the girls into their beds and read them a bedtime story? Or for that matter, how had she managed to crawl into her own bed without her shoes on, though fully dressed? She then remembered a man, a stranger. He'd entered her house. Had scared her daughters, had terrified her by making her painfully aware that at any given second he could hurt them all. Henk. Henk without a last name. Henk, the knife-wielding shirker who avoided his patriotic duty to work for the Germans. She sprang upright, surprised stars weren't circulating around her head and making her queasy.

"Easy, sister."

Henk reclined leisurely on a chair beside the double bed, his feet propped up on Luuk's side. He smiled. "You look better, but I'd go easy if I were you."

She didn't need to take advice from him, though that wasn't her top concern. "Where are my daughters?" She flung the blanket off and swung her feet toward the floor. His hand to her upper arm stopped her from standing.

"Stay right where you are."

"If you hurt them, I'll see to it that you suffer the rest of your wretched life."

His lips slanted sideways into an out-of-place grin. "You're tough for a mother living by herself." He told her he would release his tight clutch of her arm if she cooperated. "That's better." He sat down again and leaned into the chair's tall back. "Your two little ones are sound asleep. I wiped your face clean after your nearly non-stop spewing last night. Then I gave you the aspirin I found in your medicine cabinet, and tucked you into bed. I played father and read the girls story after story until they fell asleep. I'll tell you what—go back to sleep. In a few hours, I'll cook breakfast for you and your daughters. I saw eggs in the refrigerator."

Such gumption. "Why don't you get a bit of rest? You must be exhausted."

He snorted. "Nice try, Julia. One I'm not falling for."

"You can't stay here forever." She grunted. "Let alone remain awake forever."

He reached behind him, slid out a gun, and pointed it at her. Her heart pounded. She couldn't breathe. He'd had a gun all along and hadn't shown its terrifying presence until just now?

"I'll stay as long as necessary."

"What about my job? I have to go to work in the morning. Have to take the girls next door to be watched. Have to—"

"Mila—Marianne told me your sister-in-law's name—knows you're still not well and expects you to remain home."

"How does she know this?"

"Nosy Mila dropped by again last night before bedtime. Annelise greeted her aunt at the door. I was beside her, behind the door." He paused as Julia narrowed her eyes. "Don't look at me like that. I wouldn't hold a knife to a child."

"How nice. A criminal with standards."

"Don't call me a criminal. Not when the true criminals are the damn Nazis trying to take control of the world." He stared hard at her. Testing her to see if she'd respond? She remained silent. "And as for your job, Julia, let them fire you for all I care. We're staying right here. And we'll play house until it's time for me to go on."

17

"Tell me, Julia," Henk had said on the second night of his uninvited visit. The girls had gone to bed; it was just the two of them seated across from each other at the kitchen table. "What's your husband like?"

"What concern is it of yours?" she asked.

"You're quite defensive of Germany, and so far, I haven't heard you say one bad thing about the Nazis and the state the Netherlands is in. Unless, of course, it's all an act—"

"Don't dare accuse me of a dreadful ruse, especially when you know squat about me." She couldn't take the chance of this awful intruder second-guessing her. "There's no reason for you to consider what I've said as anything but the truth."

He cast her a sly grin. "I'm curious about the influence your husband has on your beliefs."

She leaned over the table. "I love him. He signed an oath to the Nazi Party, and if it's good enough for him then it's fine for me."

"You're not concerned about what's happening to non-Aryans?"

"To Jews?"

Henk lifted a brow. "Hitler's also against others outside the Jewish population."

"Regardless, I'm thankful my husband, our daughters, and I are of Aryan blood and need not worry. I have enough on my mind these days that is of more concern."

He leaned his palms flat against the table's edge. "How can you be so heartless and close your eyes to what's happening to innocent people around you?"

If he only knew what truly was on her heart and mind. Married to Luuk—being the man he was—she had acted the way she'd done so for a reason. Actually, longer if she considered her life before the current war upheaval. A woman had to do all that was necessary to survive, if not for herself, for those she loved. Wary of this stranger's uninvited presence, she stared into his eyes. "Why are you concerned about what I think? It's the other way around—I should be concerned about you and the way you think." She studied his dark complexion and broad features. "You say you're a Dutch nationalist, but perhaps you're really a Jew on the run. Or are you Romani? My husband has warned me about these wild gypsies. Hitler doesn't like them either." She chuckled, enjoying giving back to this intruder a bit of the adversity that he'd shed on her family. She touched her temples. "The way you've acted, you might have a touch of mental illness. Our friend, Hitler, also doesn't like the troubled or the weak."

"You're being spiteful, let alone prejudicial."

She chuckled. "Can you blame me?"

"Tell me about this man of yours. Is he good-looking? If I were a woman, what about him would I notice first? Do you think he's coming home again?"

Was he trying to find out more about her or her husband? He could be a homosexual, an asocial according to Hitler, who had banned homosexuality back in 1935. Not about to answer Henk's question, she was about to shake her head, but he stopped her by gripping her hands. She tried to pull away but he held tight. His large hands were dry and warm and reminded her how a long time ago Luuk had made her feel like a woman. She cursed herself for noticing.

"It's a discussion we're having, that's all," Henk said. "It will be a long day if we can't converse with each other, don't you think?"

"I'll answer your question if you answer mine first."

He gave a curt nod. She asked him why he was on the run.

"I've told you. I don't want to go to a German factory and get blown up into countless pieces. Do you not understand the need to survive?"

She thought about Luuk, about what she was trying to avoid telling this stranger. "Oh, believe me, I do understand the need to survive. But you're leaving out a part or two. Don't tell me otherwise."

He lifted his hands in surrender. Unfortunately, a mock gesture. "Ah, you've figured me out, I see." He paused for countless seconds. "As I've said, I'm on the run. From the Germans. From my family. From my pregnant girlfriend. And her father who is after my life unless I marry her and give him 10 more grandchildren despite having no income to feed them."

"Your best bet is to actually disappear in Germany."

He laughed. "Tell me about your husband."

Aware she'd not escape his query, she mused how and what she could reveal about Luuk. She peered into Henk's blue eyes. "Unlike your eyes, my husband's eyes are of two different colors. One brown, the other green. That was what attracted me to him, the complexity. I'm happy to say that the physical aspect is the only variation one will find in him. He's a good and kind husband and father, always speaks in a soft and comforting voice, hardworking, generous and most ambitious."

"Interesting you list ambitious last."

She smiled. "Yes, he's confident and wants to provide well for his family. It's not a personal drive to be the best. He just wants the best for those he loves." She stood, ignoring the faint wave of dizziness. "Pardon me, but I need to check on my two sleepyheads."

He stood. "I'll be right behind you."

"Sadly, I'm counting on it."

Their forced camaraderie to each other as the days ticked by unexpectedly helped to ease the tension. By nature, children were resilient and usually adapted to change better than most adults she knew. Her daughters were no exception. They played quietly, happy to be home with her, despite Henk's presence. With her constant smile and reassurance that all would be fine, they didn't appear to worry like she did, though who knew what they thought about. Without showing up to work at the bakery, her position would have been terminated by now.

The sixth day of Julia and her daughters' captivity was no different for them, though Julia noticed that Henk was becoming more twitchy and shorter in patience. Julia liked to think of herself as sympathetic, and though she was curious about what fueled the man to take her and her family hostage, anger, disgust and resentment brewed even more rampantly. After tucking the girls into bed, she startled upon seeing Henk leaning on the doorjamb. She rubbed at her pounding heart. "Were you watching us all this time?"

Henk grinned, a look that under different circumstances, Julia could imagine many young women as seeing him as charming. "It's refreshing to see sincere maternal love."

Uncomfortable with the close space they shared, she dodged around him then faced him again. "That's an odd way of phrasing what should be natural between a mother and child."

He puckered his lips and kept silent for a few seconds. "Not in my world."

"Is that part of why you're on the run, hiding? Are you looking to improve your lot in life?"

He titled his head from shoulder to shoulder and she heard a distinct crack. "We've been together for six long days, Julia—the last thing I expected from you is this pretense of concern over me. Let's call it a night, shall we?"

Without a word more, she started toward her bedroom. Hearing the floorboards creak behind her, she turned to see him following. "Are you planning to spend the night outside my bedroom door again—because you won't like what I'll do to you if you think you're coming inside with me—and keep guard over me?"

He paled. "Exactly. It's a shame, but no shock, that after all our lovely time together you still don't trust me."

Julia replied not in words but by a push to the door, entering her room, and locking the door behind her, though she knew she wouldn't sleep a wink that night.

At midnight, after reading a paragraph in a book for the third time in an attempt at comprehension, Julia sprang out of bed when she heard a crash that sounded like it came from downstairs, followed by intense pounding at her bedroom door.

"Let me in, Julia—they're here for me," Henk pleaded. "Let me in or I'll... Keep away from me...I did nothing wrong."

Julia heard her brother-in-law Liam asking about her and her daughters. She didn't hear Henk's reply. Another man's command for Julia to stay put inside of her room sailed through the closed door.

"You can't arrest me!" Henk shouted.

Another man informed him that the three of them were police officers and that he was under arrest for being a deserter of serving the Nazi Party. Sounds of a struggle then reached Julia's ears. A slam against the bedroom door shoved open the door and Julia shrieked when she saw Henk fall inside the room, apparently unconscious. Eye contact with Liam alerted her to remain right where she was until Henk was removed. Seconds later, after the three officers had rousted Henk, they got him to his feet and dragged him out of the house. Liam immediately was beside her.

"They've arrested him, Julia. You won't be seeing him ever again. Are you okay? The girls?"

As if on cue, Annelise and Marianne ran into the room. Anni cried out first. "Mama, is he really gone? Are we okay now?"

Julia pulled her daughters into a hug. "We're fine. You don't have to be afraid again, understand?" Her daughters, in a wartime occupied country, had many reasons to be afraid, but right then, they were alive and well. And Julia had all the hope possible that they would see a tomorrow, possibly a much better one than the past six days.

Julia peered over her daughters' shoulders at Liam. He smiled —something she couldn't recall seeing from him in a long time.

Awakening early on a dark November morning, alone in her bedroom, Julia turned from one side to another, trying to dodge the new morning ritual of longing and praying for Luuk's safe return home, a desire that had become amplified after Henk's forced entry into her house. She wanted her husband home, safe and sound. She thought she might be a bit braver and stop imagining what it would be like for her and the girls to endure another soldier's desertion and subsequent break-in if she would just receive a letter from her absent husband. Not one word came from Luuk. She hadn't a clue where he was stationed or whether he was in combat with the Russians or fighting the Brits or the Canadians. Perhaps he was digging burial ditches in Libya while others fought to control access to oil from the Middle East and material goods from Asia. Luuk had made good on his promise—of course—and sent his soldier's remittance to her. However, his brother received it first. Julia trusted that the cash Liam gave her on behalf of Luuk was the full payment. Vexing, though, was Liam's refusal to reveal Luuk's location. More skewed emotions from this anxiety often sent her to bed hours earlier than she would have retired otherwise and always brought Julia to face the truth: more than wanting Luuk by her side, she didn't want to be alone. Oh, she had her daughters, but she needed an adult who would understand her situation and champion her strength, worth, and most of all, to reassure her that she wasn't crazy.

The doorbell blared. She hurried from her bedroom in the hope the annoying buzzer wouldn't awaken the girls. She stopped halfway to the front door. What was she thinking? Without a side window to glance out of to check on the caller or a peep hole, she had no idea who stood on the other side. If she opened the door a crack, the person could push his way indoors. Of course, she could ask about the person's identity, but then she'd give away that there was no man beside her, one who would ordinarily respond in this kind of situation. *Curse Henk.* She had fewer fears and concerns before his forced visit.

Frantic pounding snapped her from her thoughts. "Police. Open up."

A razzia! Although she understood that houses were raided with the intent of rounding up Jews to ship out to camps, this was the last thing Julia needed right now. She fastened her snug-fitting bathrobe and stepped to the small chestnut stand beside the door. She withdrew the identity papers she'd become accustomed to show these days, though a personal response to a demand of this nature was a first.

"Open up immediately," a shout came.

Fears aside, she had no choice but to unlock the door and permit the officer inside.

"*Gibt es hier Juden*?" a uniformed man shouted at her, though she stood right in front of him.

"No. There are no Jews here. Never will be, either."

He pointed his gun at her. "Are you Jewish?"

She'd just told him there were no Jews in her household. What did he want from her? Panic washed over her. Sweat at the base of her spine dampened her robe. She thrust the papers at him. "I'm not Jewish. Nor my children, who are in their bedrooms, asleep."

The officer called to another man and ordered him to search each room while he reviewed the identity cards documenting that she and her daughters were registered Dutch citizens and not Jewish. He lowered the gun, gave her back the papers, and then called to the other man. Without a word of explanation or apology —not that she was expecting either—they left the house and headed next door toward Liam and Mila's.

"Mama," Marianne called as she ran toward her, "did he hurt you or the baby?"

With one hand, Julia stroked her belly, and with the other, she pulled her youngest to her side for an embrace. "We're both fine."

"The policeman asked if we were Jewish," Annelise said as she entered the hallway.

"What did you tell him, Ani?"

"I said no. Marianne said no too."

"You did the right thing. Go to your room and get dressed. I want to peek out the window."

"But, Mama," Marianne said, "you can't. They don't want you looking."

Julia and all her neighbors had received instructions not to look out their windows if there was a raid, but she needed to see for herself if the authorities had left the street. "Do as I say, girls. No delays."

Fortunately, when Julia heard the piercing shrill of a whistle seconds later, Annelise and Marianne had left the parlor for their bedroom. She stepped to the window.

"You are forbidden to look out your windows," a clipped voice blared outside. Julia wedged a finger between the curtain and the window casing, just enough to look out despite the order not to. Passing by was a truck with a large swastika banner fastened to its side; loud speakers hung on each corner of the vehicle. "You are forbidden to stand by a window. Move further inside." *The less witnessed, the better.*

About to pull away, Julia saw them. Men, women, and children. Pale faces, downturned mouths and brows. Toddlers clinging to mothers. Men with arms around the hunched elderly. A swarm of yellow badges with stars pinned on coats, shirts and blouses, depending on if one was fortunate enough to have grabbed an outer garment to combat the cold. *Fortunate*? These people—these Jews—were being herded toward the tram stop. Would they board a train next? Where to? As if she was outdoors herself and November's damp bone-chilly air had her in its grip, Julia began to tremble.

A crack of a gunshot. Glass shattered.

Julia leaned closer to the window. A soldier stood outside her house; his rifle aimed at the neighbor's house across the street. Meneer Bakkum's second-story window was no more. Julia suspected neither was Meneer Bakkum. She smacked a hand over her mouth against the waves of nausea chopping at her stomach. Aware she wouldn't make it to the bathroom, she retched into a garbage pail beside a nearby table. The putrid smell caused one dry heave after another. She squeezed her eyes shut. Unable to block the truth from parading before her like the rounded up people she'd just witnessed, she knew this time it wasn't her pregnancy to blame. Rather, it was the utter despair across the faces of the multitudes clip-clopping before her window. Memories of her grandmother's loving smile flashing before her didn't help to soothe her either. In another time and place, she could have been marching, too, toward an unknown fate. One without the promise of hope for tomorrow.

When a cold numbness blanketed her mind and quieted the churning acid in her belly, she stood and leaned against the table. Her husband was missing. For reasons she couldn't imagine, he'd failed to make direct contact with her. She had two daughters. Another child would be born in six months. Although she could rely on Liam and Mila, she was essentially alone in a war-torn country falling apart before her own eyes. She couldn't do this, couldn't live as the only adult in this house, not with the terror of tomorrow's unknown arriving soon.

18

Anniversaries were meant to be special and to commemorate a meaningful time that had become embedded in one's memory. This was not the case for 10 May 1942. Too much had already happened since the German invasion of the Netherlands two years ago in 1940. Back then, Charlotte had been opposed to the separation of her family, which she feared would ultimately break up and destroy them permanently. Now? With an intensified passion, she hated that mothers across this adopted country of hers were faced with this wretched decision of saying goodbye to their precious ones. Worse, the last time she'd seen Helmut, she'd vowed to go into hiding with their daughters, but hadn't. When she thought about it too long, sweat broke out on the back of her neck and her heart raced.

She wedged a finger between the parlor curtain and shade for a peek outside. These days, she seldom dared to fling back the curtains or lift the shade to allow sunshine and some hints of the world into their little haven of an apartment—a place she prayed daily would continue to remain a sanctuary, though she feared that an abrupt change would soon find them. When a hand rested upon her shoulder, she turned and smiled at Edith. In November, she'd turn 16—a teenager on the verge of adulthood. Her daughter nearly matched her in height. Unlike many others, at least they had food and her daughters had a chance at staying healthy. "Yes, love?"

"Krista wants to go for a walk and I offered to go with her. May we? Just around the block?"

"It's not a good idea. Stay put where I can see you."

Edith stepped back and slipped her hands into her skirt pockets. "Why? It's not like we have to wear the stars on our clothing like the Jews have to. Who is going to bother us?"

Charlotte opened her mouth to speak but then snapped it shut; her jaw pinched from the reality she faced on two fronts. The first, nationwide, was her daughter's reference to the painted black six-pointed star against the yellow cloth background and inscribed with the word *Jude*. Ordered in late April by the general commissioner for security and the higher commander of the SS Police, they were to be worn by all Jews. These yellow badges—*Judenstern*—were made in Poland in the Łódź ghetto, likely by Jews suffering by the Nazi hand, and distributed by the Jewish Council. The second, since she and the girls were hiding in plain sight under the guise of non-Jews, the Nazis and the Dutch working on behalf of the Germans, weren't distinctly observing them. Yet, though he'd used his true name—Kurt Weber—her husband was on the run because he hadn't denied his Judaism upon arrest and was wanted by the Dutch police working on behalf of the Nazis. She'd promised him to go into hiding with her daughters. But she hadn't. She couldn't. To do so, would not only mean to risk permanently losing their current identities, but they also risked becoming separated from each other. Would they ever find their way back to each other? Charlotte would fall apart if she didn't have her girls to watch over daily, to nurture their growth, to see to their happiness, to encourage them to believe in a future.

She looked into Edith's sky-blue eyes, the same as her sister's. Her oldest was already smitten with boys and daydreaming of becoming a teacher, marrying her Prince Charming and having lots of children. Her youngest flirted more and more with independence as each day marched on. That was unless life would drastically change for them as it had done for most Jews in the Netherlands. Her daughters needed her more than ever. And she'd be a fool to deny that she needed them as well.

"Mutter," Edith said, stamping her foot, though Charlotte recognized it as an act of playfulness. "You're lost in your daydreams. What am I going to do with you?"

"Leave Mama alone," Krista called from the sofa. "She's probably thinking about poor Papa."

Charlotte felt the color drain from her face.

"Look what you've done, Krista." Edith's brows slanted inward. "You've gone and upset Mutter, you little fink."

"Enough," Charlotte said, not quite a snap, but certainly not a pleasantry. This buildup of tension between the three of them, resulting from staying indoors too long, would not benefit anyone. "Let's all go for a walk, together." Upon seeing a smile spread on both girls' lips, she made one stipulation clear. "I don't care if you see a friend or a cute stray kitten. Keep by my side. Agreed?"

Krista nodded. Edith bounced on her toes and then gave her a hug as if she'd just offered to host a party for her daughter and she could invite all the boys she wanted. Their merriment vanished as they walked down the stairs. Charlotte couldn't help but hear the conversation between her daughters.

"Have you told Mama about what's upsetting you?"

"No, she wouldn't understand. She doesn't have to worry about being fired from her job like Marta's mother."

"Because Mama no longer is Jewish?"

"That's right."

"And your friend Lilah?"

"It's so sad, Krista. Her father isn't allowed to be a doctor anymore because he's Jewish. "The Jews have no rights to do as they please like the other Dutch citizens—like us."

Before the front door to the building, Charlotte gripped the door handle so hard that it bit into the palm of her hand. In not wanting to upset the girls, she swallowed back a groan. Why did children think their loud-whispering would not reach parental ears? She spun around, prepared to rail against their wayward thinking. She'd tick off their faulty statements one by one on her fingers to show them a thing or two: they shouldn't hide things from her, especially scary fears and doubts that she'd understand; she could indeed be fired from her job no matter what her religious beliefs were, even if she denied she was Jewish; that just because she'd escaped having to register as a Jew to the government and having to wear the Star of David in public didn't mean that she had no sympathy or empathy to Jews or the downright fear of being discovered and handed over to the authorities for being Jewish but proclaiming a false identity. She couldn't say any of these things, couldn't behave so miserably and morally contradictory, let alone maternally mean. Instead, not daring to provoke a squabble among them, she opened the door and stepped outside. She breathed in a soothing breath of fresh air and waited until her daughters walked out. Then, like any other mother looking forward to a lovely afternoon outing, stepped between the girls and hooked elbows with them. "Do you have suggestions for where you'd like to walk?"

"Can we visit Rembrandtplein?" Edith said. "I love the shops there. Well, when they used to be open." Charlotte countered that it would be too far of a walk, considering all that was happening. "Then let's go to Noordermarkt. There's bound to be one or two merchants open for business."

"Oh?" Charlotte was surprised by the lack of hesitation. Edith had always preferred to soak up the sun, and it had come as no surprise that she'd first suggested Rembrandtplein despite the lengthy walk, but to quickly jump to another location, one least favored, was a wonder. "Sweetheart, you might find Noordermarkt a disappointment. The once-fun place to shop isn't the same since the Germans have—"

Edith groaned. "I'm so tired of hearing about the big, bad Germans."

"Edith, love, must I remind you of our origins?"

Her daughter rolled her eyes. "Of once upon a time being

Jewish and German? Our past that you and Papa say we..." Her voice had cracked when mentioning her father; tears streamed down her cheeks. Thankfully, no one was around to see this outburst and disrupt their privacy. "Of our past that you both insist must be forgotten?"

"Your father and I never said to forget," Charlotte said softly, "but we must hide certain facts if we are to remain together and sadly, our faith is one to conceal." She withdrew a handkerchief from her purse and blotted Edith's face. "We're not acting from shame but from a need to survive. If we can just make it through this war, we stand a chance of making a good future for all of us."

Edith pushed away Charlotte's hand. "Should we become Jewish again and see what God wants for us?"

Charlotte didn't care if her daughter didn't like her mothering touch, but she again wiped the girl's cheek with the handkerchief, relieved Edith didn't pull away. "It's not God's desire for Jews—or believers of other faiths—that worries me. Instead, it's what mankind desires, and to what extreme they'll go to get everything they want."

"I just want to be me." Edith stared into Charlotte's eyes. "Whoever I am these days."

Life was going to change. It had to. Whether by force or choice was unknown. Without a word more, Charlotte grasped her daughters' hands, and they proceeded toward Noordermarkt, the same square where the first public meetings were held to organize last year's strike to protest the deportation of Jews by the Nazis.

Krista brought up the noticeable change that Charlotte had fought all week to deny to herself: fewer people were riding bicycles. "Is it true, Mama? That Jews are no longer permitted to own or use bikes?"

Charlotte reached for her daughter's hand. "Yes, dear." They were also forbidden to ride on public transportation, own land or property, and they had to observe a curfew past eight in the evening until six in the morning. Though her daughters were aware of this discrimination, Charlotte couldn't begin to explain these regulatory mandates over a select group of people who once had rights like the others in this country, because in her mind it was all gibberish. It made not one iota of sense. These were the mandates she and the girls would have had to obey if they'd confessed the truth about their faith. "Let's turn around and return home. We've done enough walking for one day."

"Enough?" Edith's forehead furrowed. "How can I meet..."

Charlotte stopped walking. "Meet whom, Edith? This isn't the time or place to mingle with friends."

"She hoped to meet Guus," Krista said.

Edith narrowed her eyes at her sister. "Be quiet."

"Girls," Charlotte said between clenched teeth, "behave."

Having decided to continue, she and the girls stepped up their pace and arrived at the market five minutes later. At first, Charlotte wondered if she mistakenly guided them to another market, one she hadn't known about. Sadly, this was the correct place. The once-lively market that she and Kurt had visited when they first arrived in Amsterdam during the summer of 1939, teeming with piles of goods strewn across table surfaces, did not remotely resemble what was before her eyes right now. One sole tent. A handful of tables. Scraps and second-hand items for sale. This hub of commerce now resembled the rest of the once-bustling and thriving city that had become unrecognizable like an old, hunched-over woman who remembered her younger, better days and mourned that she couldn't enjoy that existence a day longer.

"I'm going to have a look around." Edith started to walk away, but Charlotte grasped her shoulder and tugged her closer. Edith pointed to a nearby table of textile goods. "All I want to do is look at the pretty material. Can't I at least dream about sewing blouses for myself one day in the future? Or is that a new crime too? Oh, wait. We aren't Jewish. So that's not a concern." She squirmed free of Charlotte's hold and ducked under the tent.

Charlotte began to follow Edith but Krista reached out for her hand. "Mama, Edith wants to have fun, that's all."

"Your sister was quite..." Rude. Immature. Self-centered. She could be attracting unnecessary attention to all of them.

"Silly?" Krista suggested.

Charlotte glanced at the table where Edith stood. Her daughter was holding up a pink flowery material while eyeing two teen boys walking on the other side of the street. Her daughter was normal. Alive and healthy. Doing what girls her age had done since the beginning of time. What wasn't normal was this new standard imposed on a select group of people, or her own extreme diligence to remain on guard over herself and her daughters against a slip of the tongue or an action that would get them slapped with a condemning star they'd be ordered to fasten to their clothing.

"No one is watching us," Krista added. "No one cares about us."

"You're right," Charlotte said. Her words likely didn't reach her youngest's ears since Krista had strayed away to a neighboring table laden with books and toys.

"They're lovely girls."

Charlotte turned to see a woman with attractive dark features, brown-blackish hair cut in a fashionable bob, and one of the nicest smiles she'd ever seen.

"My name is Johanna Süskind."

"I'm Charlotte Beck. Nice to meet you. I detect a German accent. I speak German if you'd like to continue that way."

"*Das ist gut*," Johanna replied and smiled once again. She jutted her chin in suggestion to chat in the corner of the tent.

"I'm just browsing." Charlotte chuckled. "I would rather enjoy the company and conversation of an adult." They moved to the privacy of the corner.

"These days, I browse more than I shop as well, especially with a little one at home."

"Ah," Charlotte said. "Pardon my forwardness, but I thought you were beaming like a proud mother."

Johanna went on to tell Charlotte how Yvonne was three years old and how she, her husband, her mother, and mother-in-law moved from Germany to Holland in 1938. She leaned closer to

Charlotte. A bit too close for a stranger, yet Charlotte sensed the woman trusted her. "We were enjoying Amsterdam until recent changes."

Charlotte glanced about—would either of them ever again enjoy a lifestyle that didn't require constant awareness and observation of who stood nearby, watching and listening? "Yes, I know exactly what you mean."

"Do you?" Johanna studied Charlotte's clothing. She then shifted her shawl. A large yellow star appeared. How Charlotte hadn't detected this earlier was beyond her. "I don't see a star sewn onto your clothing. Good for you and your daughters, that you don't need to worry."

Charlotte's face heated in shame.

"I don't mean to distress you, Charlotte. I should leave."

"No, please stay. It's not you. There's plenty I'm upset about these days."

Johanna nodded. "I see a ring on your finger. Are you married?"

Charlotte turned numb. "He's missing."

Johanna grew quiet as she peeked at Edith and Krista. "I see," she said after a few long seconds. "Lately, quite a few husbands have disappeared and for various reasons. Do you work?"

"I take care of children in a crèche in Plantage."

"Ah, no wonder you're so patient with your daughters."

"They would say otherwise." Charlotte grinned. "Being a mother of two teenage girls is a daily challenge."

"Of course." Johanna rifled through her purse and withdrew a small piece of paper and a pencil. Using the purse as a firm surface, she jotted a note and handed the scrap to Charlotte. "This is my address. If circumstances permit, would you like to meet my husband Walter and my little girl?" She glanced about. "I promised my mother—who is watching Yvonne—not to stay out late. Of course, with the curfew in place, I must return home, anyway."

"Yes, meeting your family would be nice, Johanna." Charlotte watched the woman walk in the opposite direction from which she and her daughters came. After a few minutes passed, she crossed to where Edith was weaving her hand through a small pile of flimsy cotton material. "Let's go." She guided Edith toward where Krista stood flipping the pages of a book and announced it was time to return home.

"Must we?" Krista said, her voice whiny and testing Charlotte's patience that, minutes ago, Johanna Süskind had praised.

"No more questions. Let's go home." *Let's go home while we can.*

19

On a lovely late May day, the last day of school for the season, Krista appeared healthy in Charlotte's eyes, not ill as she'd stated. Like the majority of the Dutch, herself and Edith included, her youngest daughter had lost weight due to the shrinking availability of food, especially the nutritious provisions like beef, milk and vegetables. If the war would continue much longer and the unavailability of food worsen, would they all die from starvation? Yet, her youngest's complexion was good. She didn't appear feverish. No complaints of pain. It was unlike Krista to miss out on the excitement of the end of the school term celebration that was planned.

"But I'm telling you the truth." Krista looked pleadingly at Charlotte. "Please don't send me to school. I won't go. I want to stay with you."

It was her daughter's last three words and her tone that squeezed Charlotte's heart like a clamp. They weren't spoken in a shrill-tone but rather, were tinged with the sharp twists of anxiety and the bite of fear. Charlotte silently cursed the German occupation. Krista was 13 years old. She was of the age and mindset that, at times, wanted to stray away from Charlotte's side, but still of an age when she needed a mother's care. Yet, no child, of any age, should have to worry about what was to become of her and her loved ones. They were in the kitchen and Charlotte glanced at Edith sitting at the table. Her eldest had a mouthful of dry toast—they hadn't enjoyed butter or jam for months—while she pushed the remaining food on her dish from one side to the other with her fork.

"And you, sweetheart? Are you well enough to attend this special last day of school?"

"Yes, Mutter," Edith said.

Charlotte was relieved to hear this, of course. Yet she now had another dilemma—what to do with her daughter while she had to work. "Good. Gather up your schoolbooks and help me get your sister dressed."

Krista pulled away from Charlotte's embrace and leaned against the oven, crossing her arms. "Don't make me go. I want to stay home."

Out of options, Charlotte slipped her fingers through the child's once glossy hair. The lack of nutrients was already paying an awful toll on everyone in this country under siege. "You must choose," she said softly. "Either attend school or sit quietly in the crèche while I work. You can't stay here alone."

Krista averted her gaze. "I'll go with you."

"All right. Be ready in five minutes. We have a good 40-minute walk ahead of us."

Considering Krista's claim that she was feeling unwell a scant few minutes ago when she dreaded going to school, the first change that grabbed Charlotte's attention was her daughter's lively step. The second difference was that fewer people were walking in the streets. And most of them were women, since Dutch men had been either conscripted to fight on behalf of the Germans or face the consequences of not fighting by joining the ranks of the slave-labor forces sent to Germany or to western Holland to build the Atlantic

Wall against the enemy. Charlotte grasped her daughter's hand. "Have I ever told you what Oma did one day when a group of boys followed behind me as I walked home from school?"

"No. Were the boys nasty? Did they throw rocks?"

"They didn't hurl rocks, probably because rocks are visible and they could easily be caught and gotten into lots of trouble with their parents. What they did throw at me was just as painful though —names. They called me mean names. Names attacking me for being a girl, for being Jewish, for having the parents I had, and for living in the particular house and neighborhood my family loved."

"That's silly. You were born a baby girl. You didn't choose your parents or house or religion."

"That's right. Keep in mind though, I loved all three of those things about my life."

"What did you do? Did you fight with those boys? Yell at them? Run from them?"

"Neither of those. There were four boys and only one of me. I couldn't win a fight with them. Yelling wouldn't help—if I did yell, it probably would have encouraged them to call me more names, and they would have made fun of me in worse ways. As for running, I was never a fast runner and knew they'd easily catch up with me. The last thing I wanted was for them to hit me. So, step by step, I proceeded home. Fortunately, my mother—your grandmother—was outdoors in the vegetable garden and saw me approaching. She ran toward me, her arms pumping the air up and down and making her move mighty fast. When she caught up with me, she snatched me away from the boys and shook her fist at them. Under no certain terms, she told them, were they ever to bother me again, or she'd report each of them not only to their parents but to the local priest."

"She wasn't afraid of the boys or their parents?"

"Krista, fear had nothing to do with it. Believe me, my mother would have looked anyone in the face and told them to leave me alone. She loved me, and I loved her. Her only concern was me."

"But Oma was Jewish. Why would she go to the priest?"

"My mother was a smart woman and caring mother. Because of their wrong behavior, those boys feared the consequences and humiliation that their priest would dole out. She would have done nothing differently that afternoon, even if it meant that she had to face punishment to save me from harm."

Krista squirmed free of Charlotte's hand. "I have a friend in school. Elsje."

"Oh? You've never mentioned this friend before."

"She's new. Elsje and her family moved to Jordaan a few months ago. She was upset yesterday. At lunchtime, I asked if she wanted to tell me about what was wrong."

"It was nice of you to offer a listening ear to your friend."

"She couldn't eat her sandwich. I couldn't eat mine. We went to the corner of the lunchroom and talked. She told me she was pretending not to be Jewish."

"Did you mention to Elsje that you were also Jewish?" she murmured to Krista and held her breath for the reply.

"No, Mama. You said to never tell the truth about my religion."

"Good girl." They approached the corner of Plantage Middenlaan, where they would turn left and would reach the crèche across from the Hollandsche Schouwburg, the once glorious theater that the Germans had gutted when occupying Amsterdam. Charlotte had to hurry Krista's story. "What more did she say?"

"That... that her brother..." Krista's eyes brimmed with tears.

Charlotte cupped her daughter's cheek. "Tell me," she said gently.

"Her older brother was sent a notice. To report to the train station today. He was supposed to be sent to Westerbork."

Krista's usage of past and present tense had Charlotte's mind swirling. "And?"

"They all went away today. I'll never see my friend again."

"What do you mean by went away? Where did they go?"

"Into hiding. Elsje's parents are afraid someone will tell the authorities that they're Jews with false papers. She said they loved her and her brothers and that's why they are all going into hiding. But Mama..."

Charlotte squeezed Krista's shoulder. "Yes, love? You can tell me."

"Elsje's sad because that means her parents, two brothers, and she will have to hide in five separate places. They may never see each other again."

Charlotte wiped her daughter's tears with her fingertips. "Tell me. Is that why you didn't want to go to school today? Because you won't see your friend?"

"Yes, because she won't be there, ever again." Krista looked away. "And no, because you don't love me and Edith enough."

"I don't understand."

"Why won't you put us into hiding, like what Papa wants for us? Why do we pretend to be people we aren't? Don't you love us, Mama? Like Elsje's mother loves her? Maybe if Edith and I are in hiding for the summer, by the time September comes, the Nazis might leave, and everything will be okay again. Then we could come out of hiding."

Enough talk. Charlotte leaned closer to her daughter's ear. "Let's go into my workplace. You are not to speak one word about this to anyone. We'll talk later, at home. Yes?"

Krista nodded and they entered the crèche. Charlotte counted on its demands to keep her occupied for the next eight hours or so. She hoped that the heavy work load would give her enough time to think about whether or not to alter all of their lives, conceivably on a permanent basis.

20

After hours of reading stories to the nursery children, playing with them, and changing countless stinking diapers of crying babies who were weary, hungry, and in need of attention, all Charlotte could think about that early December day was food. While she was delivering an assigned child to her home, she indulged in a daydream about a dinner she would cook if food was of no concern, but that was far from the reality in the Netherlands. Yet, while the basic foods like milk, flour, meat, grain, cheese, and precious sugar declined by the day, talk amongst Dutch citizens about going into hiding divided many. A few refused to hide, no matter the consequences. Yet, there were families, single young adults, students, and the elderly who disappeared mysteriously into the inky darkness of night. To complicate matters more, while one segment of the population refused to help conceal Jews or others in need of escaping the Nazi eye, others mumbled within the listening range of family and a few trusted friends that they'd hide a person for a price or open their doors free of charge.

The fact that she couldn't even think about food without linking it to the increasing horrors occurring daily, Charlotte knew it was time for *onderduiken*, for her and her daughters to go into hiding. She'd arrange for Edith and Krista's safety and then would look into her own escape route. But how? Back in late November, she'd started to hear whispers about a Dutch reverend who went by the name of Frits de Zwerver, a man known for leading resistance groups against the Nazis. His specialty was hiding people. That month he was conducting a meeting in Driebergen-Rijsenburg, a town in the province of Utrecht, but at the time, Charlotte couldn't arrange to attend the meeting. Actually, she didn't dare, the ironic misfortune of a woman living without a man, responsible for two daughters, and most of all, a Jew pretending to be an Aryan.

Frustration, like an uncontrollable thermostat, heated within Charlotte. This was wartime, not just nationally but from what she heard, globally, since the moment the United States entered the war last December. What she faced—the threat of imprisonment and death of her family versus the destruction of the very fibers of her family—was unthinkable. And what did she have to do at this very moment? Carry on her job as if all was fine—that was also bizarre. But she had no other choice. While standing in the girls' lavatory waiting for a four-year-old child to finish up, someone tapped her shoulder. She thought she and the girl had been the only ones in the room. Dread, her default emotion as of late, tightened her muscles.

"It's me, Charlotte," Johanna Süskind said in German, "I'm glad to see you once again."

Charlotte faced the woman and replied in German, a language she knew the child would not understand. "Nice to see you as well, Johanna. I hope you and your family are well, as well as can be. I'm sorry I haven't taken advantage of your lovely offer to visit you at home."

"Don't think twice about it. I've been busy too. Normally I stay away from across the street. But I had to deliver a message for my husband to your supervisor because Walter's regular worker wasn't available." Johanna smiled at both Charlotte and the child. "I saw you duck into the lavatory and thought I'd catch up with you."

The little girl slid off the toilet. Charlotte guided her to the sink, thankful that Johanna followed them. She ran the water and helped the girl soap her hands. "From across the street? Do you mean the old theater?" As soon as the overly inquisitive questions were out of her mouth, Charlotte's cheeks flamed. "Sorry. I didn't mean to pry."

"Yes, the Hollandsche Schouwburg. Walter was assigned there by the Dutch Jewish council."

Walter! Despite speaking in German, Charlotte glanced at the child and cringed. What had come of this world that she had to worry about what she said in front of an innocent four-year-old child? "The... council..." Of course she knew about the Jewish Council. It was what the council might know about her true identity that was more disconcerting. Complicating matters further for the director of the nursery, Henriëtte Henriquez Pimentel, the Nazis, just as they had mandated many employers to fire their Jewish employees, ordered her to dismiss all non-Jewish colleagues. Fortunately, with Charlotte's paperwork in order, she was able to continue to work with Henriëtte, at least for now. With the German occupation, one could never count on what the next day might bring. Another major change was the Nazi order that the nursery must house the children separate from their parents confined to the former theater where they awaited deportation to Westerbork. Rumor spread quickly that the Nazis had a low tolerance for crying children.

Now Charlotte knew exactly who Johanna and Walter Süskind were, and she hated herself for thinking the way she did. This paranoia, this lack of trust in others, this assumption that the other person could and would turn against her had grown terribly destructive. She only wished she hadn't connected Johanna's husband's given name Walter to his surname Süskind—if she had leaned on the side of naiveté, she could have maintained a budding friendship, though, of course, she always would have to be on her guard. Then again, it was a perilous time and not a time to worry about forming new friendships. Yet, she liked Johanna. Her instincts told her this woman could be trusted. Charlotte sighed.

This not knowing who was on which side—the Nazi side or the Nazi's enemy side—was too complex for her. She just wanted to love her fellow human beings—if only each person could behave humanely.

"Ah," Johanna said, "it's no secret that Walter is on good terms with SS officer Ferdinand aus der Fünten."

Charlotte nodded, barely. She wondered whether it was best to separate her association from Johanna that very second after all.

"It's all right. You can trust me, as well as my husband. My instincts say I can trust you as well." Johanna glanced at her watch. "I must report back to Walter before he becomes anxious. Would you and your daughters like to come for dinner this evening?" With her head up, shoulders back, and a smile on her lips, she radiated confidence. "It won't be gourmet, though one of the perks about Walter's job is to get a little more food than others—I hate to confess. He likes to joke that the Nazis are fattening him up for the kill. Between you and me, each time Walter says this, I want to kill him."

An unexpected chuckle snuck from Charlotte's mouth. "Forgive me for this laugh."

"Well, it is a macabre subject. A laugh—as dark as it might be—is better than crying all the time. It saves one's sanity." Charlotte nodded. Johanna patted Charlotte's shoulder. "It's all false what they say about Walter and Aus der Fünten. Although they were schoolmates in Germany, Aus der Fünten is a dedicated Hitler man while my husband is dedicated to saving lives, particularly Jewish lives. You can trust Walter. He will do whatever is necessary to help those in harm's way—even if it means putting up with this old acquaintance of his." Johanna smiled at the little girl who stood by the sink, a Jewish child whose parents awaited deportation across the street in the old theater—a child who was forced to attend this nursery center because the Nazis couldn't tolerate crying children. Johanna turned her attention back to Charlotte. "I suspect you're concerned about your daughters and that these interests are quite worrisome, to say the least. Walter and I may be able to help you. Our place, Nieuwe Prinsengracht 51, is an easy three-minute walk from here, but unfortunately a little longer from your home."

Charlotte's lips tugged into a little smile. "I walk to work all the time."

"So, you'll come for dinner?"

It was as if Johanna sensed her need to put her daughters in hiding. Charlotte was relieved this new friend was reaching out to her with an offer of help. "Yes, I'm looking forward to it."

The house on Nieuwe Prinsengracht was an inviting three-floor brick building with lovely rooms, all with little furnishings though the pieces that adorned each were elegant. After what was referred to as a modest dinner of roasted chicken, potatoes, and sauerkraut with a few slices of carrots—a feast compared to what Charlotte and her daughters had grown accustomed to—Johanna's mother ushered the children into another room so Charlotte could talk privately with Johanna and Walter. Seated at the table, Charlotte's hands grew clammy and she wrung her cloth napkin on her lap. Johanna exchanged looks with Walter sitting opposite to her.

Walter cleared his throat. "I trust you enjoyed your dinner, Charlotte."

"Yes, thank you. It was delicious. I can't recall the last time we enjoyed chicken or for that matter, potatoes and a vegetable in one meal."

"Quite unfortunate. As is everything these days." Walter leaned closer to her. "What I'd like to talk about must not be relayed to the Jewish Council. I need your full trust in me as well as your agreement that not one word that we exchange will be mentioned to the council or to anyone."

"Yes, of course."

"I won't ask why—nor do I want to know—but if you need to go into hiding, I can help you and your lovely daughters. First, tell me how I can fully trust that you will keep this operation and my arrangements secret."

Charlotte summoned a soft but determined tone. "My name is Herta Weber, not Charlotte. My husband is on the run for a crime he did not commit. We are Jewish, from Germany. Stranded on the St. Louis, we arrived in Amsterdam in June 1939, homeless. There. I've told you everything that the Nazis can use against me. That's how desperate I am and how much I trust you."

"Are you willing to hand over your daughters to complete strangers to provide them with a place of safety? Are you willing to do so without the promise that you will ever see them again?"

"I have no other choice."

"How old are your children?" he asked.

"The oldest has just turned 16 and the youngest is 13."

"Do you want to hide?"

Charlotte pushed past the knot constricting her throat and ignored her watering eyes. "I am prepared to do all that is necessary so that my daughters will live a good life, well into their elderly years. If that means they go into hiding, and not me, that is perfectly fine."

"There is a way I can help. Working with your director, Henriëtte, and the director of the teacher training college that shares a courtyard with the crèche, we have a way to help your girls find safe houses."

"Houses? Plural?"

"Depending on Nazi raids, living conditions at these houses, the owner's preferences, and to be frank, money, it's not uncommon for children to have to go from one place to another. The thing is, Charlotte, it would be best and more practical to route Edith and Krista separately. With Krista being the youngest, and most vulnerable, she shall be sent off first to a new aunt and uncle. Then we'll find a place for Edith, though at her age, it might be difficult. But I will find a way to place her." He paused to glance at his wife. Johanna reached over with her napkin and dotted Charlotte's wet eyes and cheeks. "You though..." Walter continued, "we might not be able to find a place for you. Our main focus is on the children."

Charlotte sniffled. "I completely understand. How long until... until they leave?"

"Can you have Krista ready tomorrow morning at nine? She should come with a sack of the bare necessities and any cash you may have to spare."

Tomorrow. She had to say goodbye to her youngest child so soon?

Johanna touched Charlotte's arm. "You know this is for her best?"

"Yes, I do." Her stronger, more resolute voice did not surprise her. It was inevitable that this day would come, sooner or later. There were no other options if she wanted to secure a possibility for her daughters to live through this war.

"Bring her to work tomorrow. I'll talk with Henriëtte—we'll take care of all the arrangements. Behind Henriëtte's stern appearance is a woman with a large, kind heart, especially for children—someone who can be trusted."

Charlotte now realized that the woman she worked for had a lot more responsibility and took far more chances than the older woman she had envisioned going home at night, kicking off her shoes, and climbing into bed. Charlotte sniffled. "Do I wait to hear from you again before leaving for work tomorrow morning?"

"No. Consider the arrangement firm."

She was about to ask how she should answer questions about Krista's disappearance, but she stopped herself with the truth: she need not worry about explanations because no one cared enough to ask about Krista, or subsequently Edith. This was war. People disappeared all the time. Instead, she listened carefully to Walter's directions for tomorrow, possibly the last time she might see her daughter.

"Will we see each other again?"

On the day her daughter was born, Charlotte never would have imagined that this day, this monstrous moment in time when she would have to say goodbye to her precious Krista, would arrive because of hatred and prejudice. She pulled Krista up from the breakfast table and into a hug. Her daughter had asked the same question last night when Charlotte had gathered the girls to talk upon arriving home from the Süskinds' home. They'd sat on the edge of Krista's bed; Charlotte, sitting between the two, had wrapped an arm around them both and revealed what was to happen the next day. Krista said she was ready to leave and that she'd be brave. Now, this repeated question of Krista's must be a call for reassurance. Charlotte couldn't blame her.

She grasped Krista's hand. Not wanting Edith to hear what she was about to say—not yet—she was relieved when Edith had excused herself to the bedroom. "God put us together as a family, and God will find a way to bring us together again. I believe this with all my heart. Will you believe this too, my love?"

"Oh, yes, Mama." Krista placed her hand over her heart. "I will keep you and Papa and Edith right here."

For her daughters' sake, Charlotte willed her tears away. "You're a beautiful and strong girl, Krista. One day you will fall in love with a kind man who will marry you, and you'll have the most adorable babies and make me a proud grandmother."

Krista smiled wide. "I would like that."

Charlotte kissed her sweet child, trying not to wonder about when she'd see her youngest daughter next. She tried not to fret over whether or not the strangers taking in her daughter would be gentle and considerate of her. She tried not to worry about the war not coming to an end or how many years would go by while her daughter lived with strangers and would forget her mama's face.

Charlotte gestured at the table. "I see you've eaten all your eggs and toast."

"Mama, it was only one egg and one slice of toast." Krista

quickly rubbed her belly as if to say she had eaten plenty. "It was good."

"If you like, I can give to you the egg I was going to cook for myself."

"No." Krista twirled one of her curly locks of hair. Charlotte hoped that neither scissors nor blonde hair dye would be required to disguise her little one. Then again, if it would help Krista keep alive and thriving, then so be it. "You eat the egg, Mama, or give it to Edith."

Charlotte bent and kissed her daughter on both cheeks. "You've grown wiser and more kind since yesterday. I am so proud of you, and I love you with all my heart."

"Mama, I'm about to go on a special journey. I promise to wait for everyone I love. Don't worry." Krista offered a serene smile. "I'm going to tell Edith that it's time to go." Without delay, Krista dashed to the bedroom she shared with her sister—the room she'd likely never see again. Charlotte heard her tell Edith that it was time for Edith to leave for school and time for...

And it's time for me to go to the crèche with Mama. But those words weren't spoken. At least, not loud enough to reach Charlotte's ears. What she did hear was her youngest telling her oldest that Edith had to stop crying, to help Mama, and most of all, to be brave. Because, Krista said, if she could be brave, then so could Edith, since it was her turn to leave now and Edith would be next.

Charlotte's heart shattered into smaller pieces than she had ever thought possible. How was she alive? She groped for the back of the nearest chair. Why couldn't Kurt be with her on this day? Had he wondered whether they'd gone into hiding since the time he'd asked a while back, and whether he'd see his family ever again? Was he still alive?

"Mama?" Krista said, and touched her arm. "We must leave now. I want to hide. Please take me."

With Edith heading north toward her school, Charlotte and Krista started south on their walk toward their old Plantage neighborhood where the Vereeniging Zuigelingen-Inrichting en

Kindertehuis—or the crèche, as Charlotte simply thought of it—was located opposite of the Hollandsche Schouwburg. In these two places, she'd never imagined people trying to save Jewish children's lives. For the first time in the longest of times, she had hope again for her daughters. Arriving, she asked Krista, "Do you remember what to do?"

"Yes," Krista said softly. "I am to wait for the tram to stop between the two buildings. Then, I'm to hurry into the teachers' school. And you go to work."

"Correct."

"And you must walk into work right away."

"Correct," Charlotte said, wiping away the single tear barreling down her cheek. More welled in her eyes. "That's exactly what I will do."

"Then go, Mama. Don't cry. You must be brave. For me." Krista turned away, looking for the tram.

A squeal came, announcing the tram's arrival. Charlotte did just what her daughter urged—she walked into the nursery school. Alone. Her little one had asked her not to cry, but that was the one thing she did. Tears ran down her cheeks like a storm-tossed, uncontrollable river. Brave, she was not.

21

Her daughters were gone. Charlotte would always remember when and why she had to say goodbye to Edith and Krista, one by one. How could she forget this cruelty? Forced by Nazi hatred, carried out by her own hand. And the love of her life, Kurt, was away from her side as well, because of this absurdity of perpetuated evil. As she left the apartment on an early February morning, she couldn't imagine what the rest of 1943 would be like. More thoughts of her family wrapped around her heart and accompanied her: Kurt, running from the Dutch authorities and the Nazis for the past year and a half for a crime he didn't commit; Krista, in hiding for two months; and Edith in hiding since the day after Christmas, both because they are children of Jewish parents.

The one thing she never expected to obstruct the peace and quiet she needed to think about her husband and daughters were the daily challenges. With developments and changes taking place under the SS supervision at the crèche, she was no longer employed as a nursery aide, which meant she no longer had contact with her supervisor or the random chance of meeting the Süskinds; it had become too dangerous for arranged meetings. She kept her ears open to learn about possibilities for her own hiding, but with each day thundering by, none came. The news that did reach her ears served to dishearten her further: recently, 1,200 Jews were deported from Apeldoorn to camps now believed to be more than just work camps, and the attack on a German officer in Haarlem triggered more than 100 arrests and 10 executions.

She wanted to think positively—of Krista tucked away in a cozy warm bed in a land of plenty and peace, far from Amsterdam and from the claws of the Nazis. Would she fall asleep at night anticipating a breakfast of fresh strawberries, bread topped with sweet *hagelslag*, currant buns with cheese, and lots of milk to keep her bones strong? Would her strong-willed sister, Edith, less than a handful of years away from becoming a woman, help her hostesses with chores while keeping tabs on a good-looking teenage boy? Had she taken on the responsibility of helping with the younger children in hiding? And Kurt? Had he taken up pipe smoking? Seated on a cushioned window seat beside a fireplace in an apartment in Zurich after a day's work, was he enjoying a good book and a smoke? Or, would he be unable to focus as thoughts about her and their children roamed through his mind? As Charlotte began to walk down the street, she wanted to envision her absent family enjoying their life, not suffering. She took no comfort in knowing that she wasn't the only troubled soul wandering absently.

The streets were frosted, making the cobblestone slippery, and the winter sky was gray and heavy with gloomy clouds. Passersby with burdened minds like herself never smiled or glanced her way. The *hoot ha-ha* of a seagull drew her attention to the bird landing on the nearby canal bridge. The sight of two girls caused Charlotte to pause. She leaned against a lamppost and watched. The youngest child, though easily a good six or seven years Krista's junior, flooded her with a new wave of sorrow. She'd forgotten Krista's birthday in January, forgotten her youngest had turned 14. Even if she'd remembered, with herself here in Amsterdam and her beautiful daughter far away from her, Charlotte would have whispered a *happy birthday* and *I love you* for no one but the air to hear. But she'd forgotten. Too occupied? In sorrow? Worse—had it been too painful to remember? How could she be such a horrible mother?

"Mama, look at me," the imp by the bridge called. She flapped her arms. "I'm a seagull. I want to see the bridge."

"Leave her alone," the older girl said and pointed at the woman, evidently their mother. "She's busy with Ada."

The woman turned toward the girls and spoke to them. A reprimand, judging by the girls' serious faces. The woman appeared to be in her late twenties, possibly early thirties. Her straight blonde hair, trailing halfway down her back, was on the unkempt side, either from poor nutrition or, speculating by the baby in her arms, she was too busy with her three children to fuss over herself. She must have indeed been functioning on little energy, hopefully not with a lack of food as well. Where was her husband? She seemed both familiar and not. Charlotte couldn't quite place her.

The baby, about seven or eight months, broke out in a staccato wail that ripped through the air. The oldest child cupped her ears while the youngest resumed flapping her pseudo bird wings. The child circled her older sister, mother, and the baby. The mother, rocking the wee one, appeared not to have realized that the middle child had jumped onto the low stone wall bordering the canal. A smack of water ripped through the air.

"Mama, look! Marianne! She fell!" shouted the oldest girl.

The woman turned in time to see Marianne bob up once and then sink below the canal's surface. Charlotte dropped her purse, shook off her coat, and ran. She jumped into the water and dove under. Under no condition would she dare leave the canal unless that child was in her arms, preferably alive. A minute or less later, Charlotte surfaced with the unconscious child draped over her shoulder. Having transferred the baby to her older daughter, the child's mother extended a hand to Charlotte and helped her out of the water.

"Is she breathing?" the woman said in Dutch.

With no time to respond, Charlotte lay down the girl on the slushy ground, lifted the child's arms over her head, and began to apply chest compressions with her palms. She ordered the sister to fetch the coat she'd shed on the road so they could keep the soaking-wet girl warm. With the baby in her arms, the older girl obeyed and ran after the coat.

"Breathe, Marianne." The mother dropped to her knees alongside Charlotte. "Live. Live for Mama."

"Marianne," Charlotte repeated the girl's name. She continued in Dutch. "Breathe, Marianne. Breathe for your mama."

Marianne sputtered. Mouthfuls of water discharged from her small mouth. Charlotte helped her to her side, and the child coughed up more water. She then tried to sit up. By that time, the older girl had reached them with the coat, which Charlotte grabbed and covered Marianne with. Careful to not jar Marianne in case of internal injuries, but wanting to get her off the frozen ground, she stood and lifted the girl, still bundled in the warm garment. It didn't escape Charlotte's notice that the mother had her hand on Charlotte's arm, helping her to stand and guiding her so that she wouldn't topple over. "I'm Charlotte. And you?"

"Julia. *Dank je—*"

Two gray-haired men ran up to them, interrupting Julia in her thanks. The one with an overcoat whipped off the garment and placed it around Julia's shoulders. Julia had begun to tremble, likely in a state of shock. Added warmth would help.

"We're here to help. Let's get this little darling to a warmer place." The taller man reached for Marianne from Charlotte's arms. He looked first at Charlotte then Julia "Where to, Mevrouw?"

"Down the alley," Julia said, pointing to a passage between a boarded-up chocolatier and a post office. "Then right, two houses over."

When they turned right, another woman ran out of the first house. She reached for the baby. "I'll take Ada now, Annelise." She then reached for Julia's arm and helped steady her. "Dear God, what happened to Marianne?"

"She fell... fell into the canal," Julia said as she motioned for the man carrying Marianne to enter the house before them. Following in quick steps, she said over her shoulder, "I think she'll be fine now, Mila, if we can warm her up. And Charlotte—get her some of my clothes and show her where to change." Mila said of course she'd do that and with the baby in her arms, took off into the house without delay.

"Oh, no need." Touched that Julia, as distraught and distracted as any mother would be over nearly losing a child, would think twice about her, warmed Charlotte more than a blanket. "I'll be fine. I don't want to intrude."

"Warm clothes are the very least I can offer you." Julia's large blue eyes were a mix of desperation, worry, and loneliness—traits Charlotte recognized easily. "I could use the company of the woman who saved my daughter's life."

Unease shrouded Charlotte, but she accepted the invitation and stepped indoors to see Marianne settled on the sofa. The two men hovered over the child. After fetching a plain skirt, sweater, and socks, Mila steered Charlotte into a downstairs room to change her clothes, then excused herself to tend to the wood stove. When Charlotte returned to the room, she noticed the men had left. Julia was changing Marianne into dryer clothes. Without worrying about formalities, Charlotte gathered a throw blanket piled in a heap on a rocking chair and covered the shivering Marianne.

"You need warmth as well, Charlotte," Julia said without looking away from her daughter stretched across the sofa. "Why don't you put your wet clothes on the chair and stand by the stove. You'll be warm in no time." A polite suggestion, not a curt command.

"I'm Annelise," the older girl said as she steered Charlotte toward the stove. Charlotte introduced herself by her first name only. Then, aware that Julia was listening, she added her new last name.

"Can you open your eyes for me, Marianne?" Julia asked when the child's eyes fluttered seconds later. "Wake up for Mama. Tell me how you're feeling. Are you hurting, sweetheart?"

"No hurt." Marianne looked at her mother and shook her head. "Cold. Tired."

"Should I run for the doctor?" Mila asked.

"It doesn't appear necessary," Julia said. "Thank goodness." She smiled at her daughter. "I love you, sunshine."

The way Julia beamed at Marianne reminded Charlotte of the time when she first met Johanna Süskind and had told her that she'd sparkled with the smile of a mother adoring her child. War was an incredibly odd time. While two or more man-made sides battled for the blood of perceived enemies, children were born and life continued. Johanna—a mother of a young girl barely out of her toddler years. Julia—a mother of three girls. Herself—a mother of two daughters. Johanna was Jewish, like Charlotte. At this point, there were no indications about Julia's faith, but unlike Charlotte's, Julia's children were tucked under motherly wings. Life is never fair during wartime.

"Let's have tea to warm us all up, and we'll talk more," Julia said. She explained that Mila was her sister-in-law who lived next door and asked Mila if she'd fix them tea.

"I want tea too," Marianne said.

"Yes." Julia kissed her daughter on the forehead. "A hot beverage for you is perfect. Mama will talk to our guest, but later the two of us will talk about how little girls must at all times stay away from the water and slippery bridges."

After Mila served the tea, with apologies about the strength as well as the lack of sugar, cream, or lemon, she excused herself to return to her own home. "If you need my help, Julia, do knock at my door without hesitation."

Julia thanked her sister-in-law. "I don't expect to need a thing." Once Mila was out of the house, with Annelise singing to her baby sister in a distant room and Marianne still on the sofa, sleeping, but thankfully alive and breathing, Julia turned all of her attention toward Charlotte seated on a chair close to the wood stove. "You've saved my daughter's life. I can't thank you enough."

"I did what any other person would have done in this situation."

"You were nothing short of brave. How did you learn resuscitation like that? Are you a nurse?"

"No, just a mother." Charlotte winced. She hadn't meant to mention her children. A question asked here and there about a subject she couldn't talk about would lead only to trouble. "When I began working in a nursery, I was taught how to resuscitate a child in need. Your daughter is the first one I've ever helped."

"It's good that you received that training. Again, thank you. As for your children, do you have sons or daughters or both? Where are they?"

"Two daughters." She wanted to scream at herself for revealing this basic fact. She needed to always stay on guard—the less said, the better. Lost in flashes of Edith and Krista's faces appearing before her, she hadn't a clue that she'd broken out in tears until Julia stood from the sofa and patted her shoulder.

"I didn't mean to upset you, Charlotte."

Charlotte had a split second to reshape the truth: tell this stranger her girls had disappeared, in the hope that Julia understood and respected the implied meaning of having gone into hiding or to opt to speak far worse. With this relationship new and fragile, Charlotte couldn't gauge whether Julia could be trusted. She decided on the latter of her choices. As she thought about it, one really was not that different from the other. Either way, she'd likely never see her daughters again. "My daughters are dead. Along with my husband. We were in Rotterdam visiting my husband's family the night of the bombing." She rocked forward, swept away in the true emotions of loss, heartache, and empty loneliness. "I barely lived, but I clung to life, though I'm uncertain of its worth at this moment."

Julia gasped. "How sad. I'm so sorry. Do you live alone? Where?"

"Yes, but the place doesn't matter." What she was about to say was a truth Charlotte wished was a lie. "My landlady is about to chase me out of the apartment building—I lost my job a few weeks ago and can no longer afford rent and barely anything else."

"Then stay with me."

Julia had spoken the invitation so quickly and had shaped it around the word *me* instead of *us*—exclusive of her daughters—that Charlotte wasn't sure she heard correctly. In hesitation, she peered at Julia; the woman's look of fixed determination erased her doubt. "I can't do that. This is not the best of times—you have enough mouths to feed. Surely your husband—"

"Do not concern yourself about my husband." Julia made an odd sound, halfway between a snort and a chuckle. "As for concerns, he hasn't been one of mine for quite a time. He doesn't even know about our baby daughter."

"You're not expecting him home?"

"No, I'm not. Nor is he welcome here. I can use another woman's company, to be honest. A friend is good these days, *nee*?"

Charlotte looked about the two-story house. From where she sat, she couldn't tell if there was a spare bedroom in the modest house or how she could avoid becoming a nuisance, but the ugly truth—that she was about to lose her own place to live—was a looming fact she couldn't ignore. Julia hadn't interrogated her about her faith, heritage, or political stance, and though Charlotte knew better than to assume the best of people these days, she had a hunch that Julia wasn't concerned about Charlotte's background. Likely, Julia also had a few things to hide, par for the course in the middle of a war. If she accepted and the living arrangement turned for the worse, she could always leave. "Your invitation is quite lovely, Julia. Thank you. I won't get in your way?"

"I can offer you the small downstairs room my husband uses for storage—the same room where you changed into my clothing. It won't take long to clear out. There's a cot in the shed out back. If you help me drag it indoors, it's all yours."

"That would be fine, though I don't have the means to offer compensation." Charlotte blinked in debate with herself. "There are a few possessions in the apartment I can try to sell—the cash I receive I'd be happy to turn over to you. Perhaps there would be a little extra left for food for you and your children."

Julia smiled; the warmest one Charlotte had received in some time. "And for you, as well!"

Charlotte would gain the means of sustenance if she accepted Julia's offer. Nourishment. Shelter. Company. Children to cheer her up. This was definitely better than living on the streets and begging for food. With no prior arrangements for herself to hide in a stranger's house, if she chanced walking about, she'd likely be taken in by the police or the SS and then ordered onto a transport train to a work camp in the east, and doing the kind of work she didn't want to find out about. "Yes, Julia," she said in a firmer commitment. "I'll be happy to accept your generous invitation to live with you and your family."

22

Julia should have never taken the baby out of the house a week ago in cold weather, nor, for that matter, the two older girls. If Luuk had been home that awful day, he would have rebuked her until he became hoarse. *I married you because you were kind and beautiful, but you've become a monster. How could you think so little of our daughters and subject them to the miserable cold? Do you know what people will think of me, that my wife has stopped loving me, her children, and has lost her mind?* Between the constant squabbling between Annelise and Marianne, the 24-hour care of all three children, and the stale indoor stuffiness, she had to get out of the house that day. Not wanting to again ask Mila to watch them, she'd bundled up the three and ventured outdoors, eager for the touch of fresh air on her face, the first in a few months. She never expected Marianne to slip into the canal.

She heard her husband's dissatisfaction once again: *I'm so disappointed in you, Julia.* But he hadn't been home, not then nor when she'd learned she was carrying his third child, nor when Henk intruded into the house and held them captive by gun and knifepoint, nor when Charlotte moved in with them. Luuk hadn't been home for nearly a year and a half, far too many days for her to continue obsessing about what he'd think about her or how she ran the household, doing the best she could, while he was off killing people in the name of advancing Hitler's powerful name. Yet, she couldn't shake herself free from Luuk's haunting ghost—her constant companion. Maybe that would change for the better with her new guest.

With Charlotte watching Ada and reading to the girls in the parlor, Julia turned from the changing table where she'd just placed a stack of Ada's freshly washed diapers onto a shelf and stepped toward the window to soak up the little sunshine streaming through the curtainless bedroom window. With more dark, gloomy days lately than bright ones, she squeezed her eyes shut to block out all that was upsetting. The opposite happened. Instead, in her mind she saw brown and green—the colors of Luuk's eyes—streak through the sky like lightning. She heard feet stomping, coming from over a thousand teenage boys and university students marching on the pavement en route to a transport for slave labor. She tasted the fear, bitter like old Brussels sprouts, of those wondering how Seyss-Inquart would retaliate against the Dutch churches that sent a letter of protest against the Nazification of society. Too much.

As if waking from a horrid dream, Julia opened her eyes and rested her forehead against the window glass, cold despite the sunshine. Tears stung her eyes, but she batted them back, seeking a balm for her broken spirit. Music. Yes, that would do nicely. She summoned her Oma's favorite piece of music, Franz Schubert's Arpeggione Sonata in A Minor. Hearing the cello's trill in her mind helped her to slip back to her childhood days of frequent visits to her dear Oma's house. Oma, who had played the cello professionally in a string quartet, encouraged Julia's piano playing by accompanying her. Thinking of how she used to playfully tease Oma by saying that the Schubert's Sonata was her favorite piece of music—not Oma's—brought a smile to Julia. Though, it also made her acutely aware of how that warm glow of joy had paled during the majority of her adult life since she'd married Luuk. Oh, there had been pleasant enough times between her and her husband. Luuk's defiance of his parents' displeasure of him wanting to marry Julia. The little getaway honeymoon to Paris, using the last guilder in Luuk's pocket, and his confident reassurance that when they returned to Amsterdam he'd prove right away that he would be a fine provider and she wouldn't have to worry about a thing. He was wrong. She found it overwhelming, especially when the children started to come along, that she had to learn how to become thrifty in her spending. The thing was, she couldn't share her feelings with him or he'd retaliate by blaming her for the faults he refused to correct, and his ways physically hurt at times. At least he tempered his explosions with a charm that always took her by delighted surprise and filled her with horrid guilt of ever thinking of him negatively. Hand-written romantic poems tucked alongside her breakfast dish. Singing to her while she bathed. Wringing a warm washcloth over her back to rinse off the soap, invariably leading to planting sweeping kisses from her neck to her breasts to a tug out of the tub and into his eager, naked embrace. The countless wildflowers he'd present her with; the generous minutes of his time reading bedtime stories to Annelise and Marianne.

It was worth it, staying married to Luuk—a confused man, not a beast. As she remembered the sweet music she loved, peace filled her soul. She began to sway, then stood on her toes, twirling like a porcelain ballerina figurine on a music box. Luuk appeared to be transporting her back to their days of courting. The good, kind, and gentle Luuk, this time, not the ranting, demanding one. Not the one who was always right while everyone else was always wrong. He led her to the dance floor, clasping his left hand to her right hand. Their fingers loosely interlocked.

"If you marry me, Julia, I'll make you happy. You will want to put aside all the things you once enjoyed."

The Schubert sonata quieted, readying itself for the next crescendo. "How will you accomplish this, Luuk, darling?"

His eyes sparkled. "By giving you a whole new batch of wonderful life moments to tuck into your memory."

She giggled like the young woman she indeed was, one innocently believing all people were good and kind. "You make it sound as if you're giving me a scrapbook, and I am to fill the pages to look back upon from time to time."

"Exactly. I promise you a lifetime of no regrets. I will make you proud to be my wife."

"Your wife?" She stopped dancing, though the music continued to play. "And how do you know if I want to marry you?"

The most charming and seductive smile she'd ever seen on a man spread his lips wide. "Because I am certain that you will enjoy life with me as much as I will with you."

The bedroom door squeaked open, jolting Julia back to the present.

"Oh, pardon me."

Standing in the middle of the room, clearly alone, Julia dropped her hands to her side when she saw Charlotte with baby Ada tucked in her arms.

"Sorry. I intruded on your privacy, but when you didn't reply to my call, I grew concerned. You've been so tired lately, and I wanted to see how you were." Charlotte smiled at the baby. "Ada misses your company."

Julia reached for her baby girl. "Is she fussing over food?"

With an expertise Julia believed she never had, despite Ada being her third child, Charlotte placed Ada in her arms in one fluid and gentle motion so that the baby looked at her as if to say: *I'm happy you've held me all this time, Charlotte.* A pang of jealousy flittered within Julia's chest, but like an annoying gnat, she mentally swatted it away. She couldn't afford to lose Charlotte as a friend.

"I don't believe so," Charlotte said. "See that smile? She just wants your company. As for the other two, Annelise and Marianne are playing nicely in their room."

"That's a nice surprise." Julia walked to the double bed and placed Ada in its center. "Come join us." She watched Charlotte sit on the bed's edge and make a silly face at the baby, encouraging her to move toward her. An early crawler, Ada pushed onto her knees. Julia and Charlotte oohed and aahed.

"And goodness, Charlotte, no need to apologize for entering my room. This is your home too. I tend to get lost in my daydreams and forget there are others living in the world along with me. Not a good thing for a mother to do." Remembering Luuk, dancing with him—at least, this apparition who stepped in for her husband—while all along wishing the real Luuk would continue to stay away, was another reason why she was glad for Charlotte's companionship. About to tell her this, she paused, taking in the woman's silence, her focus riveted at the window. "Charlotte?"

Charlotte looked at Ada, now on Julia's lap. "Were you imagining your husband? Were you dancing with him? You looked incredibly happy, Julia. You must miss him."

Julia debated whether or not to talk about Luuk, the good or the bad, or not one word. If she and Charlotte were to remain housemates, it would be polite to tell her a little about her husband. "Yes, we were dancing, at least in my imagination." She surprised herself with a dreamy sigh. "We haven't danced since… since… Oh my. Since the time right before he disappeared from me and his daughters."

"You looked as if you were in heaven."

She doubted that if she was ever fortunate enough to make it to the everlasting resting place, she'd dance with Luuk if he was there too. Then again, wasn't heaven a place where not only God forgives one's sins, but one would also forgive all transgressions that had occurred in their lifetime, from all who had committed these misdoings? Such as an insult. Humiliation. The constant threat of abandonment. And the worse ones. "Luuk had his moments." There. That was a safe way of phrasing it.

"Ah, Luuk's his name." Charlotte feathered her fingers across Ada's cheeks. "This is the first time you've mentioned his name. Although, as you've said when we first met, he has yet to learn about little Ada, so I don't blame you for your mixed feelings."

Mixed feelings. A mild description of her reaction to the

complexities of her relationship with her husband. The discomforting blend of confusion, resentment, and loss hovering over her from thinking about Luuk knotted Julia's stomach. She looked at Charlotte. "Tell me about your husband. You haven't mentioned his name."

Charlotte wrapped her arms around her middle. "Helmut was a good man, the best."

"Oh, dear. That's right—you'd said that he and your two daughters had perished in the Rotterdam bombing. So unfortunate and tragic." She patted Charlotte's hand. "Forgive me for bringing up such a sensitive subject."

"No need to apologize, Julia. The ability to talk freely and confidently to each other will determine whether we're simply housemates or friends. Don't you think that's true?"

She gave a little nod.

"Good," Charlotte said. "Please, don't worry about whether or not to talk about Helmut. He is—was—a wonderful, loving husband and father. I will never forget him, never stop thinking about him. Nor do I want to, because in my mind, he—and our daughters—will stay alive, forever."

"And your daughters' names? How old would they be now?"

"My oldest, Edith, a November baby, would have been 16," she said in a soft tone. "My littlest one, Krista, would have turned 14 last month."

She still continues to celebrate her precious ones' birthdays, Julia thought. Who could blame a mother? A wild idea crossed her mind. "I can tell you love your daughters as I love my girls." She looked at Ada and smiled. "Let's have a birthday celebration for them. Ani and Marianne adore parties, not that we indulged in elaborate celebrations while their father was home." A weight slid off her shoulders, streaked down her arms, through her fingers, and dissipated into the air. She sat straighter. "It makes no difference what my missing husband thought or had done in the past. Let's celebrate the beauty of your daughters tomorrow. We'll have a grand time, I promise." She stood with Ada, kissed the baby gently on the forehead, and tucked her into the bassinet she kept beside the bed. "Well, that is if you don't mind a possible cry or two from my bundle of joy here?"

"That would be lovely. Thank you, Julia."

"*Gefeliciteerd!*" Annelise shouted as Charlotte entered the parlor. Not prepared to be outdone by her oldest sister, Marianne jumped from her chair and repeated the congratulations in an excited squeal. Julia hoped the shouts wouldn't awaken Ada, who was asleep on her lap. Then again, it was nice to see her daughters happy. She swept her attention toward Charlotte, who had joined the birthday circle in her honor. The poor woman appeared a bit surprised and troubled by the greeting, though who could blame her? Both her daughters were dead, and had been for nearly three years. What a long time.

"Aren't you going to say *gefeliciteerd* back to me?" Marianne asked. "To all of us?"

Charlotte fingered the V-neckline of her dark green sweater. "Oh, of course, darling." She offered her congratulations to each one of them. "My goodness," she said when Annelise thrust a cloth-napkin-wrapped gift at her. "Thank you. I wasn't expecting this." Worry lines crossed her forehead, her mouth sagged into a frown.

Annelise bit her bottom lip. "You don't like the napkin we used? Mama said there's no pretty paper."

"Oh, no. That's not it." A weak smile overcame Charlotte's frown then faded. She glanced at Julia. "Your Mama's suggestion yesterday to celebrate my daughters sounded lovely. But thinking about my girls makes me sad."

"Open the present," Marianne said. "It will make you happy again."

Charlotte stroked the gift as if running a finger under a kitten's jaw. "How about I open it a little later?"

"No, silly. You're supposed to open it right away." Marianne looked at Julia. "Right, Mama?"

Julia shifted to accommodate Ada. "Yes, dear. But please be respectful of Charlotte, our special friend."

"Sorry, Charlotte."

"And I'm sorry I didn't open this gift yet." Charlotte sat on the vacant chair between the two girls. "I wasn't expecting a present. That's all."

Marianne started to speak, but Annelise elbowed her younger sister in her side. Short on sleep and patience, Julia narrowed her eyes at her daughters, urging them silently to behave. She shifted her attention to Charlotte. "We thought this homemade gift might lift your spirits."

Rather than replying, Charlotte untied the string around the clothed package. "Oh, my."

"Don't you like it?" Annelise asked.

"It's custom to show us all," Julia said softly, the nudge more for her daughters' satisfaction than for her own, especially since she'd put the girls up to it after they sat around the breakfast table without a clue as to what to do for the party.

"Why yes, of course." Charlotte lifted the gift for the girls and Julia to see. "It's precious, like my own two daughters. It reminds me of them. Whoever drew these two lovely girls is a most talented artist. And whoever designed the cutouts of their new dresses and outfitted them is indeed a budding seamstress or a fashion designer. How clever and considerate."

"Mama?" Marianne's lips twitched. "What does Charlotte mean?"

"It means she likes the gift you two made to honor her daughters."

"No," Charlotte said, firmly. "I absolutely love this gift. Thank you, precious darlings. No matter where I live, I'll keep this gift in a special place for all to see."

Marianne slid off her chair, took one step toward Charlotte, and hoisted herself onto her lap. "Aren't you going to live with us, forever?"

"Girls," Julia said. "That's enough questions for Charlotte. You remember what I'm always reminding you about?"

"Ask about what doesn't concern you and get answers that won't please you," Annelise murmured.

"Correct." With Ada awakening, Julia lowered her head to the baby and made a happy face. "Your little sister is waking up, so please be two dears and get the birthday cake your Tante Mila baked this morning."

Both Julia and Charlotte watched the girls skedaddle from the room into the kitchen. Once they had the parlor to themselves, Charlotte set the picture back into the wrappings. "I truly meant what I told your daughters, that this is the loveliest of gifts and that I'll always treasure it. Thank you for thinking of me."

"It was Ani's idea to draw the picture. Hopefully, it resembles your daughters a little. Marianne wanted to actually dress the two girls. I suggested they make cutouts to fold and tuck around the girls." Julia pointed at the picture. "Look carefully. See the tiny slits for the clothes tab? They want to make a whole wardrobe for your picture-girls, and I expect that will keep them plenty busy over the next few days."

"That would be lovely. Julia, your daughters are so sweet. If Edith and Krista were alive and here, they'd become the best of friends with your daughters."

Julia kept silent for a moment, toying with how to say what was on her mind. She couldn't think of a delicate way to frame her words and spoke out, hating herself for being blunt like her husband. "You aren't Dutch, like you've said, are you?"

Charlotte rocked back.

"Sorry. And to think moments ago I'd reprimanded my daughters about asking questions that don't concern them. It's just that you appear confused about the birthday party. Grant you, it's uncustomary to have a celebration for the deceased, as dear to your heart as your daughters were to you." *If indeed she had daughters.* As best as she could with a baby on her lap, Julia leaned closer, as if sharing in confidence. "But you were taken back by the offer of the *gefeliciteerd* cheer."

"It's been—" Charlotte jabbed two fingers between her eyes.

"Don't worry, my friend," Julia said. "Each one of us has a secret. You can trust me with yours, whenever the time is right for you to share. Or not. True friends also respect each other's need for privacy."

Charlotte gave the tiniest of nods, though shot her a questioning look. "Yes, that's true. But I was going to use the word *difficult*. That it's been quite difficult, this loss of my daughters and husband."

She looked so sad, rightly so, that Julia thought about placing Ada in her arms. What woman didn't perk up from holding a baby? She passed Ada to her and delighted in Charlotte's smile. "It would be beyond difficult for me if I were to lose one of my children or all three of them."

"Not your husband?"

"Here's your cake," Annelise announced as she walked into the room with the cake carefully centered on a tray yet wobbly in her clutch.

"And I have chocolates," Marianne said, showing the treats in the cup of her palms. "Tante Mila always has sweets."

Julia stood, whispering her thanks to Charlotte for holding onto the baby. Wanting to grab the cake from her daughter's hand before it plunged to the floor, she scooped the small but beautiful-looking cake from her oldest. Once the cake was secured on the dining room table, she called Charlotte.

"This looks scrumptious," Charlotte said.

"It should." Marianne crawled up on one of the chairs clustered around the table. "You didn't eat your breakfast like Ani and me. Mama says we won't grow unless we eat our meals."

"You have a smart mother." Charlotte gave the baby back to Julia and sat next to Marianne. She looked directly at Julia. "May I have the first slice? Although it's tradition that the one who is celebrating the birthday should serve the cake to everyone else, my mouth is watering for this delicious-looking treat."

Surprised but relieved that Charlotte was aware of Dutch birthday customs, after all, Julia gave a small nod of approval. She regretted thinking wrongly of Charlotte earlier. Julia glanced at the cake. "What would I do without my sister-in-law, who not only bakes and cooks for us against my protest, but can manage to find ingredients for an apple cake just like one the good Nazis feast on?"

23

For Charlotte, the time passing by since she'd last seen her daughters was the worst part about living in Julia's house. Since she'd become a housemate of this family that was not her own, she appeared safe from the dangers that Jews throughout the Netherlands faced daily. For this she was grateful. Yet, inconsistent with the comfort she'd found living with Julia and her daughters for a month now, the uncertainty of her daughters' welfare grew heavier and more hurtful to bear. Also concerned about Helmut—her attractive, strong and intelligent Kurt—she could only reason that, hopefully living in another country, he stood a better chance of surviving this war than if he had remained behind. Glancing at the alarm clock ticking beside her cot, Charlotte sprang up from the thin, but ample enough mattress. It was time for her to do something other than sit around and imagine the worst.

She had no idea whether the director of the nursery school where she used to work was still employed there, but if anyone could give her a sprinkle of information, of hope to cling to, about her daughters, Henriëtte Henriquez Pimentel would be the one. On her knees, she poked a hand under the cot and pulled out her small valise. With a puff, she blew off the dust, snapped open the two tabs, and then went to the chest of drawers where she kept her clothes plus the handful of extra garments Julia was gracious enough to loan her. She couldn't guess whether her endeavors would reach her daughters, but trying was better than not trying. It was the absolute least she could do. Into the valise she tossed all her socks except for two pairs, her sole nightgown, two pullover sweaters, and two summer blouses, which meant she'd have to find a job for extra cash to purchase more clothes—if a shop was open—or for all she cared, wrap herself in a bedsheet.

"What are you doing?"

Charlotte jerked her head up from the valise. With raised brows, wide-open eyes and mouth, Julia stared at her as if she were a child planning to run away and was caught packing for the trip. With three quick strides, she crossed the narrow room and stood by Charlotte.

"Please, tell me you're not leaving. Goodness, Charlotte. I thought you liked it here with us. What did I do wrong?"

"Julia, you're a lovely friend. Have no fear, you've done nothing wrong, nor am I leaving."

"That's a relief. I've been enjoying your company, and my girls too."

My girls. Charlotte had two daughters as well. Alive and healthy, she could only hope.

She shoved the valise aside and sat on the cot, inviting Julia to join her. "I've been thinking about Edith and Krista."

Julia glanced at the valise. "I imagine you think about them daily, if not each minute."

"Yes," Charlotte murmured. To speak louder, she'd risk sobbing, not that crying in front of Julia would be horrible, but she wanted to remain strong and clearheaded. "I miss them terribly. At times it's more than I can bear."

"I appreciate your honesty." Again, Julia eyed the valise. "But the clothes you were packing?"

"I thought that since I'm no longer able to take care of my darlings, I could at least take provisions to—"

"To whom, Charlotte? Tell me you weren't thinking about taking them to a bunch of Jews. We've been ordered to stay away from them for a reason—the few obvious ones that are left these days. For our own good, for the good of our country."

And what would be wrong with taking needed clothing to Jews, she wanted to ask. Was helping the persecuted, the hunted, those no longer considered human beings, a crime? Julia might not have stated accusations against Jews in direct words, but she hadn't expressed out-and out-concern for them either. Did Julia also have her share of concerns over her? If Julia were to learn of Charlotte's true identity, and if Charlotte chose to be mean and fabricate lies about Julia, conceivably, either one of them could betray the other to the Nazis. Thankfully, the more Charlotte learned about Julia she didn't believe that her new friend could be cruel and betray her even if she were to discover Charlotte's history. She'd saved Julia's daughter's life, which meant everything to Julia, though the only thing that Charlotte was concerned about at the time was aiding the little girl so she could enjoy a future. Then again, Charlotte had to remain vigilant for dangers and difficulties. Charlotte sighed to herself. When would this threat of deception ever end? The German occupation had changed the once beautiful Dutch spirit into a land of minefields containing hatred and cruelty that stripped a person of basic human rights that all should have and enjoy.

Thinking that Julia was the one in need of comforting, not herself, Charlotte grasped the woman's hands. "I want to give my daughters clothes, food, and the boundless love I have for them." She paused, trying to come up with a way to shove aside the fact that her next words were a stretch of the truth. "But since Edith and Krista are gone from this lifetime and I can't help them, can't see them grow and mature into fine women, can't help them survive this dreadful wartime that impacts both the Jews and non-Jews, I thought the least I could do was hand these few things over to the director at the crèche I used to work at in Plantage in the hope that it would help those in need."

"Don't be foolish."

Charlotte released Julia's hand and wrapped her arms around her middle. She needed a hug. She needed to give a hug. To her husband. To her daughters.

"Sorry," Julia said, with a curse at herself riding on a heavy breath. "That sounded worse than I intended. Will you forgive me?"

"Of course, I forgive you."

"I shouldn't have snapped. No need to copy my husband's antics." Julia fidgeted with the fringe of the bedcover. She frowned, as if deep in contemplation. "I'm worried about you, that's all. It's not safe to walk such a distance, especially by yourself. And carrying a suitcase will bring the kind of unwanted attention that will have the authorities pick you up like a Jew on the run, and deport you to a camp. Believe me, denials and paperwork won't get you ahead these days."

"I hadn't thought of that." Charlotte truly hadn't. Images suddenly crashed through her mind. The sharp click of boot-stomping Nazis as they marched down the streets. A shrill whistle of the police upon a cornered enemy, followed by a poor person's gasping breath as he lay in a pool of blood. Charlotte cleared her mind of those horrid sounds and visuals. Julia was right. The days of strolling here or there and walking non-stop to the crèche had slipped into funereal bleakness, countering a yesteryear that no longer existed. The minimal goal she'd had in mind was to request from Henriëtte updates on Edith and Krista, and to give her the valise in the hope that she could smuggle it to her daughters. Now Charlotte saw her plan as ridiculous and dangerous. When had mothering and loving become an offense?

"Charlotte, to repeat in blunt language: if you're found walking on the streets alone, you'd be seen as a dead ringer for someone on the run rather than a good Dutch citizen." Julia blotted her teary eyes with her fingertips. "Look at me—I'm crying over you as if you're my long, lost friend. And I hope you will be my friend, not a mere acquaintance. I also have to tell you—with my husband gone and three little ones, honestly, I've been feeling a bit safer here since you've been living with us."

"Although I would have come back after dropping off the clothes, with your in-laws living next door, I'm surprised you're uncomfortable here."

"His name was Henk."

"Pardon?"

"A stranger. He broke into my house two years ago and held us hostage at knife and gunpoint. He did this regardless of Mila and Liam being my neighbors."

A chill shot down Charlotte's spine. "That must have been terrifying. With the little girls and..." Charlotte blinked. "Oh, my—you were expecting Ada."

"Yes. Fortunately, it was early in my pregnancy and I doubt Henk was aware of it. He didn't hurt us, thank God." Julia inhaled deeply and let out a slow breath. "The strange part was that Henk was a Nazi, not a Jew. Imagine that! Turned out that the louse was a traitor to the same party that wanted to make life good for him."

Charlotte swallowed back her confusion. How could Julia give thanks to God and then seconds later support a political party that wanted to wipe those who worshiped another faith off the map of Europe—or the whole world? While hatred and prejudice against others was nothing new since the dawn of mankind, and as much as she badly wanted peace and an end to this war, she wasn't a fool. Another war, with another variation of hatred spewing left and right, was likely already brewing. What about herself? She was Jewish, not hiding in an attic or on the run, but living with someone she really didn't know all about and in a German-occupied country. One false step could misfire and cause her never to see her family again or to lose her life. Whether Julia was a hardcore Nazi sympathizer or a non-Jew that blindly accepted Nazi changes and mandates without question didn't matter in regard to her motherhood. Julia's will to survive and to think of her children made her incredibly similar to Charlotte. It made Charlotte question whether to take her chances and leave this house. Problems and obstacles had an awful way of dictating how one responded to threats. Without a place to live or to hide, and without family or friends to turn to for help, she needed Julia as much as Julia needed her.

Julia reached for the valise and lugged it onto her lap. "Will you remain here today, Charlotte? Will you promise me not to take the chance of being wrongfully arrested?"

Charlotte held back a flinch at Julia's last two words that described precisely what had happened to her dear Kurt. She thought about Julia's husband and how she rarely mentioned him. Was he the source of her insecurities?

"Yes, Julia. I promise." In all likelihood, if she had safely managed to bring the valise to the nursery, the clothes probably would never have reached her daughters. "I'll stay put. But I'd love to learn more about you, especially if you were to value our friendship."

"Oh, yes. I'd like for us to become good friends. Learning more about each other is a must. Let's begin with your husband. Then I'll tell you about mine."

Be careful, Herta. That's what Kurt would have cautioned. She looked into Julia's eyes. "His name was Helmut," she said softly, the mention of her husband's fake name leaving a bitter taste on her tongue.

24

Charlotte had thought that with Annelise and Marianne next door at their aunt and uncle's house for a post-dinner visit and with Ada sound asleep in Julia's bedroom, she and Julia would have an easier time with this conversation. Instead, they sat opposite each other at the kitchen table, both cradling a cup of tea. Both keeping mum.

Excuses of ending this failed discussion began to tramp through her mind. *I could say I'm exhausted, that a headache is making mincemeat of my head. Claim that the earlier conversation about family has reprised a depression and it would be best to retire for the evening. Or, with plans for a job search early tomorrow, anxiety is kicking up, and I need time alone to think of a strategy.* The thing was, if she were to claim these excuses as the truth, she wouldn't deviate from reality.

Julia shot to her feet. "Who are we fooling, my friend?" She gestured to the two untouched servings of tea on the table. "We need a drink stronger than this barely flavored lukewarm water." She crossed the dining area in quick strides to the small sideboard. Opening the door, she said, "In the past, Luuk forbade me to help myself to his stash, but he certainly isn't around right now to command me."

"Yes, that's correct. I'm glad to hear you sound more in control."

Julia pivoted away from the cabinet and lifted a half-full bottle of liquor and two shot glasses. "Shall we enjoy some *jenever*?"

Charlotte smiled, despite that the offer of the drink brought back the memory of Kurt sharing the news of the brutality following the college professor protesting against the Nazis at Dam Square, and how she and Kurt steadied their nerves with the strong drink. "Let's do that!"

They moved to the sofa that Julia had inherited from her parents, a piece of furniture from the late 19th century. The faded green damask may have had a few lumps, but like its curvy mahogany frame that wrapped around its corners, their conversation flowed smoothly as they exhausted the topic of the dreary weather, Ada's newest antics as she discovered her world, and the latest cutest thing that either Annelise or Marianne had shared.

"Here's an idea," Charlotte said as she wondered how much longer she could tolerate Julia's fidgeting with the fringe from the throw draped over the back of the sofa without becoming twitchy herself. "Let's begin on a positive note. While we both might have difficulties thinking this way, let's name one good thing that we've both learned about ourselves since becoming more independent."

Julia shook a finger at her, though the little grin toying with her lips indicated amusement, not annoyance. "You always have an interesting way of phrasing things. You, my dear, should become a diplomat. If you do, there might be hope for each of us, after all."

Charlotte half chuckled and half groaned to herself. If she would have to save her life by attempting to use diplomacy with a group of Nazis, being considerate of and sensitive to their needs and outlook on life, she wouldn't live five minutes. Likely, even less. She looked at Julia. When was the exact moment amid this bedlam of the German occupation that all aspects of life started to center around the fact that one distinct group dominated the majority of the population? Was it when she and Kurt were first awoken by the blares of the sirens signaling the alarm of a foreign attack? When they first started debating whether or not to go into hiding, let alone whether or not to deny their faith and heritage? When she had to say goodbye to her husband followed by the farewells to her daughters fleeing for their lives? She remembered the life milestones like her marriage and the birth of each of her daughters. Warmth embraced her heart as if it was yesterday. However, the past events in the Netherlands were no occasion for celebration. Truth be told, that was why she and Julia were drinking *jenever*: they drank because they needed to forget their anguish. Sometimes, the right relief could soothe the worst of pains. The combination of wartime and absent husbands certainly required attention.

"Charlotte, are you getting too serious?"

"You're the perceptive one. Perhaps we shouldn't drag ourselves down in the dumps of our past."

"No way, you aren't getting out of this one." Julia giggled. "Shall I begin or…"

"Or me?" Charlotte supplied Julia's missing words.

"*Ja*. You read my mind. Not hard to do, in my current state."

"Oh, please. You must not be hard on yourself." Charlotte leaned back, resting one arm on the sofa's back. She was surprisingly relaxed, but didn't connect it to the *jenever*. Rather, it was the atmosphere—the acceptance into this stranger's home and being appreciated by not only Julia but also her daughters. "I'll go first. I learned that I can indeed open jars without having my husband around to help me."

The silence between the two hissed in Charlotte's ear a little too long. Just when she thought Julia might have interpreted her attempt at humor as rude and coarse, resulting in Julia wanting to suddenly push her out onto the streets, Julia burst out in laughter. So loud, that Charlotte turned toward Julia's bedroom where the baby was sleeping, expecting the little one to awaken and cry.

"Don't worry," Julia said between snorts. "If Ada can sleep through my blubbering at night, she can sleep through my laughter."

Julia cried herself to sleep? She might not admit it, but she must truly love and miss her husband. "Oh, my. I'm sorry, Julia. I didn't mean for this topic to circle back to traces of sadness."

Julia waved her hand. "No need to apologize—I didn't take offense. You're so funny, though. I just wasn't expecting this from you since you always appear contemplative. But, thank you. I needed a good laugh."

"Helmut would often say that I was pensive to the extreme. He'd tried to coax me to loosen up—to look at the brighter side of things. This was before the war began, before—" She stopped herself in time. Of course, this was before the war started. She'd told Julia her sob story about losing her husband and children in the bombing of Rotterdam, thus proving that keeping up with lies could be a tripwire to one's detriment. "There I go again—silly me. Call me Mevrouw Too Serious." She pushed herself to go on before Julia could say a word. "On a more significant note, the one thing I learned about myself—and actually am shocked by—is that I haven't broken into countless pieces all this time while living on my own."

Julia bobbed her head. "I cannot imagine what you've gone through. Luuk may be away, but he has reassured me it's for a good cause. Although at times I have my doubts, there's this part of me that believes he'll come home to me. He does love me and our daughters. I'm hoping that what they say about love is true—that it overrules the disagreements in life. But you? You're an amazingly strong woman, and I envy you for discovering this necessary trait." She slumped back onto the sofa. "Meanwhile, I teeter between thinking I can make it through one more day caring for three young children by showing a positive and calm attitude and losing my patience, let alone my sanity."

Charlotte leaned forward, balancing her elbows on her knees. "All women fear that they are failing as a wife, a daughter, a mother... as a person. Wartime or not. Tell me, Julia. You must have discovered a few amazing strengths about yourself during your husband's absence."

Julia lifted the *jenever* to her lips but stopped short of taking another sip. Instead, she murmured into the glass.

Charlotte cupped her ear. "Pardon?"

"Yes." Julia pulled the shot glass away and looked at it as if it had offended her. She set the drink on the lamp table beside the sofa. "I deserve more respect than Luuk claims I do."

About to ask what she meant by that, a knock at the door gave Charlotte pause. Considering that a war was spreading havoc across the globe and that no one of good merit would call at night, especially uninvited, ratcheted up suspicion. Yet, it was Julia's sudden downturned eyebrows and pale face that robbed Charlotte of words. Julia sprang to her feet and tugged Charlotte's hand. "Quickly, go to the children's room."

The visitor on the other side could have been a Nazi acting on orders to search the house, though absent was their customary pounding and barking orders to open the door immediately. "Why? Who do you think it is?"

"Charlotte, do as I say. And once there, hide."

The odd mixture of fear and reluctance to obey covered Charlotte's arms with gooseflesh. This was Julia's house. She knew best, right? Pushing aside more questions, she rushed to the girls' bedroom without looking back over her shoulder. On the one hand, Julia, on the inebriated side, couldn't effectively confront a caller if that person turned out abrasive, yet it was her home. If Julia gave her a warning to hide, then Charlotte should obey her wishes.

Without further hesitation, Charlotte pushed open the door, relieved that Annelise and Marianne were next door with their aunt and uncle and that she didn't have to explain her sudden intrusion, let alone hiding, to the little girls. She didn't dare switch on a light, allowing brightness to slip under the door and alert visitors. Just as well. The last thing she wanted to see was the sight of the twin beds, adorned with the stuffed teddy bears and forever-smiling dolls that shouted *we belong to two girls who are alive and happy to live in their own homes.*

Having been in this room enough times to be aware that she didn't have decent options, she slipped under a bed. Flat on her back, she tried shifting a few times to relieve the soreness from an object wedged under one of her shoulder blades. She ceased moving when the door creaked open.

"Charlotte?" Julia called. "It's safe. Come on out."

Curious, she clutched the pesky nuisance and wiggled out from under Marianne's bed.

"There you are." Julia giggled. "Just like my girls—they always hide under their beds."

From what? Or, was it from whom?

"Sorry to cause alarm. The caller was Mila, no Nazi raid. She said the girls fell asleep and that if it was fine with me—and it is—that she'd keep them for..." Julia reached for the light on the dresser and switched it on. "What are you holding?"

Intent on learning more about Mila's visit, Charlotte had forgotten she'd held onto the unknown object. She lifted the item in question. A gold necklace chain. Although its pendant was missing, it reminded her of the beautiful necklaces and pins that Kurt had crafted, like the butterfly pin that he had gifted her many painful days ago. A gasp clawed its way up her throat, but she managed to swallow it back.

"That necklace chain?" Julia said. "Why in the world did one of my girls take my favorite necklace and hide it? And what did they do with the pendant?"

To play. To imitate their mama. Who wouldn't want a piece of jewelry to help forget about the disasters of reality, of war? Charlotte handed the chain to Julia. "When I dove under the bed to hide, something kept irritating my back. I had no idea about the culprit until I crawled out of the hiding place." Aware that she needed to divert the attention from herself and return the focus onto Julia, she swallowed dryly, pondering the words she was about to say. "You were awfully alarmed when you heard Mila's knock at the door—I'd never seen you so frightened. Although it was just Mila, it could have been a raid to check if you were hiding anyone you weren't supposed to. You warned me to hide, which I find confusing because I have documentation showing I'm not a concern to the Nazis. Why is that, Julia? Who did you want me to hide from, and why? Am I an embarrassment to you?"

Julia sat on the closest bed, Annelise's, and picked up a doll with golden ringlets from the band of toys gathered around the pillow. She set the doll on her lap, stroking its nose, fingering a curl, smiling at it softly as if the doll was alive and waiting for her attention. "Do you want the truth? It's not pretty."

"Yes, of course. If we are to be friends, we must share the truth at all times."

Julia nodded but remained quiet. Charlotte sat opposite to her on Marianne's bed. She'd wait as long as it took, giving Julia the crucial seconds or minutes to sort out the truth in her mind and decide the exact amount of facts that she could afford to share. In wartime, no matter which side one was on, everyone clung to secrets.

"Since you aren't Jewish," Julia said softly, "I'm not concerned about the Nazis finding you in my home. They're not my enemy, nor am I theirs." She inhaled deeply and released her breath slowly. She looked Charlotte in the eyes. "You're right. I do fear someone—my husband."

Charlotte's instant concern for Julia had her springing onto her feet then dropping onto her knees before her. She folded Julia's icy hands in her warm ones. Tired, and with no patience left, she needed to get to the point, but with decency and respect. "The tears running down your cheeks tell me you have quite a few mixed feelings about your husband."

Julia pulled her hands from Charlotte's hold and blotted her tears with her fingertips. She sniffled and nodded.

"I suspect," Charlotte continued, "he's hurt you, and you don't know how to react, whether it's guilt or anger or frustration or all three." She paused, watching Julia's face for telltale expressions, yet none came. "If I'm wrong—and I'm overstepping my boundaries—please let me know. I've certainly been wrong before."

"Luuk says and does certain things for my own good."

Charlotte sat on a rug and drew her knees up to her chest. "Is this what you believe or something that Luuk has led you to accept?"

"He's said this quite often to me, reminding me that I can't seem to remember how to behave like a good wife, saying…" She began to rock back and forth.

"Julia?"

"He insists that it's for my own good."

"What's for your own good? What does he do or say to you?"

Julia's gaze drifted to the dollhouse sitting on the floor in the corner, its mother figurine in the kitchen serving dinner to the father seated at the table. Two little girls sat on a bed in a bedroom on the opposite side of the house. A snippet of home-life, Charlotte assumed. At least, how it used to be for Julia's family.

"He tells me his reminders are for my own good." Julia crumpled across the bed, burying her face in the array of dolls, stuffed animals, and pillows. Her body shook with sobs; she twisted and her hair swooshed and lifted off her chest. And that was when Charlotte saw the scar that spanned a half of a hand's width, close to Julia's heart.

Charlotte gasped. "That's a horrid scar. Did he take a knife to you? Threats, warnings, and actions like that are not done for your *own good*. Don't you see, Julia, this is physical abuse?"

Julia stopped crying. She propped herself onto an elbow and rubbed the spot that Charlotte had asked about. "This?"

"Tell me. What did—does—Luuk do to you?"

"I deserve his discipline. And more."

"Discipline? You aren't a child that needs discipline. Husbands have no right to hurt their wives." Charlotte tugged Julia into a sitting position. "This is physical abuse. If Luuk hurts you in any form or degree, you need to get away from him and fast."

"You've said it yourself—there's a war going on." Julia closed her eyes for a few seconds then opened them. "I can't leave. What about my daughters? My baby? Where are we supposed to go? And what about you? I can't put you out on the streets."

If Julia knew she was lying—keeping back from her the truth about her faith and her family—would she understand and sympathize or hand her over to the Nazis? Right then and there, the answer to that awful question eluded Charlotte. However, it was obvious that Julia had suffered terribly from this husband whom she believed she loved, a man who evidently knew pathetically little about loving or cherishing another.

"Can you answer my question, Julia? Can you tell me what Luuk did to you without telling me that you deserve it? Just tell me the facts."

"He drank a bit on the heavy side that night. Started having his doubts again."

Doubts? All around them a war raged on, propelled by the evil forces of Nazism and Fascism. This source of evil was fueled by a population of those who either had no qualms about supporting laws and illegal acts against human beings they'd categorized as non-humans, or by those in society who were recruited to carry out this evil. "What do you mean by doubts? I have plenty of doubts. I'm sure you have too. But we don't go around hurting other people."

"That he'd never amount to any worthwhile position in society. He's big on getting respect from higher-ups, you see. Tragically, these important people don't perceive him as having the desired ability to contribute on the same level." She groaned. "Please, if you meet Luuk one day, don't tell him I told you this. He'd deny it and make trouble."

Charlotte cringed at the desperation in Julia's tone. "So, he grabbed a knife?"

Julia shook her head. "No... no. I said a few unkind words. At the time, he said that I should have supported, not ridiculed him. He asked me what was going on in my brainless mind—his words. Outraged and hurt, I snatched his glass, full from another round of *jenever*, and threw it against the wall."

A keen understanding about where this revelation was going shook Charlotte. "He retrieved a piece of the glass?"

Julia nodded, again rubbing at the spot on her chest. "He said that since I broke his drink glass, that I should be broken a bit more as well and cut me with a shard of glass. He's done this before—cut me with glass—and he'll probably do it again. If he ever comes home."

"What did Luuk mean when he said you should be a bit more broken?"

"All the troubles he has are not of his own making, don't you understand? Other people cause his problems. And since I live in his house, it's my fault and he must try his best to correct me, for all our sakes." She squeezed her eyes shut, then opened them. "My misdeed that night, my choosing to behave shamefully, carried consequences."

"You broke a glass. It's not like you purposely set the house on fire." Charlotte eyed Julia from head to toe, then sat beside her. What other physical and emotional scars did this woman conceal? "Has he cut you elsewhere? Hurt you in other ways?"

"Sorry." Julia palmed the sides of her head. "I can't talk further about this tonight... maybe never."

"If you believe this foolishness, you'll never be free to enjoy life."

Slowly, Julia peered up and into Charlotte's eyes. "In my husband's absence, I've grown more confused and uncertain what to believe. Besides, what difference would it make? There's not one thing you can do or say that will change him."

Charlotte gave in to a little grin teasing her lips. "But it's not Luuk I'm interested in helping to change. Here's the thing about me, Julia. I help others, especially kind souls. And I won't accept a no. I want to help you become the strong and beautiful person that I know you are."

Julia lifted a brow. "Despite the potential consequences?"

"Especially despite negative consequences."

25

27 March began as a typical Saturday, or as typical as a Dutch citizen not wanted by the Nazis could appreciate in the year 1943. As Julia took care of Ada in her bedroom, Ani and Marianne played in the parlor, their tones hushed but content despite the delay in breakfast. They were such good girls. Since their sister's arrival, the girls didn't act out in jealousy or resentment or demand more of her time. If they had, Julia would have been uncertain how to offer them more attention with a newborn to care for. If she wanted to truly ruin her relative peace, she could work herself up in a tizzy if she thought further about Luuk. Ever since Charlotte and she spoke about how she'd gotten the scar on her chest from her husband, she'd worked on ending her fantasy of Luuk as a doting father. She was still unsure how to grasp the other extreme—his temperament—that could easily ignite like dry kindling. She thanked her lucky stars that he wasn't around these days. At this point, she couldn't care less that he was serving his country. If indeed his patriotic duty was the truth. It was best not to think about him. All that counted was his absence, from her, and from his children.

What failed to appear normal that given moment—that was,

the new normal—was the lack of hearing Charlotte's voice. Often, her friend spent the early mornings chatting with the girls before beginning her job search. Although Charlotte never complained about the Nazi mandate that all abled-bodied citizens needed to work longer hours, Julia wondered about the little effort Charlotte was putting into applying for work. Yet, it wasn't her place to encroach on her friend's privacy, and she refrained from inquiring. As for her own work circumstances, the one good thing Luuk had overseen before he departed was to reverse his thoughts on her working outside the home. With a firm decision that Julia needed to care for their young children, he had made last-minute arrangements to ensure that Julia would be exempted from working. She hadn't taken advantage of that status until she'd lost her job at the bakery, courtesy of Henk, and discovered that she was expecting Ada. Since she'd revealed a little about Luuk and his ways with her to Charlotte, Julia had been the one to distance herself from Charlotte, and for a good reason: if she pressed Charlotte to tell more about her past life, she should expect to reciprocate with the truth of her own past, including the past few years married to Luuk. All of it. She wasn't ready. There was a good possibility she may never be. That was the price of concealing for years the truth about how weak and pitiful she was. After hiding under thick layers of false identity, she couldn't stand up for herself because she'd forgotten who she was and what made her unique. But forgetting, not dwelling on the past, was good. It was safer that way. For all.

There was an oddity about this near-spring morning with its teasing brilliant sunshine and the singsong of birds chirping happily flowing in through the open window. All of this brought a sense of normality, despite the war, despite people killing for the right as well as the wrong reasons, despite her chaotic household life. She couldn't quite pin it down, though. With Ada dressed for the day in a hand-me-down outfit of Marianne, she gathered the baby in her arms and bent closer and smiled, glowing with joy when Ada smiled back. "I love you, baby girl. Let's go check on your sisters. They might know Tante Charlotte's whereabouts." As soon as she'd uttered her housemate's name, and referred to her for the first time as the children's aunt, Julia shuddered with a realization that burned a hole inside her: she was more concerned about Charlotte and whether she'd return, than she was about her husband.

"Mama," Marianne said as Julia walked into the parlor. The smiling child lifted the big doll that she shared with her sister. "Look. We're playing nicely." She gave Annelise a quick sideways glance. "Right, Ani?"

Annelise nodded. "I wish Charlotte was here. She likes to play tea with our babies and us."

Babies. Julia sat on the sofa near the girls, poised to clap Ada's hands and sing the traditional Dutch nursery rhyme of *Witte Zwanen, Zwarte Zwanen*, a song about a white and a black swan. The song's words about wondering who might sail to England with her never reached her mouth. Was that foreign country across the North Sea not far from the shores of the Netherlands, safer and fuller of saner folks enjoying a normal life? A flash of a memory of a woman whipped past her. The stranger wore a Jewish star and trotted at a good clip as she pushed a white and navy baby buggy that looked leftover from the Great War days. Julia had seen this same look on many people, an expression of sharp lines. At the time, Luuk had tried to explain that the woman's six-pointed star had to be sewn onto the clothes of all Jews, worn on the left side at chest height. "See, my dear," Luuk had said while looking deep into her eyes with a delighted smile on his lips. "This is for security's sake. We're being protected against these worthless occupants of our country. Thankfully, the Nazis are acting on our behalf to safeguard us." When she'd asked Luuk about which official carried out this decree and whether he mattered to her husband, he shook his head slowly as if tsk-tsking a child. "He's the Netherlands' representative of Heinrich Himmler, and I had the honor of being introduced to him during that last meeting I had with Seyss-Inquart. Need I say more?" At least she didn't have to indulge his belittling attitude further by asking about Himmler—one of the Nazis' household names.

But it was the conversation she'd had with Charlotte one late evening only a week ago when they both couldn't sleep that had made her think long and hard about Jewish mothers and their babies. They were sitting on the sofa, sipping weak tea and nibbling the last of the cheese Mila had brought over earlier. They were talking about motherly things. One topic led to another, and the subject of babies brought to Julia's mind the sighting of that Jewish woman she'd seen with the baby carriage. She shared this with Charlotte. She then relayed what Luuk had said about the Jewish star badges and how their own safety was more certain now that one could easily distinguish Jews because of these stars. When she added that Luuk had emphasized that one day and hopefully soon they would no longer have to think twice about Jews, Charlotte dropped her gaze to her lap.

"Julia," Charlotte had said, "for the purpose of conversation, let's put aside the social debate of Aryans versus non-Aryans. If you were born to Jewish parents rather than Roman Catholic, grew up and fell in love with a Jewish man and had a baby, wouldn't you want the best for that child?"

"Of course," Julia snapped. As if an insult had been hurled at her, she'd flushed apple red. Perhaps her reaction stemmed more from shame than guilt, though the two feelings were nearly always connected. It wasn't the first time that Julia had thought about that reverse situation that Charlotte had posed and of its implications that left her questioning her own humanity.

Now, before her daughters, she hugged Ada close to her breast, the surge of maternal desire to love all her children multiplying within her heart. To love all children, no matter their faith or race? Could she dare? With the image of that Jewish woman wearing the star in her mind, and Luuk's sly rebuke, and Charlotte's question replaying in her ears, Julia sucked in a deep breath. She glanced at Ani and Marianne. Her girls were alive, healthy, beautiful, and so innocent, and yes, as innocent as that baby in the carriage that had no comprehension of the hardships their mommy faced solely due to the Nazis.

"Girls, did you see Charlotte this morning? Or was she already gone when you came out here to play?"

"We stopped her when she opened the door," Annelise said. "We told her not to go."

Marianne shook her head. "We told her to never go because this is her home."

"So, she is here?" Julia looked about the room. "I don't see her."

"Mama, is this a new game?" Marianne giggled. "She's gone."

"Oh, dear. Did she say where she was going or what she was going to do?"

Both girls faced each other, their brows lifted in question. Julia thought she'd made herself clear that it was unsafe for Charlotte to wander the Amsterdam streets alone, especially if she wasn't heading to a job or on a specific errand. Although she had her identity papers on her at all times, this was an early weekend morning and she'd be seen as a suspicious woman. Not good. "Let's get the three of you girls off to Tante Mila's. I want to catch up with Charlotte."

Marianne pulled at her bottom lip. "Is she in trouble?"

"I'm sure she's fine." Lately, Julia wasn't able to determine what qualified as fine. "Please, let's hurry."

With bicycles and cycling prohibited by the Nazis, Julia proceeded by foot to Plantage, where Charlotte had told her she used to work. Since Charlotte had not too long ago packed clothes in a valise with the intent of bringing them to her former place of employment, Julia reasoned she might have headed that way this morning. She must find Charlotte before harm came her way, and she also needed to think of what she'd say if stopped by officers or the SS demanding an explanation as to why she was outdoors and by herself. *I need to feel the sunshine on my back, officer.* During these times of war? *I need the exercise.* She could, of course, use her lucky card and inform the officers who her husband was and how much he—and she—were devoted to the Nazi Party, hoping she wouldn't stutter when it came to mentioning her own degree of support. Whatever she said, she couldn't utter the truth: that she took the risks of venturing outdoors for the sole purpose of finding her friend—the only friend she had, when she stopped to think about it—before harm came to her. To do so would bring unneeded attention to Charlotte, something that Julia didn't want.

Was this war truly a necessity? Did all non-Aryans and political protesters need to be put in their place—just like Luuk had told her? While her thoughts went up and down, one constant was her wish that the bloodshed and the perpetual worry over who was watching her every step would end. With summer on its way, all she wanted to dream about was slipping on her favorite blue cotton dress that she could wear to the park when she brought Annelise, Marianne, and Ada to soak up the day's warmth. They'd watch men, women, and children on their bicycles, pumping their tires at a leisurely pace and taking the time to wave and smile at others. When hungry, she'd unpack a heavenly full picnic basket stuffed with assorted cheeses, meats, biscuits, and lots of healthy fruits. A little candy treat would be packed secretly on the bottom, only detected once their lunch would be gobbled up. And who knows—Charlotte might still be living with them. How splendid her company would be on that most beautiful day.

"*Halt houden!*"

Julia looked up to see where the German-accented Dutch command came from—an SS officer. She obeyed and stopped walking. Unsure of what to do with her hands—raise them above her head in surrender as if guilty of a crime or keep them by her sides, surely not cover her pounding heart—she compromised by lifting them slightly by her sides, showing she was unarmed.

"Identity card."

Without hesitation, she slipped a hand into her skirt pocket and withdrew the requested papers. Aware that she had nothing to worry about, she couldn't help but swallow dryly while the officer studied the paperwork that stated that she was a Dutch citizen, and noted that there was no black capital *J* stamped on both sides of the card to indicate that she was a Jew.

The uniformed and notably armed officer handed her back the card and advised her to move along without delay. She thanked him, hurried on. She reached Plantage and turned left onto Plantage Kirklaan. Adjacent to the entrance of the Artis Royal Zoo, in front of the civil registry office housed in a former concert hall, stood Charlotte. By herself, she appeared on a stroll rather than a mission. Good. Unlike the stories circulating about town of men and women working underground to topple the Nazis in the Netherlands, Julia never thought her housemate would be one of those resistance-women fighting on behalf of the Jews. The last thing Julia wanted was to learn that Charlotte wasn't the woman she claimed to be.

Julia's arrival here—essentially to spy on Charlotte—was oh so wrong. What had she been thinking all this time? About to leave the poor woman to her privacy, Julia turned to dash away before Charlotte could see her. Too late.

"Julia?" Charlotte smiled despite arched brows of surprise. "Is everything good at home? Are the children—"

"We're all fine," Julia said, her tone laden with the clumsy punctuation of deceit. "They're with Mila. Are you out on a walk, like me? Lovely day."

Charlotte straightened her purse strap on her shoulder. "Yes, but it's a long walk to Plantage for you."

Julia could say those exact words back to Charlotte, but resisted. "This morning, when the girls asked for you, considering the circumstances we're all facing, I thought I should look for you. Remembering what you said about once working in a Plantage nursery, I got as far as the zoo, where, fortunately, I found you."

"I was hoping to find an old friend or two." Charlotte's stare skipped about. The poor woman. No doubt she was haunted by her memories of her lost family. She tapped her left index finger on her bottom lip. "No, that's not true. It's just that I see them all the time here in Plantage."

"If not your friends, who? Your husband? Your daughters?"

"Yes. Their images in my mind become real in this neighborhood. It's like I see Edith and Krista walking together and talking... laughing. That's why I came here—my girls loved this zoo. They adored the elephants. And then there's my husband, who also appears. I see him often leaning against a post. He motions for me to come nearer so he can whisper to me. He used to do that all the time... get me to come over to him as if he had a great secret to share only to then pull me into his arms and say over and over again that he loves me, each time louder, oblivious to who might listen." Charlotte sighed, more dreamily than distraught. "Do you think I'm silly?"

"Not at all. Family is a constant, always with us whether in life or death." Julia gasped. "Forgive me. I didn't mean to bring up missing family members. When I stop and think about it, that's why I hear Luuk singing his silly songs in his rich, vibrant voice and why I accept his invitation to dance with him while only I can hear him humming in my ear. I choose to dwell on the positive times spent with him. I need to do this so I can continue on." She leaned back, alarmed over her dizzying thoughts about her husband. Did she love him or hate him? "We should return home before trouble finds us. We can talk then if you like."

"Yes, good idea." Charlotte remained rooted in place. "Did you run into anyone during your search for me?"

"An SS officer stopped me and asked for my identity card. Though my paperwork was checked and he deemed it fine, his questioning unnerved me."

"How frightening. I should have remembered your advice about being out on the streets by myself. The last thing I want to encounter is an officer and endure an interrogation."

Julia gestured with a sweep of a hand toward the direction that would lead them both to her beloved Jordaan home, a place she appreciated more and more. "Shall we go home?"

26

After hours of tossing and turning, Charlotte stumbled from her cot and padded barefoot into the parlor. As dangerous as it was, yesterday she'd come so close to strolling through the zoo in the foolish hope of visiting and thinking about the memories of her dear Kurt and precious Edith and Krista. With each day apart from her family, it was becoming harder to see their faces in her mind, to hear Kurt's deep voice or the girls' laughter that always reminded her of a blue-sky and flower-blooming spring day. The question of where Kurt might be—whether he was living, either freely or hiding in another country—and whether their daughters were safe in hiding and their new uncles and aunts were treating them well, only made her more heartsick. Should she mourn their absence or look forward to the day they'd be reunited? She wanted to do the latter, to be of good and optimistic cheer. But on her own and incredibly lonely, despite living with Julia and her children, despondency often came to visit. Some mornings were more difficult to manage; others were a breeze. This morning, awakening before the others, she'd march into the kitchen to see what she could cook up for breakfast. Although these days, with food rations in place, choices were few and they ate what they could. Even Marianne and Annelise had stopped whining about a heartier breakfast, a midday snack, and sweet desserts. Poor darlings.

"Charlotte!"

She turned to see Marianne at the kitchen's entrance. Her sister, Ani, as the older child preferred Charlotte to call her, was adorable in her own way, but it was Marianne who stole her affections. Ani's independence set a boundary of sorts between them. With her bubbly personality and her golden ringlets, Marianne reminded Charlotte of her curly-haired Krista when she was Marianne's age and made Charlotte more tender toward the child. "Yes, sweetheart?"

Marianne placed a hand on each hip; a serious expression pushed aside her usual smile. "Are you going to eat breakfast without me?"

"I'd love your company! Want to be my big helper?" Charlotte extended a hand. "Let's see what we can stir up and surprise Mama and your sisters."

"Let's not wake them up. It's nice just you and me."

"You're a sweetheart!" Charlotte took the little girl's hand and guided her around the corner toward the table. A loud pounding came to the front door. Both Marianne and she jumped, then looked at each other quizzically. She told the child to stay put as she asked for the caller's identity at the door.

"It's me—Liam." Mila's husband—Luuk's brother. Whereas she liked Mila, her guard went up around Liam despite Liam always treating her well. It was the association with his brother that made her uneasy. Yet, since this wasn't her house and Liam was Julia's family, she opened the door and greeted him.

"Would you like me to wake Julia?" she asked.

"Yes, without delay." Liam walked in and stood with his hands behind his back. Charlotte was aware that his hands had been badly injured and that he self-consciously tended to hide the mangled stump of his left hand, as well as his right that fortunately had an intact thumb and fourth finger, though the others were gone. But the way he'd positioned himself came off as intimidating, as if he concealed a weapon behind his back.

"I'm awake," Julia called from behind them. She signaled for Marianne to come to her side and eyed her brother-in-law. "I was just waking up when I heard your knocking. What's wrong, Liam? Is it Mila?"

"We're both fine. I came here to caution you to not to step a foot outdoors on this miserable day, as well as tomorrow. We'll have to wait to see what happens."

Julia cinched her bathrobe tighter. "What news is this that you're tiptoeing around?"

"There was a raid last night at the Population Registry in Plantage, the building adjacent to the Artis Zoo."

"Yes, I'm familiar with the Registry." Julia glanced at Charlotte. Her words—*do not reveal that we were just there yesterday*—were unnecessary to say aloud. Charlotte heard each one without a struggle. "Why is this a concern of ours over here in Jordaan?"

"Mila says I'm overreacting, but I don't think so." Liam shut the front door and leaned against it. He narrowed his gaze hard on Charlotte in a way she'd never experienced. She held her ground and didn't flinch. "It's believed that members of a resistance group led by Willem Arondéus dressed up in police uniforms faked a search, injected a sedative into each person in the office, dragged them into the zoo, and then set fire to the cabinets containing files of important lists of people's names and other documentation all showing Aryan-condemned religious and political persuasions. A good deal was lost, but not as much as they probably had hoped. Those idiots may be on the run, but imagine what's going to happen when they're caught like the dirty rats they are?" Liam shifted his gaze toward Julia. "There's always the chance a Nazi patrol may search house to house to find these men. And who knows what a few offered guilders for one's cooperation will bring out. Listen to me carefully—I know Luuk well enough to say confidently that he'd want safety for you and your children. You must stay put." He cast Charlotte another look. "And you might want to stay inside as well. Understand?"

Charlotte nodded. What else could she do—say she hoped these resistance people escaped without capture, punishment, or other repercussions? Say that as a Jew, she would pray for their safety and success for future resistance endeavors? That if she could, she'd be more than happy to provide them shelter? "Yes, Liam. I understand."

As soon as Liam left, Julia locked the door and released a long sigh. She bent over to tousle Marianne's hair and asked her to wake her sleepyhead sister Ani for breakfast. Once the girl trotted out of the room, she faced Charlotte. "Do you think anyone saw us yesterday while we walked home and suspected we were part of this group?"

Charlotte's heart squeezed; her shoulders tightened. She willed herself to stand straight, to carry a look of nonchalance. "It's not safe for anyone, though not being Jewish or politically active counts highly on our behalf. The truth is, we certainly did not do anything wrong. We weren't aware of this group or their plan."

"You're right. The two of us will carry on as we've been doing all along during this stressful time." Julia glanced about the foyer with its plain pine table and matching hat tree. "I'm going to change into day clothes. Check on the baby. Then I'll meet you in the kitchen."

"I'll see what I can scrounge up for a breakfast feast." Charlotte expected Julia to give a curt nod and head toward her room, not to stay in place and to stare at her. "Julia?"

"It's getting so difficult."

Charlotte knew the answer to the question she was about to ask, but from the need to have another woman—another mother—validate her own thoughts, she continued. "What is difficult?"

"This putting on our masks of life-is-fine for our children's sake." Julia's breath hitched. "I'm sorry. I didn't mean—"

Charlotte raised her hand to pause her. "I understand. If my own daughters were beside me, I too would have my share of concerns."

"Suggestions?"

"As you say, my friend. We must carry on, positive in spirit, for the sake of our children, whether our own or all the innocent little ones suffering or in danger."

Four days after the registry building was raided by the resistance, the city of Rotterdam was again bombed. This time, it resulted in 401 casualties. Ten days later, more than 85 percent of the Dutch students refused to pledge loyalty to Nazidom. And the next day, Sunday 11 April, Charlotte returned to the house after dropping off Annelise and Marianne next door at their aunt's. Now that the search for the resistance members responsible for the raid two weeks ago had simmered down in the Jordaan neighborhood, she and Julia were free to shop for badly needed groceries and supplies. Whether or not they could find daily staples was a different matter. Charlotte entered the kitchen through the side door and heard an unfamiliar male voice. Instead of telling Julia they were ready to shop, she leaned against the doorjamb, listening to this new person while ignoring her pounding heart.

"After all this time, Julia, you haven't a smile for me?"

"Of course, I do—I wasn't expecting you home, that's all."

"And why's that, darling? If you weren't expecting your husband, then who were you hoping to see?"

Luuk had come home! Possibilities and scenarios raced through Charlotte's mind: She could turn, retrace her steps through the door she'd just entered and run and run and run from this house. Or she could stay and make sure this husband of Julia's won't hurt her. Acting on pure instinct, she pulled a kitchen drawer open as quietly as she could manage, grabbed the meat cleaver that hadn't been used since she'd arrived—there hadn't been meat to cut. Then she slipped into the walk-in pantry to hide. She pushed her way toward the back but not so far that she wouldn't be able to continue to hear the conversation through the wooden door she'd left open a crack.

"Don't be silly, Luuk. I wasn't expecting anyone. And I'm happy to see you again. Really, I am. It's just that I haven't heard from you in an awfully long time. I had no idea where you were, what you were doing... if you were hurt in combat. Are you home for good?"

"Do you want me to be?"

"Yes, definitely. I've missed you."

"Is that so? You sound defensive for a lonely wife who misses her husband."

"Please, Luuk. You must believe me."

"Then it's time for you to believe me as well. Time to stop doubting me—"

"Ouch! That hurts."

"Then stop squirming away from me—I'm just hugging you. It's been a long time since you've been in my arms."

"It's just that... you kind of grabbed me a bit firmly and dug your fingernails into my arms."

"What are you talking about? I touched you. Why are you making a fuss? Why are you so schoolgirl-shy with me all of a sudden?"

"Sorry. I don't mean to upset you. I guess I've become unfamiliar with your ways. I've missed you, Luuk. It's been more than a year since we've seen each other. It's been so scary lately."

"Well, here I am, on a short afternoon break from helping the Führer's cause. I won't be able to stay home, though. I'll tell you why, but first tell me—where are my lovely daughters? I want to see them, want to hear them shout Papa again."

"Let me get you a drink first."

Within her hiding place in the pantry, Charlotte ordered herself to stay still. Not an easy task, not when Julia's words from not too long ago clattered in her memory. Luuk had told her that she deserved discipline, that she needed constant reminding of how to behave correctly as a wife. Yet, he'd been away from his family fighting for the Nazis. If she were to see his ugly face, she probably had enough disgust seething in her veins to spit in his face, a detriment—certainly not a boon—for either Julia or herself, especially if he discovered her Jewish faith and heritage. Her stomach twisted. What had happened to her desire for everyone in this world to respect one another? She knew the answer: she couldn't respect anyone, let alone a belief system that dehumanized other human beings for having varying faiths and interests and that wanted these people harmed, annihilated. What Hitler was propagating was far more than just his personal opinion. That was why her beloved Kurt had gone missing; why she put her own daughters into hiding; why she took on the name of Charlotte and hid in clear sight in—what she was discovering was—a Nazi-loving home. And right now, Luuk, a Hitler follower, stood under the same roof as her. In an attempt not to cry out loud, Charlotte pressed a finger against her mouth and continued listening to the conversation between Julia and her husband.

"Julia, what's happening here? First, you act skittish around me, and then you're keeping mum about Annelise and Marianne—my daughters. Are you hiding another man—a lover?"

"No. Honestly, don't think twice about that. There's no one else."

"Well then, after all this time apart, I thought you'd think about me and about how to improve things between us. You must always support me and never ridicule me. Or do you need a reminder, my dear?"

"No, please… let go of me."

"What? You don't like me holding you nice and tight against my chest like a good husband should hold…" He swore. "Stop resisting me. Or is this some sort of romantic game? I too can play—easily!"

"You're right, Luuk. I didn't mean to upset you. You're finally home after what must have been a grueling time of stress and hardship. I'd love to hear about what you've encountered on the front."

"I can't tell you about battles on any fronts. I only came home long enough to say hello, to say I love you, hoping to hear those same words from your lips—not to receive your cold shoulder."

"I do love you. Please don't doubt me. I'm just confused. This short visit of yours—is that why you're not wearing your uniform?"

"There is no damn uniform! Never was. I must be a sorry sight for your eyes."

"I didn't say that. Let's sit on the sofa, Luuk. We have a lot of catching up to do." A moment of silence followed Julia's invitation, and Charlotte figured they were moving into the parlor.

"Julia, let's go into the kitchen instead. You can fetch me that drink you offered. A *jenever* would be nice. I can use it."

Charlotte closed the pantry door and shoved as far back as possible.

"Luuk, wouldn't you be more comfortable in the other room—on your favorite chair with your feet up on the ottoman?"

Instead of a reply, a squeak came. "Why is the back door open?"

"Goodness. I must have left it open after bringing the girls next door. Silly me." The door banged shut. "Sit. Relax, honey. You sound tired. I'm sorry for any misunderstanding between us. I'm just a little anxious."

"Come sit on my lap. I miss holding you."

"If you don't mind, let me sit at the table, across from you, so I can concentrate better."

"You can concentrate on me. I'd like that."

"Luuk, please, tell me about the missing uniform. You said there never was one? I don't understand. I saw you wearing one with my own eyes. I saw you strip free of it that last night when we made love. Tell me. I want to understand what has happened to you so I can tell you my own news. Exciting news—news you will enjoy hearing."

"Ah, it's so nice to hold your hand again. Soft and tender, just as I remembered. Just as I had dreamt about all these past months without you."

"Luuk—"

"I never joined the German army. Never was part of the SS or any service for Hitler. They didn't want me. I didn't want them."

"I don't understand. I saw your uniform with my own eyes."

"There are lots of things I don't understand. Things I no longer take trouble over. Things I can't tell you about. Things I won't tell you about. Don't push me. You might not like what will happen."

"But you've sent money home through your brother. Does that mean Liam knew all this time and that he has been lying to me as well?"

"Liam's done exactly what I've requested of him. No holding grudges against him—understand. If it wasn't for my brother, I doubt your pretty little self would have survived as well as you have."

"Oh, I have my own way of handling things. I've changed since you left me. I had no choice." Still within the pantry, Charlotte sucked in breath hoping Julia wouldn't become careless and mention her. "Let's move this conversation back to you. Tell me what you've been up to."

"Why? So that you can stop imagining me as a hero fighting on behalf of the Nazi cause? To help bring a golden lifestyle to the Netherlands? I didn't abandon our marriage. Didn't abandon our children. I had no choice but to join the forces to secure this country from a bunch of worthless non-Aryans."

"Luuk, I never said you—"

"No need to voice what's written all over your face."

"If you believe in Nazism but never joined their ranks, then where have you been? Why weren't you fighting in combat?"

Raucous laughter exploded.

"You're laughing at me, your wife?"

"Shut up, Julia." He laughed more. "Let your exhausted husband laugh. This conclusion of yours—that no uniform means no Nazi support—is the funniest thing I've heard in a long, long time." Luuk and Julia kept silent. After a minute or so, phlegmy hawking filled the awkward gap. "Are you going to fix me a meal to go with that drink that has yet to materialize?"

"That's the funniest thing I've heard in a while." Julia didn't laugh. "Where have you been all this time? Most households don't have food, and if they do, there's little variety." Footsteps. A clunk. "Here's a glass of water. Enjoy!"

"You're right—you've changed. It makes you sexier."

Again, Julia kept quiet.

"Don't look at me that way. All right. I'll tell you my story with the happy ending, but I need to shorten it because I'm expected at a meeting. As I said, I never joined the army, which means I never helped to build the West Wall or fight on the eastern Soviet front only to freeze my butt off. I'd borrowed the SS uniform to impress you—what I don't need from you are suspicions and doubts. Here's good news—I ran into an old friend who introduced me to a fellow by the name of Wim Henneicke. Ever heard of him?"

"Can't say I have."

"Good. Forget that name and everything I'm about to tell you. The less you know, the better we all will be. Wim started up a group, and I've joined forces with him. Simply put, I'm doing exactly what I hoped to do under the worthless Seyss-Inquart—I'm hunting down and trapping Jews, all of whom have a nice bounty on their miserable heads."

A scrape of what sounded like a chair dragged against a wooden floor reached Charlotte. She then heard Luuk tell Julia to sit back down.

"Stop looking so shocked, Julia. You and I have both been supportive of the Nazi movement. We're both opposed to the Jews and believe they need to be controlled—not the other way around. What? Are you going to tell me you've had a change of heart? That you actually care about this group of non-humans? That you are more than eager to stand on a soapbox and preach love and good-will for all?" He snorted a mocking laugh. "Are you going to tell me that you've taught our daughters to respect and cherish Jews, Gypsies, and homosexuals? Or the mentally disturbed, for that matter. Forget it. I don't care what you think. Just tell me where Ani and Marianne, my little darlings, are. I want to see them before I leave."

"You can't, Luuk. You shouldn't. They're next door at Mila's because I needed to search for food. Both girls are sick from the chickenpox."

Chickenpox? Charlotte wondered why Julia was lying, but she trusted her. Well, at least she wanted to trust her, though after hearing Luuk call Julia a hater of Jews, she wondered who exactly she'd been living with. As for Luuk, the Jew-hating bastard that she'd suspected him to be all along, she definitely didn't trust him.

"You need to be careful, Luuk, since you haven't had the pox—I understand it's quite bad for adults to endure."

"No worries. I won't go near them, much to my regret."

"As for me, don't concern yourself over my beliefs and alliances. You know fully well where I stand on what Hitler wants. I know he wants the best for my native country."

"Why are you staring at the clock, Julia? Nervous?"

"Take my hand. Let's go to the bedroom... Luuk! Wipe that silly grin off your face. I just want to show you our new daughter, Ada."

"Our..."

"Yes, a new baby girl! She was your farewell gift to me from our last night together before you left. Ada is healthy, adorable, looks like you, and is a true blessing."

"Another child to feed? I've wanted a son for the longest time..."

"Luuk? Why are you so disappointed with having a new baby daughter, with me? We both know how babies are created and can't control whether it's a girl or boy. Why can't you be happy for us?"

"You're right. How are you? Are you well after..."

"The pregnancy? Yes. Thank you. And the birth wasn't as laborious as the past two deliveries. Ada is a joy and I love our little darling. Her sisters adore her as well."

"While I have no misgivings about leaving for the reasons I did, I'm sorry I haven't been here for you and the baby."

"You did what you had to do, right? And you should have no regrets—as you just said. So, that's that." The sounds of low heels clicked on the floor. The pantry door opened a crack, just enough for Julia to reach inside. "Ada is asleep, or at least the last time I checked, in her crib in our bedroom. Judging by the time—which is why I was staring at the clock—our baby girl should be waking up about now, and I'd love for you to meet your new daughter. Speaking of which, I meant to grab detergent to wash her diaper, but I forgot." Julia groped for the bottle on a side shelf. "Found it. Let's go."

"Can Ada catch the pox from her sisters?"

"Yes. But you must trust me—that's why they're staying with Mila and Liam, who, fortunately for them as well as us, had the disease as children. And so have I. But you, my dear, haven't and must keep away from them."

"Yes, I hear what you're saying. Getting sick at this time is like a bullet to the head. God only knows the number of Jews left in Amsterdam that I need to get rid of. Let me see the baby, and then I'll hurry out. You won't take it the wrong way?"

"No. I understand your responsibilities better now. Come on, let's go see little Ada."

After they left the kitchen, Charlotte counted to 50. She then pushed open the pantry door. She assumed Julia had left it open for her, believing she must have come home through the side kitchen door and had hidden in the pantry since there was no other option. Without hesitation, Charlotte dashed through the same door she couldn't have waited to enter minutes ago. She ran through the neighbors' yards, meat cleaver tight in her grip.

27

Charlotte ran across a canal bridge and raced around two corners. She couldn't care less about who saw her and what they thought. She'd left behind the smattering of her personal belongings at Julia's house—a couple of blouses, a skirt, another pair of slacks, socks, and undergarments. None of it mattered. Her dignity, yes, that did matter. The one photograph of her family? Well, she'd regret that terribly. Always. Out of options, though, she'd fled from the Jew-hating house permanently. Never would she go back. That was when it hit her. Wobbly, she needed solitude and ducked into an alleyway. There, she leaned against the brick building, but more angst washed through her. Like a heavy cloud bursting open. Turmoil, not the relief she had hoped for, rained down upon her and soaked her from head to toe.

She squeezed her eyes shut, wishing the haunting images flooding her mind would dissolve and leave her with what was left of her sanity. The image of Kurt, when they had exchanged their last goodbyes and he'd left after telling her to close her eyes, was one she couldn't shake. This too had happened in an alleyway. What was the use of having hope? She should walk directly to a police department or a Nazi headquarters—if they weren't one and the same these days—raise her hands in surrender, declare that she was Jewish, and plead for them to put her into an internment camp, or worse. She'd lost her family. And just when she thought she was gaining a friend in Julia and seeing the promising shore of optimism on the horizon, she'd lost that too. There was no sense in fighting for your life when there is no reason to survive.

She jumped when someone tapped her on the shoulder. When she opened her eyes, she wished she hadn't.

"Thank goodness I found you," Julia said. "I've been looking all over for you."

"Where's your husband? Is he with you?"

"No. He took off, again, preferring to fight for his cause rather than to stick with his family. I put two and two together and knew you were hiding in the pantry and did my best to keep Luuk from discovering you. He wouldn't have understood why I'd let you come live with us and why I didn't ask his permission first, though how could I when he was away? I assumed you had a good reason to hide from him and I tried to protect you." Julia sighed. "I'm babbling like a little girl. Sorry. That man of mine unnerves me at times. At least I found you. When I stopped an older woman and described you to her, she said you ran into the alley between the barbershop and the shambles of what was once a fine cheese market."

Although Charlotte was thankful for the brick wall supporting her, she was sandwiched between the woman she'd run from and the building. She couldn't easily squirm out of Julia's sight. "Get away from me!"

"I can explain. Just hear me out."

"Why? It's quite clear—at least to me—that your husband controls you. I fear he is abusing you, and I'd hoped to help you, but you've neglected to mention that he was a Nazi and that you too support Hitler."

"Why would you assume that about me, and why would that matter to you? Apparently, it's not clear to you what was said between Luuk and me—the lies I told him, like Annelise and Marianne having chicken pox."

"What about Luuk's aggression toward you, or your personal beliefs? No wife deserves to be treated poorly by her husband. As for you being a Nazi follower, after hearing what you and your husband talked about, I'm horrified that you kept these beliefs from me. It makes me question our budding friendship; makes me question your respect for others. And if you have no respect for others—no matter what they believe in—I question how you could trust me or how we can be friends."

"I do trust you, Charlotte. But I also trust my husband. No. I trusted my husband. Past tense. I've done my share of pondering in his absence. He would be upset if he were to learn about the occurrences under our roof this past year. Right now, what's more shocking is your third-degree scrutiny toward me."

"I care about people. It makes no difference whether they're Jews, Christians, or what country they're from. As long as they treat others humanely, that is all that matters. Your husband showed a far different side than I'd hoped to see." Charlotte swore when Julia shifted and fingered a strand of hair that revealed a horizontal wound beside the top of her ear. From what she'd learned, this gash —mere centimeters from her left carotid artery—spelled life or death in a matter of seconds. "What is this? Another fresh cut? This wasn't here before I brought the girls to Mila's. Is it courtesy of your caring, adoring husband? Don't try to fool me by saying otherwise."

"Oh, this." Julia lifted her hand to the wounded area but didn't quite touch it. Although not freshly seeping in blood, Charlotte suspected it was tender to the touch. "Luuk doesn't know his own strength. He's like an excitable puppy at times, but with a mightier strike. He just grabbed me the wrong way, that's all."

"Are you aware of your own excuses and coverups for Luuk?" Disgusted, Charlotte shook her head and nicked her cheek against the brick. Blood trickled from the cut, and she winced.

"There," Julia said. "We two aren't different, after all. We both bleed."

"What are you talking about? My cut is from me being reckless, whereas yours is from the hand of your husband. Don't tell me it's a little bruise—that's an out and out wound. Good thing you didn't bleed to death! Tell me what this brute of yours did." Charlotte glared hard. "And tell me why you're living a life of denial."

"It's just his way."

"From the look of your watering eyes, I can tell you're not fond of his way."

"All right. I'll tell you." Julia stood taller, squared her shoulders, and set her jaw firmly. "This was Luuk's parting message for me as a reminder to be a good little wife while he's away. Fortunately, he waited until after he saw his baby daughter for the first time. Afterward, we walked back into the kitchen where I thought you were still hiding, and he insisted on having that *jenever* of his. He took one gulp, smashed the glass on the table and then cut me with a shard." She pulled back her sweater, and Charlotte noticed for the first time Julia's blood-splattered blouse. "He has always been up and down to the extreme when it comes to his emotions and anger. I should be used to his little reminders of how to be a good wife, but while he's been away, I've come to the conclusion that I can't tolerate him a minute longer. Nor do I want to try. Although, the guilt burning within me is quite unsettling." And just as Julia's anger had spewed out, she began to cry. Apparently, as she'd just intimated, she too rode the seesaw of up and down emotions. No wonder she and her husband had once been an inseparable pair.

Charlotte couldn't afford to gamble with Julia's oscillating state of mind. Her own life was at risk, especially if Luuk changed his plans and was combing the streets for his wife. Thinking she could flee from the upset woman, she ducked around her supposed friend and hostess.

Julia hooked her elbow. "Don't run from me. I need you."

"Let go of my arm, Julia."

"Why did you run from the house? You were safe there. Luuk wouldn't have gone into the pantry. Not when he expects me to wait on him. And why would you want to run from me? Friends don't do that. The bigger question is why were you hiding in the pantry? So what if Luuk had found you? It's not like you were a thief or a murderer? Even Luuk understands my right to have friends. And for heaven's sake, you're Dutch and have the documentation showing you're Aryan and have a right to live here." Slack-jawed, Julia crossed her arms. "Are you indeed who you claim to be?"

"You say you need me, then let's talk about you. You're married to a controlling monster. He makes a great Nazi, Julia. When exactly were you going to tell me that little fact about your husband? Or for that matter, when were you going to mention that you too are a Nazi supporter?"

"I didn't think that mattered to you, especially since you were desperate and needed a place to stay. And I figured since you weren't wearing a Jewish star and were enjoying walking about in relative freedom without looking nervously over your shoulder to see who was watching, that you too sided with the German occupiers and just didn't bother voicing your opinion. But, after Luuk's visit and hearing from his own mouth about what and who he sides with, why would you ask such questions? You aren't Jewish, are you?" Julia slapped a hand over her mouth. "I didn't mean to sound so… so—"

"Antisemitic? Hater of all non-Aryans? The thing is, you're embarrassed. Apologetic in asking those questions. If you were truly a Jew-hater, your guilt wouldn't be so obvious. What difference should it make? You either like me for who I am and go against the ideology of a sadistic tyrant and madman or continue to take the side of your husband who worships this nut in Germany. But considering the admissions to your husband about Nazism that I heard with my own ears back at your house, apparently, you hate Jews as well. As far as my faith, beliefs, and origins go, they're my business and don't need your approval."

"Come home with me, Charlotte. I'll explain. I promise Luuk isn't there. I doubt I'll see him for a while, if ever again."

"From the sound of it, despite his inability to treat you kindly, your husband treasures you. And for the life of me, because I don't understand it, you love him despite his abusive aggression. Believe me, that's not how husbands should cherish their wives." She calmed her choppy breathing to push out a bigger concern of hers. "How are you certain that Luuk won't be waiting there after all, or for that matter, won't visit?"

Julia stepped closer toward Charlotte. "There are certain things one should not say outside of one's home. I can tell you more once we return. That is if you trust me?"

"Do you trust me? I haven't answered your question about my background."

"Charlotte, it's like you say—what you truly are shouldn't matter to me, especially if we're friends. I value your friendship. It's my husband I'm having mixed feelings about." She stared at Charlotte's hands. "Who were you prepared to use my meat cleaver on?"

"On anyone coming after me with hatred glaring in their eyes."

Charlotte surrendered to the grin tugging at her lips. The woman across from her was tipsy—or worse. Thank goodness the children were next door.

Julia pushed aside her drained glass and smiled at it. "Drinking Luuk's beloved *jenever* behind his back is quite satisfying. Want another round, Charlotte? Charlotte... Charlotte. I wonder if that's your real name."

"I have plenty, thank you. You were going to tell me about why you are certain Luuk wouldn't be venturing home again. Odd, since he's your husband and this is his house."

"I'm so tired of him." Julia gulped down more of her *jenever*. "Tired of his orders to be quiet. No, that's not quite it. He told me to shut my worthless trap. That I never know what I'm talking about, that if it wasn't for him—and his fine German-Dutch family—that I'd be living on the streets or shacked up with a bum who dodged the Nazi call of duty."

"That he's said all this in disregard that you're his supposed beloved wife, mother to his children—three precious daughters you've cared for in his absence—is proof that he has no respect for you." Charlotte looked hard into Julia's eyes, silently ordering her friend to sober up, to think clearheadedly before it was too late to talk about their concerns. "Julia, Luuk's behavior—his aggression—toward you is sadly nothing new. From what you've said, I sense he's intimidated you to agree with his Nazi beliefs. Or, at least you chose to go along with the pretense of placating his anger." Julia averted her gaze, a sign that Charlotte might have finally hit a sensitive chord. She pressed on. "And from what I've heard with my own ears while I was tucked away in the pantry, he plays with your emotions just like how his own emotions must play havoc on himself. Yet, I can't help but wonder about the part you're leaving out."

"The part about Ada." Julia paled. "I was shocked when Luuk came home, but then I thought that if I introduced him to his new daughter, the good Luuk would be visiting, not the bad. See, I'm always thinking this way... how to play him as he plays me." She groaned. "I'm as bad as he is. I deserve his discipline—"

"No, you don't, Julia." When Julia remained quiet, Charlotte decided to nudge her to continue. "What happened when Luuk saw the baby?"

"He screamed at me. Accused our adorable dark-haired Ada as being another man's mongrel—his word, not mine—saying I cheated on him. He then said the unimaginable—he questioned whether Annelise or Marianne were also his children. I swore to him the honest truth, that I hadn't made love with any other man, that Annelise, Marianne, and Ada were his children. And then you know what else he said?"

There was more ugliness? "I can't imagine."

"He asked me if I lured Jews into bed with me for extra money." Charlotte gasped, but Julia continued. "That's when I dodged him—I'd wanted to steer him away from the baby—and rushed back into the kitchen. Silly me—I thought that if he had a drink, he'd relax enough to talk sensibly with me. So, I offered him the bottle of *jenever* and he grew more hysterical when he noticed that someone had been drinking the liquor. That's when he broke the bottle and cut me. That's when he threatened that if he ever learned the identity of our children's father—or fathers—that their lives might be in danger, if not mine. And that's when I told him to never come home again." She paused for a handful of seconds. "And Charlotte, that's the God-honest truth."

There had to be more to this matter than Julia was telling her. She had a hunch that soon Julia would tell her everything. Then again, to be fair, these days it was difficult to discern the truth from lies, whether the lies originated from callousness or from the need to cover up and survive. For a myriad of reasons throughout history, not all mothers had prioritized the welfare of their children. Fortunately, they were not the majority. Quite a lot of mystery remained around Julia; Julia certainly didn't know all about her. One thing about Julia—this woman who sat beside her, who had welcomed her into her home when there wasn't anywhere else to live, who fed her when there was a shortage of food, who didn't interrogate her upon her moving in—was that she wouldn't have fabricated a lie saying her husband threatened their children's lives. "I do believe you, Julia. I'm just sorry about the circumstances that have made me accept this truth. Throughout time, we women have been the stabilizer of relationships. Whether with our parents, our husbands, or friendships, we've sought neutrality. Oh, I'm sure there have been countless exceptions, but for the most part, we women are the peacemakers in relationships. However, that doesn't mean we should accept losing our dignity, let alone souls, to anyone who takes advantage of us. Husbands are no exceptions."

"Deep down in Luuk's jumbled mind, I'm certain he realizes that he's gone too far for too long and was wondering when I'd come around to challenge him." Julia lifted her fingers to her recent cut from her husband. "I can't take his violence anymore and told him that. And told him to keep away from me, his children, his house. He didn't protest or make another threat—just stormed out.

It's not like he signed an oath to keep away, but I believe he'll respect my wishes."

"For your sake, and your children's, I'm relieved that you're done taking chances on him. Yet, what will you do if Luuk comes back with apologies rolling off his tongue, with promises to love you and your daughters? These very well can be lies, again. He'll likely hurt you, both verbally and physically, starting the whole circular process once more. Lies are the calling card of abusive husbands. While society doesn't do much to protect women, it's women that need to protect themselves. And let's face it, this is his house and—"

"Honestly, since Luuk's surprise visit that just happened, I haven't thought about him coming home if he should decide not to honor my wishes." Julia stood and took her glass to the sink. "I'm not worried. He lives for Hitler. I doubt he'd be back soon, if at all. Luuk has no interest in his family or me. He wants to bump up the power ladder, and if he can't do it by the means of the army because they've rejected him, it comes as no shock that he found this Wim Henneicke—chief of bounty hunters, from what I gather." She sucked in an exaggerated gasp. "Oh, dear. Looks like I didn't forget this fellow's name, like Luuk ordered me to, after all. I'm a bad wife!"

Minutes ago, Charlotte wanted nothing more than to depart this house—away from Julia. Now, she leaned back, surprising herself that she was thinking twice about it. Julia had offered her a place to stay at a perilous juncture in her own life when she was without a family, without a home, without a promise of safety—no questions asked. Yet, she had hidden in the food pantry earlier out of fear of Luuk, because her instincts told her to take cover in the name of survival. She'd heard him speak about his hatred of Jews. And horrifyingly, she'd heard from Julia's mouth that she abided her husband, or at least, tolerated his beliefs. Then again, what woman who was abused both physically and emotionally by her husband wouldn't say or take precaution—especially within his presence—to keep him calm and from lashing out at her? That became a habit, and habits were difficult to break. "No, Julia. You're not a bad person, and certainly not a bad wife. After learning more about you, I'd say you are hurt and confused."

The yowling from one of the feral cats that roamed the neighborhood sailed through the kitchen window. Julia frowned. "That has to be one of the saddest sounds ever." Recognizing an intentional delay, Charlotte nodded and waited for Julia to continue. "The poor thing's homeless, like so many these days. You were homeless too, Charlotte, but not now. My home is your home. Would you like to tell me your real name? And who you really are, where you're from, and your religious beliefs?"

Charlotte couldn't deny that she wanted to like Julia and wanted to be her friend. Yet, she knew that if the woman sitting beside her couldn't—or wouldn't—accept her for who she was, that she'd leave this house immediately. Taking her chances on the streets of Amsterdam was as risky as staying under the Arzt roof.

The Singelgracht Canal. Papers dropping. An SS man fetching them. Luuk introducing himself with just his first name. It all flashed before her eyes as if it happened for the first time.

"Charlotte? What's wrong, dear? You look like you're about to pass out."

She struggled to her feet and gripped the edge of the table to prevent toppling over as more memories flashed before her eyes. She rubbed at her throat, at the bare spot where the butterfly necklace Kurt had made for her would have hung if it hadn't been stolen. "Julia, what color are your husband's eyes?"

28

"Luuk's eye color? Of all things, Charlotte. Why should you care?"

"Tell me the color of his eyes. Now."

Julia gestured for Charlotte to sit. "If Luuk's eye colors interest you that much..." She smiled, despite the strained conversation. "Ah, I just gave it away. My husband has different-colored eyes. His right eye is brown and his left is green. This may sound bizarre, but it does happen. I once found it quite attractive... once found several things about him appealing."

"Has he ever given you a butterfly necklace?"

As if she was wearing the necklace in question Julia grasped the bare spot on her neck. "Well, yes. A couple of years or so ago, he surprised me with a lovely necklace. The chain was rather plain, but that only accented the jewels and artistry of its butterfly pendant. Why do you ask?"

"Did Luuk say where he'd purchased it?"

She shook her head. "I tried to get it out of him, but he wouldn't tell me. At the time, I thought if I pumped him further, he'd turn against me... in his usual Luuk way that you're discovering. And I didn't want to cause tension between us because he'd made me feel like a queen with that gift—a rarity from him."

"May I see it?"

Julia sighed. Another thing she'd meant to do, but never got around to it. "I wish I could show it to you because it's so lovely and remarkable that I can only imagine it's a singular piece of art. But I can't show it to you because I'm uncertain where it is. You see, that gold chain that had poked your back that time you hid under Marianne's bed when someone knocked at the door and I told you to hide, is the one with the missing butterfly pendant. I suspect the girls had played with it and then hid it, not wanting me to find them fooling around with the jewelry I warned them not to touch. Tomorrow morning, after a night's sleep, I'll ask Annelise and Marianne what happened to the pendant."

Charlotte stood and rushed toward her bedroom. Julia, about to call out to her and ask what was happening, too confused and startled, surrendered the notion. It didn't matter—Charlotte darted back into the kitchen.

"Here!" Charlotte sat beside her again and unfurled her clenched hand.

The room swirled before Julia. She braced her hands on the table in hope to stop her dizziness. Before her was a dazzling piece of art in the shape of a butterfly pin. It matched her necklace exactly, gem by gem, color by color, and arrangement by arrangement. She gasped.

Charlotte glared at her. "Is this what your necklace, the one you're hesitating to show me, looks like?"

"Hold on there. You're upset, and though I fail to understand why, please don't take your frustrations out on me. My husband gifted me the necklace. It's not like he stole it from you. Julia narrowed her eyes. "Explain this sudden curiosity over my husband's appearance and a necklace."

"One day after work, before I met you, I was crossing one of the bridges and collided into a uniformed SS man. He said his name was Luuk. He distinctly had two different-colored eyes that matched the ones you just described to me."

"And the necklace?"

"My husband, before we left our native country, Germany—"

"So, you aren't Dutch by birth?"

"My husband made me this butterfly pin." Charlotte folded her fingers around the butterfly pin as if it had become alive, and she wanted to prevent it from flying away. "Right before Germany invaded the Netherlands, he'd come home, angry—which isn't like him—to tell me that the matching necklace he'd just finished was snatched by a man that he'd chased but to no avail."

"And this man your husband ran after, his eyes matched the colors of Luuk's eyes?"

Charlotte nodded. "Though… Helmut didn't know the thief's name. I cannot imagine that it is a coincidence."

When Charlotte had hesitated seconds ago, Julia suspected that she might have stumbled over her husband's real name. If so, what other truths was she hiding? Were they in Rotterdam when the bombing occurred and her husband and daughters were killed, or were they home, in Amsterdam, alive and comparatively safe? That was the trouble with lies—they had an awfully sneaky way of trapping a person further into the quagmire of more complex ruses without a way out. Ironically, she knew this from her own tales.

A cough came from the kitchen's entrance. Both Julia and Charlotte glanced up.

"I saw Luuk race out of the house and wanted to check on you," Mila said. "Sorry to interrupt. I'll leave."

Julia pointed to a chair. "No, please stay. I need your sanity and reason." She looked about. "Where are Ani and Marianne?"

"With Liam." Mila tugged at her loose-fitting blouse hanging over baggy slacks—a standard look these days. "They adore their uncle, and with his spellbinding storytelling, they're in no hurry to come home."

"Stop fidgeting and join us. The girls will be fine for a little while longer." Julia waited until Mila sat. Her poor sister-in-law was so nervous that she was making her uptight. If it weren't for the serious topic at hand, she'd march into the other room and turn on Luuk's radio in the hope of catching one of the schmaltzy cocktail tunes she adored. Instead, she looked at Charlotte, whoever she truly was, and then at her Mila. "Well, Charlotte had just informed me that a while back, her husband had crafted her this pin." She asked Charlotte to show Mila the piece of jewelry.

Mila gasped. "This butterfly is identical to your necklace!"

Julia murmured an *oh-God* under her breath. "Well, Charlotte, apparently Luuk had helped himself to this necklace in question when he shouldn't have. To be honest, I've wondered about where he acquired the money to purchase such a lovely gift for me. Back then, we were—still are—living modestly."

Charlotte jumped to her feet. "I beg you both to pretend you never saw me. I'll slip into the dark of night and disappear from your lives."

"What would that accomplish?" Julia grasped Charlotte's arm. "Stay. Before Mila came over, and before this unfortunate business about the butterfly necklace's origin arose, you had just said that you believed me, that you trusted me. Why this abrupt change?"

"Because I now know who your husband is. Not only have I heard Luuk admit his allegiance to Hitler, but I've seen him with my own eyes wearing that awful SS uniform on that canal bridge—"

"A uniform that he told me was borrowed and not his own."

"It doesn't matter. Your husband's a Jew-hater and, what's more, a Jew-hunter. If we should meet and he decides he doesn't like me, he could harm me at his whim and then take it out on you as well."

"Charlotte," Mila said, softly, framing her name in tenderness. "Julia and I have years together in family and friendship, far longer than you've known her. She's a good woman. In all honesty, you've modeled a higher example of humanity than she's ever seen from her husband. Consequently, Julia has changed—matured—for the better. She wouldn't be telling you half these things if she didn't trust you, or if she doubted her inclination that Luuk would not show his face for another visit."

Julia had been Julia Arzt, proud wife, mother, and native Netherlander and pretend Nazi Aryan for so long that when Mila's soft touch came to her arm, she couldn't keep the truth buried inside her any longer. She was relieved. "Charlotte, I want to tell you about a recent development that, in spite of Luuk's visit today, he's unaware of. I've sought counsel from our priest about divorcing Luuk."

"Divorcing Luuk?" Charlotte echoed. "I'm not Catholic, but it's common knowledge that the Church sees marriage as a sacrament that cannot be broken."

"Though oddities do happen," Mila added.

Julia couldn't help but notice that a slight grin twisted her sister-in-law's lips, as well as the little nod of agreement from Charlotte. "You're correct. Although his Reverence has expressed a desire to help me, divorce is an impossibility. He asked me to come back for further talks to learn about how I could please my husband and improve my marriage. I suppose in theory this would be the correct thing to do, but all the talk in the world won't change Luuk or his behaviors toward me." Julia touched her fresh cut and winced. "Actually, I'm getting desperate. I'm not as concerned about myself as I am about protecting my daughters and seeing them grow into fine and happy women."

"Well, you should be concerned about yourself as well," Mila said.

"Yes, I agree," Charlotte said. She turned toward Mila. "Does your husband know about his brother's aggression toward Julia?"

"No," Mila said without hesitancy. "Out of all their brothers, Liam is the closest to Luuk, yet keeps a certain respectable distance. I'm afraid that since his work injury that nearly killed him, my husband has also become a changed man in that he tends to let things slide a bit more than he used to."

"So, he turns a blind eye on Luuk—only sees the best in him?"

"That's Liam, all right."

"Does he also look away from his brother's political alliance?"

Mila coupled her hands on the table. "Although Liam is more open-minded than his brother, especially about different faiths and beliefs, we don't talk about politics. Whether it's the right moral thing to do or not, this omission of subject has become our way of coping with what's happening around us, and Liam's way of dealing with his pro-Nazi brother."

Charlotte straightened in her chair. "This woman-to-woman talk we're having is good, but why should I believe either one of you? Why should I stay a minute longer in this house and believe I'm safe when this place is owned by a man who abuses his wife? And if he should discover that I'm secretly living here, he could do more harm. I think it would be best if I were to leave."

Julia looked at Mila, who nodded her consent to speak for them both. "Let's just say that Luuk's mistreatment—"

"Abuse, Julia," Charlotte said. "His mistreatment of you is pure abuse."

"His abuse... of me is one thing. But as I've explained to you, I will not tolerate his mistrust about who fathered his children or his subsequent behavior against them, though I'm confused as to what to do next."

Mila patted Julia's arm. "We are still thinking about it."

Charlotte took one step back from the table. "Julia, you're Catholic and you married a Catholic. Despite this conversation, I can't imagine you divorcing Luuk. You also have three little girls to care for." She glanced at Mila. "And Mila, I suspect you have the full intention to stay with your husband. You appear to have a good marriage, plus the two of you have nothing to worry about when it comes to satisfying Hitler's standards for Aryanism. That alone thickens the complexity."

"That's an odd way of phrasing it." Julia sighed. "What stirs the pot of complexity is coming from you, my friend. If you aren't Jewish, then Luuk isn't a cause of personal concern. You could at least remain here until you find another place, until you think things over. Let's all face the facts, together. You don't have another place to stay, and neither do I. Nor Mila. So, we aren't different. We must stay put and defend our home against... against..."

"Against the enemy?" Charlotte suggested. "Whether it's your husband or whoever else may crash through the door and tell us what to do and when to do it?"

"I don't blame you for not fully trusting me—yet—especially after you've heard what I said to Luuk." Julia stood up from her seat at the table. She couldn't imagine her life without Charlotte as a friend, nor did she want to. "I will have to find a way to establish a solid trust between us. Meanwhile, Mila and I have talked on and on about Luuk. The time has come to put words into action. In the meantime, I want you to remain here, where it's reasonably safe for you compared to anywhere else. When you're more comfortable trusting me, you'll share about your past. Meanwhile, with documentation stating all the facts about Charlotte Beck that would pacify the Nazis, you will, no doubt, be fine right here."

Charlotte's expression softened. "I admit I've chosen to share particular things with you. Let's leave it at that. At least for now. But I don't want to put you or your children in danger." She looked at Mila. "Or you and Liam."

"We will all manage," Julia said. "And do you know what I wish to do for you?"

Charlotte lifted a curious brow. "To make this war end?"

"If I could, I would. Without delay." Julia glanced at the clock, then back at Charlotte. "I suspect that your husband and daughters are alive." She held up a hand when Charlotte's mouth dropped open. "Let me finish. What I'd love to do for you is to help you find your family so you can be reunited with them. Let me gather my little chicks from Liam's likely poor, spinning head, tuck them into bed, and then the three of us can talk in more detail. So, will you stay?"

Charlotte nodded. Julia stepped toward her houseguest, her friend, and pulled her into an embrace. Mila strode over and placed a hand on Julia and Charlotte's shoulders.

"We're in this together," Julia said. "Remember this."

29

On Thursday, 13 May 1943, barely a month after Luuk showed his face at his home, the Germans ordered all the Dutch to surrender their radios. Whether one was a Nazi supporter or a Jew in hiding did not matter. That was the day Charlotte knew she had to talk with the Süskinds before they disappeared. It was happening more and more often—people were vanishing all the time, as if they never existed to begin with. At first, it had been one by one, like her own husband, followed by her subsequent decision to send Edith and Krista into hiding. All painful disappearances. Whoever the Nazis declared as their enemy were rounded up in droves—a multitude of innocent people. Unlike cattle that had no clue they were being taken to their own slaughter, these unfortunate victims knew what misery awaited them. That was what happened days ago on the 5th when Wilhelm Harster, commander of the SD—the intelligence agency of the SS—ordered the final phase of the deportation of Dutch Jews. Three thousand Jews were corralled and sent into Germany. Their friends and the remaining family didn't expect to ever see them again.

At seven in the evening, when Charlotte left her newly assigned workplace at one of the Fokker aircraft factories in the north of

Amsterdam that the Nazis had commandeered for their own industrial war goals, she bypassed Julia's house and rushed straight to the Süskind's Plantage residence. With each frantic step she took she knew she'd put herself at risk, as well as Johanna and Walter, yet she couldn't turn around. In case she would be stopped by the Dutch police or the SS during a routine check, she always carried her documentation that showed that she was Charlotte Beck. Although, if she made one false move—a nervous eye twitch, a spasmic swallow, a misspoken word or a nervous-sounding stutter—she too could be deported, and like a cloud of smoke, dissipate into nothingness. If she would be caught on her way to the Süskinds, she might put them all at risk. It would be a guilt she'd always carry with her, especially if she misguidedly sabotaged Walter's future missions to rescue Jewish children. But she had no other option. Not with the Nazi clock ticking in their race to control Europe, if not the world. She was a mother of two children in hiding. She needed to know about her daughters' health, their chance of survival, their hopes of a new day that would bring them happiness.

Standing before the Süskinds' front door of their elegant brick house, she wondered whether Johanna and Walter still lived there. Images of a stranger opening the door instead of her friends—perhaps of a Nazi superior—filled her imagination. It was a haunting, surreal moment as well, since it was the last social event she and her daughters partook in together when she accepted the invitation to have dinner with the Süskinds. Edith and Krista's faces flashed before her... Edith's flowing, long, straight hair, dark as a raven; Krista's curly reddish-brown locks, bouncing with each move she made. Oh, how her youngest child had tons of energy. Her littlest one loved to sing and dance and delight Kurt and her with impromptu skits and performances. Would she be an actress one day? And her eldest? Edith was her serious child. Not only had she always done the expected, like researching a topic in school without the prompting of a teacher or surprising her parents by cleaning house, cooking dinner and then shooing them out for a walk while she watched Krista at home, but she did so with gusto.

Charlotte squeezed her eyes shut. This thinking of her daughters tugged at her heart. Her two loves in life that she'd given birth to and looked forward to seeing throughout the years—whether at family dinners, holidays, or their eventual weddings and the birth of their own children—always centered her world. Without them, she truly was at a loss about how to carry on. For that reason, she lowered her finger to jab the doorbell, yet suddenly couldn't bring herself to impose on the Süskinds. Thinking she'd slip away from this house after all, and dart across the street, she turned and stepped away. The door creaked open.

"Herta?" Johanna, her hair tucked under a blue kerchief and with surprise edging her expression, glanced up and down the street. "Please," she said in German, "come in."

Upon hearing her friend speak her true name and then hearing her native tongue, Charlotte breathed only slightly easier. Here, with friends, she could be Herta, again. "*Danke schön.*" She hurried in and Johanna closed and locked the door behind her.

"It's lovely to see you again. It's been a while. Do follow me inside. Walter will be happy to see you as well."

"It has been a while," Herta said as she kept pace with Johanna. She thought back to that cool and rainy December day when she'd brought Edith and Krista over for dinner. The roasted chicken with fresh vegetables and potatoes had helped to chase away the dreariness of the weather, though not the occasion. "I'm relieved to find you all here."

"Altogether?"

She wanted to smile for this special woman but couldn't. "Yes, and that too," she murmured. This lovely woman had a sharp intuition. Herta asked about her daughter.

"Yvonne is fine and thankfully healthy. Would you believe she's turned four already? She keeps us all busy!" Johanna stopped short of the parlor. Herta ceased walking as well. "I'm so sorry. I shouldn't have mentioned my daughter's doings when your two are away in hiding. Please excuse my indiscretion."

"You've done no wrong." Herta reached out to Johanna's arm. "These are sad times we live in when one must have regrets talking about one's child. Actually, that is why I'm here to talk with you and your husband."

"Well, please have a seat." Johanna motioned toward one of the four chairs, two on each side of the coffee table; gone was the lovely damask sofa she'd seen earlier during her first visit. "Pardon me while I tell Walter you're here. Without a meeting to attend to, for a change, he's fortunately home." It was only seconds later when Herta heard two sets of footsteps.

"It's a pleasure to see you again, Herta." Walter enveloped both of her hands. "Though, of course, I'd hoped the next time would have been with your husband and daughters."

Johanna placed a small dull silver dish with a handful of peppermints on the chipped oak coffee table between the mismatched armchairs. Had they sold the better pieces of silver, as well as furniture, to fund their efforts to help others go into hiding? To purchase food for themselves, and as she suspected, to give to others?

"Have a sweet, Herta. Would you like tea? I'm afraid we no longer keep coffee in this house."

"Coffee is scarce gold these days. But even if you had a secret stash and had offered me a cup, I'd have passed. Sleep is hard to come, lately. Thank you, though."

"Are you here to inquire about your children?" Walter asked.

"Walter!" Johanna stared at him. "Please, our friend must have a lot on her mind."

Herta lifted a hand and gave a little wave. "No concerns. That question is perfectly fine. And yes, I'm here because of my daughters. I want to see them. I need to see them."

Johanna, who sat beside Herta, patted her on the shoulder. "I can fully understand. When—if—I run into the mothers who have put a child into hiding, they all inquire about seeing their children.

They're all full of regrets and worries. More so than the fathers, for the most part, though I suspect they're trying to act stoically for their wives' sakes. I try to offer comfort by reminding them it was the most favorable thing they could have done for their young ones, but naturally, these words offer no comfort."

"Papa!" A rosy-cheeked Yvonne, wearing red pajamas, bounded into the room. She swung open her arms in what Herta recognized as the expectation for her father to lift her onto his lap. That, Walter did. Herta couldn't tell who sparkled more—the proud father or the adoring child. Without prompting, Yvonne said a darling hello to Herta and then smiled at her mother.

"Well," Walter said, "this little surprise visitor has just made it more difficult for me to say what I was about to say." After Herta encouraged him to continue as best as he could, she was relieved he did. She concentrated, or at least tried to, on his words while fighting the memories parading before her eyes of Edith and Krista when they were younger, like Yvonne.

Edith dressed in a maroon jumper with a white blouse, ready for her first day of school. Krista cried in frustration when, after brushing her hair for two minutes, she couldn't get her curly hair to straighten like her big sister's hair. Or the time when Herta sewed matching red and white-plaid holiday dresses for both daughters, not only because they would look adorable, but because they'd entered a phase of fierce jealousy.

"So, you see," Walter said. Herta realized that her roaming attention had her miss Walter's last words. She listened more intently in an attempt to pick up the thread. "It is impossible to locate your daughters. Krista originally went to Arnhem and then north into Friesland and Edith the opposite. She started off in Den Helder, but the last time I was informed, she was relocated to Nijmegen. With the frantic action these past few weeks by the Nazis, between razzias and deportations, we've not only lost track of our earliest missions but believe it is fortunate not to know details. It's much better this way for the children's welfare that we're uncertain of their exact location." He shifted Yvonne onto his other knee and whispered into her ear. The child smiled. Herta imagined that Walter had told her that she was growing into a big girl. How she missed telling her own daughters the little things that made them smile from ear to ear. "However, we do have the confidence to say that they're in better, more caring hands than otherwise... No, that didn't come out right. Not to compare your own loving hands—"

"I understand," Herta said. She looked at the child sitting on her father's lap and smiled, remembering the stories she'd heard about hiding children's new 'aunts' and 'uncles' giving less food to these children and more to their own flesh and blood, or the tales of an abusive hand, or how several hidden children could no longer remember the sound of their mother's voice. How these tales came about, no one knew, since families hadn't been reunited. At least, not yet. Hopefully, one day, and soon. Were the tales merely hearsay or the truth? "No offense taken. I'm sure what you meant in comparison was the alternative of..." She struggled to say the awful words that dried her mouth, but she pushed them out. "The alternative of winding up in a deportation camp. Or worse, according to the horrid stories about the eastern camps in Germany and Poland."

Johanna stood, took two long strides to her husband, and scooped up her daughter. "Time to go to bed, sweetie. Say goodnight to our guest." She invited Herta to stay and continue the conversation with her husband for as long as she needed. Then, with the promise of reading a storybook, she took Yvonne upstairs to tuck her in for the night.

Walter waited until his wife and daughter left the room and were out of listening range. He then scooted forward in his seat. "If I can't help you in the manner that brought you here, how else may I help?"

A wise and kind man, he was. Herta hoped that he and his family remained out of harm's way. She couldn't imagine, nor wanted to, this world without Walter. "I want to be reunited with my daughters, let alone my husband. It's like I'm in a purgatory of emotions, like I can't mourn for them because I don't know if they're dead and I can't celebrate because I also don't know whether they're alive and well. As much as I strive to be positive, it's terribly difficult especially when the stories of evil and its destruction reach us and etch wider the perimeters of a grim, new reality."

"I imagine you feel powerless." His furrowed brow smoothed out. "What would you like to do?"

"If I can't find and help my daughters, I want to help other Jewish children."

"I see," he said in a soft tone. Could he continue speaking without his voice cracking with emotion? This must have been extremely difficult and painful for him, as well as his wife—not only helping others to survive, but in constant awareness that they too could one day face the consequences other Jews in this country faced on a daily basis. "We've helped as many as possible to go into hiding. There are those less fortunate, those left behind by parents who shoved them onto the streets in a last resort of hope before the adults were rounded up and deported. They're called *straatkinderen*."

Herta nodded, though she didn't want to accept the term for street children. No child should have to live on the street like a stray animal. What was this world coming to? "I've heard of this."

"The older children shelter during the day and only come out at night—after Nazi bar hours end and the lunatics need to sleep off their benders before duty calls their names in the morning and they have to begin their reign of terror anew."

"I'd love to help these unfortunate children, or even the little ones."

Although no smile crossed Walter's lips, Herta sensed he was pleased. He stood, and with the promise of returning within seconds, excused himself to retrieve papers from his desk upstairs. A man of his word, he returned before she had a chance to think twice about her new set goals, not that it mattered, since she wouldn't be changing her mind. If she couldn't help herself or her daughters, she certainly was not about to waste a precious second by pitying herself, not when others needed a helping hand.

"Charlotte," Walter said upon entering the room. She looked up, surprised by his sudden use of her other name. "Your current identity, coupled with the documentation supporting it in place, is perfect for this operation I'm going to connect you with. However, I need to ask you a question, and I'd appreciate your honest reply." She sat back and waited for him to continue. "If you take on this responsibility, the stakes against you are high. If you are caught by the powers that be, whether by sight or if snitched on, the least that can happen is that you would be arrested, interrogated—semi-civilly or by means of torture if you don't cooperate—and then tossed into a rat-infested cell. And that is if luck is on your side and your false identity of Charlotte keeps. If not, and they discover you're a Jew, you will be immediately on your way to one of the Dutch transport camps and then packed onto a train to take you to another camp in the east." Though Walter didn't shift, Charlotte sensed that his whole body tensed before her eyes. "We have no evidence of any person who has made it back from these eastern camps to confirm the full scope of what's happening there, but we have high suspicions that they're not camps of gruesome work but are actually death camps."

"Death camps?"

"Centers of mass production-line extermination." He fisted his hands. "Are you still willing to take the risk to help these orphaned street children?"

There was no other choice if she wanted to live with her conscience and maintain her morals, dignity, and hope. As she'd said to her daughters often, one must cling to hope when darkness threatens. She stared into Walter's eyes. "Yes."

"Very good, then." He handed her a piece of paper. She expected the group's name to appear on the stationary scrap. Instead, only a woman's first name, Geertruida, and an address in the Oud-West district was written on the piece of paper. She instantly understood the secrecy involved in this transfer of information. "Is Oud-West too far for you to go? Alone? Especially at night?"

"Night?" Charlotte echoed, then immediately shook her head. "Of course not. I'd walk kilometers all night long to help anyone I can spare from the Nazis."

"Good. I will contact Geertruida and tell her you will meet her in two nights. Nighttime is the only time you will find her. Actually, I should say morning. At two, precisely speaking, so you must be on time. Do not knock on the door of this address. Rather, go into the alleyway three buildings to the right of the address, walk to the rear toward the canal, and there she will be." After she stood and thanked him, he lifted a hand to pause her. "Charlotte, if a stranger approaches you, swallow the paper with her name and address without hesitation and start walking the other way." She promised to do so and asked Walter to convey her goodnights to his wife and daughter. As he escorted her to the door, she wondered if this might be the last time they would see one another. As if he'd read her mind, he again enveloped her hands firmly as he had done so earlier that evening. "Don't think about what's ahead or what occurred in the past. These aren't the best of times, and though you haven't solicited my advice, I strongly suggest that it is best to stay in the present. That's how Johanna and I have chosen to cope with the fact that we, and our precious daughter Yvonne, can also be carted off to a camp."

"Are you saying that you've chosen to face each day as it arrives?"

"Yes, we face each moment as it comes. *Het leven moet verder gaan.*" Walter paused, then looked her directly in the eye. "Indeed, life must go on."

With the threat of tears flooding her eyes, she could only bob her head in agreement. She reached for the doorknob.

Walter opened the door and then quickly shut it, separating them, at least temporarily, from the harsh hatred and bloodshed that occurred in the name of war. "I nearly forgot to tell you—Geertruida knows me by the name of David. No last name. That is the only name you are to use." He opened the door, peeked left and right, and motioned for her to leave.

Charlotte stepped into the cool night air. One foot forward. Then the next. She could do this. She could take the necessary steps back home—to Julia's house at least—where she'd resume her next couple of days as Charlotte Beck, obedient servant to the Nazi Party as far as they were concerned, and a Dutch-born resident who worked in a factory on their behalf. She'd try not to think about much else. In a short while, she'd meet with this leader of the covert operation that Walter was arranging for her to aid. It was the least she could do during this awful time of unadulterated evil.

She passed her old workplace—the nursery—hurried past a toy shop with an *Out of Business* sign hanging tilted in the filthy glass window, dreadfully reminding her of an executed victim that no one claimed recognition of. The sad sight was ironic considering she'd taken Edith and Krista to this same shop upon moving to Amsterdam for a little treat to take the sting away from moving to a different country rather than to America like they'd hoped. America... Did her friend Zofia and her son, Eban, the ones she'd met on the ship sailing to Cuba, ever make it to New York? Were they happy and healthy, living a life free of war and strife? She and her husband must be reunited by now. But what about that friend of hers—the deaf one—who lived in Poland and had remained behind with Zofia's husband's family? What had become of them when the Germans invaded Poland in 1939? Could they all one day meet and celebrate the beauty of life?

A clang shot through the air and pulled Charlotte's attention a few steps ahead. A man stood beside a trash can heaped with garbage. Its lid faced downward on the ground—he must have knocked it off of the can. Stooped over, his choppy-cut steel gray hair covering his eyes and a ragged white-gray beard revealed that he was old, but masked further identification. It was evident that he'd been foraging for food scraps. The poor man. He was likely homeless and spent his days and nights staying away from Nazis who were unsympathetic to the elderly who couldn't contribute—

workwise—to the Aryan cause. If he was a drunkard or mentally ill, or for that matter, physically unwell, that too would be used against him. Walter's warning flashed like lightning through her mind—that upon contact with a stranger, she should swallow the scrap of paper with Geertruida's address. And flee. So soon? She'd already memorized the contact's location. She crumpled up the paper, swiped her hand across her mouth, and ingested the information. Yet, she decided to not immediately alter her path like Walter had urged her to do. Instead, she continued to face the stranger, poked her hand quickly into her pocket and withdrew a guilder. Most likely, this old man was harmless. He too had the right to live and that meant the right to nourishment that didn't come out of a trash can.

"Here," she said and extended her palm. "Please take it." The man didn't look at her, nor did he reach for the coin. He grunted his refusal. She placed the guilder on top of the lid that remained on the ground. "I'm going to leave this here. I can't blame you for not trusting me, but it would make me happy if you could use it. I'm going to leave. Stay safe." She continued on, step by step toward Julia's house, toward the next part of her life, with the distinct feeling that the old man watched her walk away. She hoped he had seen many better days in his past. As she continued back to the Jordaan, she prayed that if she couldn't further help this stranger that she'd just met or find her husband and daughters, she could at least be successful at helping the left-behind children forced to live on the streets of what used to be the fine and kind city of Amsterdam.

30

Plans, by definition, were sensible and helpful. Yet during wartime, as Charlotte discovered, they were the most ridiculous things ever, let alone frustrating. On the evening of her clandestine meeting, as she finished peeling the one carrot leftover from the four rationed vegetables, she again looked at the clock. In less than six hours, she'd be on her way to Oud-West.

"Blending this stale bread with two measly potatoes isn't going to fool my young and hungry daughters." Julia shoved the bowl of potatoes aside and wiped her hands on her apron. Her usually rosy-colored cheeks had paled in the recent weeks, and she radiated nervousness. Everyone did, no matter what age or gender, no matter what race or religious beliefs. War favored not one soul. "You've been the quiet one since Mila and I had our little discussion with you last month. If we've upset you, please speak up."

"It's not you. I have a few things on my mind that I'd rather not talk about. What about you, Julia? I have two good listening ears if you need to share any burdens." She glanced at the clock again. "With the girls entertaining Ada, we have a few minutes to ourselves."

Julia pulled out a chair from under the table, flopped down, and leaned on her elbows. "I just heard from the neighbor on the other side of Mila's about a new Nazi edict. Actually, not new, but it's the first time I've heard about it and I find it upsetting. It's been ordered that Jews married to non-Jews must be sterilized. On the 19th of this month, the churches united in protest, but I have a hunch that this protestation fell on deaf ears."

Charlotte, despite not being in the mood to chat, grew curious. Might Julia's reaction derive from her personal concern? Charlotte couldn't imagine. Considering Julia's husband's political stance, she searched her mind for the right, cautious words. "Are you upset because of its social implications?"

"It upsets me that a governing power has the authority to decide —to permit—who is able to love one another and ultimately who can have babies. I regret that it has taken me so long to start thinking of others." Julia mumbled a curse. Charlotte couldn't hold back the untimely grin. "You think it's funny? Or me, do you find me amusing?"

"Not at all, Julia. You remind me of myself, that's all. My husband always says—said—that I come across as clean-cut and wholesome but, pushed too far, and alone under my own roof, I could set his ears on fire with my sailor-talk."

"That's what Luuk says about me."

Charlotte believed it was safer not to talk about Julia's husband. "As for the topic of forced sterilization of Jews in mixed marriages, sadly, you're right, it's nothing new. Back in 1935, Germany passed the Nuremberg Race Laws." She waited for Julia to nod in recognition, but instead, she maintained a blank face. "I'm referring to the laws that say intermarriage and sexual relations between Germans and Jews—basically, between Aryans and Jews—are verboten. This came before the invasion of Poland, mind you. Even before the Race Laws, Hitler had put into place government sterilization for what they view as hereditary illnesses like mental illness, epilepsy, deafness and blindness and—and, believe it or not, alcoholism. One of the goals of Nazism is to create a purely bred Aryan race by zeroing the chance of any imperfection, as Hitler sees it, to occur.

I'm not at all surprised they want to stop Jews in Holland who are married to non-Jews from having babies as if it's their right to play God. Next, they'll probably round up street children and sterilize them for all the imperfections they've picked up from living on the filthy streets that would contaminate their Aryan blood purity and—"

Julia touched Charlotte's arm. "What's wrong? I've never heard you speak so strongly on a subject."

Charlotte nodded. "I'm quite upset! As a woman, I think an authority, whether on a national or community level, that determines whether or not a woman has the right to bear children based upon her religious beliefs and heritage should be viewed as criminal, let alone as pure evil. I'm sorry about the rant, but this is one thing I'm passionate about."

"I see that, and I appreciate your honesty. Luuk and I haven't talked about having more children. Ada was a complete surprise. A wonderful gift that I don't regret, but still, a child that we hadn't talked about having right away. Not that the decision has to do with my concerns or wishes, as far as he goes. Whatever Luuk says should happen in our marriage, indeed does happen. That explains his reaction to Ada's birth." Julia glanced toward the direction of the parlor where her two older daughters fussed over their baby sister. "Luuk was resentful about another daughter. He's terribly old-fashioned and believes he's not a man without a son. Argh, what am I talking about? I don't want Luuk back in my life, let alone have more of his children, and I love children. At one point in my life, I'd dreamed of having a whole brood of little ones... like six... or eight. But of course, if Luuk does stray home, I'll have no say in the matter. Why should I think about forced sterilization when my own husband forcing himself on me is more probable?"

It was all so crazy, this war, this survival of the desperate from the ones playing a god of the absurd and controlling others. Though a modern way of thinking, Charlotte believed that Julia should have a say in whether or not she wanted to have more children. But the sad part is women had no say in the matter. The raging war had prompted a few governments to persuade or control —if it wasn't one and the same—which women could and should produce children. The husbands of these countries either were eager to comply or gave in to the pressure. Mussolini's urge for Italian women to produce babies was eerily similar to Hitler's goal of increasing the Aryan race. Babies in the other category of non-Aryans faced separation from their parents and eventually death if Hitler continued to have his way. And Herta Weber? She had to perpetuate what her forged identity papers claimed: she was Protestant Charlotte. It was no one's concern that she had to give her daughters away in an attempt for them to survive. Nazi edicts dictated that if she and her daughters were discovered as Jews, the Nazis couldn't care less about whether her beautiful, innocent, loving children might live. Or, whether or not she desired to bring another child into this world.

Although she longed to share her burdens and concerns with another woman—another mother—she couldn't talk about this subject any further, especially not with Julia. And not when she was prepared to meet a stranger in a few hours and put her life at risk to save homeless children's lives. She stood. "Pardon me, Julia. Exhaustion has finally caught up with me. It's been a long day. I'm retiring early for the night."

"Sleep well, my friend."

Julia's last two words froze Charlotte in her place. Despite standing on opposite sides of the enemy line, she wanted to be friends with Julia. If the world was inhabited by more friends than enemies, it would indeed be a better place for all. And to think that of all topics— freedom, or not, to birth children out of love rather than controlled by the hand of authority—should unite them as friends was a curious wonder. She needed to latch onto the olive branch she sensed that Julia was sincerely offering. "You as well, my friend."

The alarm clock ticked to one AM, but Charlotte, awake all night, had no reason to turn the alarm off since she'd never set it. Having never changed into nightwear, she was already dressed and ready to go. And out the back kitchen door she flew, careful to be light on her feet and to avoid brushing against objects that could clatter. As she rushed down the streets and crossed canal bridges, leaving the Jordaan and snaking her way through the twists and turns that would get her to Oud-West, she readily understood why this time of night was best for saving children: for a Nazi-infested city, the streets were oddly empty. Nazis, the police, or someone like Julia's husband who was looking to earn some extra guilders by capturing Jews, were likely indoors at this time, tanking up in the one or two hotel bars still open for business, if not in secret pubs. Determined to reach Geertruida and help this initiative succeed, she walked on.

Just on time, she reached the address Walter had told her about. Veering right, she strode past three buildings, turned down the alleyway, and proceeded to the canal. No one was there. This couldn't be. She glanced left and right, but didn't see anyone. Across the water? Not a soul.

"Henny!" A whisper? A bat's screech?

Charlotte spun around and squinted, more out of caution than because of the drab night sky. She saw no person or animal. When someone tapped her shoulder, she managed to hold in a scream. She turned to see a woman. Taller than her, slim like most people these days who ate poorly, the woman appeared to be in her young forties. She pressed her index finger over Charlotte's lips. "Are you here because of David? Just nod or shake your head."

Charlotte immediately recalled Walter Süskind's warning that Geertruida would refer to him as David. She complied with a nod, and the woman steered her toward a side door that, due to it being tucked behind a bush, she hadn't noticed before. Once inside, she expected the woman to turn on the lights, but instead, the stranger continued to lead her down a hallway and then through the door of a room. There, without stumbling about, she switched on a table light. Although dim, there was enough light in the windowless room for Charlotte to look around. A table by the door, one narrow bed—empty, though from the looks of the ruffled blanket, it had been occupied not long ago—and an empty wooden crate beside the bed, occupied the otherwise empty room. There were no chairs to sit on, so they remained standing and stared at each other, one woman sizing up the other.

"I'm Geertruida. Do not tell me who you are. I do not want to know about you. You are now Henny." She crossed her arms, and that was when Charlotte... Henny... realized Geertruida was likely not the woman's real name. "Is that okay with you?"

"Yes, of course." While she would have enjoyed telling Geertruida that one of the first acquaintances she made upon arriving in the Netherlands was of a lovely and caring woman by the name of Henny, and for that reason alone she'd always liked that name, she had no doubt that Geertruida was someone with a no-nonsense mindset who wasn't fond of idle chatter. That was a good thing, considering the circumstances and its dangers.

"Henny, you will be assigned to various tasks as I see necessary. The *straatkinderen* must always come first, not your needs. No excuses that might jeopardize a child's life will be tolerated, meaning that I don't care if you're hungry, late for work, or in need of a toilet. Understand?" Henny nodded. "Good. Then follow me."

Expecting that Geertruida would lead her back outside, Henny was surprised when she took her to the adjacent room and opened the closet door. "Your eyes will soon adjust to moving about in the darkness. We are the ghosts of the night. Mark my words. You will get onto your hands and knees and enter the closet. On the bottom to your left, there are two barrel bolts. Unlock them and they will open a panel. Crawl into the space and continue until you see a dim light. Follow the light, and you will enter a passageway that will take you to another room. There, four children should be sound asleep. They are between two and six years old. The six-year-old girl is easily frightened and often cries; the youngest is the bravest, but I think it's because he tends to relax around other children—"

"Probably misses his siblings." When a soft groan escaped

Geertruida's lips, Henny understood this meant *listen to me*. This was apparently intended to be a one-way conversation and she was glad she didn't start about her nursery school work experiences that were already on the tip of her tongue.

"You are to remain with them until morning," Geertruida continued. "These are the youngest of our current batch. They wouldn't fare well on the streets like the older children that we're trying to place in homes. Do you suffer from claustrophobia?"

"No," Henny admitted truthfully.

"Good, then I will secure the locks to the tunnel as soon as you pass through. There is a clock in the children's room. You will not be able to get out of this passageway or the room until five in the morning when I will open the latch. Then you are to wake the children, if they aren't already up, and feed them the food that I leave for them. Then you are free to go for the day. There is a water closet and a sink in the room. I will see you again tomorrow night, at the same time."

Henny realized Geertruida had phrased a statement, not a question. "Yes. Will I do the same tomorrow night?"

"Most likely, but only until I gain a sense of your capabilities." *And until she earned Geertruida's trust*, Henny assumed. She couldn't blame her one bit. "It's not good for the children to become dependent upon a particular person, not during this time of instability, especially with people dying or disappearing left and right. The aim is to have you work the streets with the older ones. More on this later. *Goedenacht*."

Without a pause, Henny dropped onto her knees and crawled into the closet as instructed. Groping to her left, her fingers brushed against the two latches. She unlocked the panel and without saying another word to Geertruida, entered the tunnel. Upon hearing two distinctive clinks and slides, Henny pushed away the thought of what would happen to her and the children if Geertruida was delayed—or worse. She couldn't afford to worry, not if she wanted to give the best possible care to these four children who needed her.

When she followed the dim light down this strange pathway to an unknown place where she'd meet four new little ones, each homeless and with little hope for what tomorrow may bring, Henny slipped into the role of Herta—mother of two daughters. She focused on how each of her girls were a gift and treasure from God; how on many nights Edith's cheerful tone, as she read a story to her younger sister, cheered and comforted Krista; how on one morning, back in Germany, four-year-old Krista caused the whole family to be late for the shul service when she pouted too long about wanting to wear Edith's dress rather than her own; how the day after Herta lost her dearest friend to cancer, her precious daughters made a bouquet of paper flowers that they colored with pencils, and after presenting the flowers to her, remained by her side and kept her company. Before Henny pushed the panel that led to the children's room, one last fond image produced a smile on her lips: She and Kurt sitting at the dining table with their two daughters, Kurt's former boss, an atheist, and his Irish wife, a Catholic, and their two sons who wanted to become Jewish. The adults suspected that the boys' interest to change their faith was connected to their crushes on the girls. But what did it matter? They peacefully sat together and enjoyed good food and each other's company. Each person saw the other as no more or less worthy of respect with regard to one's faith, or lack of faith. They were all people. And as Henny slipped into the room, she thought that that fundamental principle of love and respect for all was exactly what Hitler wanted to dismantle. Returning back to reality, she put into perspective what she'd chosen to do: helping others in need.

She might have been uncertain about if the children would take to her or in what condition she'd find the room, but she hadn't expected to find a girl who was the spitting image of Krista at the age of three, sitting up in a bed with ample pillows, sheets, and blankets. She hugged a doll to her chest and stared wide-eyed as Henny slipped from the tunnel and entered the room. Would the child yell and awaken the other three? Would she start crying in fear or scramble under the covers? If Henny sat down beside her, would she scratch or bite in an attempt to shoo her away? She didn't. Instead, the little darling smiled and lifted her doll and offered it to her.

In the dim light coming from a single lamp on top of a narrow table set between the two beds, Henny could see a boy beside the girl, who was apparently sound asleep. From Geertruida's brief description, Henny believed him to be the one who was the youngest and bravest. "Hello, my pretty girl," she said softly to the staring child. "My name is Henny. Would you like for me to stay with you tonight?"

The girl nodded. "I'm Thea." One by one, she held up four fingers.

"You're four years old! What a big girl you are." *May you live and one day have a grandchild hold up four fingers to show you her age as well.*

Thea yawned.

"Want to go back to sleep, darling? I'll sit right beside you and keep an eye out for your safety." Without a word or a nod, Thea, clutching her doll, cozied up beside the boy. When Henny sat beside her, the girl closed her eyes. Seconds later, a tiny snore spilled from her open mouth. Henny glanced around at the other sleeping children and rocked back, amazed that she'd stopped thinking about the war and its surrounding misery. She knew it was because of these precious children. Her heart filled with a joy she hadn't experienced in a long, long time, nor expected to feel again. She chose to grasp this sweet peace, to focus only on these children's needs, and to shove away the lurking worries about the evil surrounding all of them.

31

After Liam's visit Julia wondered about how the calm and comfort of this July evening seemed at odds with the ongoing war. He'd just told her about the events of the past few days and she was uncertain what to make of it. While she should be grateful that the RAF didn't bomb her house, she worried about how much the people of Amsterdam-Noord—just over eight kilometers northeast of her Jordaan neighborhood—suffered when the bombs struck them. The Fokker factories where Charlotte worked were the actual targets of the British bombings, though the bombs had hit the surrounding areas as well, killing and injuring close to 300 residents. Several of the factories sustained considerable damage. Charlotte would be without work for the coming time. Lately, Julia wondered about Charlotte. She was seldom home, and when she was, she appeared exhausted and kept quiet. Before the recent bombings, the few times Julia tried to engage her in a conversation about her new job, Charlotte had replied in very generic terms. *It's factory work—busy and boring. The other ladies I work with chat about the weather or other safe topics. No one dares to complain—either about the work or the war.* War. Julia's thoughts drifted back to Liam and the additional updates of the news he shared: that in addition to

Mussolini's arrest, a massive air raid had targeted Hamburg, the German port city where many had immigrated from Europe to flee the horrors leading up to the war, both the current war and the troubles that led to the Great War.

"Mama," Marianne called from the parlor. "Is Papa ever coming home again?"

Julia looked up. How could she begin to tell Marianne that she honestly did not know the answer to her question, and besides, didn't care to see her daughter's father ever again?

"Tell me too," Annelise said. She rattled a toy before Ada, who had turned one year old in June. The girls were playing on the rug. Before Liam's visit, they'd been loud, giggly, and at times squabbling over who got to hold Ada, which was all fine with Julia. She loved their happy chirps, their adoration for their baby sister, and was amazed how they could momentarily shove aside the threat and terror of war from her doorstep. This question—asked at least once a day—of whether their father would come home, along with wondering when they'd be a real family again, made Julia confused about how to respond.

Julia squatted between Ani and Marianne and tugged them into a hug. Ada, nestled in Ani's arms, squealed in delight. "Your father is on a special mission and is doing—"

"The best he can," Annelise and Marianne said in unison, finishing her sentence.

"Oh, my. I guess I've said that once too often."

Ani narrowed her eyes, looking too much like an adult at the age of seven. "Yes, you have, Mama. I want an answer. A real one. Please."

"Sweetheart, I gave you the best and only answer I have. Be a big girl about this."

"Is Charlotte on a special mission too?" Marianne asked.

"What makes you ask this?"

"Because we haven't seen her that much either."

"Well, neither have I," Julia said and instantly regretted her words.

"Mama, is Charlotte hurt?" Ani asked. Her bottom lip began to quiver. "Did she get shot? Did a Nazi arrest her?"

Think fast. Think about what would calm your daughters and avoid pandemonium. "Your Oom Liam is good at telling me what happens every day. There's been no bad news about Charlotte." She smiled. "Charlotte will keep out of trouble. You two like her, I can see."

"She's nice," Ani said. "And she's your friend. You're always happy when she's here with us."

That, Julia was. Happy. Calm. She thought back to the beginning of her marriage with Luuk, to their better days. Luuk once was a loving husband and they'd been incredibly happy together. With him, she was on firm ground and never concerned about what would happen next. That all changed, though, when he started to want more. More recognition. More status. Glory. He became convinced that Nazidom was the sole key to achieving this. That's when he began threatening her and cutting her with knives and glass, as if he built himself up while he whittled her down in size. At first, she spoke up, but when he countered with insults on her intelligence, she withdrew whenever he was around. It was safer that way, easier. The times she braved contesting him were the times she suffered most by his hurtful hand and words. Only after Charlotte pointed out how wrong this was did she realize that this was abuse and that she didn't have to accept this as normal. Since Luuk had last paid a visit—the day he'd learned about the birth of yet another daughter—she'd begun to see him as an ill man. As unfortunate as that was, she couldn't chance having him around. If not for her own sake, for that of her three daughters. Charlotte was a good and steady person. One who sadly had suffered severe hardship and loss. Yet, life was certainly going to get better for her and the day for Charlotte to move out and away from Julia would inevitably come and stir up life again for all of them. As a friend, she'd have to let her go and hope for the best for this woman who had saved Marianne's life and brought a smile to each of their faces. After the war, they'd find a way to keep in touch. For all she knew, Charlotte would meet a new husband and settle down in...

"What's that noise, Mama?"

Julia was shaken out of her reverie. About to ask Ani what she meant, she paused when she heard a door slam shut in the kitchen. "Stay here. I'll check."

Walking toward the kitchen, she feared it was Luuk, as if her thinking about him could conjure him up like an unwelcome spirit. As she stepped into the small room, her concerns about her husband coming back to cause trouble were replaced by her concerns about whether another intruder broke into the house—another Henk madman to hold her family hostage. The last person she expected to find was Charlotte. She was sitting at the table with her head on her folded arms resting on the tabletop. It was as if the poor woman had surrendered in total defeat. As softly as she could, she hurried to her side. "Charlotte, what's wrong?" When her friend failed to reply, Julia asked if she'd mind if she sat down beside her.

Charlotte glanced up. "Sit, but I'm not good company right now."

"Oh, dear. Your eyes are beet red—you've been crying." Julia dragged a chair beside her. "What can I do to help?"

"No one can help."

"Is this about the loss of your job at the factory?" Thinking a little reassuring touch might make a difference, she reached for Charlotte's arm. "Liam stopped by a short while ago and shared the details. Don't worry, my dear. Times are rough, but another work offer will come along. If you're concerned about helping financially around here, as I've said when you first moved in, it's not necessary. We've managed well all this time and one way or the other, we will continue to do so."

"That's not it, at all." With furrowed brows and a broad frown, Charlotte sat up and leaned back into her chair. The look on her face said she dreaded an interrogation.

Julia would not push her further. Yet, she didn't want to be uncivil. "May I get you a cup of tea?"

"I just witnessed a—" Charlotte's sobs made her choke on her remaining words.

About to offer what she hoped would be comforting words, Julia realized the falsehood in this shallow attempt. This was wartime. Charlotte must have just observed a terrifying tragedy to shake her to this degree. Julia placed a hand tenderly on her shoulder. "I'm here for you."

Charlotte nodded and swept a hand across her teary eyes. "I saw a child killed by a Nazi soldier."

"For the love of God, how could this be?"

Charlotte's initial silence was a loud reply: because this cruel war of evil does not exempt innocent children. She looked into Julia's eyes. "He did this intentionally. He did not warn the little girl. Did not ask her why she was alone on the street, scouring the ground for a bite to eat. Did not give her a second chance. He aimed his gun, pulled the trigger, and fired several rounds of ammunition into her. She dropped dead, her blood draining onto the ground. I was about to rush over to her when a woman, one whom I've never met, pulled me back and muffled my mouth with her hand and told me I'd get killed if I ran to the girl. Willing to take the chance, I tried to wiggle free, but her determined grip held me back."

"So, you wanted to help but couldn't. And you're troubled from the guilt of not running to the child's side?" Charlotte's snort confirmed Julia's hunch. "I suspect you feel awful because if this child had been one of your own daughters killed in this atrocious way, no one would have been beside her."

"Yes." Charlotte wrapped her arms around her middle and started to rock. "It's a horrible admission... to not only see a child killed, but to want to help but can't. This fighting the images of my own daughters in the same situation of cruel death—"

"I would feel the exact same way. Any loving mother would. You did what you could, and tried to do more. Opportunities of righting a wrong were taken away from you."

"Julia, you're a good friend. I appreciate you listening, but I need to be by myself to gather my thoughts."

"I fully understand." As Julia watched Charlotte leave the room, she was certain of two things: Charlotte's daughters were alive, in hiding, likely, and Charlotte—whoever she was—battled not only the grief and shock of seeing a child killed, but she was also full of guilt for this could have been her own child if circumstances were different.

Julia started toward the hallway, then stopped. There was one more thing about Charlotte Beck that she was convinced she was correct about: Charlotte was Jewish. Lately, it might have been a hushed conversation between women throughout the Netherlands, but it was common knowledge that Hitler detested women dying their hair or wearing cosmetics and perfumes. Ration coupons barely stretched wide enough for food and other necessities that the war had depleted, but they definitely did not cover hair dye. In the past, she'd heard about the women who worked in the ammunition plants in Zaandam and Delft and how they'd gained unintentional complexions of yellowish skin tones and matching hair color, the price tag of exposure to TNT powder. Though that wasn't an option these days. Over the past two months, when Charlotte's dark roots began to show more and her blonde hair became dingy and brunette, she'd taken to wearing her hair tucked under a scarf. Most women, including Julia, scoured the city for secondhand scarves for that reason. Before meeting Charlotte and inviting her to move in with her, if Julia had seen a dark-haired woman she'd assumed she was a Jew. Living with Charlotte and seeing the horrors of Jewish men, women, and children—of having various shades of hair—being rounded up on the streets only for following a different faith than the Aryans, Julia had come to realize just how prejudiced she'd become. And the sad, pathetic part was that she had kept in check her feelings about her husband's growing Nazi ambitions through the years. But since his last visit and his accusation that their children might have been fathered by another man, she never feared him to the degree she did at the present because of the truth—a truth she'd skirted around. Especially with Mila, who, before meeting Charlotte, was the only person Julia had trusted her heart to. And a truth she denied in its entirety to Charlotte. If Luuk were to learn about this, he would take the children from her and end their marriage. Or worse. God only knows what might occur to her precious daughters then. In many respects, if Julia's suspicions about Charlotte were correct, she had almost as much to lose as her friend if the truth about their identities surfaced.

Since May, Charlotte had been sneaking out of the house at the ridiculous hour of one in the morning. Although Julia had hoped her friend had a lover and enjoyed secret trysts, she highly suspected that this wasn't the case. For the next hour or so, she'd give Charlotte time to herself, then ask if Mila would watch the girls overnight. Later, she would follow Charlotte when she left the house. Julia knew her friend and knew that Charlotte served a greater purpose other than her own needs. She was going to get to the bottom of this. As Charlotte's friend, she was determined to help. She was determined to break the wall that separated them from becoming better friends by telling Charlotte that they had more in common than not, and more than ever, they needed to lean on each other.

32

There was no way Charlotte would attempt to sleep that late July evening. With images of the killing of the girl replaying before her eyes, as well as being held back against her will to help the poor darling by the one person she never would have guessed, there was no way she would slip under the covers. Instead, she sat on the wooden chair by the small writing desk in her room. She had figured the chair's hard surface would prevent her from nodding off, which worked, but it offered no escape from her state of mind.

The crack of gunfire booming through the air. Sardonic laughter from the Nazi murderer. The click of retreating jackboots. Silence cloaking the street. And Geertruida.

"Why did you stop me?" Charlotte asked the overseer of the resistant group she'd helped night after dark night since May. "That child needed me. She was dying. No one was by her side when—"

"And I need you, Henny. We need you to continue to operate, to help us save lives."

"But if we can't save the life of one precious child, then what good are we? What good am I as a human being?"

Geertruida, an undemonstrative tough bird, gripped Henny's arms. "We cannot control who gets killed in this war. War is full of hate, blood, and destruction. We can only try to help as many as we can. We must let go of certain misfortunes and proceed on."

"I can't. I won't pass by another one in need and close my eyes like you're asking me to."

"You must choose, and right away. Choose to help many or die helping one. But you also must realize that if you choose the latter, then you will most definitely put our whole operation in harm's way. Subsequently, you also put at risk those who you live with, those who you love. This enemy of ours has not one misgiving about extinguishing the life of those they hate. By bringing this attention to yourself—because they will be watching you—you will be luring these worthless scums to your doorstep. Do you want that?"

Charlotte chose to help as many as she could. She'd find a way to carry on after this awful day of death. If lucky, she'd succeed at relegating the memory of the murdered child into a part of her mind that would only seldom haunt her. Or, if she was unfortunate, nightmares would pay a visit on one too many occasions. But Geertruida was correct—she had to help as many innocent children as she could to survive this nightmare of death and destruction by the hand of those who played the role of god. A worthless and unreal god—a monster, a demon. For sure, not the true creator of life.

Valiant Henny, as Geertruida had donned her when she'd made the decision to not permit the slaughtered child to derail her efforts in helping the resistance group's efforts in helping the street children, rose from the chair at one a.m. She brushed her hair and teeth, chugged a few sips of water, and slipped out of her room, then tiptoed out of the house as she'd done for the past two months. She stepped outdoors, thankful for the cool night air, and for this time alone as she hurried from the Jordaan to Oud-West, which like more and more Amsterdam neighborhoods once filled with family, friends, shops, cafes, and cultural activities, and places of worship, had become more like deserted areas where even ghosts didn't dare to frequent. However, this night was different, which was perfect since it required from her a fresh dose of concentration and an effort to stay in the present. If it was up to her, there would be no more dead little girls, or boys.

Instead of continuing to care for her four charges, Geertruida wanted Henny to try her hand at becoming a courier for the group. Her first assignment was to pick up papers from a forger who not only knew the craft well, but was also quite the artist, fueled with the passion, like Henny, to help others despite the risks and consequences. She stepped into an alleyway that would take her to the back door of an out-of-business brothel, an establishment that she never imagined would shut down. Evidently, the curfew enforced by the Nazis had put the kibosh on the prostitutes peering out their windows in an attempt to entice customers. *Well, every ending is a new beginning,* Henny thought, and pushed open the door.

A young woman wearing dirty trousers with her hair pulled back in a ponytail introduced herself as Sari. She had a stern expression on her face and her eyes were hardened—more than they should have been at her age. *Ah, so this was the artist turned forger.* Henny introduced herself by her first name and made no mention of who sent her. The woman handed her a tin container the size of a small briefcase that she assumed was packed with the forged documents that Geertruida expected. Without another exchange of words, she strode to the door she'd entered and stopped short from opening it. Not only did another door creak open behind her, but an odd premonition sent chills up her spine. She spun around and recognized him immediately—the old man she'd given the guilder to when she'd last left the Süskind's house and had caught him searching a trash can for food. He was the artist behind the forgeries? She squinted as she tried to adjust her vision in the dimly lit room. Her breath hitched. From a distance, that evening, his silvery hair might have aged his image, but now, up close, she saw that his complexion was smooth, his neck skin firm, not loose. This was no old man. His fingers were stained as black as the apron over his clothing. Ink? He must have been the artist, the forger, not Sari. Struggling for air, she groped to her sides in an attempt to stabilize her wobbly balance. "Kurt?"

The man was unmistakably her husband. He narrowed his eyes and glared back. "You have me confused without someone else. Get out, get away. Never come back here."

She was swallowed into an abyss of nothingness.

Glass chinked. Henny turned her head from side to side. She opened one eye. Sari. "Where's Kurt?"

"You fell to the ground and gave me quite the scare." Sari handed her the glass that she must have heard rattling seconds ago. "Here you go, have a few sips of water. Don't be embarrassed. None of us are eating properly these days, not with the cursed Nazis restricting what we can enjoy while they patrol the streets with sizable bellies hanging over their belts. The pigs! No surprise we're all wasting away like we're living in a work camp. No wonder you passed out."

Henny sipped the water and looked around, but she saw memories flashing through her mind instead of the room's details. She had been about to exit the door when she'd turned around. She must have lost consciousness and collapsed to the floor. Sari was a slip of a woman, barely out of her teens, with little muscle to her bones. She couldn't have carried her to this... What was she lying on? A bare mattress on a floor? In a back room? Was this the place where her husband slept, without her?

"Where's Kurt?" Her repeated question had finally etched a slight smile on Sari's face, though she kept silent. "I just saw my husband after a long, forced separation. Why won't you tell me about his whereabouts?"

"I'm afraid you're mistaken. Confusion has also been striking—"

Henny sat upright, relieved the room wasn't spinning on her. "Please, no more lectures on the terrible Nazis. I'm quite aware of how they're treating us—the lucky ones they haven't imprisoned or tortured to death—and the dire consequences of bad health popping up and no doctors to attend to us. Spare me. That old man I saw was not the man he was pretending to be. That was Kurt, my husband, in disguise. Now tell me, where is he?" She scrambled to her feet. "Should I search this building by myself?"

"I'm sorry to say, Henny, but I believe you might have suffered a hallucination. There was no man. I am the one who took care of the matter that you came for." She swept her hands out to her sides. "You may search the building all you like, but I suspect that whoever sent you here will be quite agitated, to say the least, if you don't hurry off into the night with what is expected from you. I suspect that if you don't arrive back to this person in a timely fashion you will force him or her to assume the worst. You will put the entire operation in jeopardy. Are you well enough to continue?"

Henny had no choice but to return to Geertruida, especially since she held in her possession the forged documents that were needed for the placement of more street children in safe homes. She had no other choice but to cease her spiel on how she was convinced she'd seen her husband. Besides, she didn't want to take up more of Sari's time. So, she downed another gulp of water, thanked the woman, and slipped outdoors into the moonless, dark night.

Charlotte was sure that it had been her husband, not an old man, who had rummaged through the garbage can, and refused to look her in the eye or take her coin. And tonight? That was Kurt who had entered the room before she left the building. He must have been the one who had scooped her off the floor in her unconscious state and carried her to the mattress. Had he forged documents for Geertruida all this time instead of taking shelter in Switzerland or another place of refuge, as he had promised to do? If Walter Süskind worked with Geertruida, might he have also been aware that her husband was the one who used his talents and skill to forge false documentations? And if so, had he not trusted her with this information about her missing husband? There was a chance that Sari too could be quite the artist, but if anyone could pick up the trade of a forger and become such an expert that even someone like Geertruida could rely on his talents to save the lives of the street children, it would be her husband. There were more questions than answers. One way or another, she would get this resolved. She'd find him. They'd reunite. She'd help him with his forgeries, and like the perfect couple they were, they'd become an amazing team to help keep children away from Hitler's henchmen. Another miracle could be in store for them—they'd find their daughters, and like in a fairy tale, they would all live happily ever after with Edith and Krista and—

"Charlotte!"

She'd deliver the documents to Geertruida and do what was instructed. Then, since her workplace was destroyed by bombs, rather than look elsewhere for work, like the Nazis demanded, or return to Julia's to stare at her bedroom walls, she'd chance walking up and down the streets of Oud-West or the Jordaan or Plantage in search of Kurt. She couldn't care less about the number of police or SS officers she might have to dodge or how many blisters on her feet she'd suffer from by the end of the day.

Suddenly, she was seized by her back collar and pulled against the brick siding of a building she was hurrying by. With her heart pounding and regrets twisting her insides for being foolishly lost in her daydreams, she looked up. Convinced she'd see a member of the SS, she blinked. Julia?

"Where were you going, Charlotte? Didn't you hear me calling you?"

Henny, Charlotte, Herta, whoever she was, craned her neck and peered in both directions in search of onlookers. Fortunately, no one else was around. Grabbing Julia's arm, she steered her into a near doorway. Its splintered frame suggested that it had not been used for a few years. "Why are you here, following me? Are you aware of the danger you're putting us both in, let alone your family?"

Julia wiggled free of Charlotte's grip. "You're the one who left a nice, secure house in the middle of the night, like you've done each night for the past few months."

Julia knew? "Is this the first time you've traced my steps, or is this a routine for you already? Who is watching the girls?"

"First time. Mila, who else? And before you go on, tell me what you're up to."

"I can't."

"A secret mission?"

"Don't press."

"You're my friend, and I'm here because I'm concerned about you and care if you're shot dead. Please, explain to me."

Charlotte held back a cringe from the picture Julia had painted for her. Since she joined Geertruida's resistance group, she had to put away all traces of fear and horror. Otherwise, she would have lost the fervor that propelled her out of Julia's nice, secure house a long time ago. She planned to keep doing this as long as she needed to. She'd work until children no longer had to worry about being separated from their parents, or wondering when the bombs would stop falling, or going to bed hungry. This war had to end; this evil had to be stopped. "Julia, I appreciate your concern about me, but I'm careful. Believe me, I keep a vigilant eye out for danger."

Julia grasped Charlotte's arms. "All it takes is one slip, whether out of carelessness or if you fall into a horrid trap. Have you ever thought about that—another's will to sacrifice you as their stooge so they can remain safe? I need not remind you that this is war. Call me selfish, but I don't want to lose my best friend. You have to stop whatever you're doing."

Despite the darkness of the situation, Charlotte smiled. "Best friend, huh?"

"Yes, you are. There's Mila, of course, but she's more like a sister or cousin." She cringed. "I didn't mean that offensively, but despite the few ups and downs you and I have had, it's different than between Mila and me. So yes, I consider you my best friend."

"And I consider you a good, dear friend as well. First, I have a delivery to make. Then, in a few hours, I'll return home."

"Good. I have news that I must share with you."

Charlotte sensed that she could trust Julia, and needed to confide in her. "And I have news of my own to tell. So, I'll see you soon." She waited about five minutes after Julia departed, checked the streets for passersby, and then with the container of forged documents tucked in an inside shirt pocket, scrambled back to Geertruida, curious about Julia's news and wondering how she was going to explain seeing her dead husband.

33

Asleep, Charlotte became aware of a presence beside her.

"Don't be alarmed, Herta. It's me. Sleep, sweetheart. You need your rest."

Kurt? He was next to her? Calling her by her real name, not Charlotte, and certainly not Henny. She didn't want to sleep a second longer. What she did desire was to open her eyes, see her beautiful husband, frame her hands around his incredibly gorgeous face, and invite him to slip under the covers beside her. Preferably, without a stitch of clothing on. She wouldn't wait a second longer for him to embrace her. She'd wrap him in her arms. She'd whisper his name over and over, telling him how much she missed him. Without questioning him about what he'd been up to, she'd tell him to never leave her again and start kissing him with no intention of stopping. But when he failed to say another word, when she stopped sensing his warm breath caressing her neck, she knew it had all been a dream—one pitiful dream that couldn't compensate for the steely reality around her.

She opened her eyes and immediately saw Julia sitting on a chair next to the cot. "What time is it?"

"Four in the afternoon, sleepyhead."

"Four? The last thing I remember is gulping tea, saying I needed to fetch something from my room. I must have sat down on the cot and dozed right off." She eyed her clothing—the same gray slacks and blue blouse she was wearing when Julia had caught up with her after picking up the forged documents. "At least I had the presence of mind to slip off my shoes."

"I'm glad you got some much-needed sleep."

"I've been non-stop busy." Charlotte peered over Julia's shoulder at the open bedroom door. "Where are Annelise and Marianne? The baby?"

"Liam is watching them. It's wonderful having relatives next door. The girls will be there until dinnertime, so we'll have plenty of time to talk."

"What about Mila?"

Julia gestured toward the hallway with her chin. "She's sitting on the sofa reading a magazine that's three years old, if you can believe that. In fact, let's go and keep her company. Mila's a good listener, caring, and can be counted on to keep what she hears in confidence. In fact, I just shared something with her that was quite overdue in telling." She extended a hand. "Shall we? I want to tell you too."

Instead of latching onto Julia's hand, Charlotte drew her legs up and hugged her knees. "I recall that, during the night when we last saw each other, I'd mentioned that I have news to tell, but I'm not sure if I can talk about it right now, or should." She expected Julia to look shocked or disappointed, not to offer her a patient look. Charlotte sighed. "Sorry. I realize I'm not being fair. You told me you had news, then I said I had my own news to share with you, and now you're probably thinking I said what I did to shake you off and send you home." She raked her fingers through her hair that was free of the tattered brown scarf she'd worn for the past couple of weeks. Evidently, she'd also managed to slip off the head covering before nodding off. Shame and guilt brought heat to her face, and she rubbed at her cheeks as if she could wipe the fire of embarrassment away.

"Don't be alarmed, my friend. Yes, I've long ago noticed your blonde hair fade to dark brown, and long ago suspected that blonde wasn't your natural color. It's a consequence of war, all right."

It was time for Charlotte to be straightforward. "What is? The lack of hair dye, or the revelation that some of us are not who we claim to be?"

"You're right. Not everyone is truthful about their identities."

Had Julia stated a general sweeping phrase or an admission? Charlotte swung her legs to the side of the bed and stood in front of her. "Well then, Julia, who are you?"

Julia handed her a sweater from the foot of the cot. "Wear this. It's a cool afternoon and this will keep you warm. Let's go out to where Mila is. I'll make us a pot of pitifully weak tea and we'll chat."

Seated on the sofa, Charlotte lifted the teacup to her lips for her first sip and looked to Julia to begin the conversation.

"When I saw you in the middle of the night, I'd told you that I think of you as a dear friend. However, I also sense there's a barrier between us. A barricade, if you will, made of secrets. Mine. Yours." Julia suddenly looked distressed and darted her attention toward Mila. "Can you help me before I jumble matters more?"

"Actually, I think you're doing just fine, but I'll try." Mila crossed her legs and leaned over her lap. "Charlotte, I believe what Julia is trying to say is that she thinks you have valuable information to exchange with each other that would prove a tighter connection between you two—a bond, if you will—that would benefit you both. In these perilous times, a woman needs all the help and support she can get—not simply to survive but to live. Although Julia has confided in me through the years, she just told me something of importance that she would like tell you as well."

"Is it trust?" Julia asked Charlotte directly. "If you're wondering how you could trust me, especially after learning about my Nazi-saluting husband who has a penchant for hurting me..."

Charlotte's hands began to shake. She set the shaking teacup on its saucer on the table beside the sofa. "I shouldn't have intruded with my opinions—"

"Nonsense," Julia said gently. "You were right to state the obvious—my husband is cruel when it comes to me and thinks he needs to put me in my place."

"And if he has a tendency to hurt you, what's to stop him from hurting your daughters? How does he treat others from a different faith, heritage, social class, or anyone who simply disagrees with him?" Charlotte sighed. "Sorry. I shouldn't be so bold."

"Sorry? Don't be. I've wondered about these same things as well, which is another reason why I've asked Mila here for this discussion." Charlotte couldn't imagine in what direction this conversation was heading, but remained silent to give Julia the chance to say more. "But, first things first. I need to gain your full trust in me, and hopefully, your full respect, despite this secret. I hope what I'm about to say will encourage you to speak up, but if not, no worries. I've thought about this at length and am committed to telling you, no matter what your reaction will be like." Julia picked at a fingernail. "My grandmother was Jewish, which according to Hitler, makes me Jewish. However, Oma married Opa, who was a devout Roman Catholic. She converted to Catholicism and raised her children as Catholic. These days, I seldom think of myself as coming from a Jewish bloodline. One not favored by any Nazi. One that, in the hands of my own husband, may likely prove disastrous." Julia had stopped talking to stare at Charlotte, making Charlotte aware that she'd opened her mouth in surprise. "But here's the thing," Julia continued. "Both Annelise and Marianne are unaware of this hidden heritage. I need to protect my daughters at all times and if that means keeping their family background a secret—at least for now during this awful occupation—then so be it."

"Yes, I understand," Charlotte murmured, intrigued. "What about your husband?"

"I never told him about my family. I should have told him while we were courting, at least by the time we became engaged. The fact that back then Luuk had intimidated me so much it kept me from being honest with him about my own flesh and blood, doesn't sit well with me. It should have been an indication that I was uncomfortable with him from the start and that this wasn't a good sign. But I was desperate to leave my parents and their controlling ways, and didn't say a word, desperate to find a Prince Charming who would always cherish me and protect me from harm. That left me with the opposite—a domineering husband with a penchant for abuse."

"As well as living in a German-occupied country that has made Judaism a crime," Charlotte said. "And though you don't identify yourself as Jewish, nor practice the faith, you're at risk of your past catching up with you and being used against you. You face suffering the consequences of deportation to a camp like other Jews, the Roma, the mentally ill, deaf, and blind—anyone less than 100 percent Aryan. And, since you've come to realize that your husband's allegiance is to Hitler rather than his family, I imagine you're more terrified of what he would do if he were to discover your secret."

"Yes, this is correct." Julia blanched and looked down. "Not only to me, but to my daughters as well."

Charlotte scooted from her end of the sofa toward Julia and patted her hand. "You've hinted at dealing with Luuk. Do you now have a solution?"

Julia turned and looked her directly in the eye. "I've vowed to myself that I will never allow Luuk to physically or emotionally hurt me again, let alone endanger my children. It's taken me a ridiculously long time to arrive at this point, but with your help, I've come to realize that I shouldn't have to suffer at the hands of an abuser. That's not what love and kindness are about." Julia breathed in deeply and exhaled. Her face twisted as if anguish and all its ugliness had caught up with her. "So, I've decided that if he comes home once more, whether one day soon or in the far future, and starts making threats or demands, I will kill him."

"No!" Charlotte seized Julia's hands and held them tight. "I won't let you. He's a Nazi. He is connected with anyone who has Evil as a middle name. He has no conscience and cannot differentiate between what is right and wrong. What's more, he's a big man, one who—I imagine—is quite strong, and he will be the one to kill you." Tears began to run from her eyes like a waterfall, but she didn't brush them away. "I'm afraid for you, my friend. And it's not for the reason you think."

Julia sniffled. "Then why?"

"You have three young daughters. If Luuk kills you, whether intentionally or out of self-defense, then they will be without a mother. He'd likely not raise them. What man would? Rather, he'd surrender them to an orphanage. The bigger thing though would be if you killed him, even if you managed to keep it hidden from the authorities."

"Why? I don't understand."

"What would you tell your daughters? How would you explain to them that the father they love died by your hands? You couldn't. And, the baby? How could Ada grow up and not think twice about her mother killing her father, the father she never got a chance to love, or why her mother was keeping a big secret? Believe me, children are quite perceptive. Your daughters will see a link between their father's death and their mother's big secret. Right now they're too young to understand your reasoning, but later, when they're older, I doubt they will accept your actions. They'll always wonder what might have happened if you gave their father just one more chance. His death would mean the end of his abuse, but it would also destroy your family, and you don't want that, do you?"

"No," Julia said, barely audible. "But Luuk has to be stopped. I won't let him hurt me and won't take a chance on the girls either. But the big thing is, I can no longer be with him, nor do I want to."

"I wouldn't want you to." Charlotte leaned back into the sofa.

She glanced across to the chair where Mila sat, who'd been attentive but quiet, giving them all the time and space needed to exchange overdue considerations. She then turned her attention back to Julia. "We need to make plans. Agreed?"

"Yes." Julia leaned back. "First, though, it's time to reveal your true identity to me if we are to continue trusting each other, don't you agree? And tell me about the news you mentioned last night."

Charlotte got to her feet and crossed the room to the fireplace that she'd never seen used. She imagined that Julia and her husband had sat before this once often used source of warmth and ambiance and cuddled together while their daughters slept in their beds. On a note of heated passion, they might have stripped off their clothes and made love before the crackling logs. Luuk whispering in Julia's ear how much he loved her... Julia planting little kisses all over his face that she held in her hands... both sharing promises that their love would last forever and ever. Julia had hinted that tender moments had occurred between them in the past, that though their marriage had suffered and was far from stellar, there were at least a few sunny glimpses here and there. But to think that their marriage and family—their love for each other—had all been tossed aside because of Luuk's adoration of Hitler and his warped Nazidom was beyond sad. To reach this point in a marriage was a tragedy. Julia had taken a big chance by confessing not only her family heritage but also admitting her willingness to kill her husband if he abused her one more time. As for herself, Charlotte couldn't continue to live a life of lies with the person who had welcomed her into her home when she had no other place to live. She leaned against the slate mantel and looked at her friend.

"My name is Herta Weber. I am Jewish."

Julia smiled. "Nice to meet you, Herta. I have a special offer for you."

34

Julia hummed on this first Sunday of October, the day she, Mila, and Herta were all available to gather. It was past the midpoint of 1943—three long and miserable years since the German occupation. Ironically, a side effect of war was learning how to live each day as it came while hoping and believing in a better tomorrow. With Julia's daughters next door under their uncle's watch, it was a perfect setup. Mila, employing the carpentry skills that she'd honed out of necessity upon Liam's injury to his hands, sawed the wood that came from the dismantled kitchen food pantry. Julia held the fresh-cut pieces, and Herta nailed them securely in place. The hiding place under the attic stairs for the street children that Julia had offered to take in was nearly completed.

"Julia, I haven't seen you this chipper since... goodness, I don't know." Herta swung away at the hammer. "You appear to have relaxed a bit, all things considered."

"Considering my Nazi husband roams about, and that not only do I have a Jewish bloodline but my dearest friend is also Jewish and living in my house, and we're planning to hide a few children who are still living in the streets—that is, if you can even call it living—*ja*, I'm happy. I'm helping the resistance! But the real question is whether Geertruida is okay with all this?"

Herta removed the nail secured between her lips. "Geertruida is desperate for help these days, especially with less and less people available or willing to assist. Believe me, she wouldn't have said yes if she had doubts about you." She struck the hammer hard, and punched a hole in the wall.

"Oh, dear," Julia said. "We've been working non-stop. Let's sit for a short spell and catch our breath." They sank to the floor, all three of them hugging their knees. "Do you think the children Geertruida brings will manage to keep silent when Ani, Marianne, and Ada are awake and active? I'm nervous that if there's a raid or if my girls should see a passerby while outdoors, they might give away our secret. And if Ada, who is growing more curious by the second, alerts her sisters, who knows what will happen."

"Geertruida is aware of the restrictions. This is a similar situation compared to the safe houses where the children have been placed. With the constant threat of razzias, children throughout this country have learned to stay quiet if they want to live to see another day and—hopefully—be reunited with their true families." Herta winced. "That is, if they remember their mothers and fathers. I've been told that countless children have jumbled their real and adopted mothers and fathers in their minds, and this has led to confusion as to who their actual parents are." She leaned her head back against the wall they were putting up and squeezed her eyes shut.

"I'm so sorry," Julia murmured.

Herta cracked open one eye. "Why should you be sorry? You're doing what many have refused to do—opening up your home to those in need."

"Because of what you just explained in your attempt to reassure me." Julia smiled tenderly at Herta as she cursed this war silently to herself. It had to end. Sooner rather than later. "I shouldn't have brought up this issue that made you think about how the children in hiding might have forgotten their parents, not with your own two daughters out of your sight, and living in hiding. This must be terribly hard on you."

Herta stood up. "Let's get started again, shall we?"

Julia nodded but then shook her head. "Have you seen your husband again? Is he still conducting business in his shop?"

"No, and no," Herta answered softly. "After that last time I saw him—and ended up identifying Kurt to the woman who must have been his assistant—he's either been reassigned or is avoiding me or both. According to Geertruida, that shop is presently a vacant building. Kurt, as long as he's alive, will keep forging documents—or more—to help others. And, if he comes to know about Edith and Krista's whereabouts, he will find a way to bring them food or other necessities."

Julia got to her feet and stood beside her friend. "Kurt sounds a lot like you—thinking of others first. He must be a good husband."

"Was. Was a good husband. Now he wants nothing to do with me."

"Maybe he's watching out for you and needs to keep his distance. Maybe—"

"Enough. No more husband-talk. No more maybe-talk." Herta pressed another nail into her mouth, an ending to the conversation, Julia concluded.

Liam barged upstairs. "Don't worry, the girls are fine. I have news to give to you—news that can't wait."

"Do we need to endure more heartache?" Julia asked. "That you're not smiling is already telling me that the war hasn't ended yet."

"It's about Walter Süskind."

Julia had often wondered about her brother-in-law's sources of information, especially since his political stance had come to lean in the opposite direction of that of his brother, Luuk. No matter. These days, with world and national news failing to reach whoever hadn't been carted off to a camp, she was grateful for Liam's connections. "Tell us."

He glanced at Herta. "I'm sorry to tell you because I'm aware of your friendship with the Süskinds." He hesitated more, but Herta urged him to continue. "Just a few days ago, on 29 September, there was another large roundup of Amsterdam Jews. We thought we had already seen the last of these roundups, but this time ten thousand were caught and deported. With the majority of Jews already removed from this city, there's talk that this might have been the last significant razzia."

"And Walter?" Herta asked.

"It hasn't yet been verified, but it's believed that Walter, his wife, and child were part of the roundup. They might be in Westerbork as we speak."

"Walter will find a way out."

Although Herta said those words confidently, Julia noticed that she wrapped her arms around her middle. She walked beside Herta to lend her support. Regardless that Liam's news wasn't good, she thanked him for the update and watched him descend the stairs. She then patted Herta on the shoulder. "Time to get back to work?"

Herta nodded. "Walter Süskind would be quite proud of us."

"From what you've shared about him, yes, he would. And I'm proud of you too." Julia rubbed her hands together. "Since we both have work tomorrow, let's continue with this far more important and urgent project."

As October progressed, both unexpected good and troubling news arrived. First, Italy changed its political position and declared war on Germany. Then came the solemn warnings on 27 October: the food supply to the general population of the Netherlands had fallen to a dangerously low level. With winter on its way, life became more fragile and everyone was at risk, especially with stringent food rationing. The evening that Liam had conveyed the latter news, with the children asleep, the adults had gathered in Julia's parlor to celebrate the completed construction of the hiding place with the last of the *jenever*. "Here's to the children," they said as they clicked their glasses in cheer. The house was ready; just in time, since Geertruida planned to bring the first two children to the house in two days. At 10 that night, Liam and Mila stood up from the sofa to go home. Herta also rose and then collapsed to the floor.

Julia was the first to reach her. "Herta... can you hear me? Can you open your eyes?" She touched her forehead and looked at Mila. "She's burning up. I'm afraid I have no aspirin left."

"I do," Mila said and dodged next door.

Liam helped Julia hoist Herta onto the sofa. He reached for the blanket draped over the nearby chair's back. Using his wrists, he covered Herta, who was beginning to stir. She batted her eyes, then began to tremble.

"I'm freezing. What happened?"

Julia slipped beside her. "My dear, you passed out. Mila's fetching aspirin for what I suspect is a fever. Have you felt sick the whole day?"

Herta shook her head but winced. "It just hit me. I hope it's not that dreaded flu that's breaking out." Her eyes widened. "If I'm ill, Geertruida won't risk bringing the children here. I've ruined—"

"This isn't the time to fret," Julia said softly as Mila entered the room with two aspirin clutched in one hand and a glass of water in the other. Julia lifted Herta enough for her to chug the medication and water. "Easy, there."

"What are we going to do? I can't be sick. We're out of time." Herta sank back into the sofa and rested her head on a pillow.

"The only thing to focus on is getting better." She eyed Liam. "Feel strong?" As if Liam read her mind, he scooped Herta into his arms and asked Julia where to bring her. "To her own room, where she's bound to enjoy a fast recovery."

A fast return to health did not happen. Herta still had a raging fever the next day, and as she barely drank or ate, she grew weaker and weaker. On the third day, seeing Herta thrash about in a restless sleep, Julia knew exactly what she needed to do, though her friend would not appreciate it. At least, not at first. That was, if Herta was going to pull through and recover. Enough. She had to be strong for her friend. That meant relegating to the back of her mind the horrid realization that war did not necessarily kill by weapons of bloodshed alone, but also by famine and disease.

35

Five days later, free of fever but immensely weak, Herta opened her eyes that morning and quickly shut them again, squeezing out the image of the person sitting on a chair beside her cot.

"Open your eyes, Herta," Kurt said.

She couldn't gauge his tone, couldn't tell if he was relieved that she had taken a turn for the better health-wise. Was he overjoyed to be with her again or resenting each second that he was delayed in forging documents for the resistance? Or, had he been the one to initiate a search for her? "Why should I open my eyes? I'm sick. You're a hallucination... a dream." When a retort didn't come, drained of all energy, she tried to sleep. Lately, sleep was a delicious state. She didn't have to worry or dodge authorities, who, upon discovery of her true identity, likely would shoot her dead on the spot. And certainly, when asleep, she didn't have to put on a mask of bravery when in reality, she was terrified. When had she let hope slide from her grip? Had her surrender to despondency led to a decreased resistance to germs? Was it her fault that she fell ill, possibly exposing the others, possibly sabotaging the hiding of the children in Julia's house?

"Hertala."

Only one person ever had made her name into this sweet endearment, one she hadn't heard in years. She opened her eyes and saw her husband clearly. "Why are you here, beside me, and not in Switzerland hiding from the Nazis?" She attempted to prop herself onto an elbow, but Kurt, with a gentle admonishment to not tax her already weak body, helped her to lie down again. "And why do you bother with me? You made it clear that day in the shop that you never want to see me again. Did you take it up with that assistant of yours where the two of us last left off? She is—"

"Sari," Kurt said, stopping her short. He pulled at his chin, but not enough to hide his grin. "I'm glad you're coming around, even if it means suspecting me of cheating on you."

"Well, stop me from guessing and tell me what's happening. I don't understand one thing."

The grin slid from his face, his lips flattened, and his brows lifted. "That was my full intention—keeping you confused. Actually, I wanted you to believe I left you and that I only thought about myself and my welfare while keeping far away from the Nazi infestation in this country." He leaned closer, only a breath away from her lips. "Herta, I love you. Always have and always will. Because the authorities were looking for me, I had to leave. But, because I wanted to keep watch over you, I came back and lived on the streets right here in Amsterdam until I joined the resistance and, here and there, took up offers to sleep indoors."

She thought about giving up first one daughter and then the other to place them in safe houses. Of the loneliness and heartache she'd endured. About the risks she'd been willing to take because she couldn't live one more day thinking about herself and her needs. Then, she'd found Kurt only for him to tell her to leave him alone. She'd reached the point of giving up hope in getting her family back together. "I had to say goodbye to Edith and Krista when I placed them in hiding. And you, Kurt. When you told me in that forgery shop of yours to get away from you and to never come back, it was as if you said that you didn't want me in your life ever again."

He kissed her. Once. But when he lifted away, her lips tingled with a tenderness that only true love knew how to plant and nourish. "This war... this hideous time... Herta, I wanted to keep you far away from me—a wanted man. Those Nazis have tortured people using atrocities only a devilish mind could think of. I've even heard about them skinning captives alive to obtain information. Whether it's true or not, I didn't want to find out for myself, but even more—I didn't want to lead them to you. Without you, I have no reason to try to live through all this."

"What about living for our daughters?"

"Don't misunderstand me, Herta." He kissed her again, longer, leaving a taste on her lips of long-ago passion. "I love our daughters, yet it's you I live for. But after I said what I did when you stopped by for the documents... if you don't want to see me again, tell me, and I'll be on my way."

"Don't ever leave me again." She clutched his shirt. "Do you know who lives in this household?"

"A Christian woman with a Jewish grandmother and a Nazi-saluting husband?"

Herta nodded. Hearing him phrase the incomprehensible truth too neatly in one sentence made her woozy. She slipped further under the covers, closed her eyes and hoped to drift off into a quiet sleep. If luck came her way, she wouldn't awaken until the war ended.

"Herta... Hertala. Open your eyes again, my love."

Why wouldn't he let her sleep? What more could he say that would persuade her to carry on one more day, that tomorrow would prove differently, free of threats? "What?" she mumbled.

"Your friend, Julia, and her sister-in-law and her husband, we all talked before I came to your room to wait for you to wake up."

How long had he waited? She'd never asked. How long had he been prepared to wait beside her and see her either return to health or to pass on to what she desperately wanted to believe was a beautiful heaven where sorrow didn't exist?

"And?" she managed to say. "What came of this talk?"

"I volunteered—vowed, actually—to kill Luuk if he ever stepped foot into this house again."

She opened both eyes, unable to sleep.

36

Luuk hadn't come home to Julia and their daughters during the Christmas of 1943. And to everyone's amazement and relief, he didn't show his face during the wintry cold, hungry months of 1944. That was perfectly fine with Herta. With Kurt and various children sheltering in the house, hiding from the Nazi enemy, they all kept busy between caring for these children as well as Julia's children and keeping them separated, careful to keep them from becoming familiar with each other. They also kept a vigilant eye out for those neighborly friends who could easily be persuaded to rat them out for a little money. And then there was the constant lookout for Luuk, especially since Wim Henneicke, the leader of the bounty hunter group that Luuk had joined, was assassinated by the Dutch resistance.

Now, as the Christmas of '44 approached, they—this newly extended family of Julia and her daughters, Liam and Mila and Herta and Kurt—once again sat around the dinner table. Yet, that comfortable sense of family, friends, and coziness was absent. As half a loaf of bread was passed around the dinner table, and two-and-a-half-year-old Ada broke out in a maddening cry from banging her knee, Marianne covered her ears. "Mama! It's cold in here. I can see my breath. And I'm hungry." She dropped her hands and rubbed her tummy. "I can feel all my bones inside me."

Mila stood from her place at the table. "Pardon me. I just remembered I have a brick of cheddar. I'll be right back."

"I'm also hungry," Annelise said. "My friend told me about how people are dying from not eating. She said people in the countryside are walking long distances to find food at farms. Are we going to do that, too?"

Herta took the silence from Julia as a cue. Seated next to Marianne, she offered the child a big smile. "Let's play a game, darling."

"A game?" Marianne said, sounding more like an upset crow rather than an excited girl. "We just want to eat, not play."

"I'll start first." Herta winked at Kurt. *Remember this game, dearest? The one we used to play with Edith and Krista when they were troubled over matters out of their control?* She lifted her glass for all to see. "I'm grateful for this water. It's tasty and keeps me healthy. What about you, Kurt?"

Kurt looked around the table. "I'm grateful for lots of things. For my wife. For meeting all of you. For you letting me live in your house."

"I'm glad you're living with us," Marianne said as she nibbled on her piece of bread. She glanced at her mother. "When will Tante Mila come back?"

"Soon. See, we do have food. Good thing Mila remembered she had some cheese. She always finds food!"

"We can give some to the other children hiding here," Annelise said.

Julia's hand began to shake, and water sloshed over the rim of the glass. Kurt snatched it from her hand and set it on the table at a distance.

"We know about them," Marianne said. "There's one boy. And one girl. And they live in the attic wall, not like the ones that used to live under the stairs until they moved out last week. Ani and I heard them singing. Their voices come from the vents in our room."

Annelise nodded. "They sing at night, taking turns. I think it's a lullaby. They must be afraid, like Marianne and me."

Marianne lifted her chin. "I'm not afraid."

"Now that I'm home, no one should be afraid."

They all turned to see Luuk at the dining room's entrance. His hand gripped Mila's upper arm. Her face was tight and pale. He was slim—like they all were—but stood tall, shoulders squared. No trace of a smile. A rifle was strapped to his shoulder.

"Well, let me rephrase what I just said," Luuk continued. "If you have Jewish kids hiding in this house, yes, then there's a reason to be afraid." He peered at his daughters, his eyes taking in the sight of Ada crawling onto Julia's lap and burying her face from him. "Marianne and Annelise, aren't you going to give your father a big hug?" When neither girl stirred, he glanced about the room. "Liam, my brother, tell me who is this woman and man seated at my table? Would they also be Jews? I can fetch a pretty price for them and can offer you a percentage. Money goes far these days."

"They're friends living with Julia." Liam stood, matching his brother's towering height. "No need to hurt them."

Luuk chuckled, his mismatched eyes twinkling, but not from the light of the dim room. It came from within. He approached Kurt. "Ah, I remember you."

"And I remember you," Kurt said through tight lips.

Herta looked into her husband's eyes. *Be careful. Do as planned. Don't die on me.*

"Aren't you that Jew who makes jewelry?" Luuk looked at Julia. "Do you still have that butterfly necklace I gifted you a few years ago?"

"The one you stole?" Kurt stood, aiming a gun at Luuk. "The one I chased you for, but you escaped?"

Luuk laughed as he reached for his rifle. "Your bitty gun is no match to my—"

Kurt fired, but Luke dodged fast enough to miss the bullet. He punched Kurt in the face, and Kurt toppled over his chair onto the floor.

"Say goodbye, Jew." Luuk again reached for his gun but groped empty space.

A shot was fired. Luuk stared at his brother and then collapsed in a bloody pool on the floor; his blood splattered and gushed onto the chairs, table, and rug. The girls screamed. Julia gathered her three daughters and ushered them out of the room. Herta scrambled next to Kurt, bruised but alive.

"Well Liam," Mila said, stepping beside her husband, "no one could ever rightly say that your hands are worthless." She stood on her toes and kissed him. "And, never again will you have to put up with Luuk's awful insults claiming you are no match for him." They both eyed Julia as she walked back into the room.

"My brother will never hurt another person again, especially you, Julia. Mila and I will help you with the girls. We'll make sure you'll never have to think twice about today. Let's take care of him before word leaks about his… disappearance."

"I'll help," Kurt said as he struggled to his feet.

"Are you up to it?"

"Nothing will keep me away."

Herta kissed Liam on the cheek. She thought about the two children hiding upstairs. "And I'll check on the little ones in the attic and then help too, because nothing will keep me away either, from ridding the world of this believer in evil."

37

NOVEMBER 1945

Herta crossed the canal bridge over the Amstel River nearby the first apartment she and her family lived in when they first arrived in Amsterdam six years ago. She still enjoyed coming to this particular bridge. Since the war ended, she and Kurt lived in an apartment, that in addition to their own personal touches to a yet another new beginning, the cozy place was decorated with the new paper dolls that Julia's daughters had made for her latest birthday, in honor of her own daughters. They were framed on a parlor table. She'd accepted their gift along with their promise to make her new ones every year until her daughters came home. At the thought of Annelise and Marianne—and now Ada—who were growing like wild roses, and her dear friend Julia, Herta smiled. She was grateful she and Kurt lived only three streets over from Julia, still next door to Mila and Liam.

They were all changed, different people now. Having survived this war that finally ended for those in the Netherlands when the Germans surrendered on 5 May, how could they not have grown, seen life differently, and established new realities? She thought about her friend Zofia, the one she'd met on the ship they'd sailed to Cuba en route to what they all thought would be their final destination—America. Zofia had escaped the war, but at the time when they departed from each other, she was uncertain of her husband, his family, and her friend's whereabouts. Had they lived through this horror? If so, they, too, must have experienced many changes. She hoped that they were all for the good, that harm did not reach Zofia and her loved ones, the same hope Herta had for Edith and Krista, the same hope Julia had for her daughters as well.

A damp gust of wind shifted Herta's loose kerchief and sent chills up her arms. Why she had worn a sweater instead of a jacket was beyond her reasoning. Then again, much surpassed her understanding these days. A dog barked and brought her attention toward the end of the bridge where she saw Kurt; he was carrying the jacket she'd left behind. She smiled as he approached. "You've walked quite a distance. Do you have news?"

He held her jacket for her to slide her arms into. "Yes and no. Krista is still in Sweden, but she continues to recover nicely from her illness. The doctor at the tuberculosis sanatorium says she should be home next month—in time for Hanukkah."

"That would be nice," she murmured.

"Herta, sweetheart." Kurt grasped her hands, and they stared over the bridge at the beautiful historic Amsterdam buildings. Unlike the other parts of the Netherlands, they fortunately hadn't suffered ruination from bombs or fires. "We have lots to be thankful for. We know where Krista is, that she's expected to make a full recovery and will soon be with us, in our new, lovely home. Our little sweetheart is now 16 and is on her way to enjoying good health. She has a few more years at home with us before she flies the nest as an adult woman to make her own path in life."

"At least she's come around about living with us."

"Yes. I understand how hard this has been for you, and I can't blame you one bit." Kurt squeezed her hand. "It was scary for a while with Krista saying she wanted to continue to live with her foster family. I thank God that she changed her mind." He chuckled. "Ah, the will and tenacity of a teenager—we'll be blessed to celebrate another birthday with her coming January."

"I did what I had to do—put both girls into hiding in a last attempt to spare their lives." Herta buried her face in his chest and sniffled. "Each day I wonder whether they will come to terms with my choice and accept it as a mother's last-ditch effort to protect them, to see to their welfare... to see to a tomorrow for each of them. I wonder if they will forgive me. It's an awful price to pay for loving my daughters." Her remaining words choked her up.

Kurt clutched her tightly. "One way or another, we will make life bearable once again, and carry on, while never forgetting the unfortunate ones who perished."

She nodded, and then forced herself to voice one more concern, one she was sure Kurt knew was coming. "What's harder to believe, to accept, is the mystery of Edith's whereabouts. Whether she's alive or wants to live with—"

"Don't say it. We must believe she's alive and well and, of course, wants to live with us. We will find her."

"But if she is alive, she's turning 19 this month." Herta shrugged. "She's a woman, no longer a child. She may have chosen not to have contact with a mother who gave her away."

"Or, a father who, in her mind, abandoned his daughters and wife regardless of it being an effort to protect them from harm."

It was Herta's turn to comfort her husband. "Just last week I heard that Geertruida survived the war. Thank goodness! I'll search for her and ask if she can help us with finding Edith, unless our precious oldest daughter finds us first. For all we know, she might be making her way to us as we speak. Imagine, Kurt, her smile when she sees us and Krista, and gets swallowed in our hugs."

"For all we know, she's married and has a child."

"Don't say that. I'm not ready to be a grandmother." Despite the seriousness of the conversation, she smiled. "Though, if that was the worst consequence of these past few years, so be it. I can easily cradle a grandchild in my arms and spoil her with all my love."

"A baby girl?" He shrugged. "Maybe we'll have a grandson."

"Twins! One of each."

He kissed her, not in a hurry to step away. "And you do still want to live in Amsterdam, not in New York like we once had planned?"

"Yes, this is home. I love this city, this country. Although, I'd love for all of us to visit Zofia one day in the near future. Wouldn't that be nice?"

"Yes," he said, "you and I and our two daughters—our family." He leaned toward her again for another kiss.

She pressed her hand against his chest to stop him, but only for a moment. "It's good that our hope is reviving, slowly but steadily." She swung her arms around him and pulled him in for a kiss, eager to share more love with her beautiful husband.

ABOUT THE AUTHOR

Elaine Stock writes Historical Fiction, exploring home, family and friendships throughout time. She enjoys creating stories showing how all faiths, races, and belief systems are interconnected and need each other.

Inspired by her paternal heritage from Brzeziny Poland, Elaine wrote *We Shall Not Shatter*, Book 1 of the Resilient Women of WWII Trilogy. The novel has earned the Historical Fiction Company 5-star and "Highly Recommended" Review and won the Finalist Award in the Historical WWI-WWII category of the Historical Fiction Company 2021 Contest. Book 2, *Our Daughters' Last Hope*, features what becomes of Herta, a character from Book 1, and her family, in Amsterdam. Book 3, *When We Disappeared*, is the story about Herta's daughter within Nazi Germany. The audiobook for all three books of the Trilogy will be produced by Tantor Media.

Although multi-published in award-winning Inspirational Fiction, and a past blogger and online magazine contributor, Elaine now pens novels for the general reading audience. She is a member of Women's Fiction Writers Association and The Historical Novel Society. Born in Brooklyn, New York, she has been living in upstate, rural New York with her husband for more years than her stint as a city gal. She enjoys long walks down country roads, visiting New England towns, and of course, a good book.

Dear Reader,

If you have enjoyed reading my book,
please do leave a review on Amazon or Goodreads. A few kind words would be enough. This would be greatly appreciated.

Alternatively, if you have read my book as Kindle eBook you could leave a rating.
That is just one simple click, indicating how many stars of five you think this book deserves.
This will only cost you a split second.
Thank you very much in advance!

Elaine.

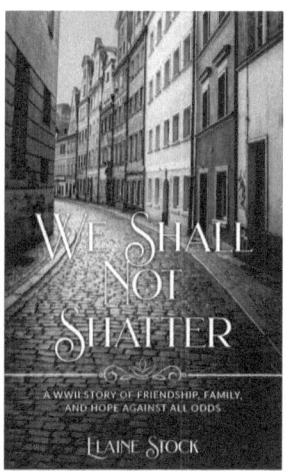

We Shall Not Shatter is Book 1 of the Trilogy **Resilient Women of WWII.**

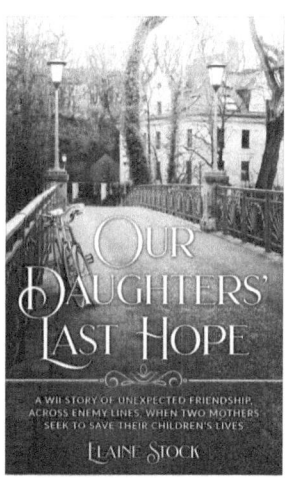

Our Daughters' Last Hope is Book 2 of the Trilogy **Resilient Women of WWII.**

When We Disappeared. A WWII Story of Two Women of Different Faiths who risk their lives to save family ad Friends is Book 3 of the Trilogy **Resilient Women of WWII.**

More information you will find on the authors website:

https://elainestock.com

READERS GROUPS DISCUSSION GUIDE

1. As she is talking to her daughter, Herta concludes: *That was one of the toxic consequences with prejudice: people welded it as a sword to attack others without fully taking the time to get to know the accused; more aggravating was that the attacker didn't want to know the target of his hatred.* How would you explain prejudice to a child?

2. Julia thinks of her husband's pride as his strength but also his Achille's heel. Discuss this trait within yourself or someone you know.

3. Upon the German invasion of the Netherlands, Herta muses that war made enemies from many and friends from a few. Do you find that during difficult times, there is a tendency to count on a few trusted individuals and to be wary of the majority?

4. In trying to comfort his wife, Herta, Kurt says that fear would uproot them faster than an enemy's threat. How large of a battle do you have with fear? In what ways to you try to combat its power over you?

5. Herta, like most women, is strong for her loved ones, yet is confronted by her own struggles, which she cannot afford to show, especially toward her children. Discuss this dual challenge that women, throughout all times, face.

6. Do you agree or disagree with Julia that the way not to fear the future is to bury the past?

7. In viewing her own troubled (and hereditarily mixed-faith) marriage with Luuk, Julia comes to view the necessity of not only receiving love but giving love. What is your definition of love?

8. As much as Luuk is set in his dedication to the Nazi Party, he's a romantic at heart. Do you know of people who are both charming and offensive? Are you able to justify their behavior?

9. While Charlotte walks with her daughters to a market, Charlotte tells Edith: "It's not God's desire for Jews—or believers of other faiths—that worries me. Instead, it's what mankind desires, and to what extreme they'll go to get everything they want." Do you agree or disagree?

10. Charlotte also proclaims that out of necessity to survive (the crisis they might face as Jews if their true identity is revealed), there is no shame in concealing one's faith. Has this been done throughout time by various faiths and communities or was it singular to what the Jewish population faced during WWII? Is this act something that you condone or condemn?

11. After Marianne, Julia's daughter, nearly drowns, Charlotte muses that war was an incredibly odd time: While two or more man-made sides battled for the blood of perceived enemies, children were born in the very definition that life continues. Discuss how ironies of life coexist, for better or worse.

12. Julia and Charlotte both suspect the other of not sharing the truth, concluding that was the trouble with lies—they had an awfully sneaky way in trapping a person further into the quagmire of more complex ruses without a way out. Discuss how this has happened several times in the story, and if it has happened in your own life.

13. Bonus Question: Walter Süskind offers the following advice to Herta/Charlotte: *"Don't think about what's ahead, or was in the past. These aren't the best of times and though you haven't solicited my advice I suggest strongly that it is best to stay in the present."* Do you personally agree or disagree that this may be the best way to handle most of life, both during the good and difficult times?

ACKNOWLEDGMENTS

One of the treasures of continuing my writing, especially the Resilient Women of WWII Trilogy, is the tremendous support from not only friends, family, and my I-thought-established set of fellow authors and writing group and association support but the blessed growing of all of these. I want to especially thank Nancy Loyan Schuemann, Roberta Decaprio, Nadine Feldman, Sue Roberts, Yvonne Gill, Lelita Baldock, Sandra L. Young, Leigh Turner, Christina Consolino, Lisa Montanaro, Mary Frey, Mary Schmidt and 2022 Debuts! There are so many more names I'd like to share, but truly not enough pages to do so.

My gratitude again goes to Liesbeth Heenk of Amsterdam Publishers—Liesbeth, it's a true pleasure working with you. Here's to the success of the full Trilogy! And, thank you to my new editor, Iulia Ivana—I appreciate all of your insights and suggestions.

Speaking of friends, thank you to all of my friends (and you know who you are!) who have practiced so much patience in me getting back to them while I squeezed every possible second out of each day. My delay in replies are not a delay in my love for you.

And, when it comes to love, friendship, and acceptance of who I am, Wally, you're the Number 1 in my universe and please, never forget that!

AMSTERDAM PUBLISHERS HOLOCAUST LIBRARY

The series **Holocaust Survivor Memoirs World War II** consists of the following autobiographies of survivors:

Outcry. Holocaust Memoirs, by Manny Steinberg

Hank Brodt Holocaust Memoirs. A Candle and a Promise, by Deborah Donnelly

The Dead Years. Holocaust Memoirs, by Joseph Schupack

Rescued from the Ashes. The Diary of Leokadia Schmidt, Survivor of the Warsaw Ghetto, by Leokadia Schmidt

My Lvov. Holocaust Memoir of a twelve-year-old Girl, by Janina Hescheles

Remembering Ravensbrück. From Holocaust to Healing, by Natalie Hess

Wolf. A Story of Hate, by Zeev Scheinwald with Ella Scheinwald

Save my Children. An Astonishing Tale of Survival and its Unlikely Hero, by Leon Kleiner with Edwin Stepp

Holocaust Memoirs of a Bergen-Belsen Survivor & Classmate of Anne Frank, by Nanette Blitz Konig

Defiant German - Defiant Jew. A Holocaust Memoir from inside the Third Reich, by Walter Leopold with Les Leopold

In a Land of Forest and Darkness. The Holocaust Story of two Jewish Partisans, by Sara Lustigman Omelinski

Holocaust Memories. Annihilation and Survival in Slovakia, by Paul Davidovits

From Auschwitz with Love. The Inspiring Memoir of Two Sisters' Survival, Devotion and Triumph Told by Manci Grunberger Beran & Ruth Grunberger Mermelstein, by Daniel Seymour

Remetz. Resistance Fighter and Survivor of the Warsaw Ghetto, by Jan Yohay Remetz

My March Through Hell. A Young Girl's Terrifying Journey to Survival, by Halina Kleiner with Edwin Stepp

---

The series **Holocaust Survivor True Stories WWII** consists of the following biographies:

Among the Reeds. The true story of how a family survived the Holocaust, by Tammy Bottner

A Holocaust Memoir of Love & Resilience. Mama's Survival from Lithuania to America, by Ettie Zilber

Living among the Dead. My Grandmother's Holocaust Survival Story of Love and Strength, by Adena Bernstein Astrowsky

Heart Songs. A Holocaust Memoir, by Barbara Gilford

Shoes of the Shoah. The Tomorrow of Yesterday, by Dorothy Pierce

Hidden in Berlin. A Holocaust Memoir, by Evelyn Joseph Grossman

Separated Together. The Incredible True WWII Story of Soulmates Stranded an Ocean Apart, by Kenneth P. Price, Ph.D.

The Man Across the River. The incredible story of one man's will to survive the Holocaust, by Zvi Wiesenfeld

If Anyone Calls, Tell Them I Died. A Memoir, by Emanuel (Manu) Rosen

The House on Thrömerstrasse. A Story of Rebirth and Renewal in the Wake of the Holocaust, by Ron Vincent

Dancing with my Father. His hidden past. Her quest for truth. How Nazi Vienna shaped a family's identity, by Jo Sorochinsky

The Story Keeper. Weaving the Threads of Time and Memory - A Memoir, by Fred Feldman

Krisia's Silence. The Girl who was not on Schindler's List, by Ronny Hein

Defying Death on the Danube. A Holocaust Survival Story, by Debbie J. Callahan with Henry Stern

A Doorway to Heroism. A decorated German-Jewish Soldier who became an American Hero, by Rabbi W. Jack Romberg

The Shoemaker's Son. The Life of a Holocaust Resister, by Laura Beth Bakst

The Redhead of Auschwitz. A True Story, by Nechama Birnbaum

Land of Many Bridges. My Father's Story, by Bela Ruth Samuel Tenenholtz

Creating Beauty from the Abyss. The Amazing Story of Sam Herciger, Auschwitz Survivor and Artist, by Lesley Ann Richardson

On Sunny Days We Sang. A Holocaust Story of Survival and Resilience, by Jeannette Grunhaus de Gelman

Painful Joy. A Holocaust Family Memoir, by Max J. Friedman

I Give You My Heart. A True Story of Courage and Survival, by Wendy Holden

In the Time of Madmen, by Mark A. Prelas

Monsters and Miracles. Horror, Heroes and the Holocaust, by Ira Wesley Kitmacher

Flower of Vlora. Growing up Jewish in Communist Albania, by Anna Kohen

Aftermath: Coming of Age on Three Continents. A Memoir, by Annette Libeskind Berkovits

Not a real Enemy. The True Story of a Hungarian Jewish Man's Fight for Freedom, by Robert Wolf

The Glassmaker's Son. Looking for the World my Father left behind in Nazi Germany, by Peter Kupfer

Zaidy's War. Four Armies, Three Continents, Two Brothers. One Man's Impossible Journey of Endurance, by Martin Bodek

The Apprentice of Buchenwald. The True Story of the Teenage Boy Who Sabotaged Hitler's War Machine, by Oren Schneider

---

The series **Jewish Children in the Holocaust** consists of the following autobiographies of Jewish children hidden during WWII in the Netherlands:

Searching for Home. The Impact of WWII on a Hidden Child, by Joseph Gosler

See You Tonight and Promise to be a Good Boy! War memories, by Salo Muller

Sounds from Silence. Reflections of a Child Holocaust Survivor, Psychiatrist and Teacher, by Robert Krell

Sabine's Odyssey. A Hidden Child and her Dutch Rescuers, by Agnes Schipper

The Journey of a Hidden Child, by Harry Pila with Robin Black

The series **New Jewish Fiction** consists of the following novels, written by Jewish authors. All novels are set in the time during or after the Holocaust.

The Corset Maker. A Novel, by Annette Libeskind Berkovits

Escaping the Whale. The Holocaust is over. But is it ever over for the next generation? by Ruth Rotkowitz

When the Music Stopped. Willy Rosen's Holocaust, by Casey Hayes

Hands of Gold. One Man's Quest to Find the Silver Lining in Misfortune, by Roni Robbins

The Girl Who Counted Numbers. A Novel, by Roslyn Bernstein

There was a garden in Nuremberg. A Novel, by Navina Michal Clemerson

The Butterfly and the Axe, by Omer Bartov

Good For a Single Journey, by Helen Joyce

The series **Holocaust Books for Young Adults** consists of the following novels, based on true stories:

The Boy behind the Door. How Salomon Kool Escaped the Nazis. Inspired by a True Story, by David Tabatsky

Running for Shelter. A True Story, by Suzette Sheft

The Precious Few. An Inspirational Saga of Courage based on True Stories, by David Twain with Art Twain

Jacob's Courage: A Holocaust Love Story, by Charles S. Weinblatt

---

The series **WW2 Historical Fiction** consists of the following novels, some of which are based on true stories:

Mendelevski's Box. A Heartwarming and Heartbreaking Jewish Survivor's Story, by Roger Swindells

A Quiet Genocide. The Untold Holocaust of Disabled Children WW2 Germany, by Glenn Bryant

The Knife-Edge Path, by Patrick T. Leahy

Want to be an AP book reviewer?

Reviews are very important in a world dominated by the social media and social proof. Please drop us a line if you want to join the *AP review team*. We will then add you to our list of advance reviewers. No strings attached, and we promise that we will not be spamming you.

info@amsterdampublishers.com

www.ingramcontent.com/pod-product-compliance
Lightning Source LLC
LaVergne TN
LVHW091711070526
838199LV00050B/2354